More praise for
PROBABLE CAUSE:

"A convincingly detailed portrayal of the labyrinth that the American legal system can be . . . Gideon Page is neither a superlawyer nor a superman, and his problem-plagued relationships with his daughter and his lovers—would-be and otherwise—and his colleagues, clients, and friends reverberate with authenticity."
—*Arkansas Democrat Gazette*

"One of the warmest, funniest, most human lawyers in the suspense genre."
—*Minneapolis Star & Tribune*

"A plum . . . Stockley's hero is a laconic, warm-hearted soul."
—*Booklist*

"Engaging . . . The verdict on this one: It's a winner."
—*The Orange County Register*

"Homespun warmth and wry charm . . . A down-home *Burden of Proof*."
—*Kirkus Reviews*

Also by Grif Stockley
Published by Ivy Books:

EXPERT TESTIMONY

PROBABLE CAUSE

Grif Stockley

IVY BOOKS • NEW YORK

Ivy Books
Published by Ballantine Books
Copyright © 1992 by Grif Stockley

Library of Congress Catalog Card Number: 92-20184

ISBN 0-8041-1133-2

This edition published by arrangement with Summit Books, a division of Simon & Schuster Inc.

Manufactured in the United States of America

First Ballantine Books Edition: December 1993

Cover photo of red marble by M. Angelo/Westlight.

To my wife, Susan Gill

1

"YOU HAVE A call from Dr. Andrew Chapman at the city jail. He says it's urgent that he speak to you right now."

Chapman? Wearily, I rub my forehead as if I'm hoping his name will come off in my hand. Not even a glimmer. I put down my pen, wishing the brief in the Davis case would go away. How do appellate judges stay awake? I flip through the Rolodex on my desk, on the off chance his name will show up. Why would a jail doctor be calling me? I haven't had a criminal case since I left the Blackwell County Public Defender's Office over a year ago. Personal injury law pays more, but it isn't as much fun. Especially if you're an associate cranking out research and the crap cases the senior partners throw like dog scraps to us once they realize the cases aren't turning into pots of gold as they had hoped. What the hell—maybe this doc'll be in a car wreck someday. "This is Gideon Page," I say, glad for any excuse to take a break. Brief writing isn't my long suit anyway. A decision was handed down by the Arkansas Supreme Court two weeks ago with my name on it (I did most of the work, though a senior partner's name went first) in which the court reversed a million-plus judgment for our client on the jury instructions. The second big case this month down the tubes for Mays & Burton. We're on a roll—unfortunately it seems straight downhill.

"Mr. Page," a deep, rich voice reverberates in my ear, "my name is Dr. Andrew Chapman. I've just been charged with manslaughter. Can you come talk to me?"

1

As if I'd gulped pure caffeine, I feel instantly alert. Mays & Burton stays away from criminal cases, but this guy could be loaded. I look at my watch. In seven minutes, at precisely two o'clock (Oscar Mays likes his associates to walk in right on the dot—he's usually on the phone, but that's okay), I have a command performance with Oscar, presumably to go over my research on the Davis case. As fast as we're losing cases, we could stand some cash flow. Maybe Oscar'll go for it. "I'll be down to see you in less than an hour." If Oscar passes on it, I'll refer the guy after I break my boss's neck.

"Thank you," Dr. Chapman says politely and hangs up.

Elated, I put down the phone and write his name down on a yellow pad. Who is he? God, lawyers are horrible. Bad news makes me feel almost as good as sex. I grab up the Davis file, but instead of heading for Oscar's office, I swing by the john. Sometimes, I think the best thing about being an attorney is being able to go to the bathroom whenever I want. If I worked in a factory, I'd need a catheter attached to my thigh.

In the head, I join Darryl Worley, who is at the next urinal. He doesn't look so hot. Charcoal-colored pouches under his already dark eyes make him look as if he has survived a physical beating instead of an emotional and financial one. He was the lawyer on the Stoddard case a week ago in which the judge snatched from us on a judgment notwithstanding the verdict after a jury had awarded our client two million dollars. "How's it going, Darryl?" I say, unzipping my pants. Darryl, ten years younger, made partner last year. He has become a friend in the last few months, and we've started playing some tennis this summer.

He smiles sadly as he shakes off, but instead of a mournful acknowledgment, he recites, "You can beat it on the wall; you can throw it on the rocks; but it's always in your pants you get that last little drop."

Damn! If people knew what some of us were really like. The guy is smooth as mercury in front of a jury, but as soon as he steps outside the courtroom he regresses into an adolescent. I laugh dutifully while he washes his hands, not having heard that ditty since high school. "Women have it worse," I say, keeping the conversation off law. If given a chance to talk about the case, Darryl will start in on Curtis Hadley, the trial judge in the Stoddard case, and I haven't got the time. I'm a little surprised he hasn't been to my office to talk to me today about it.

Darryl begins to hum the Marine Hymn as he pushes the hot-air machine button. He rubs his hands together briskly, pretending to read the instructions. "Turn on. Rub hands together. Then wipe hands on pants."

Junior associate that I am, I grin. I've seen that cartoon, too. What the hell? There's nothing new under the sun. And, according to my tenth-grade Sunday school teacher, that saying comes from the book of Ecclesiastes. Perhaps Darryl is whistling in the graveyard: truly, with his raccoon eyes, he has a sickly look about him. "Catch you later," I tell him.

"Yeah," he says, not looking me in the eye. Losing is a serious business. The firm spent over thirty thousand of its own money in experts and exhibits.

Martha Birford, who shares with me here an employment anniversary date, arrives outside Oscar Mays's office at the same time, and we go in together. She has a piece of the Davis case, too. We both like Oscar better than Chip Burton. It is no secret that Oscar was responsible for hiring us, for one thing, but also he is genuinely a nice man. He is in his sixties and seems ready to retire, but for some reason he won't or can't. If his office is any indication, he can afford it. He has a fireplace, an antique walnut desk I'd like to steal if I could figure out a way to get it through the door, and works of unknown (to me) Southern artists, who, according to Martha (incongruously, an art history major in college), for the moment are quite popular.

"Have a seat," he says affably, standing until Martha is seated, always the old Southern gentleman. It hits me that Martha and I are getting a raise. I want to tell him that I have brought the firm a decent client but have learned that Oscar likes to speak first, whatever the situation. Age before beauty, I suppose.

Age has its compensations. Oscar's suit, a dapper, baby-blue summer Brooks Brothers, in the $750 range, looks tailored and nicely hides his sizable paunch. After all these months, I've only seen the man not wearing his suit coat in the bathroom. "Martha and Gideon," he begins kindly, "I've got some bad news. Our profits, as you know, are way down, and we are letting you both go. Your work is fine. It's merely a question of finances. I'm really very sorry."

I remain perfectly still, trying to maintain my composure. My spine is so straight and rigid a bone in my lower back pops in protest. Surely this can't be happening. I've worked my butt off for this place. This time next year I had hoped to have paid off enough of my debts to be able to incur some more in order to send my daughter to college. I am gripping the sides of the leather chair and trying to relax.

Martha, who could have paid off a sizable chunk of the savings and loan bailout with what she spent for her recent wedding, begins to cry just as she did two weeks ago this past Sunday at the front of the Pine Bluff First Baptist Church. Pleasant, but with a headful of gray hair (the firm apparently likes the mature look), Martha was thrilled when her recently unemployed boyfriend of five years caved in and accepted her last ultimatum.

As if he is consoling a newly rich widow, Oscar stands and pushes a box of tissues from his desk at Martha. She snuffs loudly. I feel like joining her. Oscar, his voice registering disapproval, as if this won't do, says ruefully, "In retrospect, we should have waited to take on some new people, and of course, you're aware of the setbacks we've had recently."

The man has a nice gift for understatement. Since the place has been like a tomb the last couple of weeks and a copy of the most recent court reversal is sitting on my desk, I feel like saying that we've had an inkling that year-end bonuses might be down this time around. Yet, there is no point in leaving on a bad note: we'll still be here for a while, and I'll need a reference. "So when is our last day?" I ask, keeping my voice light and if not managing a smile, at least a nice grimace.

Oscar sits back down. Tears, he decides, he can handle. "We're going to give you two weeks' pay, but the majority of the partners voted that we don't want either of you even going back to your office. A couple of years ago we had an associate who was discharged take some clients with him. It caused us a major problem. I'll need your keys right now."

The bastards! Martha gasps. My heart begins to race, and I feel my mouth go so dry I can hardly swallow. We are being treated like employees caught stealing. I am furious. After paying bills last night, I have maybe a hundred dollars in my bank account. My hands shake as I pull apart my key ring and hand it to him. God, I hope Andrew Chapman isn't a figment of my imagination. Solo practice, here I come.

"I'm obligated to remind you," Oscar says, placing my key in a plain white envelope and then looking at me, "that taking any clients you have dealt with here is a violation of your employment contracts."

Automatically, I shake my head up and down, wondering what kind of specialty Chapman has. If I'm going to be treated as if I'm incapable of loyalty, I feel few qualms about displaying any. Am I a thief? It depends on the definition. However, I doubt that this is a story I'll brag about to my grandchildren some day.

"Personally I think this is ridiculous," Oscar says, more to Martha than to me, his wild white eyebrows wagging up and down in a show of concern. He says, "I'm sure everyone here will give y'all a good reference."

I glance over at Martha, who is finally getting herself under control. She is inspecting the damage in her compact mirror (now I know why she carries her purse everywhere). If Oscar has to say he is certain, that means she had better be careful whom she asks. I won't be needing any references.

I slide the Davis file over to him. Too late I realize it has my yellow pad with Chapman's name on it. Perhaps he won't notice it.

Oscar talks about the secretaries being available to update our résumés, but I tune him out. All I want is my check and out of here. My mind goes back to the document that Martha and I signed when we started: any client that we saw is a client of the firm's. Well, I haven't seen Chapman yet. Somebody must have clipped them pretty good. I can't wait to get to the jail.

Finally, Oscar takes two checks from his desk and slips them to us like he's ashamed of them. I look at mine. He should be. It'll cover the mortgage and utility bills. I wonder if I qualify for food stamps. I was beginning to have my doubts about the firm even before the cases were reversed. Still, it was a living and held out the hope of something better down the line. Now I know I should have checked them out better. Yet, at the time I was under some pressure to get out of the PD's Office.

"If you want to drop by later this afternoon," Oscar mumbles, "we'll have your personal items from your office boxed up at the front desk."

I've had it. "You run a class act, Oscar," I say, letting Martha precede me out his door. I give him a look of pure hatred. I hadn't realized until now how much I have sucked up to the partners. It feels good not to have to smile anymore.

Oscar's face turns the color of a bruised peach, but he doesn't have the nerve to respond, and I don't blame him.

Thirty seconds later, unemployed for the first time in my life, and beginning to realize it, I am standing on the sidewalk in front of the Blair Building, as stunned as a witness to a bomb blast. I look up at the eighth-story windows, wondering if this is a bad dream. Martha is inside, presumably still crying in the bathroom, where she fled after leaving Oscar's office. At least she has a husband. Where am I going after I leave the jail? I don't have an office anymore. Dr. Chapman, whoever the hell he is, will be impressed with his new lawyer. Well, Doctor, actually I'm practicing out of my car these days. Those bastards at Mays & Burton! American capitalism at its best.

As I cross the street at Chase and Fry, heat radiates from the pavement as though someone had poured on gasoline and ignited it. Central Arkansas in the summer is a twenty-four-hour steam bath. By the time I walk the four blocks to the municipal courts building and to the jail housed beneath it, my nicest shirt, an Egyptian broadcloth with burgundy stripes, is clinging to me through my undershirt like wet toilet paper. Fortunately, I didn't see a single person I knew on the streets, since everybody with an IQ over 7 is standing over a vent in their offices, wondering why I've chosen to stagger around outside in the middle of the afternoon in 101-degree heat.

At the window inside the municipal courts building (which has all the charm of a bus station, someone has spilled a bag of popcorn on the scuffed marble floor), I write down my home address, obtain a red attorney's pass, and clip it to the lapel of my sports coat. As I wind around the maze of offices toward the stairs that lead to the jail, I try to compose myself for my first interview in solo practice, but my mind is still in Oscar's office, as I tell him what I think of such shabby treatment after over a year of busting my balls for him and his firm. The fuckers—I hope they never win another case. At the rate they're going, it's not an idle thought.

It is only when I enter the secured part of the jail that my mind snaps back to the present. Instantly, I have my old feeling of claustrophobia as I approach the window. As a former Blackwell County public defender for a couple of years, I am no stranger to this facility, which, unlike other detention facilities in the county, has always given me the creeps. It is like being confined in a small pen full of attack dogs: too many angry people (cops, prisoners, detainees, drunks, persons with mental illness, and lawyers) compete in too small a space simply for a place to exchange information. It is the constant noise that puts me on edge. I've never heard anyone speak in a normal tone.

Though I haven't been gone from criminal practice that long, I recognize none of the jailers on this shift. Jailers don't exactly get to be a defense lawyer's best friends, but there is no sense in alienating them unnecessarily. I know some lawyers who spend hours waiting for their clients. I doubt if it is by accident.

"You'll have to talk to him on that bench," a pudgy black guy who comes to my armpit tells me, pointing with his chin to a gray wooden structure in front of us. He must be one of the civilian jailers. Why hire a rookie, spend all the money and time to train him, and stick him down in the jail to dispense medications and serve food? It only took us a couple of millennia to figure out the economics of it. "We're out of space again."

The new jail is under construction, but it isn't the sort of job there'll be a lot of overtime on to get completed. Not a real sympathetic constituency, as a friend at the PD's Office used to say. I don't argue, even though a federal case could probably be made of it. If this guy's a doctor, I should have him out on bond this afternoon. I sit down on the bench and wait, feeling absurdly pleased. I have forgotten how much I missed criminal law.

In two minutes Dr. Andrew Chapman appears before me in a bright orange jumpsuit, and I almost keel over in amazement: he is black. I didn't have a clue from his voice, a wonderful, deep baritone. One thing is for sure: Chapman is not from the eastern part of the state, the Delta, where I grew up.

"I'm Andrew Chapman," he says, holding out his right hand, which swallows mine, though we're the same height at just under six feet.

"Sorry about the bench," I tell him needlessly, sitting down. Some guys look rumpled in a brand-new tailored thousand-dollar suit: Chapman, on the other hand, is the type who can look good in a prison outfit. In his early thirties, I estimate, a decade younger than myself, Chapman has a lean, muscular body with no stomach (he'll have one when he's my age), a neat, carefully trimmed goatee, and reading glasses pushed down low on the end of his nose, all of which combine to make him look like a young Ed Bradley from "60 Minutes." The resemblance ends there. My potential client has none of the world-weariness of Ed, who is beginning to look as if he has crossed too many time zones. Despite his apparent youth, and despite this setting, Chapman has the dignity of a much older man. Sitting erect next to me on the bench, he says quietly, "Aren't you the lawyer who over a year ago got off with a light sentence the man who murdered the state senator?"

I watch the cell bars in the window across from us as a pair of black hands grips them. From here I cannot see a face, but the fingers wrapped around the metal look feminine. In front of our bench the place is a zoo, with prisoners and their keepers passing back and forth, making it hard to hear. "Yeah, that was mine when I was at the public defender's," I whisper, pleased that the Anderson case still has some mileage. It was a famous case at the time, getting me my job at Mays & Burton. Hart Anderson was perhaps on his way to becoming governor of Arkansas when he was shot down in his own home by a man who was being treated for mental illness by Anderson's wife. The plea bargain I worked out for my client, a delivery man for a food-catering service, was, under the circumstances, almost a case of blackmail, but this is not the time to be modest. "Tell me briefly what happened, so I can get a bond hearing and get you out of here."

Chapman, also watching the same pair of hands, says softly against my ear, "It's pretty complicated. Did you read about the girl at the Human Development Center who was electrocuted a couple of weeks ago?"

"Yes," I say instantly. I can't let go of the contrast to my daughter: Sarah, whose Colombian mother, now dead, was a product of a sublime mix of Indian, Spanish, and Negro blood, is stunningly beautiful, with curly coal-colored hair. My daughter, an almost spooky replica of her mother, is

Rosa's exact height, five feet four, and has the same lush
figure. The child at the Blackwell County Human Development Center, severely retarded (I can only imagine what she
looked like), had mutilated herself by constantly hitting her
face. My recollection of the *Arkansas Democrat-Gazette* article was that her death involved an attempt to stop the self-
mutilation. I am not particularly religious (although I was
raised a Catholic and got through a Catholic boarding
school), but I remember offering up a prayer of gratitude for
my daughter's wholeness. "Wasn't that an accident?" I ask,
still watching the hands on the bars. From time to time I can
see a woman's chin.

"Of course it was!" Chapman says emphatically, his voice
a boom box in the narrow hall. "But I've been charged with
manslaughter."

I lean my head back against the wall, trying to recall the
maximum length of sentence. Fifteen years. Shit! Well, that
will show you do-gooders. Must be some kind of crusade
from the new prosecutor, Jill Marymount, the first woman
ever to hold the office in Blackwell County. "Do you know
why?" I ask, my question as innocent as a first-grader's.

The digits on each side of a middle finger which is now
sticking out between the bars of the window peel back, and
a hoarse voice cries: "Sit on this, mothafuckers!"

Crinkling his brow in apparent distaste, Chapman seems,
behind his glasses and beard, truly offended. I doubt if he
has ever been in jail. He appears much too disapproving.
"That woman ought to be in the state hospital," he observes.
"Can't we talk about this later?" he asks, his deep voice as
plaintive as a farmer's prayer to end a drought.

For the first time, the full face of the female prisoner comes
into view behind the bars. She appears insane, her white hair
shooting in all directions, and I recall that prisoners who are
obviously ill are kept closer to the jailers' cage in the front.
"Of course," I say and stand. What do I expect to get from
this man right now? "Have you got some way to make
bond?"

As Chapman rises, the old woman pleads, "Get my black ass outa here, white boy! I can't stand it any longer!"

I look at my watch, wondering if I can get a bond hearing this afternoon. Chapman, his voice anxious but assertive, says, "And I can pay your fee, if that's what you're worried about."

I shrug, pretending nonchalance, but no words have sounded sweeter today. Yet if he works for the state, he can't be too loaded. Maybe he's on contract. "I'll see if I can get a hearing this afternoon."

Chapman releases so much air in a sigh he seems almost to shrink. "I'd appreciate that."

As I turn to leave, he grabs at my sleeve. "Do you have a card?"

I suppress a groan, knowing I must get this over with, before I waste any time on this case. I look him in the eye, hoping I'll know how to put this. "This is my last day at Mays & Burton," I say, trying to sound casual. "I'm in private practice as of this moment."

Against the background noise, Chapman studies me for a long moment. Fuck those bastards. He's my client, I think, wondering what else I should say to convince him to stay with me. Finally, he says, "Good. You'll have plenty of time to work on my case."

For the first time all day, I smile. "That's one way to look at it," I say, virtually admitting that I was fired. Yet, as I go upstairs, I feel confident. He wanted me, not Mays & Burton. It's a good feeling.

2

UPSTAIRS I LOOK for the municipal court prosecutor to determine the possibility of a bond hearing this afternoon. A bailiff advises me he is winding up a trial and should be available in half an hour, and I walk across the street to the county courthouse and take the world's slowest elevator to the third floor.

The Blackwell County Prosecuting Attorney's Office has undergone a major change since my entry into private practice. About six months ago, Phil Harper, who had been the head PA during my brief legal career (I didn't go to law school until the ripe old age of thirty-seven), accepted an appointment to fill an unexpected vacancy on the Arkansas Court of Appeals, and a woman from his staff was appointed to fill his place. A woman for this traditionally male job initially seemed a dubious selection, but the choice has proved astute in these days of voter sensitivity to family issues. Jill Marymount has turned the office into a crusade against domestic violence, a favorite concern of the media, since the Supreme Court struck down a statute giving civil courts broad powers to punish husbands who abused their wives.

I know Jill only slightly. While I was at the PD's Office, she was assigned to juvenile court, Outer Mongolia for an ambitious assistant prosecuting attorney with political aspirations. After Phil finally allowed her to begin handling felonies, she quickly made her reputation with a string of highly publicized child-abuse prosecutions. And when he resigned,

12

Jill, only two years ago virtually unknown, became the obvious choice to break the male stranglehold on the position of prosecutor.

However, it is not to Jill Marymount's office that I go. "Is Amy Gilchrist in?" I ask the receptionist at the prosecutor's office. Of fifteen assistant prosecuting attorneys in the office, Amy is the one I know best. While I was making my own modest reputation as a public defender in the case that has brought me Andy Chapman as a client, I learned to trust Amy, who seemed to be Phil Harper's favorite. If I approach her now before the case heats up, she can tell me what the political climate is like inside Jill's shop. Specific information about Chapman's charge can wait a few minutes. I want to get some idea of how much this case means to Jill Marymount. I think Amy will tell me, if she can.

"You can go back to her office, Mr. Page," the receptionist tells me. "She just walked in."

Flattered to be remembered by a woman I now see infrequently, I smile and make my way back to Amy's office and find her returning a stack of law books to the shelves that line the hallway.

"Gideon!" she exclaims and gives me a quick smile, her eyes as mischievous as ever. "How's the ambulance-chasing business?"

Some women make you glad to be alive. Amy is one of them. Dressed in royal blue from head to toe, Amy's firm, compact presence radiates a soothing cheerfulness. Despite an occasional flareup in the courtroom when I was going against her regularly at the Public Defender's office, we remain good friends.

"As of today, it's a one-man act," I say, following her into her office and shutting the door behind me. Her office is filled, as usual, with pictures of her parents and five older sisters, and now, obviously, some nieces and nephews. No photograph of Mr. Right. Still in her late twenties, she has plenty of time. Briefly, I explain my situation, sounding, I hope, more cheerful than I feel.

"So have you come to apply for a job?" Amy asks, tilting back in her chair that always seems to swallow her.

The question takes me by surprise. I have never considered working this side of the street. Why not? It is not a point of honor, or is it? I do not think of myself as a crusader for the proverbial "little guy" (whoever that is), but that is always the side where I end up. I lean forward and rest my arms against her desk. "I'm going to defend Andrew Chapman."

Amy nods, now understanding the purpose of my visit. "Well, you've got your work cut out for you."

This is the opening I wanted. I want to find out whether it is the police or the prosecutor who is driving this case. "Why?" I scoff, pretending indignation I don't feel. "It was obviously an accident."

Amy's normally elfin face is expressionless. "Gideon," she says carefully, "I'm not in Jill's inner circle anymore."

Surprised, I ask, "Why the hell not? I figured you'd be chief deputy, as good as you are."

Without warning and for the second time today, a woman bursts into tears in front of me. "Gideon," she sobs, "I'm three months pregnant."

I try not to gawk at her. Pregnant? I look more pregnant than she does. I study the photographs on her desk while she grabs a tissue. Stupidly, I ask, "Are you positive?"

Ignoring my idiocy, she bobs her chin. "Jill is just rigid on the subject of children. She'd like to fire me, but since she can't, she wants me to take maternity leave and have it. I'm thinking of an abortion."

I look at the picture of her father, wondering if he knows. What if Sarah brought me this news? "This is tough," I say, hedging. What do I think? I don't know. "Have you told your family?" I ask, hoping she isn't looking for my advice.

"It'd kill them," she says, honking loudly into a dry tissue, "unless I decide to have it. But even then Mother and Daddy would never feel the same about me."

Her parents, if I remember right, are hard-core Baptists. I stare at the picture of them on their fortieth wedding anniversary and see guilt being uncorked by the gallon as they toast each other with glasses of presumably fake champagne. "If you need to talk," I say, hoping to leave the subject, "call me at home. I don't have an office yet." I want to help, but I don't know what to say.

Taking my cue, Amy murmurs, "Poor Gideon. You've got your own problems."

I nod, hoping to make her feel better, but I'd take mine anyday. I stick to my script. "What is Jill running for?"

Despite her tears, Amy manages a characteristic smirk. "If you repeat this, I'll burn your house down, okay?"

I crook my right elbow at ninety degrees on her desk and hold my palm flat and stiff in imitation of a witness who takes his television lawyer shows seriously. "I swear."

Amy leans across her desk, and though I have closed the door, whispers, "The gossip I hear is that she is gearing up to run for attorney general in two years. Personally, I think she wants to be the first woman elected governor in the state."

I lean back, feeling consternation at the never-ending political ambition of lawyers. Why do we feel we are called to positions of leadership merely because some of us become highly skilled at rationalizing decisions and actions of others? My question was sarcastic, intended to probe for a less obvious motive. "Isn't her children's crusade enough? I mean, my God, how many retarded people vote? Am I missing something?"

"Gideon," Amy says, her round blue eyes serious, "she's totally sincere about all of this. Have you heard one of her speeches?" When I shake my head, Amy's voice rises as she folds her hands in front of her and begins to imitate her boss. "Every hour of each day thousands of children are being exploited in Arkansas. Not only are children the poorest population group, they are the most physically and emotionally abused segment in society; they're being provided an ever worsening education; they're hooked into alcohol and drugs; their inheritance, the environment and natural resources, are being wasted instead of conserved." Amy's voice returns to its natural pitch. "Her audiences eat it up. Children cut across class and race. It's powerful stuff."

I try to picture Jill Marymount in front of the local Kiwanis Club and fail, but then I don't have much imagination when it comes to politics. Jill is a tall brunette in her mid-thirties, striking rather than pretty, who reminds me of a high school English teacher. She scolds and shames juries more than persuades them, but I can't argue with her record. Below a certain age, child-abuse cases are almost impossible to link to a specific perpetrator. "I'll take your word for it. She sounds like a nag to me."

Amy, never modest in my presence, reaches inside her white blouse and painstakingly makes an adjustment. "She's got her statistics down cold, and she's so intense, people hang on every word she says."

I study my lap. Amy isn't far from whipping off her bra so she can get at it better. "What's politics got to do with charging with manslaughter a psychologist who did his best to keep a child from battering herself to death?"

Finally giving up or satisfied (her expression holds no clue), Amy says, "Jill, I'm sure, in her own mind, honestly believes there is no connection. She sees the child who died as simply one more example of the way children are exploited in this country. It wasn't the child who agreed to try electric skin shock—it was her mother. What adult would voluntarily let herself be zapped with a cattle prod to stop self-destructive behavior? One of her arguments is that, for example, smoking kills thousands of adults each year, but they don't go to psychologists for shock treatments to quit. Of course, she holds your client responsible, because a mother in that situation is at her wit's end and is at the mercy of the psychologist, who isn't a real doctor anyway."

So Chapman isn't a psychiatrist but a psychologist. Amy is coming on a little strong: surely Chapman didn't use a cattle prod. She is telling me more than she probably should, but I do not discourage her. Yet this may be already part of

Jill's after-dinner speech. I murmur, "So this fits right into her children's-rights theme, huh?"

Amy wags a finger at me. "Jill doesn't mention children's rights in her talks. Remember, they can't vote. She simply says that these are our children whom we make into victims, sometimes by our neglect and sometimes by our deliberate actions. Who can argue with her?"

"She sounds like she has the makings of a first-class demagogue," I say, hoping I can egg Amy on to more insights. Know thy enemy.

"She's not, really," Amy says earnestly. "Her friends say that she's been saying the same things privately for years. Now she's got a public forum and wants to see if she can take the opportunity to make some changes she believes in."

As Amy talks, I find myself wondering who the father is. Probably one of the assistant prosecutors. There are some real pretty boys over here now. "Do you know who's going to try the case?"

I know her answer before she can say it. "Jill."

"Who will assist her?"

Amy spreads her hands. "Why don't you ask up front?"

I stand up, taking the hint. It won't help Amy if anyone thinks she has been talking about the case to me. I reassure her. "Mum's the word," I say, pretending to zip my mouth.

Amy laughs. "You act so silly to be such a good lawyer."

I smile, pleased at the compliment. Were I certain of my ability, I would not need to be reassured. I have lost confidence in myself in the last hour, and for good reason. If I am so good, why was I fired?

At the front desk the receptionist calls around for me and finds out that an attorney by the name of Kerr Bowman can see me for a few minutes. She gives me directions, and I head down to the opposite end of the hall from Amy's office. I do not know Mr. Bowman, but my first impression is that I have not missed much. Though he is at least fifteen years my junior, Bowman greets me as if I were a long-lost fraternity brother. He is the kind of attorney who is always on-

stage, no matter how small the audience. The only thing I
like about him is his tie, which has alternating navy and
green stripes. He is young and cocky, with so much blond
hair he probably has to dry it with an industrial-strength fan.
Somewhere along the line a professor must have told this kid
he would make a great trial attorney and he believed it. I
look behind him and see on his wall a diploma from the
University of Texas. That accounts for some of it. Fortunately, today he is on a short leash. He pretends not to have
a copy of the arrest warrant, telling me that ''Bobba'' Stewart, the prosecutor over in municipal court, will be delighted
to make me a copy.

''We'll get one when the case is filed in circuit court after
the probable cause hearing,'' Kerr says.

I try not to roll my eyes. Kerr probably drafted it. I can't
say much without implicating Amy, so I play dumb, an easy
role for me most of the time. ''I assume, since I'm talking
to you, that you'll be handling it once it gets to circuit court.''

Kerr fingers his tie. ''Jill and I will be working together.''

I can't resist a smile. Once the case hits the papers, he'll
be lucky if she sends him out to have a subpoena served.
''Must be a big case,'' I say, feeling a pang on the right side
of my mouth. At breakfast I crunched down on what felt like
a rock in my cereal and spit it out. A part of a dingy silver-
black molar lay on the table surrounded by mush. Second
one this year. My mother's teeth. If my dick begins to crum-
ble the way my teeth are I'll be down to two inches by Christmas.

A good grunt, Kerr doesn't bite. ''It should be good
experience.''

If it goes to trial. Yet Chapman doesn't strike me as the
type to want to cop a plea. I'll find out soon enough. I head
back over to the municipal court, leaving Kerr flapping his
gums about what a privilege it is to work in front of a jury.
A minute more and I would have gagged. Could Kerr be the
father of Amy's unborn child? Surely she has too much sense
for that. The legal woods these days are full of Kerr Bow-

mans—showoffs with loud voices who are convinced a few jury trials make them bona fide lawyers. I'm not so sure. The most effective attorneys keep their clients out of court and failing that, if at all possible, away from a jury. I hope I don't have to fight Chapman over a plea. Actually, what I'd love to do is take this case and try it and win. I'm going to need all the publicity I can get.

I sit in the back of the courtroom and wait for Bobba Stewart to finish up. The prosecutor could have filed Chapman's case directly in circuit court and avoided a "probable cause" hearing—ordinarily no big deal, but under the circumstances, not a sure thing, since Darwin Bell, the municipal judge, is likely to be curious about a fellow African-American with a doctorate accused of recklessly killing a child he was trying to help. At the very least, I am counting on Darwin to set a quick bond hearing and perhaps set Chapman free on his own recognizance. The trial, a simple assault involving onetime friends, no more than a good slap in the face according to Judge Bell, who summarizes the case and then fines the defendant, a bookkeeper for a church, court costs, gives him time served (a day in jail), and then admonishes the complainant and the defendant to stay away from each other.

I come forward while the judge is lecturing the parties. Since it is now routine, the sight of a black man in central Arkansas shaking his finger at two white males as he warns them to stay clear of each other has lost its wonder (in certain parts of the state a two-headed calf presiding on the bench wouldn't draw as big a crowd) so that I can perhaps squeeze in a bond hearing before he quits for the day. After he finishes, I grab Bobba, who shrugs noncommittally at my request and accompanies me to the bench to speak to Judge Bell. I explain what I want to the judge, who listens while he is writing in the docket book his female clerk has handed him. When I tell him the name of the defendant, Judge Bell, who bears an uncanny resemblance to the late Sammy Davis, Jr., in the period of Sammy's life when he was photographed joyously embracing Richard Nixon, shakes his head and says, "You'll have to ask Judge Bruton. I have to recuse. Your client was the best man at my wedding."

Bobba grins slyly as if to say "Gotcha!" A story is told about Judge Bruton, an old man who generally hears only traffic cases, that he once said at a reception for a colleague that the country had begun an irreversible decline the day Lincoln freed the slaves. This remark must be many years old, because within the so-called "civilized center," as the *Arkansas Gazette* once referred to central Arkansas, racist remarks made in public have long been regarded as a breach of etiquette. In private, a different code governs. Five minutes later I am told by Judge Bruton's clerk that the judge, approaching seventy, has gone home for the day. My bond hearing will be no sooner than tomorrow, and I walk downstairs to tell Andrew Chapman that he will have to spend the night in jail, for no other reason than one judge likes him too much and the other one has gone home to doze in front of the afternoon soaps.

Downstairs I can detect relief by the spring in Chapman's step as he is led toward me. Damn, I haven't been on this case an hour, and I already feel guilty. Why? I think it's because I already like Chapman, even though I've just met him. Some people (not many criminal defendants) I like instinctively, and he is one of them. There is a dignity about the man that is appealing. I extend my hand formally, knowing at the moment I have nothing better to offer him. He crushes my fingers as if to reprimand me silently for allowing him to be degraded in this way. I explain his dilemma, and he listens intently. Fortunately, I didn't promise him his release this afternoon. Still, guilt, like prickly heat, jabs my conscience while I explain that tomorrow morning he will appear before the judge for a bond hearing. This man should not be in jail even overnight. If he were white, given the nature of the alleged crime, he would most likely be released on his own recognizance. He may spend one night in jail, but I'll be damned if he is going to spend another one.

"It's okay," Chapman says, consoling me. "I know you did all you could."

I shrug, not so sure. Hell, I should have called Bruton, the old bastard, at home and told him to get back down here and put in a day's work. "I'm sorry, Dr. Chapman."

He gives me a wan smile. "My friends call me Andy. 'Dr. Chapman' seems a little formal in a place like this."

I look around the human zoo surrounding me and have to agree. "Andy," I say, "my parents, God forgive them, named me 'Gideon,' and my friends don't call me 'Giddy.' "

His smile broadens. "Gideon it is."

I leave, glad I could give him something to smile about.

3

I STAND OUT in front of the jail like some derelict who has just been released from the drunk tank. The afternoon sun feels about five feet from my face. What now? So far my debut in private practice has been less than impressive. I can't even get my first and only client bonded out of jail. If I don't get out of the heat soon, I'll spend my first night in a hospital as a stroke victim. To give myself time to think, I wander back over in the direction of the Blair Building, wondering if they have had to pry Martha off the bathroom fixtures. It is beginning to sink in how desperate my situation is. If I can ever get Chapman released, the first thing I'll need to work out with him is a retainer. As if I've got something important to do, I walk against the light at the corner of Vance and Darrow. Unless you have a job, there's not much to do except window-shop—not that there's anything to buy downtown since developers figured out they could make a fortune accommodating whites who wanted to escape from blacks by moving to the western part of the county. The central business district is a checkerboard of urban blight. The closest thing to a first-rate, high-quality retail store on Darrow is a black wig shop. Actually, there is a decent-looking men's clothing store down the street, but I've never seen a white person in it. The assumption is that the stuff must be junk. And we say we're no longer racists.

I jaywalk across the street to Beaumont Drugs, which has something for everybody, even unemployed lawyers. I make the sporting-goods section my temporary office and pretend

I am pondering the eternal question: Wilson or Penn tennis balls? Bored with jogging and sick of racquetball, I have taken up tennis this summer. I wince at the price: $3.25 a can. At Wal-Mart a can costs $1.84. Given my prospective bank balance, running is looking attractive again. I find the phone booth next to the elevator and look up Chapman's address: number 5 Clearwater Apartments. Damn! The guy lives in the whitest singles apartment complex in Blackwell County. What is he trying to prove? I have thought about moving into a singles building when Sarah goes to college, but then I look in the mirror and think I'm losing my mind. The women in these buildings are young enough to be my daughters.

Out of the corner of my eye I notice a grizzled old black lady with a chinful of hair wistfully studying the phone in my hand and give her a thumbs-up sign that I'm almost through. In my new office we have to be generous about sharing the phone. I flip through the Yellow Pages, looking in the realty section, and remember an old friend in solo practice in the Layman Building almost directly across the street.

I give the old-goat lady a wink as I hand her the phone. She responds to my rudeness with a ''don't-you-be-botherin'-me-white-man'' stare, and I fairly prance out of Beaumont's, relieved to have somewhere to go. As I find Dan Bailey's name on the board in the Layman Building lobby, I begin to feel depressed again. I could write a book about what I still don't know about general practice. I am going to have to find a floor full of lawyers who will take turns holding my hand and lending me their forms. I can handle a criminal case and have learned more than I want to know from the plaintiff's side about personal injury litigation, but I can't draw up a simple deed without wanting to check my malpractice coverage. I realize suddenly that I am no longer covered by the firm. I'll just have to fly without it for a while. One crash though, and I'll be doing a forced feeding on bankruptcy law, another area I managed to avoid in school. What the hell did I learn? Confidence I do not have in abundance at the moment. As I head up to the sixteenth floor, I wonder how Dan is doing. Recently, I've come to the conclusion that he must be eating steroids for breakfast. Each time I've seen him lately, he looks as if he's gained another fifty pounds. The anxieties of solo practice, I fear. He had been in a firm after leaving the PD's Office but went out on his own six months ago. He can give me a reasonably unbiased account of the virtues (but more likely the defects) of the Layman Building.

"Is Dan Bailey in?" I ask the receptionist, a strange young woman who is slowly threading a plastic soda straw into a mouth so small her effort seems as if it might be causing her some pain.

Considering my question, she noisily slurps the remains of a Diet Coke. "Yeah, Dan's in," she says after a final gurgling sound bubbles up from the bottom of the container.

Hey, we're really moving now. "Could you tell him Gideon Page is here to see him?"

She purses her chicken lips in more thought. "Why don'cha go on back? He doesn't seem too busy." She smiles pleasantly as if she is doing us both a big favor.

This woman, her hair a rat's nest, is dressed more like a circus clown than a secretary. She is wearing green balloon pants and an aqua top. With her tiny mouth and pop eyes, she resembles some kind of prehistoric fish. Truly a receptionist from the depths. I flee down the hall until I get to 1613 and find Dan as promised, leaning back in his chair and gazing at his wall.

I walk through the open door. "Your receptionist doesn't seem particularly in awe of you," I say, taking a seat in the only other chair in the office.

He grins, his now fat cheeks billowing outward like toy sails. "It's a mutual-nonadmiration society. Thank God she's a temp. You should see the regular one—a Carol Doda look-alike." He spreads both hands under his rib cage in the now time-dishonored manner.

I shake my head in wonder at my friend's perpetual time warp. Carol Doda was, or is (for all I know), a stripper in San Francisco who surely would admit she was in her prime a quarter of a century ago, when, with all the protest marches and riots in the big cities, it seemed the country was on the verge of revolution. But Dan's most precious memory of the period is a mental postcard of two giant breasts. Yet I must have drooled over the same issues of *Playboy*. "You're looking larger than life," I say undiplomatically.

"Jeez," he complains, "if I get any fatter I'll have to be driven to work on a forklift."

I laugh, knowing I like him because I doubt he has censored a single thought since the day he got married. An hour before his wedding (a humongous affair with a catered outdoor reception at the Arts Center), he knew he was making a horrible mistake. "Brenda could handle the fact that her husband-to-be had an emotional age of fifteen," he told me once after work over a couple of beers, "but when she discovered afterward I really was only two, it freaked her. I should have called it off, but I didn't have the balls." I put my feet up on his desk and selectively rehash my year at Mays & Burton. Dan loves gossip the way my kid loves grease disguised as food.

"Shitfire!" he exclaims. "They really fucked you, didn't they?" I nod, marveling at how high Dan's voice gets when he becomes indignant. At the PD's Office we joked that if he could make his voice sound that shrill for a few more seconds he could market it as a dog whistle.

"I escaped with a client, though," I say, feeling a need not to sound too pathetic and tell him about Andrew Chapman.

His Razorback red tie choking his bulging neck, Dan loosens his collar as if my story sticks in his craw. "Aren't you a little worried," he mumbles, "that when this case hits the newspapers they might come after the fee?"

Feeling heat rising to my face, I practically shout, "He hadn't signed their retainer agreement, damn it. Besides, it was me he wanted, not Mays & Burton. The odds were almost certain they wouldn't have let me take it.''

Like a teenager wearing his first tie on a dinner date, Dan inspects it for stains. He says loyally, "You're right. They wouldn't get anywhere."

I fight down a new wave of panic. The employment agreement I signed was three pages long and covered every loophole imaginable. The assholes. I slump in the chair, feeling exhausted. "I hope the hell not."

Over a snack in the break room, Dan fills me in on the deal he has with the Layman Building. Feeling broke, I have a cup of water while he demolishes two packs of Twinkies and a Mars bar. The Secretary of Agriculture, he now calls himself, boasting that he could solve the need for subsidies to farmers all by himself.

I listen carefully and decide the price is right: I can rent a decent office and the use of a secretary for little more than three hundred a month (depending on how much typing I have). That doesn't include a phone or furniture, but Dan assures me there is a good group of lawyers on the floor who are more than willing to help each other out.

"Hell, you know that by myself I'm a card-carrying incompetent," he says, now daintily sipping a cup of coffee, "but there are five other attorneys within moaning distance of my office. Our collective IQ is probably 105, but that's more than enough to get by with the kind of nickel-and-dime crap we mostly get. You know Southerland and D'Angelo, don't you?"

I nod, sucking on a piece of ice, knowing that I might possibly find something even cheaper but probably more isolated. Not only does misery love company, in the legal business misery demands it unless you've been around forever and remember at least half of what you've learned or can lay your hands on it. Besides, I know a couple of the guys and they are pretty good, much better than Dan admits. "Tunkie" Southerland is probably one of the better lawyers I know, but like me, he is so disorganized he spends half a morning looking for his files. He writes beautifully, though, and ghosts appellate briefs for a number of lawyers in Blackwell County. Frank D'Angelo, a transplanted Yankee who couldn't get into law school up North, knows a lot of bankruptcy, so he will come in handy, too.

"If you need some furniture," Dan says, choking back a belch, "the building manager has a basement full of odds and ends that she'll rent dirt cheap."

It all seems too easy, but by 7 P.M. I'm the newest tenant of the Layman Building, and with the help of a janitor I possess some temporary office furniture. And by this time tomorrow I'll have a telephone and my name on the directory. Now, if I can just acquire more than one client. . . . Granted, my office looks like Goodwill South, but it will keep until I can drive around this weekend to some second-hand furniture stores. I know I can get some halfway decent stuff if I'll take the time to look. In the meantime, if I have any clients I can interview them in the conference room, which is only two doors from my office. Dan has told me to call the federal district court clerk's office and put my name on the list for criminal appointments for indigent defendants. The feds pay forty an hour, which is forty more than I'm getting on anything else except Chapman. I decide I will call when the phone is installed. I glance around the bare walls and realize my diplomas and other junk are at Mays & Burton, assuming they haven't dumped them into the trash. I can pick them up first thing in the morning. I've had enough of the free-enterprise system today.

4

I DO NOT pull into my driveway until almost eight o'clock. It is just as well. My daughter is at Arkansas Governor's School, a summer camp for the gifted and talented. Without Sarah, my house will be a tomb—just me and a presumably hungry dog. It is not until I have to push myself out of the Blazer that I realize I am exhausted; however, there won't be many times that I will be fired, enter private practice, and pick up a well-to-do client all in the same afternoon.

I walk across tall, scruffy grass to the house, mulling over the fact that Andrew Chapman is a behavioral psychologist, not a psychiatrist, as I previously assumed. Shrinks work with the mentally ill. I have no idea if the girl carried a dual diagnosis of mental retardation and mental illness. Wouldn't she have to be insane to mutilate herself? It is an area I know nothing about. Chapman can start my education tomorrow. Seldom has a lawyer known so little about his client. Despite my ignorance, I do know one thing, and that is this case ought to be great for business. If I can't pick up some clients from the kind of publicity this case will generate, I'm not long for private practice.

In the mailbox is the usual junk mail (Amnesty International—if they had spelled my name right I'd have given them more money—now I'm glad I didn't) and, much more pleasing, a letter from Sarah. I am thrilled she was selected to attend Governor's School but have privately wondered if her unusual racial background didn't make the difference. Granted, she is unusually bright and a hard worker, but she

28

is hardly a genius, having inherited my defective math genes. The selection committee arguably (and probably only theoretically, since she identifies herself as white) could count her as Hispanic, Indian, and black—a cornucopia of unmentioned but undoubtedly very real racial requirements.

I can hear Woogie screeching on the other side of the door. I usually make it home before seven. I won't open my letter from Sarah until I have taken Woogie for a walk. He acts so obnoxious and hyper until he's eaten and gone out, it isn't worth even opening a beer first. Tonight is no exception. As soon as I open the door, my dog, a perverse mixture of beagle and sometimes I think another species entirely (perhaps a giraffe, so long are his legs), is on me. First a fast suck on my shoelaces for old times' sake—he hasn't done that in a while—and then he backs off and makes repeated runs at me, bounding higher each time. Fortunately, beagles—even mixed breeds with long legs—can only jump so high or he would be licking my face, he is so happy to see me.

"Hi, boy," I say quietly, trying to calm him. Any inflection in my voice only excites him. "Had a big day?" I turn on some lights, flip the switch on the central air-conditioning, and head for the kitchen to fill his bowl. Rosa and I used to feed him in the mornings until he began waking us earlier and earlier to eat. While he is delightedly crunching on a bowl of what reminds me of rabbit pellets (as a boy in the Delta my father and I hunted cottontails with real beagles—it was really an excuse to get out of the house and do something together, since it never seemed to bother us when we came home empty-handed), I peel off my suit in the sweltering bedroom and slip on some shorts, tennis shoes, and a T-shirt. As I pull out my change and keys and lay them on the dresser, I glance down at a picture of the three of us—Rosa, Sarah, and me—taken outside of Graceland at Elvis's shrine in Memphis. No matter what she was wearing, Rosa always looked good. Here, just shorts, sandals, and a bright yellow T-shirt that says "Sea World" and a likeness (surely, all killer whales can be said to look alike) of Shamu, a reminder of another trip. Sarah must have been about ten at the time of the Tennessee trip, but she was already a knockout, even without her mother's sensational figure. She has it now. Genetics. She is Rosa all over again, right down to the tip of her South American Indian nose. I'm missing Sarah a lot more this third week and resist the urge to tear open her letter and read it now. But it is something to be savored over a beer. Actually, she called two nights ago, but our conversations, especially over the phone, are often awkward and frustrating, as if she would prefer to wait until she is about thirty to answer another question about her life. However, I was pleasantly surprised by her first letter, which contained more news and opinions than a week's worth of conversations around the house. When Rosa and I had a rare serious fight, she would write me a long letter, partly in English, partly in Spanish (though her English was excellent), that invariably expressed her feelings better than she did in person. Perhaps Sarah has remembered stories of these letters and has decided to use this uninterruptible and unpressured medium to explain herself. Apparently, this school is designed to stretch kids in ways they don't experience in school. In her first letter Sarah had said one of the teachers her first week made the students prove they existed. Descartes in Arkansas. Usually we are not so fond of outsiders with intellectual pretensions. It doesn't hurt to be dead a few centuries. I throw my sweaty undershirt into the hamper. As bad as it smells, surely it proves something. I call Woogie, who scurries to the front door. Outside, it seems cooler than the house and both of us are glad to escape its heated emptiness.

Typically, Woogie stops in almost every yard to piss and is a willing participant in my transgression of the leash law. Naturally, his freedom and eagerness to trespass incense the neighborhood canine population held in captivity out-of-doors, and a chorus of howls trails after us as I walk down the quiet street alternately pleading with and threatening my dog to keep up with me. Were it not nearly dark, I would have him on his leash in deference to the almost painfully law-abiding tendencies of the neighborhood, which is an unwitting model of middle-class racial harmony. In the late sixties, I'm told, a housing project two blocks east was finally desegregated, and since that time, this area has been a blockbuster's fondest dream come true, with whites selling out and blacks buying in, until, finally, the only whites left are the ones who can't afford to move away (my mortgage is 6 percent) or, perhaps, people like my late wife, who was colorblind.

As we tramp in the dust at Pinewood, the neighborhood elementary school Sarah never attended (she was bused out of our neighborhood), I wince upon hearing what sounds like a gunshot from the housing project, now called "Needle Park," located only two blocks east. I call Woogie, who is lifting his leg over some playground equipment, and we jog the two blocks back to the house. I have no desire to stop a stray bullet intended for someone delinquent on his or her drug bill. After the sun goes down, black drug dealers (there are almost no whites in the project now) control Needle Park. I don't see the point of risking an appearance on the ten o'clock news, since I should be on tomorrow night when the Chapman case breaks big time.

In the kitchen I snap open a Pearl Light and sit down with Sarah's letter, while Woogie, who seems to prefer company while he eats and drinks, laps at his water dish. Sarah's letter, neatly typed on my ten-year-old Olivetti portable, I'm delighted to see, is over two pages in length, and, in the style of her first letter, punctuated with an abundance of exclamation points:

Dear Dad,

I can't believe I'm actually sitting down and writing you another letter! Yet, so much is happening that it helps me to sort it all out if I write it down. Unfortunately, I'm finding out that I'm really kind of shallow—especially

*compared to some of these kids. In the first place, a lot of
them know so much more than I do. There's one kid who
must read five newspapers every day! For the first time in
my life I feel like the kind of girl everybody makes fun of.
You know, the dumb but peppy cheerleader, kind of like a
dumb football player! I just listen a lot of the time so they
won't find out what an ignorant person I am.*

*But it's not only that. I don't even know what I think
about religion and politics and things like that. They talk
about stuff like that a lot to challenge your beliefs and
really try to make you think about what you believe. My
problem is, I don't even know what I believe. You always
let Mom make me go to Mass, but I was too young to
understand what the priest was saying, and after Mom
died, you never made me go. I mean, I don't even know if
I believe in God! Do you believe in God? You never really
answer questions like that. You just blow stuff like that off.
I'm not trying to hurt your feelings, but I think you kind of
cop out on things like that. There are some kids here who
say they're atheists, and they can really make you think
that we're just animals and that's it! I mean, I know we're
animals, but it just knocks me out to think that's all we
are. You never talk about things like that. I don't want to
sit around at home all gloomy and have boring discussions
all the time, but I kind of feel like I've missed some things.
I think you like me not knowing what's going on. Life is
more than high school! But we never talk about anything
really important! We talk about whether I have a date on
the weekend, Woogie, whether my clothes are too tight,
who you have a date with, how dirty my room is, junk like
that!!*

*They talk a lot about Freud here—his theory that sex is
the basis of everything a person does. How civilization and
works of art come about because we sublimate our sexu-
ality. That seems so gross to me! Can't a person do something just because it's right or good? The trouble is, I can't
prove anything I say! I start to talk, and somebody ties me*

*in knots in two seconds! They question everything here.
I've never thought about it much before, but the revealed
religions like Christianity are really kind of shaky. One of
the girls in my dorm says that scientific and logical thinking has made Christianity a big joke, and she just waits
for someone to argue with her so she can tear you up. I
don't think Mom really believed a lot of the things Father
Brian said. It was a crutch for her, especially when she
was dying. (That's another thing we don't talk about!)
Freud said that religion is just a wish. When you think
about it, you see what he meant.*

*Another thing they talk about a lot up here is the Ho-
locaust. There's a Jewish kid here who's an atheist, too.
He says that if there is a God who is good and really cares
about people, He wouldn't have let the Jews and other
groups be slaughtered like that. What I don't understand
is how Germany let Hitler come to power and stay there.
They were so smart and civilized! Their excuse was that
they didn't know what was going on. Just like me! I know
you want to protect me. You want me to be happy and
smiling all the time. Like the biggest tragedy in our lives
is supposed to be if I've gone two days in a row without
making up my bed!!*

*I'll see you Saturday. Please don't wear that goofy hat.
It's no big deal you're going bald. There're a lot worse
things that have happened to people!*

*Love,
Superficial Sarah, your mindless daughter*

I put down my daughter's letter and drain half the can of
beer. I don't know whether to laugh or cry. What on earth
are they doing in that school? At this rate she'll come home
either clinically depressed or a revolutionary. As long as she
doesn't become pregnant, like Amy. Saturday, not a moment
too soon, I will pick her up for a three-day break. The first
letter should have begun to prepare me, but I'm not ready for

this new incarnation of my daughter. What's wrong with being a beautiful cheerleader? We get old and ugly and serious soon enough.

I shove myself up from the table and look in the refrigerator for something to eat. All this worrying over the meaning of life. I'll be happy if I can find a ripe tomato. I decide I only have the energy for a frozen pizza and open the freezer. So I've copped out, have I? What was I supposed to do—read Immanuel Kant to her for a bedtime story? I take out the pizza and try not to think about my failures as a parent as I pop the frozen slab of glue into the microwave. The box reads like the contents of a chemistry set. What do I believe? It depends on the time of day. In the morning I am reasonably fresh and optimistic, and so I put the odds on a God at fifty-fifty. How could somebody as marvelous as Sarah exist if there wasn't a divine spark at work somewhere in the universe? The gratitude I feel is, by itself, worth the price of admission into this world. But somewhere around six o'clock in the afternoon the odds (as I calculate them) start to go way down. By then I am exhausted, and what I've usually seen during the day is hardly reassuring as evidence of anything except that the cosmic plug has already been pulled, and if there is a God, He turned off His television set and went to bed a long time ago.

This cheery thought convinces me I need another beer to go with the inorganic meal I'm steeling myself to ingest. I gulp the last few ounces of my beer and drop it into the paper bag Sarah has insisted we reserve for cans. Too bad they can't recycle humans. When scientists are able to start doing that, the preachers really will get the shakes. I open the refrigerator again and take out another beer. What is important to me about religion is the way Sarah handles it. I'm much more interested in her being happy than in her thinking she has to discover the meaning of life. Actually, I'd rather my taxpayer's money be spent on her learning to work our VCR, but I guess Arkansas has to try to keep up appearances on this score, too.

I decide the pizza isn't so bad and chew and drink contentedly, seated at the kitchen table, while I stare out the window into the growing darkness. Saturday morning, before we pick up our kids, the parents are invited for a session to learn what is supposed to be going on, and then hear one of our U.S. senators (I forget which—like old married couples, they have all begun to sound and act alike) surely tell us how wonderful our children are, a fail-safe topic if ever there was one. I know I will not be permitted to make fun of all this sound and fury. It is serious stuff. Yet maybe I'm afraid of it (or jealous) and am minimizing my daughter's experience by making light of it.

Missing Sarah desperately, I rinse off my dish and then call Rainey McCorkle, my best friend. In an ideal world Rainey and I would be married by now, but we are still working things out. We seem to function better as friends. Since my wife's death, even the most sympathetic of observers would concede that I have behaved on the erratic side when it comes to women. Rainey, I think, would like nothing better than to be able to trust me, but like the most promising politician, I bear some watching. Apparently she has decided I am a long-term project, and since about four months ago, when we made the decision to relieve our relationship of the stress of courtship and simply be friends, we have gotten along better.

"Be sure to turn on the ten o'clock news," I say when she answers the phone. "It's been a busy day for me."

Rainey, who likes to tease, says brightly, "Oh, was there a big pileup on the interstate?"

"You can do better than that," I reply. Rainey's distaste for members of my profession is not a well-kept secret. A social worker at the state mental hospital, who, at the time we met, counseled patients I had unsuccessfully represented at civil commitment proceedings, she thinks lawyers are licensed leeches. "Actually, I was fired today, went into private practice, and picked up a client whose case is so big he's going to put me on TV, but probably not until tomorrow."

Rainey zeros in on what sounds most like the most important news to her. "What happened at Mays & Burton?" she asks, immediately serious.

I tell her the story, trying to make light of it, but I am embarrassed. The humiliation of being let go has begun to sink in. I can tell myself and others that competence had nothing to do with it, but I'll go to my grave believing that Martha and I were rookies who simply couldn't make the final cut. After all, appellate courts reverse handsome jury verdicts a good percentage of the time. It comes with the territory in plaintiff's litigation. A firm doesn't take its broom out of the closet every time a case goes the wrong way. "It's probably the best thing that's ever happened to me," I bluster. I don't want her pity. In her eyes I've already screwed up too much. Besides, she's not the type to give sympathy to someone who begs for it.

She is quiet for a moment when I finally shut up. Her voice warm and genuine, she says, "If you need to borrow some money, don't be too proud to ask me. I've got some put away for a rainy day."

I shake my head, floored by her generosity. She is offering to lend me money she doesn't have. At one point we were close enough to marriage to compare the condition of our bankbooks. Social-work salaries aren't going to drive the state into bankruptcy. "I'm okay right now," I temporize, knowing I would sooner die than take money from her. "This new client is going to be okay. I'm not kidding." I tell her about the employment agreement I had signed with Mays & Burton. This confession is at the expense of my dignity, but Rainey has seen me at my worst and can handle it. If she were the sort of woman (or man) who could be counted on to throw my weakness back into my face, discretion would definitely be the better part of valor. But Rainey doesn't hoard ammunition. She says what she thinks and moves on to the next round.

In response she merely says, "I doubt if this episode will make the chamber of commerce highlights film, but lawyers have done worse things than steal clients from each other."

I wince. It wasn't stealing at all. Yet mincing words is not part of Rainey's behavior, and I'm not really in a position to put too fine a point on my own actions. "I was furious," I say, offering an excuse since she won't do it.

"You still haven't told me the name of your big fish," Rainey says, adroitly changing the subject. She knows she doesn't need to make a speech on ethics. She has made her point.

I pause, knowing the Model Rules on ethics adopted by Arkansas technically require me not to disclose Andy's name without his permission, but by tomorrow morning everyone will know I'm his lawyer (I'm surprised I haven't gotten a call from the papers already), so a few hours don't matter. "A black psychologist by the name of Andrew Chapman, the guy who accidentally electrocuted the girl at the Blackwell County Human Development Center," I explain. "He was charged with manslaughter today. You ever hear of him?"

"I know Andy," she says in a shocked tone. "He's a real neat guy."

After this last contribution, I feel a pang of jealousy. Even in a prison jumpsuit Chapman looked impressive. "It's an awfully small world," I say, trying not to sound irritated.

"He worked at the hospital briefly as a psychological examiner, before he went back to get his Ph.D.,'" she explains. "How could they possibly charge him? It was an accident."

I nod, glad to get this response. Though she is a do-gooder when it comes to poor people, Rainey is no bleeding heart on the subject of crime. She is from the tough-guy school of criminal justice. A certain percentage of society is regrettably sociopathic. A water moccasin has a better chance of being rehabilitated than many adult criminals, according to Rainey.

"Politics, possibly, but I don't know," I say, not yet comfortable enough with Amy's theory to regurgitate it. Amy may have an ax to grind that I don't know about. "Would you keep your ears open for me?" The state is small, and the network among state employees makes it even smaller for a good number of the population. Mental health and developmental disabilities are under the same organizational umbrella, and news from one spoke travels to the other at the speed of the latest computer.

"Sure," Rainey says, shifting the conversational gears slightly. "Have you told Sarah what's happened?"

When we broke up, one of the major casualties I expected was Sarah. Rainey and Sarah became friends in a way I never thought would be possible. Rainey has come to know and love Sarah in a way I somehow can't. Half the time I come home and see Rosa standing in the kitchen (and expect far too much in the way of maturity), but when Rainey comes over, she says she sees a dazzling young woman who reminds her of no one else. For her part, Sarah has blossomed under such attention like an exotic flower. She was crushed when I came home with the news that Rainey and I didn't seem headed for the altar any longer, but they have remained good friends. I tell Rainey that I will be picking up Sarah on Saturday for a three-day break from her camp and get her to laughing over my reaction to my daughter's letter.

With a daughter of her own who has done some rebelling (though now she is a docile education major in college), Rainey is convinced that I overreact to almost everything that involves Sarah.

"Gideon," she says, "the only way you'll be completely happy with her is if you could have her stuffed and mounted on the wall in your living room."

I laugh, but there is some truth to that. I could quit worrying about what time she gets in, and it would be a lot cheaper than sending her to college. "Who's your taxidermist?"

Rainey giggles, sending a familiar, rich sound against my ear. We talk for a few more minutes, and then, sticky with a day's sweat, I hang up to take a shower. Tomorrow will be an interesting day.

The lead story on Channel 4 is Chapman's arrest. I sit in the living room in my underwear with Woogie on the couch beside me and listen as Don Roberts, who is reported to be on his way to a bigger market, reports Chapman's arrest. "Chapman, who has obtained former Blackwell County public defender Gideon Page to represent him, remains in jail tonight and will be arraigned tomorrow morning in municipal court. Efforts to contact Chapman's attorney today have been unsuccessful," Roberts says in the unctuous way of newscasters. Yawning, I walk over to the TV and snap it off. If the media can make you look bad, they will, I think irritably. Yet the only numbers they could have called are Mays & Burton and my home phone, and I didn't walk in the door until after eight. I get in bed thinking I should be relieved Roberts didn't report I was fired and will be sued by my former firm. As I turn off the light, Woogie, who has been on the floor, leaps onto the foot of the bed. Usually, he sleeps with Sarah. What is the old saying? I don't care what they say as long as they spell my name right.

That's bullshit. Mays & Burton will see that I don't come out of this smelling like a rose. The publicity will cut both ways. But even if some of the new business that it generates crawls out from beneath a rock, I'm going to need all I can get.

5

HISTORICALLY, IN BLACKWELL County municipal judges have not attracted much attention. Traffic court, misdemeanors, civil claims under a certain dollar amount, felony probable cause hearings, plea and arraignment, and bond hearings do not generate a lot in the way of legal firepower, yet this court is the venue where much of the public receives its direct exposure to the legal system, and ideally, it calls for a certain degree of decorum and dignity. Unfortunately, in Blackwell County, since these positions don't generate much excitement, some of the judges who have occupied these positions have had a way of manufacturing their own.

If you're a practicing lawyer in Blackwell County, it is painful to think of Thomas Bruton as a judge. It profits the bar more to realize that Bruton is like a tinhorn dictator in a small republic whose territory blocks access by other countries to the sea. Yet, thanks to the media, he is adored. Reporters and their bosses love judges who stick it to lawyers; instead of exposing his contempt for the law and those who serve it, the journalism community finds him colorful, if a bit eccentric. So what if he stops a trial to tell the visiting schoolchildren to his court a funny story about the stupidity of lawyers? Bruton is good press; the law itself is boring and complex. A good whiff of scandal, however, and the media would turn on him faster than pimples surface on a tenth-grader just before his first date. But Bruton, independently wealthy because of a father who was truly a fine lawyer, has no need to enrich himself financially. Like a snake too lazy and fat to venture far from beneath his rock, he is content to feed his ego with the occasional publicity that comes his way.

This morning, Bruton is plainly delighted with the attention the Chapman case is bringing him. There is no point in pretending he has a problem with setting a low bond for Andrew Chapman, but Bruton is treating my client as though he were a surly slave who would try to hook up with the Underground Railroad as soon as he was returned to the plantation.

"In setting a bond, I am troubled by the fact your client doesn't have any family in Blackwell County, Mr. Page," Bruton drawls pretentiously, peering down from the bench over his trifocals. "He doesn't have any real ties to the community here."

Unlike the Blackwell County Courthouse, the inside of the building where the municipal courtrooms are housed is without character. Functional, without ornamentation, it has the feel and look of a clean Trailways bus station. The furniture is sturdy and solid but nothing you'd want to put on a postcard. Standing beside the buff-colored defense table that looks as if it had been put together in high school shop class, I fold my arms across my chest and hide my hands under my biceps to keep Bruton from seeing how tightly I have my fists clenched. If he can see he is getting to a lawyer, he will pour it on. I want to tell him that he wouldn't be satisfied with Chapman's community ties if he had just been elected president of the Pinetree Country Club. Since there are no blacks at Pinetree except kitchen help, waiters, and caddies, this isn't likely. "As the court is aware," I say louder than I need to, "the defendant is employed by the state of Arkansas and works as a professional in this county. He lives here; the crime he is charged with makes him a threat to no one, and he would welcome a speedy disposition in this matter in order to protect his professional reputation."

With a look on his face that is intended to convey slyness but merely makes him look silly, Bruton, who only minutes ago accepted Chapman's not-guilty plea, asks, "Are you waiving a probable cause hearing then? If you are, we'll have this case bound over to circuit court right now.''

I look down at Chapman, and then back at the judge. It is tempting to advise my client to commit suicide on the spot just to get out of Bruton's court. Actually, Bruton would be disappointed if I did, since he would be out of the spotlight. The reason to go through with the probable cause hearing is to get a look at Jill Marymount's case in advance, even though the result of a probable cause hearing with Bruton presiding is foreordained. Jurisdiction, or the power of a particular court to hear a case, is a royal pain in the ass in Arkansas. Last year, for example, when I defended the murderer of a state senator, the case was filed directly by the prosecuting attorney in circuit court. Jill Marymount could have chosen to do the same here but elected to have the case originally filed in municipal court though it will doubtless end up in circuit for the full trial. "No, Your Honor," I say, "Dr. Chapman is not waiving a probable cause hearing."

Bruton's mouth, as discolored as an overripe persimmon, turns downward in a frown. "Your client's not a doctor."

I don't believe this. I whisper to Chapman, "Don't you have a Ph.D. in psychology?"

Andy nods. "From Fayetteville."

I look up and try to keep my voice even. "Dr. Chapman received his doctorate in psychology from the University of Arkansas at Fayetteville. Would the court like him to bring in his diploma?"

Looking over my head at his audience, swollen today by the media and a few curious lawyers, Bruton counters with his own sarcasm. "Mr. Page, my degree from that same institution probably says that I am a doctor of jurisprudence, and presumably, you are, too. But we do not call ourselves 'doctors,' now, do we? That would be putting on airs, wouldn't it?"

The petty little bastard. I say slowly, as if to a child, "My understanding of the law, Your Honor, is that a person is entitled to call himself anything he likes so long as it's not for an illegal purpose.''

"No, we don't," Bruton says, ignoring me and answering his own question. "And the policy in this court is that only physicians and dentists may refer to themselves as doctors.''

I look down at Andy and then back at the judge. "Would the court feel more comfortable if I address the defendant by his first name?''

It takes Bruton a few moments to catch on. He squints at me as if his patience has run out. "What are you insinuating, Mr. Page?''

That you are a racist asshole tyrant. "Nothing, Your Honor,'' I say blandly, "I'm just trying to find out how the court wants me to address the defendant." Baiting him is not a smart thing to do: judges can always get back at you if through no other way than by dumping on your client. Still, there is a fine line that I haven't crossed. Like a student who knows how far he can push a teacher, I keep my tone of voice flat and my face solemn.

At this point Bruton would rather play to the crowd than take the trouble to figure out if he can get away with holding me in contempt. A triumphant sneer comes to the old man's lips. "I don't care what you call him just as long as it's not 'doctor'!" he thunders, looking around to see the expression on the faces of his audience.

I follow his gaze. There are a few snotty grins, but mostly the faces in the courtroom are frozen into embarrassed half-smiles that tell me they find this colloquy something short of a brilliant legal debate. Still, Andy shouldn't have to put up with such blatant racism. "Your Honor, I move that this court recuse itself. By the court's failure to permit the defendant to use the title of 'doctor,' the court exhibits an appearance of racial bias.''

Chapman shoots me a look of total dismay. If Bruton dis-qualifies himself, he might have to spend another night in jail because of the delay. Fat chance. There is no conceivable possibility that Bruton will not hear this case. The last thing a bigot like Bruton will do is admit to prejudice. What I'm worried about is how high I've sent Chapman's bond by raising this issue. If I were black, I'd have more credibility. White lawyers often deal with this issue by trying to work around it—pretending racism no longer exists and then using valuable peremptory jury challenges to weed out suspect jurors. By raising this issue, I have committed a major faux pas. Officially, we are all reconstructed. Privately, nothing could be further from the truth; but, in the South, cowardice is considered good manners. Under no circumstances will we insult each other's so-called honor.

Color creeps up Bruton's neck. I have pissed him royally. He knows he is vulnerable. There are too many stories the media has suppressed in the past. "That's ridiculous—motion denied!" he spits.

I clear my throat, waiting for inspiration to strike, when I am saved by an unlikely source. Fingering red suspenders that make him look about eight years old instead of like a young sophisticated professional on the make, Bobba Stewart pipes up, "Judge, we don't have any objection to a bond of say, five thousand dollars. We don't think this defendant is a major threat to attempt to flee the court's jurisdiction."

I look gratefully at Bobba, who nervously adjusts his turquoise bow tie. If he had disclosed this when I first asked him this morning what he thought would be reasonable (I had suggested that Andy be released on his own recognizance), I wouldn't have sweat pouring down my sides now; but beggars can't be choosers.

Bruton is on the spot. If the prosecutor isn't worried, why should he be? It's not as if Chapman has been charged with an intentional act or is likely to get drunk and run out and shock another child. Shaking his bald head in disbelief, Bruton folds quietly. "If you're willing to live with that recommendation, it's fine with me. Let's set this for a hearing so we can move on."

I nod at Bobba, who is surely following direct orders from Jill Marymount. Is this a sop to the black community or what? I suppose this is Jill's way of saying to blacks that this charge is nothing personal. Obviously, she hasn't done herself any favors politically by charging a black male with a Ph.D. Blacks constitute about twenty percent of the population in Blackwell County, and it's not as if there is an assembly line somewhere in Arkansas turning out minority doctoral candidates. "Your Honor," Bobba says, "how about Monday morning?"

Bruton goes through the pretense of consulting his docket. He can bump traffic cases any time. He looks at me but does not condescend to speak after our most recent exchange. He won't permit me to believe, nor should I, that I have had anything to do with the outcome of this hearing. He has acquiesced in a low bond in spite of, not because of, my representation. "What time?" I ask, more to force him to speak to me than needing to know the time. Bruton will make it the first order of business so Bobba can get back to misdemeanor court.

"Nine o'clock Monday. Court's in recess for ten minutes," he rasps indistinctly. We are like children who have to have the last word. He rises, and still without looking at me, departs for his chambers.

As soon as Bruton shuts the door behind him, Andy shakes his head at me and says quietly, "Gideon, don't ever raise the issue of race again while you're defending me."

This instruction seems a little dramatic. I assume he is pissed because of my motion that Bruton recuse himself. I do not want to admit that it was done on the spur of the moment and out of spite. I sit down next to him so I can whisper. "You have to keep a bastard like Bruton honest or he'll run over you the entire time."

Andy picks a piece of dirt from his jumpsuit. He is not fooled. "We'll talk about it later," he says calmly. "The prosecutor saved me some money."

Instead of having to use a bail bondsman, my client saves himself five hundred dollars by putting up a cash bond. Where is he getting his money? If Bruton had jailed me for contempt, I'd be there until Labor Day; in contrast, Andy has forked over more money than I've made all summer. While we were waiting for his hearing to begin, he agreed to pay me a $5,000 retainer and $100 an hour. With any other client charged with causing someone's death, I'd be suspicious as hell. The criminal defendants I've represented don't seem the type to join the Christmas savings club at their place of employment. As I wait down in the jail for Andy to change, I wonder about his instructions not to raise the racial issue in his case. Where does this guy think he is? Throughout the proceeding, he sat as erect and proud as a king, even a bit detached from it all. Arrogance won't do at all in front of a mostly white jury in this case. The girl was white. I don't want him to beg for forgiveness; but he will have to warm up, or they won't give a damn.

Andy's clothes, now that he is out of his jumpsuit, should be badly wrinkled, but he manages to look as if he has stepped out of an ad for L. L. Bean, as fresh as a sprig of mint. He is wearing a tailored olive-green suit over a Hathaway canary-yellow shirt and a gold-and-green tie. As we walk upstairs from the jail, I notice for the first time an attractive white woman waiting for us by the door that leads back into the courtroom. I need no introduction. Olivia Le Master, as poised as a high-fashion model, looks just like her real estate ads. She is a tall, lithe woman with permed black hair that reaches the collar of a white blouse. A green peasant skirt comes to her ankles. On her feet are a pair of white Birkenstocks. Though she is too flat-chested for my taste, I think I could make an exception.

Her gray eyes, framed by dark eyebrows, seem puzzled. She asks Andy, "I missed it, didn't I?"

His eyes are on the reporters who are waiting at the other end of the hall for him to come out the front door. I have already advised him to make no comment. He says softly, not looking at her, "Just barely. Why don't we talk later?"

Following his gaze down the hall she nods and steps inside the courtroom before the media sees her. I find it extraordinary she is anywhere within ten miles of this courthouse. The nightmare it must bring back to her! Yet why shouldn't she be supportive? Andy was willing to try to help her child—perhaps the only professional willing to try something out of the ordinary. If I can persuade her to testify for him, she can be his ticket to an acquittal.

"That was the child's mother," Andy says coolly, adjusting his tie as we begin to walk toward the front door. "I'll introduce you later."

Almost immediately, we are engulfed by the media. My favorite, Channel 11's Kim Keogh, is here this morning. I have never seen her in person before, but she is even more gorgeous than on camera. All the other women reporters on television look as if they can barely hold up their heads because of all their makeup, but this woman looks as natural and friendly as a three-month-old cocker spaniel. Rainey, who watches the news more than I do, insists that Kim Keogh wears plenty of makeup but that it is so skillfully applied you can't tell. I hope she is the last one to interview me. I'd like to get to know her. As I expected, I get questions about my motion that Judge Bruton disqualify himself; but I refuse to be baited into divulging anything that will get me into further trouble, saying only that it is the appearance of bias that I alleged. If I had any guts, I'd tell them that Judge Bruton has been swapping racist jokes back in his chambers for years. Instead, I defuse the issue as best I can. With one client to my name, I don't need to have the reputation among the judges that I've become a troublemaker, even though it is common knowledge in the bar that Bruton is an ignorant fool who has no business on the bench.

I get my wish. Kim Keogh is the last television reporter to approach and asks if she can have a brief interview with me. The others, women and men alike, have come on in their questions as though Sam Donaldson had just dropped by their studios for a pep talk, but Kim is almost laid back despite being dressed to the teeth. She is wearing a hunter-green suede jacket over a full-length burgundy skirt. Her white blouse is one of those rayon jobs with the buttons at the back of the neck. Her dry-cleaning bill alone for this outfit probably cost more than my J. C. Penney suit. While her camera man is fiddling with her equipment, she asks me if I am the attorney who defended the man who shot Senator Anderson. Flattered beyond all reason to be remembered by her, I tell her that was my fifteen minutes of fame. Even her questions while the camera is on are more about me than the case, and I manage to get in that I have just gone into solo practice. I notice she is wearing no rings on the fingers that are holding the microphone in front of my face and wonder if I have the nerve to call her. It probably will depend on what she says about me.

After the interview, breathing her perfume (she smells faintly of magnolia blossoms), I ask, "How'd I do?"

She gives me a dazzling smile and says under her breath, "If this gets on the air and brings you any business, you ought to buy me lunch."

I need no further encouragement. "It's a deal," I say, wondering if she has noticed my bald spot yet. If she was in the courtroom, she couldn't miss it. The back of my head is beginning to look like a giant sand trap. She can't be more than thirty, but maybe she likes the mature type. After Rosa died, I decided that I wouldn't embarrass myself by asking out a woman more than a decade my junior. Like most of my good intentions, that didn't last long.

As Andy and I watch her walk out the door with her cameraman, he observes, "I wish all interviews were that friendly."

Andy, I've noticed, doesn't miss much. I force myself to look at him and pretend it was all business. "You're going to need all the friends like that we can get."

He nods soberly. "Would you like to go somewhere and talk to Olivia now? I know she wants to talk to you."

"Sure," I say, wishing I had known she was coming. If this case is going to be pretried in the media by the prosecutor, the mother of the victim, could, if she is willing, be of enormous help. Yet, it is difficult for me to grasp the possibility that she might be willing to get involved. After all, her child hasn't been dead two weeks. But if she talks to the media about this case, I want to have an opportunity to tell her what I think she ought to say. Doubtless twelve jurors can be found who will swear under oath they haven't heard of the case, but the presiding circuit-court judge will have an opinion, and my best hope in this case may be to keep the decision out of the hands of the jury. Unless I'm missing something, Jill Marymount will have expert witnesses falling all over each other to testify that shock shouldn't be used on helpless, retarded children. The trial judge has control over which experts are qualified to testify and whether their testimony is relevant. Before the trial judge makes this decision, I want him or her to have read or heard the mother of the victim say that her child was in such pain she welcomed someone who was willing to try to help her. Is this unethical? Surely no more so than Jill Marymount running around all over Blackwell County screaming about helpless children.

I decide to take Andy and Olivia Le Master to the conference room two doors down from my office in the Layman Building. It is an awkward walk for all of us. After I say I'm sorry about her child and she nods politely, my mind goes blank. I'm not ready to begin our interview in public, and yet small talk seems somehow out of place in the face of death. As we cross the street at the corner of Lewis and Russell, Olivia, whose stride matches my own, pauses for Andy, who has been lagging behind, to catch up with us.

"I need a shower," he says somewhat sheepishly.

Olivia nods and says, her face full of sympathy, "It must have been horrible for you."

He nods noncommittally, and I wonder about their relationship. Could it be sexual? I try to read their expressions, but if there is a special chemistry between them, I can't tell. Andy, who seems to have the grooming instincts of a cat, appears embarrassed, and Olivia, sensitive to his feelings, walks the rest of the way to the Layman Building alongside me. Yet, for all I understand at this point, they could easily be hiding their feelings. As we enter the elevator to take us to the sixteenth floor, I reflect upon the fact that sex is routinely my first explanation of human behavior. When Rainey is in her social-worker mode, she tells me that I constantly project my feelings onto everybody else.

At the receptionist's desk I have, not surprisingly, no messages in my box. The temporary, whose name I have learned is Julia, eyes me suspiciously. Great, her expression says, the first clients you drag up here are an interracial couple. "Hold my calls," I say to her as if I'm expecting to be deluged. "Is the conference room available?"

She points sullenly to a key hanging on a hook on the gray metal message box. "What does that key tell you?"

Do I remind this woman of her worst nightmare, or what? I snatch the key from its hook, resisting the temptation to gouge her eyes out with it. "Thanks," I say, giving her a fake smile. If this is not her last day here, it will be mine. I find that I do not have the courage to ask if there is any coffee in the conference room.

We make a lonely-looking trio in the conference room, but it may be helpful in stimulating conversation if we don't feel we are on top of each other. I sit at the head of the table facing the door. Andy and Olivia Le Master take chairs on opposite sides of the table. I realize I should have told Andy that I needed to visit with him alone—that there will be plenty of time to talk to Olivia. Since she is already down here and seemingly willing to talk, I am afraid to pass up the opportunity, since she may be the key to saving his rear. Now that I have them seated, I would like to be able to watch both of their expressions simultaneously, but I can't very well ask them to move together. I begin by telling Olivia that I have a daughter and can imagine how I would feel if I lost her. "Every time she's ten minutes late I start to worry about her," I say tentatively, hoping I'm not being presumptuous. I know firsthand how meaningless words of sympathy are from most people. The pain from the death of someone you love can hardly be imagined by someone else. In an effort to establish my sincerity, I add, "My wife died of cancer, so I spook pretty easily."

I have pushed the right button. Olivia's small bust rises and falls as she sighs, "How old is your daughter?"

"Seventeen," I say and, unable to stop myself, add, "she's at the Governor's School at Hendrix College for the Gifted and Talented this summer."

Her smile is genuine. "You must be very proud."

"I am," I say and stop. How callous can I be? Her child was born without a normal brain, the first words out of my mouth are how superior my child is.

Olivia's gray eyes are warm with concern as she empathizes. "I understand how you feel about your daughter. Unless she was in restraints or heavily drugged, there were times I couldn't stop worrying about Pam, and then it was a different kind of worry. When you have a child who injures herself, for months every time the phone rings after it happens you think they're calling you to tell you something new and even more horrible than before."

I have begun to nod, but I can't really even imagine what she has gone through. Almost every day with Sarah has been a joy; has this woman even had one happy day with her child? How has she endured it? As grotesque as shock sounds, a radical form of treatment at some point may seem unavoidable. However, probably only the parent of the child can say that convincingly. For the next forty minutes Olivia Le Master tells me a story that I will remember the rest of my life, for it is impossible for me not to think of Sarah while she recounts her child's tortured existence. While I listen to the predictable anguish and guilt all parents must feel upon learning their child is retarded, I think of how much I take my daughter's normality for granted. Would I have deserted Rosa (as Olivia Le Master's husband did) if Sarah had turned out to be profoundly retarded? Surely not, I tell myself, but the truth is that I would have been sorely tempted. As she speaks, I can hear my mother saying an hour before the wedding: God knows, Gideon, you don't know a thing about her background. She, of course, was not so obliquely referring to my own father's mental illness. Knowing myself, I would have tried to find a way to blame Rosa had Sarah been screwed up. How does a young mother have the strength by herself to raise a child like that at home? Incredibly, Olivia Le Master tried, but she found it was impossible alone. She had to work to support herself, and child care is difficult enough in Arkansas under the best of circumstances. For her, but perhaps not for others, she concedes, it was too much. Certain she was abandoning her daughter when she began to abuse herself, Olivia placed Pam in the Blackwell County Human Development Center when she was ten.

"You can't imagine the relief I felt when she was accepted," Olivia says, her eyes filling with tears. "I felt I could breathe for the first time since my husband ran off."

Men are truly jerks, I think. What makes us weaker than women? Is it simply that they are the ones to have children and thus come by a sense of responsibility more naturally? As I listen to her account, I imagine I am hearing the story of every women who has turned her child over to the state. If she missed a weekly visit, she felt enormous guilt. In a kind of feeble way I try to identify with her. There have been more nights than I care to remember when I have come home much later than I promised Sarah. The look on her face (anger and relief) has, from time to time, haunted my dreams.

Still, time brings a measure of acceptance of events that cannot be reversed. A healthy sense of fatalism, Olivia calls it during the interview, and though I don't believe in fate, I can understand how she does. Before Pam was born, David Le Master started a real estate business, and it was his gift to his wife when he decided he didn't want to be around anymore. "David was good at starting things," she says, a wintry smile overtaking her face whenever she mentions her husband. "I'll give him that."

Most men are, I think, glancing sideways to catch my

client's expression. He is watching her face with such sympathy I feel a twinge of guilt.

Olivia relates her daughter's tragedy without another reference to her ex-husband. In a straightforward manner she tells me what it was like when the self-injurious behavior began. With no warning whatsoever one day, Pam began beating her head with her fists at first and then later against walls, even against her bed. Not so hard that one blow would cause injury by itself but hard enough to bruise her. Left alone, she would hit herself over one hundred times in an hour. I turn to Andy and ask why a child would do this, but he says that there are only theories for this behavior, not explanations, the latest one being that self-injurious behavior is actually a form of communication. More traditionally, Andy says, slipping into jargon, it is thought to be behavior that is reinforced by attention or is an attempt to avoid a task or is even somehow intrinsically reinforcing. ''The fact is,'' Andy says, looking at Olivia, though I'm sure they have discussed this topic many times, ''no one knows for sure what prompts a child to hurt herself.''

Olivia has begun to cry. Of course there is no box of tissues for my clients in the conference room, but Olivia yanks a wad from her purse and begins to talk even while she wipes her face. ''When she first started hitting herself, I was told it might stop, but with time, it only got worse. I couldn't believe it. I don't care whether a person says they believe in God or not—you think you're being punished for something you did. Who knows? Maybe all of us were being punished— I'd be lying if I didn't admit to you that in some ways Pam's death has been a relief.''

This last sentence, understandable, and not totally unexpected, is still jarring to me. Without this last addendum about death being a release, Olivia's impact on a judge and jury will be favorable. And yet, maybe it, too, will be understood. This is not some highly emotional and distraught parent who has been overly influenced by a psychologist who wanted to use her daughter as a guinea pig for his own research. Rather, Olivia, assuming her testimony holds up, will come across as a strong, caring mother, who loved her daughter enough to inflict pain on her if that was what it took to help her.

I glance back at my client and am not surprised to find that his eyes are moist. But I do not want Olivia to admit in the witness chair that even for a moment she thought about the surcease from pain her child's death would bring. With the acknowledgment of this all-too-human motive, it might be tempting for the prosecutor to try to convince a jury that a sympathetic and frustrated psychologist deliberately went too far in trying to end her child's suffering. Waiting for her to finish wiping her eyes, I wonder how I can say this without coming across as hideously manipulative. Lawyers are directors as well as actors in a play. If we forget that for one instant, we're no longer doing the job we're hired to do. Just tell the truth, we tell our witnesses. What we mean is, just tell the truth in a way the judge or jury will believe you. I'm all for the truth, but if nobody believes it, what has the system accomplished? The trouble with being a public defender was that the witnesses for the defense were not credible even when they were telling the truth. Give me a good actor who can make the truth convincing, and I've got a chance. I don't have to tell Olivia what I need from her today. We will have the time later if she is willing to help me.

We talk about past attempts to help Pam, and I am not surprised to hear bitterness in her voice as she speaks about the psychologists over the years who refused to try shock. As she speaks, her face becomes hard, and I think I see for the first time the facet of her personality that has allowed her to take over a small real estate operation (I had never heard of River Country Realty until two years ago) and turn it into a major force in the central Arkansas area.

"The first time I heard of shock I thought I was being teased. This little Dr. Oliphant—he left the state a year before you came, Andy," Olivia says, "had the nerve to say that shock was her only hope but only a sadist would use it. He was so smug, so morally superior—I wanted to kill him. Every time I brought it up he would get this expression on his face that said I was depraved for even thinking of it. I think he wanted to try it, but he didn't have the guts.'' This last sentence is spit from her mouth, her face twisting in anger. Theoreticians do not rank high on this woman's list. Whatever I have to do to persuade her to testify, I won't moralize.

Andy's head, I notice, turning quickly to observe him, dips in apparent agreement. ''What about the other psychologists?'' I ask both of them. ''If it works, surely somebody in the state was using it.''

In a gesture of impatience, Olivia pushes her hair back from her long, tanned face. ''Though I kept hearing rumors about the use of shock in the past, Dr. Oliphant wouldn't admit to knowing anybody who had tried it who was still in the state. You know you can't make doctors talk when they don't want to—they hide behind confidentiality whenever it's convenient.''

I look at Andy and see that his wide taupe lips are tightly compressed. He must be having the same thought that flits through my mind. Notwithstanding the quality of her life, Olivia's daughter would be alive today if he hadn't had so much courage. Granted the other professionals may have been timid, but not without reason. After all, Pam died. I need to understand the circumstances better, but I'd be a monster to make Olivia sit through a story that already must give her nightmares. I ask her a few more questions and learn that it was she who had suggested to Andy that he try shock. I also learn to my dismay that he had never even been present when that form of behavior therapy had been used before. It will lend credence to the charge of recklessness that the prosecutor has to prove. Yet, as I listen to this woman, I am beginning to understand why he gave in to her. Olivia, whose intensity has grown with each moment, is both persuasive and vulnerable. As she talks about the agony Pam experienced, it is easy to believe that there was no other alternative

to shock, which, she understood and Andy confirms, is painful, yet safe, if used correctly. As I glance back and forth
between them, what disturbs me is my growing sense that
my client, though armed with the best of intentions, may
have been professionally unqualified to use shock as a technique to modify Pam's behavior. How could he have refused
to have educated himself as much as possible? Perhaps he
did, I think, realizing I know literally nothing about it.

I will want to talk to Olivia before the probable cause
hearing, but away from Andy. Though it seems unlikely, the
gratitude she feels now may turn soft before Monday, as she
begins to get some pressure to turn on him. It would be
difficult if not impossible for her to tell him while he is sitting
across from her that she thinks he should have refused to help
her. It may not be so hard to back away from him once she
is placed under oath and the prosecutor is giving her a perfect
way to escape guilt—blame the doctor, Mrs. Le Master: he
is supposed to be detached, cool, the professional. She seems
to have more integrity than that, but I will be the first to
admit that a woman has fooled me badly before in one of
these situations. Besides, from an ethical standpoint, perhaps
Andy did fatally forfeit his judgment. After all, he is presumably trained, educated, and licensed to exercise appropriate
professional discretion, and now a child is dead. A criminal,
though? Surely not.

Leaving Andy alone in the conference room, I walk Olivia
down the hall and to the elevators and tell her I would like
to call her soon. Her eyes slightly red now from crying, she
assures me she will help in any way I suggest. "He tried,"
she says defiantly, "when no one else would. All these so-
called advocates act as if children like Pam can be helped
without aversive measures. Well, goddamn it, why didn't
they do it?"

I push the elevator button for her. I have no answer. I have
no quarrel with her anger, but I want it to work for Chapman.
If I handle it correctly, the jury may understand that the real

defendant isn't on trial. I decide to provoke her with the truth, or at least part of it. "I don't know about the advocates," I say as she steps into an empty elevator, "but the doctors and psychologists are scared to death of malpractice."

A hard glint comes into her gray eyes and she stares at me, holding the door for one final comment. "All I know is these other so-called professionals weren't willing to try anything that might work," she says. "He could have turned his back on me, and he didn't, and I'm not going to forget that."

"I'll hold you to that," I say, as the door begins to slide shut. "I'll be calling you in the next day or so." I walk back to the conference room, realizing Olivia has a determined side to her that she doesn't bother to conceal. But why should she? What else does she have to lose? Besides, she is in a business that is at least as well known for its hard times as for its good times. One thing is certain: if she turns on Andy, he is dead meat. Olivia Le Master, I've decided, can be a ball buster. I just hope she doesn't decide to go after my client's.

6

WITH OLIVIA'S DEPARTURE, Andy and I adjourn for a couple of minutes to allow me to go take a leak and find us both some coffee. At the front desk Julia has a smirk on her face that says my own IQ is so low it may not be testable as she reminds me that there is free coffee in the break room, which is only one door down from the conference room. She is dressed (except for a denim skirt) in what I'd call a Hell's Angels biker outfit, complete with jackboots, and snarls through her peephole of a mouth, "Reminds me when I was a kid of my dog nearly starving one time. Blitz, our boxer, he whined at the front door for a solid day when all he had to do was walk around to the side and go through the garage."

I study her face, wondering where a bullet would cause the most pain before it killed her. I do not want to mar her precious childhood memory, but I mutter, "That's really fascinating." Applying mauve nail polish to the bitten-off stubs on her right hand, Julia stops and smiles sweetly. "It helps me sometimes when I can find something to identify with."

Thank you, Julia. "That must be difficult," I say with an equal amount of venom and head back toward the break room. Before eastern Europe totally embraces capitalism, maybe it's proponents should come take a look at Julia. What have I done to make this woman hate me? I don't usually have this effect on people. I wonder what a cattle prod would do to her.

58

Armed with two steaming paper cups of coffee, I find Andy waiting for me in the conference room with his own coffee. I shut the door in case Julia has gotten up to roam the halls. "Olivia may be the difference between you and a guilty verdict," I say, hoping my comment will get back to her. "Would you have tried shock if it had been another parent?" I ask, hoping he will answer honestly. I am not ready to ask if there is a sexual relationship between them, but if he wants to volunteer, that will be fine with me.

"The parent has to be behind you totally," Andy replies softly, peering down into his coffee.

"I don't know the first thing about what you do," I admit, seeking a place to begin. From my years repre- senting mentally ill patients in civil commitment hearings when I was a public defender, I know something about the mentally ill, but mental retardation calls up a harm- less, beautiful male giant from my childhood in eastern Arkansas who had a brain the size of a pea. This once stubborn memory has been gradually replaced with a TV image of valiant, lovable children somberly trying to cope with the simplest of tasks.

Andy nods briskly, his manner businesslike, now that Olivia is gone. He instructs, "You've heard of behavior mod- ification?"

"As in B. F. Skinner?" I ask, recalling a psychology course at the University of Arkansas when I was a sopho- more.

"Skinner was a prophet," he says reverentially, fixing me with a stare made more intense by his slightly magnified eyes, "who was so honest that few could stand his message. He demonstrated over and over again that free will is an illusion. In a society as out of control as the United States, it's lucky he wasn't lynched." With this last phrase his voice is tinged with irony.

I lean back in the comfortable swivel chair, wishing I could steal it for my office, and scratch the middle knuckle of my right hand. The permanently swollen joint is a souvenir of too many balls that bounced off the tip. A near-sighted wannabe Mickey Mantle who couldn't be trusted with contact lenses until I was sixteen, I am lucky to have my teeth. It seems strange to hear a black say, "Sorry, folks, there's been some kind of awful mistake all these years. You only think you're deciding what kind of cereal you want for breakfast each morning." I hate to tell Andy, but this decade, freedom is in. Even the most devout Marxist is trying to make a buck.

He reads my skepticism and adds, "I know what I'm saying is anathema to the legal profession. There'd be a major recession in this country if you lawyers couldn't peddle free will."

I can see a jury shaking twelve heads at once. Surely he accepts the rules of the game, or he wouldn't be in my office. "Why don't you just tell me what happened," I say, already bored with theory. Despite his profession (there is a lot of bullshit in this area), I can't help but like him. He is obviously a bright guy, yet unpretentious. Blacks who are as educated as this guy like to use a lot of big words. Andy reminds me of a good teacher, patient as a coyote and without the sarcasm and condescension that some otherwise competent professors can't manage without.

In no hurry to get to the meat, he rests his hairy chin on his fingers. "In order to fully understand my situation, you are required to accept the proposition that behavior modification is a science and proceeds on that basis."

I tap a Flair pen against my legal pad. Sure it is. Shocking a child with a cattle prod is right up there with a cure for polio. I don't blame him for not wanting to talk about what happened. "I've no doubt it was an accident," I say, smoothing his path. Rockets blow up all the time. If I can get this knocked down to a charge of negligent homicide, I'll be earning my pay.

Behind his glasses, Andy squints as if he is trying to picture the event. "It happened so fast that it still seems unreal."

Poor guy, he didn't have time to change his mind. Though he is tired, he needs to go through this. I plunge ahead. "We need to talk about what happened. What I know about electricity won't fill up a thimble," I confess. "Did you accidentally shock her in the chest, or what?"

Chapman rubs his head as if he still can't understand it. "What happened was that she grabbed the handle of the prod with her right hand, I suppose to push it away," he says slowly, "and according to the doctor who pronounced her dead, the current passed from one of the electrodes touching her left thigh and traveled through her chest and heart down her right hand, which was touching the handle. It happened so quickly I didn't realize she was grabbing at the handle."

Without realizing it, I have brought my hands together. A complete circuit. I have jumped smack into the middle, but I can always come back for details. "Didn't you have her hands tied?"

"Leon Robinson—he's an aide—was trying to hold her," Andy says, "but it was hard to keep her still, I guess."

"Was it really a battery-powered device that's used on animals?" I ask, praying it wasn't. When I was fourteen, I worked on a cousin's farm and watched a cattle prod used on sheep. I remember thinking that even through all that wool it hurt them. Of course, that was the point.

"Let me explain about that," Andy says, his voice rising for the first time since I've met him. "Once you start learning about this procedure, you're going to find that there are commercial products available you can send for to use on individuals. The problem was that I knew if I asked, I wouldn't get permission to try shock on Pam. I thought that if I showed the administrator, David Spath, what could be accomplished with Pam, he would back me and let me work with her. Shock works incredibly quickly to suppress self-abusive behavior, and both Olivia and I were convinced that he would go along with it once he saw Pam for the first time in years not hitting her head. Shock works like a miracle, and all that bullshit about it being too aversive comes to a screeching halt when, after years of keeping a child in restraints or on drugs and trying everything under the sun, you see the kid not hurting herself. Of course, it's a last resort, but the scientific literature is clear: shock works. And someone at the Human Development Center knew it at one time, because that's where I found the equipment I used. All it needed was new batteries.''

I try not to squirm with impatience. You can't expect a jury to be sympathetic when you have to tell them that your client took a device you use on an animal and used it on a human. It has to hurt like hell. ''Surely no one has used a cattle prod before.''

Stubbornly, Andy, his lips pursed, shakes his head. ''Sure they have. In some of the first published research in which shock was effective a cattle prod was used. What is recommended, and what I did, was wrap the metal case in insulation tape, so that even if the case was grabbed while Pam was being shocked, there wouldn't be a closed circuit.''

At least he seems to know what he was supposed to do. I ask, ''So what happened?''

Andy lets out a deep sigh. ''I don't know. I guess it wasn't thick enough.''

I study Andy Chapman's face, which, for the moment, seems lost in confusion. His brown eyes look puzzled, as if he has thought many times about what went wrong. The difference between me and him is that electricity scares me too much to even think about fooling around with it. Involuntarily, my mind goes back to the time when I was twelve and was shocked by an electric lawn mower. Closing my eyes, I can still feel the pain. My fingers felt like someone laid back the skin and briskly rubbed a hacksaw blade back and forth over the exposed nerves. ''Couldn't she let go of it?'' I ask, thinking of a movie I saw with Martin Sheen where, in the first five minutes, his wife was accidentally electrocuted while using an electrical appliance. Her muscles contracted, and she couldn't let go of it.

His face takes on the hardness of a clenched fist as he remembers, "I released the button as soon as I realized what was happening, but it was too late."

It sounds so grisly I feel my stomach turn. "What happened then?"

Andy stares over my head and says in a monotone, "I tried mouth-to-mouth resuscitation, and the emergency-room technicians said the doctor worked on her for thirty minutes after they got her to the hospital, but I think she was dead before then."

I nod, feeling steadily sickened by the portrait he has painted. Perversely, but perhaps not unexpectedly, given my eastern Arkansas background, what is most vivid in my mind is an image of his black lips blowing into the girl's mouth. When I was entering puberty in eastern Arkansas my best friend, Jeffrey "Draino" Cummings, "made" me choose between what our adolescent minds agreed were the two worst choices in the world: having sex with one's mother, or in Jeffrey's words, "sucking snot from a dead nigger's nose." I remember saying primly that I'd choose the second. Jeffrey, who obtained his nickname because of an experiment with a frog, hooted in derision until I changed my mind. "Was it just you and the aide?" I ask, wondering if Leon is also black.

Andy closes his eyes as if the memory is too much for him. "Olivia was there, and I had a social worker there to write down the exact number of shocks it was going to take, and also count how many times Pam hit herself before she stopped."

I am stunned by the news that Olivia was watching. She is even tougher than I imagined. "How could a parent watch her own child being shocked?" I blurt.

Andy does not seem to take offense at my tone. He says mildly, "Olivia's one hell of a strong woman. She insisted that I shock her, too, so she'd know exactly what Pam was feeling.''

Once again I can imagine the jolt that radiated through me as I tried to splice the electric cord that summer morning in the backyard. It had to be over thirty years ago, but the memory of the pain has reappeared as if a skillful therapist had uncovered a traumatic incident from my childhood. My stomach queasy, I take a sip of my coffee, wondering if I'm about to throw up. "Did you try it, too?" I ask.

Somberly, he nods. "One of the descriptions from the journals is that it is like having a dentist drill on a tooth without first having your mouth numbed. Frankly, I think it's worse than that, but it's also true that the pain goes away as soon as the current stops. It's local and doesn't radiate through the body.''

"Jesus Christ!" I exclaim. "Why couldn't you have started with something milder?" I do not add that if he had, Pam might be alive today.

Perhaps irritated by my tone, his voice less patient, Andy says, "They can get used to a lower voltage. It can be reinforcing. The literature says that if you're going to use shock, not to hold back on the intensity.''

But a cattle prod? Nonplussed now by the image of Andy and Olivia shocking themselves a single time, all I can do at the moment is blink at this comment. Some comfort that must be to a retarded teenager. As a child, I used to be terrified when my mother made my sister cut a switch for her that she would then use on our legs. The fear of what was coming was somehow worse than the pain. Of course, that was part of the punishment. Can a jury handle this so-called treatment? On "60 Minutes" recently they did a segment on the comeback electroconvulsive therapy was making in the treatment of suicidally depressed mental patients after years of bad publicity. Why? It works when nothing else does, according to the shrinks on the program. Yet there is a difference. The electricity itself (no one seemed to know how) has a therapeutic effect; here, its only function is to inflict pain. A theory as subtle as the one in the Spanish Inquisition. Doubtless, its defenders would howl in disagreement. I try to focus on what it is supposed to accomplish: the cessation of pain, the prevention of injury, maybe it can even save a life when it isn't taking one. Andy would be so much better off if he could have obtained someone's permission to try shock. It begins to sink in that maybe his boss, David Spath, knew what he was up to, but they made a deal: Andy could try it, but if it didn't work, he would have to walk the plank all by himself. Why else would he be so confident that his boss would agree to let him continue working with Pam and using a method that can't stand the light of day? "I'd like to talk with your boss and the other two who were there," I say casually. "Do you think they'll be sympathetic?"

Andy spreads his hands and then slaps his legs softly. "They don't want to lose their jobs."

I begin to doodle on the pad in front of me. Maybe they should lose their jobs. I doubt if what they helped Andy do is in their job descriptions. I anticipate him by saying, "They were just following your orders."

Andy nods too quickly, convincing me that he has told them something similar. The problem was that this defense has already failed—at Nuremberg. Yet usually nobody cares about the peons. They probably need all the warm bodies they can get at the Human Development Center. He says, "I wouldn't even bother with David. I'm just lucky he hasn't fired me. I'm sure from the governor on down, they've put pressure on him to get rid of me immediately."

I wonder if they are all black, but I will find out soon enough. David, whoever he is and whatever his color, must be quite a fellow. How does someone get into this business? I suspect not too many kids say they want to be an administrator of an institution for the retarded when they grow up. I write his name down, hoping he is white. The testimony of a black boss won't mean much, since the jury will assume blacks stick together on everything. Thinking about the issue of race reminds me of Andy's admonition after the probable cause hearing not to raise it again. I ask, "We need to discuss your problem with planting a seed in the jury's mind that you might be the victim of racial discrimination. If we can even get one juror to hold out, I don't think the prosecutor would retry it."

Andy shakes his head vigorously, as if I'd suggested that he try to bribe the judge. "Don't you see that all you do is reinforce the belief that blacks are inferior by raising the issue of race?"

I rock back in my chair, totally dumbfounded. "Are you crazy? You should know better than I do that it's not going to break this prosecutor's heart if some members of the jury are racists. She wants a conviction."

Andy sets his chin and neck as if he is locking them into position. "I've spent my entire adult life refusing to reinforce white or black racism. Each time a black asks for special treatment, he reinforces the behavior of whites who think we can't make it by ourselves."

I can't believe my ears. This guy sounds as if he was programmed by Ronald Reagan. "It's not special treatment to demand a fair trial."

A frown passes over Andy's face. "Neither you nor the prosecutor want a fair trial. You just admitted that. All you want to do is win."

This guy can't be for real. "This is your fucking life at stake!" I bark at him, slapping the table for emphasis. "You can't think you're going to use this trial to reform society. All you'd do is let them get away with what they've been doing for years—which is screwing blacks simply because you are black!"

The louder I get, the calmer he becomes. "Every minority in this country from Jews to Japanese have been discriminated against," he says, his voice barely audible, "and the way they have overcome it is by outworking you."

The bitter coffee makes my stomach hurt. Suddenly, I realize Andy is the worst kind of client—a martyr. "There's no comparison between blacks and Jews in the United States. Jews weren't degraded by being brought to this country in chains and bought and sold. They didn't have laws here literally branding them as less than human beings."

Andy begins nodding his head again. "I don't want you even implying to the jury that this case is about racism. If I had wanted to do that, I could have gone to a number of black attorneys who could do a much better job of it than you. What you don't really understand is that the first thing a black child understands is that his entire society thinks he is inferior. This is drummed into his head day and night. Every time we use the excuse of racial discrimination we allow society to confirm and reinforce our worst suspicions about ourselves. I've resisted that with every fiber in my being, and I'm not going to let this trial play into that trap. Do you hear me?"

I stare at him, wondering how he got to this planet. A black Don Quixote. Logically, he doesn't even make sense, but a part of me sees what he's getting at, and I begin to feel a grudging admiration for him. Though I think he's dead wrong, the stubborn son of a bitch has the ridiculous idea that he can help make this a color-blind society by pretending it is one. I shrug. This is absurd. If all blacks were like him, maybe I could see his point, but they're not. Yet, as I think about it, I realize I have been let off the hook. Though I would have done it, I wasn't looking forward to arguing that he was being singled out because he is black. Arkansas juries, like everyone else, resent being told they're racists. "Okay," I say. "I can live with that if you can."

"Good," Chapman says simply. Abruptly changing the subject, he volunteers, "I'll get you some material on the theory of punishment, if you want."

I give him an absent nod. "Including whatever you used." An involuntary sigh escapes me. Isn't "Do no harm'' the first rule? But maybe I can argue to a jury that what Andy did is no different from the invasive procedures doctors inflict upon critically ill patients to keep them alive. Aren't those people often comatose and without a meaningful choice? The motive is no different—it is all for their benefit—to keep them alive. God, we fear death in this country. I look up at him and see a crack in his usually stoic face. "I'm sorry," I say. "It must have broken your heart to go through this."

For an answer, he raises his head and looks through the blinds at the sky. He does not tell me that the heart is merely an organ that pumps blood to the rest of the body. He says, "You have no idea."

The truth is, I don't. And I'm afraid no juror will either. I decide not to try to find out more today. When I was first starting out at the Public Defender's Office, I used to try to wring every detail out of my clients in the first interview. It took me a while to admit this meat-ax approach was often a mistake. People talk when they're good and ready. He has more to tell me, but perhaps not today. There are interviewing techniques they try to teach you in the clinical course in law school to deal with client reluctance. He and I have come a long way since yesterday, but we're not through yet. I say, "I've got some other things I have to do this morning. Do you want to continue now or talk later?"

He pushes back from the table. "I'm more tired than I realized."

Who wouldn't be in his position? Regardless of what I can do for him, his career may never recover from the charge. I look up from my worthless notes. "Andy," I say, feeling weary even though I haven't lived with the story I've just heard for more than an hour, "I can't imagine sleeping a minute in the jail."

He gives me a sad smile, his brown eyes as mournful as a clown's.

After Andy leaves, Dan waddles into my office, as if on

cue, munching on a bag of popcorn and carrying under his left armpit a couple of manila folders spotted with grease. "At least I have a client," I say, thinking I may not be able to do much more than plead him out to negligent homicide.

Dan collapses into the cheap chair across from my desk. Ten more pounds of pressure on the back of it and I can sell the chair for firewood. "What a shitty way to make a living," he complains mildly. "People think lawyers are all rich. I wouldn't know a corporate client if one grabbed me by the balls."

As gross as Dan is, I can't imagine it either. "The business is out there," I say hopefully. "The trick is to get a reputation."

Dan drops the files on my desk. "There're all kinds of reputations," he reminds me. "In twenty years, when I'm in for my third bypass, I don't want the nurses sitting around figuring out ways to torture me because they heard I'm a scumbag lawyer."

I wonder if I'm a scumbag for walking off with Andy Chapman. By the plain black phone that obviously had been hooked up while I was in court this morning, a wadded-up pink message slip with Oscar Mays's name on it is staring me in the face. I've got to return the man's call and get it over with. Surely Andy Chapman isn't worth trying to sue me over. I'm not normally the philosophical type, but I can't help remarking, "We didn't invent the free enterprise system; we're just paid to defend it."

"Bullshit," says Dan amiably, hitching up his pants to keep them from binding him. "Lawyers like you and me fight over the crumbs. With the kind of clients we get, we don't really make money practicing law; if you can't get ahead enough to invest what little windfall occasionally comes your way, you're gonna end up like old man Sievers."

I feel a shiver sweep the back of my neck thinking of Cash Sievers, who was still trying to represent clients until his death earlier this month, although he was senile. With no investments, no Social Security, he was the Blackwell County bar's oldest and most visible legal disaster. The story was that nobody had the heart to blow the whistle on Cash, and lawyers spent entire days cleaning up his messes. Though ancient and stooped, even toward the end he still attracted clients, but rumor has it that he represented most for nothing, presumably on the hope that they would give him something at the end of their case. Judging by his office and the clothes he wore, they didn't give him much. "Thanks for the vote of confidence," I tell Dan, who is missing his mouth with the popcorn as often as he is hitting it.

"Find a rich widow or divorcée—there's so many women looking for men out there you can almost advertise for 'em," he advises, "and then bird-dog her till she drops. You're just the right age."

I laugh, but with Dan you never know. His wife's family has money. I have no doubt that Dan's home near the Pinetree Country Club wasn't paid for by him. The thought of marrying for money is sickening, but my usual thoughts about women aren't all that noble either. "To paraphrase St. Augustine when told he had to give up sex for the church," I tell Dan, repeating a story I heard told by a Catholic priest when I was in boarding school at Subiaco after my father's death, " 'Can't I wait a few years?' "

At the mention of sex, Dan snickers, his sophomoric humor always waiting for the opportunity to surface. "As long as you possibly can, but if you lose too much more hair, you're gonna be playing in the minor leagues the rest of your life."

I pat my bald spot. Is it my imagination, or has it expanded another finger's width since I got up this morning? "You know anything about Kim Keogh?" I ask.

Dan wipes the grease from his mouth with the back of his hand. "Do dreams count? What a fox! If they'd let her anchor the ten o'clock news, I'd have a reason to make it past nine-thirty. Jesus Christ, isn't middle age the pits?"

The odor of popcorn before lunch is starting to make me nauseous. The grease, I suppose. I brag, "She interviewed me this morning. She's not married, is she?" I say, knowing she's not. I didn't see a ring.

A gleam of envy comes into Dan's sparkling blue eyes, his only good feature now that he's hidden the others. "Damn! This time last year you were about to get nailed by that social worker at the state hospital, weren't you?"

I think of Rainey and smile. "We're just friends."

Dan drops the empty bag into my trash. "Kim Keogh, huh?" Dan muses. "You look at these women on TV and wonder what they're like once they've washed their faces. Did you see *Postcards from the Edge*? I lost all my illusions about Shirley MacLaine."

So did I. Those old broads will do anything to stay in front of the camera. I can imagine Mike Nichols coaxing her, "Come on, it's for art's sake." Shit. Maybe it is. But I hope she won't start taking her clothes off. "That was the point," I acknowledge. "It's all fake, but nobody said the male species had any brains."

His face red, Dan chuckles as he struggles to his feet. I can imagine his heart exploding through chest someday. "You about ready for lunch?" he asks.

I look at my watch. It's only a quarter after eleven. Dan would get more work done if he moved his office down to the cafeteria. "I got a call to make," I tell him. "I'll see you down there in a few minutes. Don't forget your files," I add, shoving the two folders at him.

He wags his head. "I need you to take a couple of cases for me. One's a DWI and the other's an adoption. I got the money, but I haven't done anything with them. A check's in there for them. I'm kind of stacked up right now. I'll talk to the clients. They'll be excited they're getting a star."

Bullshit. He's giving them to me because he knows I need the money. It's not much, but it's more than I brought with me, if I don't count what I stole. "Thanks," I say softly. "I appreciate this."

In a gesture of dismissal, Dan's hands twitch outward. "You're doing me favor."

Sure I am. I holler after him, "If you want to do me a favor, get rid of Princess Fishmouth out front."

He comes back to the door, and shows me his dimples. "You need to kiss and make up. We just heard our Miss Twin Peaks called in and said she's taking a job at a health spa. The good news"—Dan leers—"is that she said all the lawyers on our floor can get a free workout if we come when she's on duty."

"From the way you describe her," I say, playing to Dan's fourteen-year-old side, "that wouldn't be hard."

"At our age," he deadpans, "it doesn't get very hard."

I laugh obligingly. "Speak for yourself." As if on command, Dan opens his mouth and closes it. "This I can do," he says and, turning to leave again, repeats solemnly, "this I can do."

While I wait nervously for Oscar Mays to come to the phone, I reflect on my friendship with Dan. In part, perhaps the major part, of our affinity for each other is that if given the opportunity, we'd just as soon be back in junior high.

Oscar Mays sounds as if he had just buried his wife. "Gideon," he says sorrowfully after the most perfunctory of greetings, "I'm really disappointed in you. I thought you had more integrity than to steal a client from us."

I say nothing, uncertain how to respond. My desire to lash out at him for firing me is balanced by the need to take whatever action I can to limit any potential repercussion. The pause becomes too long, and I say weakly, "I wouldn't call it stealing under the circumstances. He didn't want the firm of Mays & Burton; he wanted me."

An angry tremor comes into Oscar's voice for the first time since I've known him. "You signed an agreement! When you give your word on something, doesn't it mean anything to you?''

Lawyers! We hide behind pieces of paper like cockroaches. He can treat me like a used sheet of toilet paper, and I'm supposed to feel guilty because I was coerced into signing a document that at the time meant nothing to me. I was so eager to leave the Public Defender's Office when I came to Mays & Burton that I would have signed my name in blood. Why? The memory burns my face as I listen to Oscar pontificate on the sanctity of a contract. I was terrified that Carol Anderson would tell my boss I had slept with her. I would have been fired on the spot for getting involved with a woman, who, had the case gone to trial, would have, in effect, testified as an expert witness for my client, who was accused of murdering her husband. Our way of life, Oscar preaches, depends on human beings' keeping their agreements. My experience is that if the bastards can squeeze you by the balls, they will not hesitate to do so when it is in their self-interest. In our society lawyers are brought in to do the heavy-duty squeezing. I recall my own righteous indignation from a case earlier this year in which I collected a debt for a client for Mays & Burton. I was about to take almost every last stick of furniture the defendant owned when he finally filed bankruptcy. The nerve of him! My realization that if I were in Oscar's situation I wouldn't be acting any differently tempers my tone but does not prevent me from slamming down the phone after I mutter, "So sue me!" Fuming over this conversation, I lean back in my chair and try to relax. I won't be sued. It would embarrass them too much, and, anyway, I might win. As much as the law reveres a contract, it favors competition.

After lunch with Dan and two other lawyers in the building, I walk the four short blocks to the courthouse to look at the prosecutor's file on Chapman. When I ask for Kerr Bowman, I am told that Jill Marymount would like to see me. The Queen Bee herself. This is awfully early in the case to be having tea with the prosecutor, but not all work the same

way. Some are like generals and won't get their hands dirty
until the actual battle, relying on subordinates to do the work;
others, like Jill, have a reputation for interviewing their potential witnesses from the very beginning. An ironclad argument can be made that a prosecutor in as large an office
as Blackwell County doesn't have the time to do her own
pretrial investigation. Basically an administrator, she is
being paid to exercise her professional judgment, not run
up mileage on her car for her expense account. We've had
prosecutors in Blackwell County who almost never tried
cases once they were elected. But Jill's approach allows
you to get a feel for a case you wouldn't have unless you
got your hands dirty. You get ideas about motivation you'd
otherwise miss, and you obtain a real sense about credibility
of witnesses.

After a moment Jill comes for me herself, even though I
could have found her office. She is dressed more informally
than I expected. She is wearing a light blue plaid skirt and
could be headed for a barbecue after work. Her simple red
top is sleeveless, and she is wearing flats. I realize I was
expecting full battle armor. Bare-armed she looks more feminine than usual.

She smiles as if we're old enemies, though we've never
tried a case against one another. "Gideon, I hear you're
in solo practice," she says, letting me know she's aware
I was fired. She offers fingers and a palm that are cool
and dry.

As we walk side by side to her office, I say, "Thanks for
the help on the bond. I was about to ensure that my client
stay locked up for the duration of the trial."

As we turn into her office, she demurs, "Your client
isn't a martyr, and I didn't see any point in making him
one."

If you only knew, I think. The last time I was in the
Blackwell County prosecuting attorney's office the walls
were covered with diplomas and awards. Today, children's
themes provide the most unusual motif I've ever seen in a

lawyer's quarters. It is as if I have wandered into a museum of child poverty. There are literally dozens of black-and-white photographs of children in extreme conditions: reproductions of Walter Evans photographs, sallow beanpole kids standing in front of Appalachian shacks; children from the Delta, black toddlers playing in front of a housing project; pictures of modern urban teenagers receiving some kind of group drug therapy; a white girl who can't be more than junior high age but is surely in her last month of pregnancy; Down's Syndrome children smiling into the camera, perhaps taken at the Blackwell Human Development Center, for all I know; a Native American teenager, his long black hair silken and shiny even behind the metal bars of what must be an adult jail; Third World nightmares, all manner of starving children with enormous eyes and distended stomachs. On an adjacent wall are pictures of children of affluence. American, Japanese, and European teenagers in designer clothes simply facing the camera, the girls carefully made up, their arms and hands gleaming with jewelry; some of them, mostly the boys, are seated behind the wheel of sports cars, mounted on snow skis, driving boats the size of tanks. The juxtaposition of wealth and poverty is effective. I cut my eyes back and forth between the walls. From behind her desk Jill watches patiently as I take these in. The wall opposite her desk is her constituency, the pictures shriek. I think about what Amy said. Kids can't vote.

"Great photographs," I say sincerely, noticing the expensive matting behind one picture that shows a child with AIDS or perhaps simply starving. "These ought to be in a museum."

She goes to the wall with the rich kids and adjusts a frame that has begun to tilt to the left. "Some of them were. When people learn of my interest in children, they send them to me."

There is a knock at the door, and Kerr Bowman enters, carrying a file. Men working for women. It is still a rare sight in the South—especially in the law business. Kerr smiles at me as if I were best man at his wedding. "Hi, Gideon," he says and pumps my hand for the second time in twenty-four hours. "Nice to see you again!" Maybe he is running for something, too. All this friendliness is beginning to make me want to gag.

"Would you like to sit down at my workbench?" Jill says, ignoring Kerr's glad-handing. Kerr, her expression implies, is like a gorgeous but brainless secretary, nice to look at but not to be taken seriously.

For the first time I notice her desk. A "workbench" it isn't. I sit down at one of the loveliest pieces of furniture I've ever seen. Most lawyers' desks are as functional and ugly as the floor of a public men's room. This looks like a French antique from the seventeenth century. The ornamentation on the sides is so delicate I can't imagine how she got it in here without breaking it. This is a desk a king's mistress would bend over when writing her lover. As I sit down across from her, I run my fingers over the surface. I'm not much on decorating, but I love wood. "This is exquisite," I acknowledge. This woman, I'm starting to realize, is a cut above the usual occupant in this office.

"Thank you," Jill says simply, and takes the file Kerr had handed her. She looks down at it. "I don't know how much you know about the death of the child. Have you seen a picture of her?"

"Not yet," I admit. I should have asked for one from the mother, but I may not have wanted to see it.

Jill hands me a five-by-seven-inch black-and-white. "The back says it was taken a couple of years ago."

I take the picture and study it. I don't know what I was expecting, a freak maybe. But Pam, though not pretty by a long shot, is not hideous either. My guess is that she was in restraints at the time this picture was made. Her shoulders are square to the camera, but since it is mostly of her head I can't be sure. Her brown hair, with bangs almost to her eyebrows, is combed. She seems to be grimacing rather than smiling. Her teeth are her worst feature. As strapped as the state is, I guess I shouldn't expect to encounter the work of an orthodontist. Since I know she is retarded, I think from the picture it is obvious. But I'm not sure I would know otherwise. Fourteen is not the most attractive age for any kid, and there were plenty of round-faced girls this slow-looking in Sarah's high school yearbook. There is no resemblance at all to Olivia. What I want is a picture of Pam after she was dead, to see if her face is swollen or bruised from blows she might have inflicted on herself before shock was applied. That is the photograph I want the jury to see, so it will understand why shock was necessary.

This is no autopsy report. The decision to treat the death as a crime obviously has come in the last few days. The body had been cremated. A statement signed by Travis Beavers, M.D., the doc who pronounced Pam dead, concludes: "Apparent fibrillary contraction of heart secondary to electric shock." There are straightforward statements from Andy and the others present about the accident. I learn Olivia and the social worker were watching behind a one-way mirror. The damage comes from a statement by a psychologist by the name of Warren Holditch, who is identified as a member of the staff at the Bonaventure Clinic, a psychological consulting and testing group in Blackwell County. Holditch, a Ph.D., rips Andy a new one with each sentence. I scan it hurriedly, but even a cursory reading tells me Andy is in trouble. I ask Jill for a duplicate of the file, and she tells me I am looking at my own copy. Evidently, she is waiting for a reaction from me, but until I have studied the report of Holditch and done some research of my own, she won't get a peep out of me. I smile and tell her thank you and get up to leave.

Jill is studying me as if I were one of the photographs on her wall. "You're not going to be able to blackmail this office this time around," she says, her voice sweet and innocent like that of a child announcing she is ready to be tucked into bed.

I stand up straight and pretend to look at one of the pictures on the wall to give myself time to think of an appropriate comeback. I know she is referring to the Hart Anderson case. I want to stick it to her in the worst way, but down the road I will have to deal with her office many times, and I manage to bite my tongue. I turn back to her and say brusquely, pretending anger I don't feel, "Of all people, you ought to be aware there was more than one side to the way the Hart Anderson case got dealt down. You were in this office then."

She doesn't blink. "Don't waste your time asking for a deal, Gideon. You won't get one."

I leave her office then but manage not to slam her door. A tough bitch if there ever was one. Why had I ever thought of her as a schoolteacher?

7

JULIA, DRESSED TODAY like a circus clown, in green polka-dotted pants and a ruffled orange collar like crepe paper around a lime top, greets me loudly as soon as I enter the reception area. "Last night on TV I saw you and that black dude who fried that poor kid," she says, her tone almost respectful for the first time. "None of the dudes on our floor who call themselves attorneys have ever even been in a commercial. The phone's been ringing off the wall for you, and it's not even nine o'clock."

I rest the box of junk I have picked up from Mays & Burton on the edge of the reception desk as I pick up my messages. As crude as she is, Julia at least is honest. The receptionist at Mays & Burton, a young woman I had considered a friend, just treated me a few minutes ago as if I had joined a leper colony instead of having taken a client they never would have represented in the first place. "Good for business, huh?" I say, fishing out four messages from my slot. Three are from women and one is from a guy at the county jail. Nothing beats free advertising.

She nods, unwrapping a stick of Juicy Fruit. "Yeah," she advises, and begins to work the gum vigorously as if it were a piece of candle wax. "Listen, if you're gonna be on TV, you gotta get some decent suits. Those pants yesterday were so shiny you could of signaled a cruise ship into dock with 'em."

From one clothes horse to another, I think, glancing down at her to see if she is serious. She smiles magnanimously, as

79

if she had given me a sure tip on the ninth race at Oaklawn in Hot Springs.

"I'll see what I can do," I say. "Maybe there'll be enough money for both of us."

A puzzled look comes over her face, making her mouth look like the dot at the bottom of a question mark. "That woman's here to see you," she says, pointing with her pencil to the corner of the waiting room.

I follow her eraser. A slightly built young woman is eyeing me anxiously, "You're Mr. Gideon Page," she says, rising and coming toward me. She is in her late twenties, attired in baggy jeans, flip-flops that most people wear only around the house, and a black T-shirt that obscurely reads in script, "Let Being Be!"

Buoyed by the prospects of new clients and the absence of hostility from Julia, I want to say something really atrocious like "the one and only," but manage instead, "And you are . . . ?"

"Mona Moneyhart," she says, staring up at me with pale blue eyes the size of dinner plates. "My husband is suing for divorce. Can I talk to you right now? I have a summons."

I mouth to Julia to hold my calls. Let being be? What the hell does that mean? Maybe this is how young, rich society matrons dress these days. Her last name sounds promising anyway. "Nice to meet you," I say, picking up my load. "You want to follow me back to my office? We can talk there."

Like a proud parent, Julia smiles happily as if she is seeing us go off on a first date. "Would you like some coffee, Ms. Moneyhart?" she chirps.

I can't believe my ears and don't dare turn around. Julia offering to get coffee? Am I in the right office building?

"No, thanks," my potential client says in a barely audible voice and then asks me shyly, "Would you like for me to get you some?"

"I'm fine," I say, noticing Mrs. Moneyhart is no taller than a large child. How bad could she have been? And why divorce her? It might be easier to wait until she vanishes entirely. "Thank you, Julia," I call over my shoulder.

In my office she flips on my light switch for me and clears a spot on my desk. I'm tempted to ask her to fluff up my chair and take off my shoes.

"Have a seat," I tell her, "while I read this." This will be my first divorce case ever. At Mays & Burton the firm specialized in personal injury cases, and at the Public Defender's Office, of course, we just had purely criminal cases, so I'm flying by the seat of my pants. I didn't take domestic relations in law school; now, I wish I had. What courses did I take? Did I really go? I leaf through the complaint and summons and then force myself to go through it carefully. It looks straightforward enough: her husband wants custody of their three children, possession of the house, temporary child support, attorney's fees, and court costs. Three children? How can this woman have had one? Her pelvis is so narrow I can't imagine how she could have given birth to even a credit card.

"I got the summons last week," Mrs. Moneyhart says, still on her feet. She has edged around my desk and is hovering over me.

I put the papers down on my desk. "I can read this better if you'll just relax a little and sit down."

Nervously patting her stringy brown hair, which is tied by a red ribbon behind her head, Mrs. Moneyhart whimpers apologetically in a wispy tone, "Sorry." She sighs and flops back to the chair.

"I know you're upset," I say, wondering how to calm down this woman. She is beginning to get on my nerves.

Perched on the edge of her chair, Mrs. Moneyhart begins to cry. "He wants a divorce because he thinks that I deliberately burned rats in the oven! That's not fair!"

I put the papers down and rub my eyes. Is this really my first divorce client? She better have some cash. I lean back in my chair and try to keep from sighing audibly. "Did you,"

I say, not believing I'm asking this question, "accidentally burn some rats in your oven?"

She pulls up the bottom edge of her tee shirt and wipes her eyes, revealing a milky-white waist no bigger than one of my thighs. For an instant I think she is going to pull her shirt over her head. I've got to get a box tissues for my desk, or I'll end up being charged with some kind of sex crime. She sniffs, "They must have started getting in through the back somehow. It was real cold this winter."

I close my eyes. I don't know much about ovens, but mine doesn't have a special entrance for rodents. When I open my eyes again, Mrs. Moneyhart is on her feet once more, edging closer to my desk. I am beginning to feel claustrophobic. "How could that possibly happen?"

Mrs. Moneyhart interlaces her fingers and holds them up in front of me. "My theory is that this screw that held this metal strip around the base in the back came out," she says, flicking her index finger at me, "and they worked in that way. Anyway, when I took out the pan there were these two humongous rats up to their necks in blueberry muffins, just cooking away. Steve said that was the last straw."

I can imagine. If she gets any closer, I think I will start screaming. "I don't think," I say honestly, "that I'm going to have the time to help you." Nobody has that kind of time.

Abruptly, she pulls up her T-shirt again and snatches a wad of bills from under her bra, which I can't help noticing is black. Her chest, already frail, visibly shrinks as she showers them on my desk. There must be a thousand dollars in fifties. "I knew it was coming to this," she says, her voice a shrill giggle, as she stands over me again, "so I cleaned out our cookie jar at the bank the day he moved out."

I suppose she means her bank account. I think of the check I wrote on the Blazer this past weekend to Allstate Insurance. No wonder they're all smiling in their commercials. I've got to find some health insurance now, too. "If you will just go take a seat," I say, unable to take my eyes off the money, "I'll check my calendar."

An hour later I don't know much more than I did to start, but, God forgive me, neither does my client. I don't even own a set of Arkansas statutes yet, so I can't do much more than listen and nod wisely. For his grounds for divorce, her husband's complaint alleges only the barest legal conclusions, "general indignities," as if his attorney, a man I've never even heard of, is too embarrassed to be more specific. Try as she may, Mrs. Moneyhart, who has somewhat grudgingly consented to again trying to remain seated, can't think of a single thing her husband has done to merit us filing a counterclaim. No affairs, no abuse, a good job, great in bed, her husband seems only guilty of bad judgment in having married a fruitcake.

Doodling on a yellow pad (since she has given me nothing to write), exasperated, I ask, "Can't you think of anything bad about him? Doesn't he have some annoying habit?"

Mrs. Moneyhart adjusts the ribbon holding her hair, tightening her skin in the process. "Well, he's started"—she begins to nod shrewdly—"to complain a little about my cooking."

After another fifteen minutes of mostly fruitless inquiry (she is happy to share custody of the children), I promise to call her the next day after I have contacted her husband's attorney to see how serious they are. Actually, I need the time to look up the divorce statutes. As I stand beside her waiting for the elevators (I want to make certain she gets on), I have to ask, "What does your T-shirt mean?"

Carelessly, she looks down at the fading white script, which now that her money is gone, lies flat against her chest. In a voice obviously offended by my ignorance, she says, "Surely you've heard of Martin Heidegger?"

I stare at my client's chest. I called a plumber once by the name of Marvin Heidelman, but the only thing he talked about was money. "I guess I haven't," I say nervously, wondering if she is going to demand her money back.

"The philosopher, silly," she says and reaches up to kiss my cheek as the elevator door slides open. Five men in busi-

ness suits watch as Mrs. Moneyhart waves goodbye at me.
"I know you'll rip his balls off for me!" she hollers as the
door closes.

Sweating profusely from nervous exhaustion, I go back
inside the glass doors, now remembering Heidegger's name
from an introductory course in college. My philosophy professor (he was probably quoting another professor) once said
Heidegger spent his entire life meditating on the philosophical concept of Being. And now I know his conclusion after
a life's work: Let Being Be! I can live with that. Despite her
T-shirt I don't think Mrs. Moneyhart is going to be quite so
tolerant. At her desk, Julia is holding up Mrs. Moneyhart's
file by two fingers. She must have been looking at it. She
says solemnly, "We'll call this one the rat-burner case."

It is only mid-morning, but I feel as if I have been at work
a week. I can't wait to start returning phone calls. A cattle-
prod killer and a rat burner. I'm off to a great start.

"Mr. Page?"
I nod. The girl speaking to me must be one of Sarah's
dorm assistants. She is wearing a red T-shirt and looks serious and responsible. I have brought the Blazer around to
the dorm to pick up Sarah and now am trying to find her in
the crush of girls and their parents. I squint at the girl's name
tag. Jenny Lacey.

"I just wanted to say how much I like Sarah," she says,
smiling. "She's doing fine."

"I'm glad to hear it," I tell this child as if she were Sarah's
physician instead of a college student somewhere. Actually,
this news is not unappreciated. Since I have been up here on
the campus of Hendrix College for the parents' session to
learn what Governor's School is supposedly all about and to
take her home for a three-day break, Sarah has been uncharacteristically anxious. "It must be quite an experience," I
say, eager to confide in the girl in order to gain information
about my daughter. "She's written some interesting letters."
At the session this morning for parents, a panel of her teach-

ers stressed that they were not trying to break our children down! The man next to me leaned over and whispered that it was nice to know we haven't sent them off to a concentration camp.

Jenny, whose dark eyes are magnified by lenses framed in red, says blandly, "It can be a real eye-opener. Sarah's handling it pretty well though."

I nod but look around for Sarah. Handling what? Have they told her she has terminal cancer? One of her social science teachers, a guy who teaches at Southern Arkansas University during the year, smugly told us that after three weeks many of the kids were beginning to learn how to justify their prejudices in a rational manner. As solemn as owls, the parents (myself included) eagerly moved our heads up and down in unison as if he had announced that a cure for AIDS was imminent. I wondered but did not have the courage to ask if there was some inconsistency in this statement. Can a prejudice be justified rationally? I got a C in a course in formal logic in college, so I kept my mouth shut.

I see Sarah by the door waving at me and I catch up with her as she says fervent goodbyes to friends she has known for three weeks at most. She will be back in three days, but she is behaving as if she is departing on a jungle expedition and is not expected to survive. She insists on driving but then falls silent until we are on the main drag in Conway. "Did you get my letter?" she asks, checking the mirror. To judge Sarah by the clothes she wears, you would never suspect that she is stunningly beautiful. She is wearing cut-offs with a hole on the thigh, and a T-shirt that says "Lobotomy Beer."

"I get it," I say, pointing to her shirt. "Is that what smart kids drink?"

Sarah glances down at the stitching and grins. "We trade clothes a lot, I guess. I think one of the guys got it in Florida."

Great. At their parties do they undress in front of each other and hand over their underwear, too? I am beginning to wonder if Governor's School is getting out of hand. I fight down a desire to tell Sarah about my friend Amy Gilchrist. Alcohol and sex have a way of ending up in the same bed. "Your letter made it sound like you talk about some pretty heavy ideas," I say, hoping that I have not used a hopelessly outdated expression.

Sarah tilts her head and instantly becomes distressed. "I'm a real idiot. Even those kids from real small towns have thought about stuff I've never spent five minutes on."

I clear my throat, apparently hoping to scrape up some wisdom. Instead all I get is a mouthful of phlegm. Reluctant to gross out my daughter in the first minute, I swallow it. "Sarah, a lot of these kids are probably pretty shy and introverted and don't do much but sit around and read all the time. You probably have a lot more friends."

This is not the right thing to say. Sarah looks at me as if I've just voiced the most trivial concern ever uttered by a human being. She says crossly, "My friends at home and I don't talk about anything but who likes who, and how mean our teachers are, and what we're going to do on the weekend, which is nothing."

I look out the window at downtown Conway and see two teenagers standing idly on the corner and resist the temptation to roll down the window and yell at them, "Which way to the public library?" Adults talk about the same things, and the world is still spinning, but I don't say this. It would just confirm her worst suspicions. I offer, "People have been thinking deep thoughts for at least three thousand years and the world is still in a mess. I don't think we're going to be able to think our way out of it." As Martin Heidegger allegedly said, but I don't say, Let Being Be!

Sarah turns onto the street leading to the interstate. How would you know? her expression says. I wonder whether I should tell her that I was fired. I guess she was too busy thinking to see me on the tube the last couple of nights. I hate to worry her when she sounds so depressed.

"That's the problem!" she says passionately. "Nobody really thinks. They just shoot off their mouths, and if it's glib enough, people go all to pieces like they've really heard something special.''

Glib? Not one of Sarah's words. At least not around me. One of her teachers? Or one of the words from a misunderstood small-town genius? Possibly the owner of a can of Lobotomy Beer? I'll have to start doing a glibness check before I speak. As we pull onto I-40 and head east, I say, ''It'd be kind of quiet if people had to first figure out before they opened their mouths whether their words had a decent shot at immortality.''

Sarah laughs, the first sign of normality since I've seen her, but she says, ''That's exactly the kind of flip remark I'm good at. I can make people laugh, but that's all. Nobody takes me seriously, and I don't blame them.''

Her cheeks are red. If I weren't in the car, she'd be crying. This is absurd. ''You wouldn't have been selected if they thought you were the village idiot,'' I protest.

She shakes her head but does not take her eyes off the road. ''I got nominated partly because the teachers like me. Besides, I probably count as a minority.''

I have thought this, too, but so what? No matter how you slice it, there's more to success than just brains—even in a so-called gifted and talented program. I have never really thought of Sarah as a member of a minority before. At the rate my career is going, I won't care if she claims to be a full-blooded Hottentot if it will help her to get a scholarship to college. But maybe it bothers her. ''If that's true,'' I ask carefully, ''does the minority part bother you?''

She clinches the steering wheel. ''I don't know,'' she says. ''I've never thought about what I am. I have Negro blood, don't I?''

''Some,'' I say. ''Is that a big deal?''

Sarah runs her right hand through her curly ebony hair. She surprised me by getting it cut short before Governor's School. Her haircut shows her ears and looks good. For fifty bucks it ought to. I wanted to choke her when she told me how much she had spent. But it was her own money. She got

a job in the spring at Brad's Health Shoppe as a checker/
bagger. "Dad, there's a camp I want to go to as soon as
Governor's School is out. It's just a week. It's sponsored by
the Arkansas Conference of Christians and Jews. A lot of my
friends from Governor's School are going."

I study my daughter's profile. Her light-brown skin makes
me wonder how much African blood actually flowed in her
mother's veins. Rosa said she thought her great-grandmother
had been brought to Cartagena as a slave. I have never told
Sarah, nor, to my knowledge, did Rosa. "Where do you fit
in?" I ask, knowing this is going to lead to religion. We
might as well cover the waterfront while we're on the big
questions.

Sarah bites at a fingernail on her left hand. I notice for the
first time her nails are not painted. What has happened? Before Governor's School she wouldn't leave the house unless
they practically glowed in the dark. "Thanks to you," she
says irritably, "I'm not sure."

Shit. Guilt begins to seep into the car like carbon mon-
oxide. I look out the window at fields of soybeans and think
back to Rosa's agonizing death. If that was a part of somebody's divine plan, spare me the other details. If I'd been
smart, I would have made Sarah attend Mass, and by now
she would have been sick of it and quit. Most kids do. I did—
especially after being made to go off to a Catholic boarding
school. "You can go to Mass any time you like. It's not like
they have it just once a year," I say defensively.

"They let people who are atheists go to Camp Anytown,"
my daughter says. "You don't have to be religious."

An atheist! That sounds so lonely. Sarah has been the sort
of kid who hasn't demanded that kind of clarity from life.
Events have turned on a narrow radius of school, boys, and
friends. "So you don't believe God even exists?" I say, making certain she knows I'm taking her seriously. One false note
from me, and the radio will come on. The radio! The absence
of her music is surely a measure of the weightiness of this
conversation.

"So you're a deist?" she asks, turning on the blinker to pass a truck.

I haven't really thought about this subject for ten minutes since I left Subiaco, but a deist sounds safe enough. God minding His business; humans minding ours. Let Being Be! "Sort of, I guess. Thomas Jefferson was a deist," I say, wanting to put myself in good company.

Sarah smiles at my old trick of clothing myself with authority.

"I think deism is a cop-out," she says finally, taking a wide swing around a mud-caked moving van in front of us. "What's the point of believing anything if all you're going to believe is that God created the world?"

That sounds like a good week's work to me, but I dare not make fun. Her expression is suddenly too grim. The truth is, if I have to put a name to it, deism is probably about all I can manage, and if I can believe what I read, science may be about to debunk that, too. Just because I don't understand electricity doesn't mean I'm not an ardent believer in it. And when some night Dan Rather, wearing his most pompous expression, announces that some scientist has discovered how the universe began, I'll believe that, too. "After your mother died the way she did," I say truthfully, "religion hasn't been an easy subject."

For the first time since she has been driving, Sarah turns and looks at me full in the face. Her eyes are flashing as if she is angry. "That's what I thought, but you never talk about her dying."

I feel irritated by this interrogation. What is there to say? It was horrible, but tragedy happens to most people sooner or later. That's the only consolation I know, and it's not much. "I thought it would be upsetting to us both, and all the talking in the world won't bring her back."

Her face is in profile again. "I'm really sorry for you," she says, her voice a whisper. "I know how much you loved her. I think some of the things you've done just means you haven't gotten over her."

How patronizing! I feel my jaw tighten as I think of how to put her in her place. What does she know about what I do? I'm not so bad. The arrogance of children is amazing. She goes off three weeks and comes back Socrates. If the unexamined life isn't worth living, then, all I've got to say is, sometimes the examined life isn't so hot either. What does she know about life? Yet, I know what this is about. After Rosa's death, I went a little crazy and brought to the house some of the godawfulest women. Just thinking about some of them makes my face itch. It wasn't until I met Rainey that I began to calm down. "It's easy to be perfect when you're seventeen," I tell her, making my voice as snide as I can. "But even you, Sarah, may develop a few warts before your life is done."

Sarah doesn't speak, but I can see her lower lip beginning to tremble. Hooray for the old man! He hasn't seen the best person in his life in nearly a month, and ten minutes later he has humiliated her.

"I'm sorry," she mumbles, trying unsuccessfully not to cry. Noisily, she sniffs moisture back into her throat and begins to choke, so intent she is on trying to remain poised. It is no use; my snottiness has broken a dam.

I find tissues in the glove compartment and hand them to her. Why can't I keep my mouth shut? Is my self-esteem so low that I need to attack my child? She is crying so hard I'm afraid we will wreck. I resist grabbing the wheel. I can see the headlines: IRATE FATHER CAUSES CRASH, KILLS TEN. "I'm such a bastard," I say loudly over her honking. "I ought to be put to sleep." I pat her shoulder. It feels papery thin, as easy to crush as her ego.

She laughs at my hyperbole and chokes again. Fortunately, I-40 is clear as we wobble back and forth across the intersected line like a pair of drunken ice skaters. "I'm sorry," I say, needing instant forgiveness.

"It's okay," she says, wiping her eyes with her knuckles. "I shouldn't have said anything."

The truth is that neither of us can stand for the other one

to be mad for even a minute. We want to please each other too much. We'd make a great teacher and student but in some ways are a poor father and daughter. We worry about each other's feelings too much to be honest with each other for longer than fifteen seconds. This mutual protectiveness is presumably a result of Rosa's death: the rare moment of candor I squelch. Suck it up and be a man for once, I think miserably. "I tell myself I don't talk about your mother to protect you," I say, "but it is me I want to spare. I hate to admit how many good times I had with her, because I can't imagine even coming close to being that happy again."

"Oh, Dad," Sarah says, now crying for me instead of herself.

I feel myself close to tears and wonder if I'm romanticizing Rosa. Perhaps, in some ways I am. She had a fiery temper, and occasionally she could be obstinate as a Colombian burro. But when we were in sync, it was bliss. She was pure emotion, alive in a way few people are, even for one minute of the day. Too, there is no way I can or should describe to my daughter the sensual pleasure her mother brought me. I tell her what I can. "Remember how she used to mug for us? To be so beautiful, she could be incredibly silly. I'd come home from work and drag around the house and she'd start dragging, too. And remember how she'd pretend to be Woogie and get down on her hands and knees and pretend to charge you? You'd squeal and run jump on your bed."

My daughter laughs with me, and a host of memories comes flooding back. These are easy—ones we've polished a dozen times. Like a tongue avoiding a sore tooth, I know how to stay away from the pain of Rosa's death. Sarah's laughter is perfunctory today, however. "Was she afraid of dying?" she asks. "Did she feel bitter about missing so much?"

I look out at the green, teeming fields. Sarah is bursting with life. Why this talk about death? Of course Rosa was angry at first. Who wouldn't be? I explain the pop psychology of death. "Supposedly, there are stages a person passes through. First, there's denial; then you try to bargain with God for some more time, but finally there may be some acceptance. I think it was harder for me to accept than for her. Do you remember all of us crying on the bed together one night right before she died?''

''Not really,'' she says, twisting a lock of hair. ''What happened?''

How can she not recall the most emotional night of our lives? I give her a hard look to see if she is trying to remember. ''It was about a week before she died. You slept with us that night.''

Sarah hunches her shoulders in irritation. I see that by not talking about that night, I may have deprived her of a valuable memory of how much her mother loved both of us. Maybe a memory more important than a story about how happy we were. Yet, until this moment I had forgotten that Sarah had been on the bed, too. It had upset her to see me cry. Or that was how I interpreted her reaction. I was in sheer panic that night. Denial, still. What about the stages of death for those of us who go on living? That's what religion is supposed to help you with; but if your wife dies young, to hell with it. Maybe, Sarah wasn't as scared as I thought, just sad. Afterward, I got therapy for myself; it never occurred to me to take Sarah. Now, by not talking about Rosa's death, I realize perhaps I have taken from her the opportunity to grieve for her own mother. We've never talked much about how Sarah felt. I figured she felt sad enough, so whenever the subject of her mother came up, I sentimentalized Rosa so we both would be left with a nice, warm glow. I have short-circuited her death so as to avoid the pain for her. As usual, it was for me, not her. I decide to take the plunge. My heart pounding, I say, ''Believe me. You were there. It was after supper, and we were all in our bedroom. Your mother was in a lot of pain. I started crying and remember trying to leave the room, but she wouldn't let me. She said something like, 'For God's sake, I'm dying! Stay and face this.' It made you start crying, and we all just sobbed. We ended up sleeping on the bed with her. Woogie, too.'' My breath has started to come in short gasps, and suddenly tears are running down my face.

Sarah reaches for my hand, and her chest heaves. ''Didn't she go back to the hospital the next day?''

And never came home again. I nod. ''After she was admitted, some stupid bitch tried to make you stay down in the lobby because you were only thirteen.''

Something triggers the memory of that night for her, and Sarah, too, begins to cry.

''Let's pull off the road for a moment,'' I say, glancing behind us to make sure no car is about to rear end us if we slow down. I help guide the Blazer to the shoulder, and both of us cry together for the first time since that night. What have I been trying to accomplish by trying to pretend my daughter hadn't seen me lose it? I've made Rosa into some kind of plastic saint. I'm surprised I don't have a little figurine of her on the dashboard.

Her head on my shoulder, Sarah begins to hiccup. Finally, she says in a tiny voice, ''Mom was a lot stronger than you, wasn't she?''

Maybe it is time I admitted that. I swallow but a sour mass seems lodged in my throat. ''Somehow, she had the courage to face her own death and wanted me to face it, too. I didn't want to. I guess I still don't want to. That's why I never talk about it to you. Just the marshmallow stuff.''

Sarah presses her head hard against my shoulder. ''It's okay. I can take it.''

I wipe my eyes. Maybe character, too, is genetic. My life has been spent trying to avoid pain; my daughter seems ready to wade into the middle of it. ''Your mother,'' I say, trying to remember what Rosa really believed and failing, ''wasn't the type to use crutches much. To her, the subject of God was more of a religious mystery than a crutch, and knowing she was dying didn't change that.''

For some reason, Sarah seems to brighten. ''Why haven't I remembered this before?''

I lean against her as cars and trucks whiz by us. Their drivers probably think we are lovers who have pulled off the road to neck. "Probably because it was too painful, and you knew I didn't want to talk about it. I don't really know about her religious beliefs. She always said it was more important what a person did than what they thought, and I guess I took her at her word."

"Mom was an existentialist, huh?" Sarah says thoughtfully.

She already has a new vocabulary in three weeks. If I had tried to use a word with five syllables when I was in high school, my friends would still be laughing. "If that's what that word means, I guess so. She always said that talk was cheap."

She turns and draws back to see if I am making fun of her, and apparently satisfied that I'm not, says, "I think she wanted to talk to me, too, but I was so scared."

I touch my daughter's bare arm in protest. "You were only thirteen!"

Sarah, her face as severe as an angry judge's, reprimands me, "She was dying!"

My stomach feels as if I'd swallowed my belt buckle. Surely this is a burden she doesn't need. My mind races to the day when I was about her age and I lay on my bed all day when my mother and sister drove from eastern Arkansas to the state hospital to see my father, who was dying of craziness. I couldn't make myself go visit him. I tell her about that day. "You shouldn't expect so much of yourself, babe," I say gently. "It took me thirty years to forgive myself for not going to see my father."

Sarah listens, but I can feel her judging me. "We miss so much that way, though."

I sigh. She's right, but some people have more character than others. Some of us seem only to be able, as the song says, to do whatever it takes to make it through the night. I suppose I am of that ilk. I apologize. "I should have spent more time worrying about how you were coping."

My daughter pats my knee. "You did all right. We're both in one piece."

More or less. I try not to think of the nights I came home late to find Sarah sitting on the couch in the living room wrapped in a blanket pretending to watch TV while all she was doing was watching the clock. Most of the time she was so glad to see me she didn't mention that I stunk of bourbon, cigarettes, and the smell of a woman's genitals. Some of the women I had the nerve to bring home. Sarah never gave them a chance. They weren't bad—just lonely, alcoholic types you can occasionally pick up in a lounge if you work at it hard enough. "You want me to drive?" I say. I worry about the Blazer overheating. The air conditioner already sounds under normal conditions like a 707 reversing its engines.

"I'm okay," she says and checks the rearview mirror. Instinctively, I turn my head to make sure no cars are coming, a habit from the days when she was learning to drive. She notices and frowns.

The rest of the way home I try to talk to her about what her mother was like as a real person, not some icon we have worshiped. I reveal to her for the first time that her mother was fired from two jobs at hospitals because of her temper. "She couldn't keep her mouth shut when she thought a doctor was screwing up. Once, right in front of the patient, she exploded and told a surgeon he was prescribing too much medication. They fired her on the spot, and she never admitted she might have at least waited until she got out in the hall to ream him out. I had decided to start law school by then, so it wasn't a cool move from the standpoint of money."

Her eyes on the road, Sarah listens intently. Rosa, for all her reality therapy when she was dying, usually protected Sarah as much as I did. So that she wouldn't worry, Rosa made me promise that we not tell her the time she was fired. Now I think Rosa was embarrassed. Naturally, since qualified and competent nurses are typically rare, she had a new job two weeks later, so it was no real strain. Sarah grins. "She sounds like she had a lot of guts."

"But no tact," I say, determined to be objective. "Her strengths were her weaknesses and vice versa."

Sarah ignores my observation which, in fact, sounds as soon as it is out of my mouth like a slogan from Orwell's *1984*: "War is peace, slavery is freedom. . . ." She says, "I hope I'm as assertive as Mom was."

Hell, I hope she is, too. My reaction at the time was one of delight that Rosa had stuck it to the arrogant son of a bitch. "There's a right and wrong time for it," I pontificate.

Sarah glides onto the access road off I40 to Rison Drive, which will eventually get us home. "Did she lose her temper at you much? I don't remember you having any real big fights."

I can't either. Despite my best efforts I'm having trouble painting over my dead wife's memory and giving her the warts she surely had. I look out the window and notice an attractive woman behind the wheel of a beat-up old yellow Volkswagen Beetle in the lane beside us. Damn, poor or rich, women are everywhere. For my daughter's sake, I try not to stare. "You remember how she was," I say, reluctantly turning my head toward her. "If something was wrong, she got it off her chest immediately; nothing built up that way." Her directness took getting used to, but I found I preferred it. Like me, Sarah broods too much.

"I saw you looking," she says, the barest hint of a smile playing at her lips.

When we are finally home, I pull out Sarah's suitcase from the backseat. It weighs a ton. If she has done her laundry even once, I'll be surprised. Within seconds Sarah is on the phone with her friends, and I am left at the kitchen table to ponder how to tell Sarah I was fired. In five minutes she is back in the kitchen to tell me she needs the keys to visit her best friend, Donna Redding. I start to protest she hasn't been home a minute, but I know she is dying to go see her friends.

"I've got a new job," I say casually. "I'm in solo practice, and I've already got a big murder case."

Sarah is not fooled by my tone. "Why didn't you tell me?" she demands, standing in the kitchen with her hands on her hips. Woogie, delighted she is home if ever so briefly, wags his tail beside her, hitting her bare legs.

"It's no big deal," I say, knowing now I've deliberately tried to avoid this subject. I resort to sarcasm to defend myself. "If you'd bothered to watch the news the last few days, you'd seen me on TV. I've even been interviewed by Kim Keogh," I brag.

Sarah sits down opposite me. "Did you get fired?" she asks, her voice reminding me of her mother's when she was worried.

"It was more of a layoff of lawyers," I say and tell her about Martha. "Poor woman. She had just gotten married the week before."

Sarah's face is flushed. "This is exactly what I'm talking about," she says, leaning forward on her elbows. "A disaster occurs, and you try to protect me! You should have called me."

What could you have done? I think. Sarah has begun to twist her hair, a characteristic sign of frustration. "You're overestimating the significance of this," I lie. "I've already got a half-dozen clients." I do not add that none except for Andy and Mona Moneyhart are worth discussing in terms of the money their cases are generating. What good will it do to tell her that I am scared to death of not being able to pay our bills, much less sending her to college? If she wants to worry about God and the meaning of existence, that's okay with me, but she's not my wife, and I'll be damned if I'm going to treat her like one. I reach in my wallet and bravely take out a ten. "You're going to need some money this weekend."

She flinches as if I had pulled out a condom. "I've still got some money from my job," she says uncertainly.

"That's supposed to be for clothes this fall," I said, thrusting the money into her palm. I had given her some spending money before she went to Governor's School. What has she done with the thirty I gave her? Spent it on Lobotomy Beer, I suppose.

"Are you sure?" she asks, nervous now. She takes the money and puts it into a wallet crammed with pictures of her friends.

"I should have gone out on my own two years ago," I lie, thinking of the marginal status of some of the attorneys on the sixteenth floor of the Layman Building. "I've been on TV this week because of this new case I picked up."

"When and how did you get it?" Sarah asks innocently.

As much as Sarah worries, I'd rather not have to parse the niceties of contract law. "He remembered the Hart Anderson murder," I say, answering only half the question.

"You're looking at the new Chet Bracken," I say, throwing out the name of the most famous trial lawyer in Blackwell County.

"You didn't like him much," my daughter reminds me, "in the Hart Anderson case." She stuffs her wallet into her purse, which looks weighted down with slugs. What does she carry that weighs so much? I have learned not to ask. It's none of my business.

"I respected him though," I say weakly, remembering how he intimidated me until I finally stood up to him. Maybe I just think I did. Lawyers have the psychology of dogs: in our dealings with each other we are much more conversant with the emotion of fear than affection, though in public we sniff each other and trot around together as if we are the best of pals.

"You couldn't stand him," my daughter says, now slinging her purse over her shoulder. "You said he was a bully."

I said a lot worse out of her presence. Chet Bracken works at being an asshole twenty-four hours a day, but if I got charged with a crime, he'd be my first phone call. It disturbs Sarah that difficult people can be so competent. When Sarah stops expecting virtue to be rewarded, I'll know she's grown up. "Wooly, bully," I stand and sing, shuffling my feet and swinging my hips and arms in an effort to pretend I'm dancing as I remember a song that was popular when I was about her age, or so my memory conveniently lies. "Watch it now, watch it now. . . ." These inane words are all I think I can recall of the song, but it is enough to make her smile and forget a period of my life when I wasn't particularly sterling silver myself.

"Do you act silly when you're here by yourself?" Sarah asks, a familiar, indulgent smile settling in on her face. This is the old man she is comfortable with—an affectionate buffoon who is tolerable as long as he controls himself in public.

"Not as much," I say, and pivot on my toes, one of the Temptations. "Woogie isn't much of an audience."

When I'm finally still, she gives me a quick hug and then she's out the door in her Lobotomy Beer T-shirt, leaving me to sit at the kitchen table and wish I had some of Chet Bracken's ability to convince a jury that his client is really the victim, regardless of the crime. Who will believe that a black psychologist was the victim in this case when Jill Marymount waves a cattle prod at the jury? Given the identity of the municipal court judge, old Tom Bruton, the outcome of Monday's probable cause hearing is already a foregone conclusion. I have decided against giving Jill even a whiff of our case and will not cross-examine her expert witness, Warren Holditch, who will testify that Andy should never have attempted shock. Had Darwin Bell, who is black, not felt obliged to recuse himself, the probable cause hearing might be Andy's best shot at an acquittal, and I would be working nonstop on the case now. Since I know this case will get to a jury, I have resisted the temptation to rush the process and will begin to conduct my investigation after I hear their witnesses at the probable cause hearing Monday. I wander over to the refrigerator to see what kind of lunch I can throw together. One slice of lunch meat, a jar of reduced-calorie mayonnaise. Almost bare bones, like Andy's defense so far. Four days isn't enough time to find an expert who will testify how wonderful shock is. I close the refrigerator door, realizing I can't go to the store until Sarah comes back with the car. Monday will be a long day. So what else is new?

8

FOR HIS PROBABLE cause hearing, Andy looks sharper than his lawyer, a feat not particularly difficult but embarrassing none the less. When I was a public defender, even I managed to dress better than my clients, but in private practice I am expected to look better-dressed than I do today: a blue pinstriped summer suit that fits as though I stopped at Pinehearst Cemetery on the way downtown and robbed the freshest grave I could find. It has shrunk, but I have not. Not without a trace of envy, I glance at my client. White linen suits on black males historically have a way of arousing my suspicions. In eastern Arkansas, where I grew up, a black man who put on a suit that wasn't the color of midnight was assumed to be up to no good. Hoping to spruce up my wardrobe this spring, I tried on a white suit at Dillard's that made me look like Moby Dick. It was just as well. Five hundred dollars goes a lot further at Sears. In contrast to his lawyer's ill-fitting attire, Andy's suit looks tailored. Where in the world is he getting his money? If Jill Marymount asks Olivia this question, I will object like hell. Maybe I am wrong, but I did not believe Andy when I asked him earlier this morning. Despite the withering look he gave me, I think he cannot admit that Olivia has agreed to subsidize him. I think, too, that there is at least a good chance they are having an affair. As we walked into the courtroom this morning, I caught an agonized look before she realized I was watching her. It seems odd to me that there are far fewer interracial liaisons today than in the days of slavery, but perhaps it is not so strange now that I think about it. Before the Civil War, black women had no choice in the matter, and today desirable eligible black men are so scarce a white woman would have to risk censure not only from white men but also from black women.

I turn and look over my shoulder at my daughter, who, to my great surprise, asked if she could come down to watch. Never before has she showed the slightest interest in seeing her old man leave the house except to take her somewhere, but she has heard that during the second half of Governor's School a mock trial is part of the curriculum. Hardly an original idea, but to a teacher it must sound good. Surely the national fascination with lawyers will fade when TV moves on to something else. The only thing it hasn't done, and it's surely only a matter of time, is a program called "Bankruptcy Court." Sarah gives me an embarrassed nod, but she can't very well pretend I'm not in the same room with her today. She is sitting by an old woman in the second row, and wearing a yellow sundress that had prisoners riding up in the elevator with us rattling their chains. The media are out in full force for the hearing, and I wouldn't put it past one of the males to find out that Sarah is my daughter and try to interview her. I suspect she is the best-looking young woman in this courtroom in a long time. Beautiful people don't make many appearances in municipal court.

Taking a beating in court isn't my idea of fun, but Andy needed little convincing that we have no chance in front of Bruton. We could have waived the probable cause hearing, but I wanted to see and hear Warren Holditch and Jill's other witnesses testify and perhaps do a little discovery as well. Holditch is most of Jill's case today, though I suspect that for the main event she will have lined up more than one expert to hammer home the point that Andy knew he didn't have any business trying shock on Pam.

Jill and Kerr Bowman walk in together. I almost expect him to be carrying her briefcase, but his hands are empty except for a yellow legal pad, as if she doesn't even trust him to lug her stuff around for her. Jill, trailed by Kerr, comes by the table, and I feel forced to make introductions. I say snidely, "Dr. Chapman, this is the woman who is prosecuting you, Jill Marymount."

Graciously, Andy has risen to his feet (I wouldn't have if I were in his shoes, and rudely I remain seated). Jill has the nerve to extend her hand as if she is out campaigning for votes. "Sorry to meet you under these circumstances, Dr. Chapman," she purrs. "Believe it or not, I'm aware of what I'm putting you through."

The hypocrisy of such a statement makes me want to puke, but Andy nods deferentially as if she were a dignitary who had thoughtfully stopped on the street to offer condolences on the death of an aged parent. Kerr, behind her, has to clear his throat to be acknowledged, but I let Jill introduce her own flunky. As he and Andy go through the same charade of civility, I notice Jill looks untypically feminine. Usually, female attorneys have their own battle dress—suits and high-buttoned blouses that make them look as formal and forbidding as their male counterparts—but today Jill is wearing a beige silk blouse over a red skirt that might be more appropriate for lunch at the Blackwell County Country Club. She has deliberately dressed this way for Judge Bruton, I realize. The old bastard hates woman lawyers and once sent home a woman who dared to show up in his courtroom in pants. If Jill has to play a part to get along with him, she will gladly do so.

Jill's first witness is Leon Robinson, the technician who was trying to restrain Pam when she grabbed the prod. Leon, in his twenties, is hard for me to figure. I have talked to him briefly over the phone, but he seems to have a streak of bitterness in him toward Andy that extends beyond getting him involved in this mess. Had he been able to keep Pam's arms pinned, as directed, none of us would be here today. Undoubtedly, he feels guilt and is defensive about his role in this tragedy. Leon is pure country. With sideburns and an inky pompadour he reminds me of Conway Twitty, the country singer who, legend has it, took for his first name the town where Sarah is attending Governor's School. He is wearing a blue work shirt stuffed into faded jeans that are, in turn, jammed into cream-colored cowboy boots. Despite a washed-out junk-food look (too many years on the road), he walks with an ex-athlete's grace. In a low, sullen voice, he relates how Andy asked him to help with Pam the day before. He hadn't really known what was going to happen. All he was told was that they were going to try something new to keep Pam from hurting herself. Andy leans over and whispers to me that he had shown Leon the cattle prod and had told him exactly what would happen. So what, I think glumly. Andy should never have asked him to get involved in the first place.

It comes out that Leon had become quite attached to Pam. When she was in restraints, which was most of the time, he fed her, talked to her, even brought his jam box to work to entertain her. None of this is relevant, but it occurs to me that he has insisted that he be allowed to say this before he testifies about how she died. Despite Bruton's look of impatience (what does this boy's feelings have to do with the case?), Jill lets him run. "I went to her funeral," he says, finally winding down. "If I had known how bad it was gonna hurt, I would of realized how hard she was gonna try to get away."

I could be objecting to this, but I want Leon to commit himself to the best memory of Pam he can muster. At the trial I want a jury to see that Pam meant a great deal to the people who worked with her. This wasn't an experiment on a mannequin. Pam was real, somebody to help if you could. And you didn't have to be her mother to think that way.

Finally, he gets to the actual event, which, because of the emotion in his voice, brings me and Andy, I notice, to the edge of our seats. Dr. Chapman told him to take Pam into the treatment room with the one-way mirror. He didn't even see Yettie Lindsey, the social worker, or Mrs. Le Master until all hell broke loose. He talked to Pam until Dr. Chapman got there and then Dr. Chapman told him to remove her restraints, which he did. His face balled into a frown, he says, "She started hittin' herself on the side of her face just like I knew she would."

Leon pauses as if he is trying to get control over himself, but he does not quite manage to do so and speaks now in a scratchy, hoarse tone. "He told me he was going to shock Pam with this electric rod he had, and it would make her quit hittin' herself. So when we got in there he said to hold on to her hands so she wouldn't get free. When he touched her with the prod, it was like she had been struck by lightning she bucked so hard. She just went wild and pulled out of my hands, and that's when she grabbed the prod. She fell down after that and he hollered for me to go call 911 and get an ambulance. I did, and when I come back Pam was dead." He surprises us all by bursting into tears. Astonishingly, this kid, doubtless a redneck, cares deeply about Pam. Jill offers him a tissue, and he takes it and wipes his eyes.

Before he sits down, Jill gets him to identify the cattle prod that killed Pam. It is an ugly thing, much longer than I imagined, probably about three feet in length. I assume it is that length because an animal, either out of pain or rage, would be in a position at close range to take the arm off its tormenter. I notice the black insulation tape that was supposed to keep this accident from happening and realize that if it had been me, I wouldn't have trusted myself to know how much tape was sufficient.

Jill turns to me and says blandly, "Your witness."

As I get up, I introduce myself to him. He rolls his eyes back up in his head as if he has seen his share of lawyers. During a short conversation on Friday over the telephone, he went into a bit more detail. I had wanted to talk with him in person, but he claimed to be much too busy to visit with me. I decide not to do too much with him, since I run the risk of reinforcing his testimony.

Grudgingly, Leon admits that Andy had explained to him the night before that Pam would try to pull away. "I didn't know she'd go crazy though like she did," he insists. "It was like she had superhuman strength all of a sudden," he exaggerates. Knowing I will have another crack at him, I ask him a few more questions to get him to admit that Andy had taken some pains to explain to him what he was trying to accomplish and let him sit down.

Jill wastes no time in calling the doctor who pronounced Pam dead. Dr. Travis Beavers, a GP who was doing an emergency-room stint at St. Thomas, licks his lips and testifies verbatim from the statement he gave to Jill that the cause of death was due to "an apparent fibrillation of the heart secondary to a reported electric shock."

Dr. Beavers, baby-faced and nervous, can be jumped on with both feet. There was no autopsy report, and her heart had stopped beating by the time he saw her, so for all he knows Pam might have been poisoned. I would just as soon not have the testimony frozen in stone at this point and so I do not object to what is obvious hearsay. Common sense suggests that it was the shock that caused her death, but there is no formal proof. There isn't much to work with, but it might give a stubborn juror something to chew on in the jury room when the time comes.

When Dr. Warren Holditch takes the stand and begins to speak, I forgo trying to make my usual gibberish of notes (we can obtain the transcript), and sit back and watch so I can try to figure out how to cross-examine him when the real shooting starts. A small, wiry man who looks like a runner, Holditch has none of the polish of the professional witness, which is probably in his favor. As he establishes his credentials, he stumbles over words as if English is a second language. He is nervous, but this is practice for him, too. He says he is from "Pine Buff" for "Pine Bluff" and I hear someone titter behind me. If he can't even get his hometown right, we're going to be here for a while. I find myself itching to get at him, even though I know it would be counterproductive as well as futile.

However, once Jill gets him into the substance of his testimony, Holditch's voice gradually takes on an authoritative tone. Working up a head of steam, he begins to tattoo Andy. There is a view among some psychologists, he says, that extreme punishment of the developmentally disabled for treatment purposes, as was used here, is unjustifiable because decisions are made for the retarded that we would never make for ourselves. For example, tobacco kills thousands yearly in this country, but Holditch testifies he knows of no treatment in which an adult has consented to be shocked in order to stop smoking. As he talks, he looks directly at Andy as if he is the cross his profession has to bear. If shock can ever be justified (and in his view, it cannot because of its dangerousness and severity), there have to be safeguards that were not present in this case. Now Holditch turns his head and begins speaking directly to Bruton, who has been eyeing the courtroom suspiciously, as if he were afraid that we had conspired to set off some racial incident. Holditch's voice, small and shy when he began, fairly booms off the walls. He says that it is elementary that aversive procedures, especially shock, not be tried on a retarded person until a psychologist demonstrates that he or she has tried less aversive techniques or has conducted a review of the literature and found that a particular procedure would be futile.

As he speaks, Andy leans over and whispers, his voice angry, "We don't have the staff to try what he's going to suggest, and he knows it." He adds, his voice rising, "He knows those procedures don't work with people like Pam."

Holditch begins to feel comfortable enough to slouch slightly in the chair as he talks. "In a perfect world, there would be no need for punishment. Rewards would be enough, and certainly it is often easy to increase appropriate behavior by devising a program of reinforcing activities. I hate to slip into jargon here, but to use correct terminology, one of the most obvious but effective ways to work with retarded persons is a DRI procedure. DRI stands for differential reinforcement of incompatible behavior. It simply means that you reinforce a behavior you select for the person to engage in which is physically incompatible with the behavior you want stopped. For example, a teacher takes a child who is banging herself on the head with her fist and gets that child to work at a task using her hands.''

Andy pushes his chair against mine and whispers, ''When a child bangs her head a hundred times an hour, think of the staff ratio you would need even if it worked completely with these kinds of cases, which it doesn't. Do you think Arkansas would pay for that?''

Dr. Holditch, now that he has the attention of the judge, turns his head back toward Andy as if he is lecturing a wayward student. ''However, my opinion is that in order to decrease or eliminate certain behaviors, it is sometimes necessary to use punishment as a procedure. But the principle of least restrictive treatment dictates that you try the least aversive techniques first. If you want a cite of the professional literature, see Dr. Richard Foxx's basic training manual entitled *Decreasing Behaviors of Severely Retarded and Autistic Persons*.''

Bruton acts as if he is Holditch's favorite pupil and begins to take notes. I can barely refrain from snorting out loud. With his reputation for shooting from the hip, Bruton probably hasn't written anything except his name on a paycheck in the last twenty years. Holditch dips his head slightly as if to indicate he approves of the judge's willingness to do something besides sit there and pretend he is listening. Of course, Bruton could be writing himself a note to remind himself what time Geraldo Rivera comes on. Holditch continues, ''Now, it should be mentioned there is a school of thought that says aversive techniques of behavior modification are unnecessary in addition to being immoral.'' Holditch pauses and wrinkles his nose before disagreeing. ''Some educators hold to the idea that you can replace a destructive behavior with a skill without having to first eliminate the destructive behavior, but, quite frankly, in some real difficult cases, I think this is simply pie-in-the-sky rhetoric. As I said, in an ideal world there would be no techniques that we call punishment used to decrease unwanted behaviors," he continues, "but we aren't there yet for serious self-injurious behaviors—at least I'm not aware that we are in Arkansas."

I look at the satisfied expression on Jill's angular face and realize that she has slashed the odds against making her case. By going with a conventional psychologist who condones aversive techniques of behavior management (albeit allegedly in a judicious manner) she has slipped from my hand a weapon I would have been happy to use against her. So far as I can tell from the admittedly limited research I have been able to do in the last three days, the case for strictly nonaversive means to eliminate self-injurious behavior is a matter of much debate. By not turning this case into a propaganda film in which outside experts will be trooped into the state to show our backwardness, she has strengthened her hand immeasurably. I realize now that my friend Amy exaggerated Jill's zeal to reform the system. Jill will be content to show that Andy hasn't met the professional standards for psychologists in Arkansas, a much easier task, since it is clear that he ignored the hell out of the usual protocol.

Jill takes Holditch through Pam's records. It is appalling how little had been done for her since she began to hurt herself when she was twelve. As Holditch drones on about the restraints and the drugs that had been an inseparable part of Pam's adolescent years, Andy writes on the legal pad and shoves it at me: "The turnover and vacancies on the staff makes it impossible to do anything but keep kids like Pam in restraints or on drugs."

Holditch says that one of "Dr. Chapman's" major errors was the failure to obtain the approval of a "human rights committee," standard procedure in institutions before highly aversive techniques are tried with a retarded individual. Andy whispers loudly that it was "moribund" at the Blackwell County HDC and hadn't met in months. I make a note to work on somehow minimizing this. It seems it would have been a simple matter to arrange to have his ass covered by a group. Holditch says there is no indication from his review of the records that any committee was consulted.

Jill runs Holditch through a number of recognized behavior-modification programs that he says Andy should have tried before shock: "Extinction," which, according to him, simply means ignoring the behavior (Holditch concedes this would have been dangerous, given the fact that as soon as she came out of the restraints Pam began to hit herself); "Timeout," which would have placed Pam in a room by herself with a one-way mirror for a few minutes at most; "Overcorrection," a procedure in which the teacher or trainer may actually guide with his hands the offender's body in movements that "overcorrect" the maladaptive behavior (Holditch explains, as the judge scratches his head, that, as an example, when Pam began to hit herself, she would have been required to fill a bag with ice and hold it against her head). Finally, he says that forms of punishment other than shock should have been tried first. For example, Pam could have been required to do exercises each time she hit herself. Andy shakes his head as if Holditch has suggested aspirin to cure cancer, but this seems like such common sense I make a note to ask him about it later.

Jill, who has been appropriately unobtrusive in her questioning on direct examination, asks Holditch about the use of a cattle prod, and it is the introduction of this subject that at a jury trial will do the most damage. Average Arkansans may be skeptical of all the psychological mumbo jumbo but talk about electrocution will wake them up, no matter how bored or confused they have become. Bruton thrusts his chin forward as if now we are getting to an area he can understand.

"If shock can ever be said to be appropriate as a method of behavior control, and it is still used by some professionals, according to the literature," Holditch says, tapping his fingers together prissily, "one thing is for certain: using a cattle prod to administer the electric current never is. Anyone who familiarizes himself with the literature knows that."

Again, I feel Andy's breath on my right ear. "The man who pioneered the use of shock in this area used a cattle prod."

But would he use one today? I wonder, as I listen to Holditch name a number of commercial products that have been specifically designed for use on humans. "As far back as 1975, an article was published in the journal *Behavior Therapy* warning against the use of cattle prods. In fact, my research shows that the hand-held shock apparatus is probably rare today. Remote-control devices are more widely used because they don't have the generalization problems that are encountered with hand-held products."

Ramrod straight behind the podium, Jill asks, "What is a generalization problem, Dr. Holditch?"

Holditch, increasingly comfortable in the courtroom, nods patiently. "It is not at all unusual that unwanted behaviors which have disappeared in one setting, for example, the treatment room, reappear in another. If shock is going to have any meaningful application, the child must be able to live in a normal environment. It is nothing short of cruelty to a child if the behavior soon resumes. In other words, children learn to associate the individual who shocks him or her with the stimulus. According to the literature, and in my own experience, when that person is not present, the self-injurious behavior will typically recur. For that reason remote-control devices have been developed which help prevent this problem from developing."

Jill asks softly, "Is there evidence that any other apparatus or device was used to shock Pam Le Master other than a cattle prod?"

Holditch shakes his head. "Not from the records I've been given to review."

Jill asks, "What, if anything, is wrong with using a cattle prod?"

Cattle prod. Cattle prod. If Jill is beating it to death today, wait until she has a jury. Holditch frowns, as if the question pains him. "According to the literature," he says, "the type of device used on an animal may not regulate the voltage or current. This type of apparatus can deliver more than eighty microamperes, which, if the current travels through the heart, can produce ventricular fibrillation. By the way, the pain produced has been likened to having a dentist drill your teeth without benefit of anesthesia. Before coming here, I applied a shock to myself, and in my opinion, the pain is worse than that."

Instinctively, I rise to object, but realize once I get to my feet that the severe pain produced by the shock of a cattle prod is intentional. While I am standing, Jill chooses this moment to ask, "Do you have an opinion concerning Dr. Chapman's use of shock on Pamela Le Master?"

I can make objections here, but they will do no good at this hearing, and I pop back down in my seat like a jack-in-the-box in reverse, while he says, of course, that he does, and then proceeds to say how reckless Andy's actions were and more or less repeats his earlier testimony. It is recklessness that the jury will decide this case on, and the room is hushed when Holditch finishes, and Jill says tonelessly, "Your witness."

There are weaknesses in this testimony, and I have to bite my tongue when I decline to cross-examine him. Even Bruton's eyes bulge in disbelief when I say, "No questions."

I call Olivia as my only witness. I had talked with her briefly on Friday (she surprised me by declining to meet with me again before the hearing), but she seemed as resolute on the phone as she had after the plea and arraignment hearing. Despite my urging, she has made no public statement and has refused all comment to the press. Andy, who has accepted the inevitable outcome of the probable cause hearing with his customary aplomb, had not wanted me to put Olivia through a court appearance any sooner than we had to, and argued as late as last night that she would not waver from the story she had given to the prosecutor's office and to me in my office. Perhaps, she won't, but I think I know better than Andy the pressure she will endure between this hearing and the trial. Getting her on the record now will remove the worry once and for all.

For the hearing she is dressed surprisingly informally. She has donned a navy blue picnic skirt with a simple indigo sleeveless top. Because of their general stylishness, I had not thought to ask her or Andy to wear something more formal. We do not have to impress a jury, but the press and TV are sure to pick up on their seeming casualness.

Her testimony, as I had secretly feared, is cooler than it was in my office. Though the words do not vary, her tone is quite different. I do not know if she is sounding this way intentionally, but she seems detached, almost as if she has begun to question her own involvement. Though she admits that it was she who had suggested shock to Andy her words are tentative, as if it was a treatment she had only heard mentioned, instead of one that she had spent some time trying to find out about from others. I now feel as if I am tiptoeing through a mine field. I ask her if she was aware that he had never tried shock before; and, as she had in my office, she talks about the difficulty she had finding anyone who would even admit it was an option; but this time there is uncertainty in her voice instead of conviction. I rush her through the actual event, fearing she will say something that will implicate Andy; but her story, when she is finished, is almost identical to Leon's. She does volunteer that Andy tried mouth-to-mouth resuscitation; but, had her direct testimony been given in front of a jury, the impression would have been that she was a reluctant witness.

Jill appears almost gleeful that Bruton had denied her objection that the mother's consent was irrelevant as she steps in behind the podium to cross-examine Olivia. Yet now that Olivia has performed miserably on Andy's behalf, she proves an obstinate witness to Jill. Instead of agreeing that Andy had failed to inform her of the dangers of shock, Olivia says that, on the contrary, Andy had warned her that electricity was always dangerous. Jill asks her if Andy had told her that he was going to use a device designed for use on animals.

"Absolutely," Olivia says. "He gave me an article to read showing the results of prior experiments. I knew that what he was trying to do was to show the administrator that shock would work so that he could get permission to buy and use remote-control equipment. He explained that the pain would be intense and that I should experience it, and I did. He said the research showed that if the stimulus wasn't painful enough, some children it had been tried on had adapted to the pain. He explained about the tape being wrapped around the metal part when I asked if it was safe."

Burned worse than I have been, Jill decides not to push any further, and I also decline the opportunity to redirect. Olivia leaves the witness stand dry-eyed and cool. So much for my star witness. I had hoped for a stirring defense of Andy, and only got it when I wasn't asking the questions. Yet maybe I shouldn't be surprised. Putting a person under oath in a witness box has an unpredictable effect.

After brief arguments from Jill and myself, Bruton rules almost in a perfunctory manner that there is probable cause, and he binds the case over to circuit court. Once we are outside the courtroom the media engulf us, but Andy obeys my instructions to make no comment. Despite my best intentions I can't keep myself from saying that it was pointless to cross-examine the state's witnesses.

John Winter of Channel 4 eggs me on. "Was your decision based on your belief that your client can't get a fair hearing in Judge Bruton's court?"

Now that we are in circuit court, I have nothing to lose, but instead I ignore the question and say that we will present the case to a jury. No matter how much they might agree with me, the other members of the judiciary in Blackwell County will resent it if I continue to go after Bruton.

It is only afterward upon entering the Hardhat Cafe, a local burger place, with Sarah that I find myself at a loss for words. Ignoring the stares of men twice and three times her age (though I can't), she asks, "If you think the judge was biased against your client, why didn't you say so?'' She seems annoyed with me even though I had told her our strategy on the way downtown this morning.

I squint in the smoky room, trying to find a table. I think of several rationalizations I could offer up to her. She folds her arms and waits. I could tell her I have to make a living; I don't want to get in trouble with the professional-ethics people; I don't want to hurt my client. Finally, I say weakly, ''The practice of law is mostly one compromise after another. I guess it's a habit.''

Men in suits (professionals enjoying the illusion of a macho atmosphere) are shooting pool with construction workers in the back of the restaurant, and I get us a table so we can watch. Sarah is interested in talking about the hearing and asks me questions until I fear she is beginning to think about becoming a lawyer. ''Dr. Chapman seems to me like a really nice guy,'' she says as the waitress brings over fries, cheeseburgers, and Cokes.

I agree. Before we left the courthouse I had introduced her to Andy, and he went out of his way to treat her like an adult instead of a child. I reach for the bottle of ketchup. ''He's pretty sophisticated,'' I say, thumping it on the side. Dan, who must run through a bottle a week, has instructed me, after a lifetime of thumping, that a law of physics prevents ketchup from coming out if you hit it on the bottom. Dan would be hard-pressed to name the law, but typically he is right about the results. Like a river of lava from an active volcano, the ketchup flows thickly but steadily.

Sarah carefully removes the onions from her patty. ''You sound surprised. Can't a black male be sophisticated?''

''Of course,'' I say hastily. Sarah still thinks of me as a liberal. Her own idealism, which has mushroomed in the last three weeks, seems almost quaint to me these days. I have to be careful not to sound like a racist. ''But you have to admit there're not many black psychologists in Arkansas.''

Sarah, about to bite into her sandwich, puts it down and replies, ''That's not their fault.''

Why the hell not, I think, irritated by Sarah's knee-jerk response. I bite down on a piece of gristle and have to reach into my mouth with my thumb and forefinger to remove it. What's wrong with me? I should be proud of her defending blacks. After all, how many whites really believe blacks are ever going to catch up or really even give a damn whether they do or not? I can count the ones I know on one hand, and it's not mine. What happened to me? It's the times, I guess. Still, I can't bring myself to tell my daughter I'm no longer a child of the sixties, not that I really ever was. But she has this image of my going off to save the world which I am loath to disturb. Despite my recent soul baring, I feel that Sarah needs a few illusions, and, if she wants to think I'm still a defender of the underdog, I'm not going to disabuse her. She'll find out the truth soon enough. I sip at my Coke to rid my mouth of the taste of grease and say, "You're right about that."

She nods, though I think a little disappointed I won't argue with her. Why should I? There'll be plenty of people to do that.

As I am paying the bill, Martha Birford, my partner in humiliation at Mays & Burton, accompanied by a man I do not know, comes through the door. I wonder if she's found a job. I hope so. The times I saw her in court Martha was quicker on the draw than her opposition. As we make our way out through the crowded tables, I introduce Sarah, who pleases me by lighting up the joint with one of her hundred-watt smiles.

Acknowledging my daughter with only the barest of nods, Martha says coldly, "Gideon, I see you've landed on your feet as usual."

Too stunned by her rudeness to think of a comeback, I mumble, "I got lucky," and hurry out the door. Martha and I were, if not close, in the same boat as middle-aged associates who didn't make the grade. Maybe she has resented me all along, and I was too stupid to notice.

"What was that all about, Dad?" Sarah asks. "She didn't seem very friendly."

"I don't know," I say truthfully, squinting into the bright glare. Jealousy, maybe. She knows she's a better lawyer, but as a woman she might never have an opportunity to prove it.

Outside on Davis Street, as we walk back to the Layman Building where Sarah will call a friend to come pick her up, an old black woman is commanding the center of the sidewalk. Obviously mentally ill, she is muttering to herself. Wearing blue scrub pants underneath a tight knit dress with holes in it, she is cursing every other word as she pulls at her wild white hair, which explodes from her head as if she had set off a bomb by biting into it. There is something disturbingly familiar about the woman, but it is impossible to work downtown and avoid these people. I probably have seen her half a dozen times and only notice her now because of Sarah who is staring in fascinated horror at her. As we pass her, the old woman squints at me and croons, "You the white man that got me out of jail!" She smiles at Sarah, revealing jagged gray stumps that once were teeth. A hideous stench reminding me of rotten Chinese food permeates the damp air between us. Instinctively, I grab Sarah's arm and say in a low voice, "Don't look at her. Keep walking."

The old woman calls after us, "You defendin' that ho, white man?"

Sarah giggles nervously, and I take her arm and march her across the street against the light at the corner so we can get away from the old woman. "Dad, was she really your client?"

The raspy voice and wild hair come together. I saw her in the jail cell across from Andy the day he called me. "She's insane," I explain needlessly. "She saw me once down in the jail and for some reason must think I helped her get out."

Sarah looks back over her shoulder. Even now almost a

block away we can still hear her. "How awful! Why isn't she in the hospital?"

"I don't know," I say, unwilling to pursue this subject. There are no good answers to most of her questions, but I am reluctant to tell her that, since I still want her to think somebody's in charge in this country.

9

FROM A DISTANCE the Blackwell County Human Development Center looks like a college campus or some fancy prep school. Ancient brick the color of a four-day-old hematoma is stacked in institutional splendor in front of me as I drive under a silver arch onto the grounds. As I wind around a narrow asphalt street, I wonder how often the residents try to run away into the wooded area that surrounds the campus for miles. Trees give Arkansas its natural beauty, but here I wonder if they could be a hindrance to the security of the residents. Surely a severely retarded person would in some ways be safer lost in the city than in the country. But I suspect few residents, judging from the lack of activity outside on this unusually mild July day (it must be no more than eighty degrees and it is almost eleven), spend much time outside these musty old buildings I am passing.

I ease the Blazer between a Bronco and a Chevrolet pickup outside of what I take to be the central office. Andy has told me I must sign in first before I come to his office. What would institutions do without a sign-in book? Inside a small waiting room I look at the names and addresses before me: Rogers, El Dorado, Helena. This place is not your neighborhood school. Relatives must travel hours for a visit, so I can assume that residents are grouped around the state by level of severity. As I write my name, a man of about forty taps me on the shoulder. He is, I hope, a resident: his eyes are crossed; he has a hump a camel would be proud to own, and from the sounds he is making he is without intelligible speech. He is holding out his hand, and though I have represented many mentally ill people who acted much stranger, I feel myself flinch.

"Homer," the woman behind the glass says mildly, "what're you doing down here? Does Mr. Trantham know you're down here?"

Homer, who is dressed in jeans and a red, long-sleeved western shirt, makes more sounds I can't understand; but there is no mistaking the friendly grin on his face.

To me the woman says, "He wants to shake hands."

There are food stains on Homer's shirt, and I find that I am reluctant to touch this man who seems delighted by my presence. No telling where those hands have been, but with the woman watching me, I have no choice but to extend my hand. He pumps away, and I steel myself to really look at him closely and find that I am not as grossed out as I thought I would be. Of course, I have seen retarded people before, but not so close I could feel their breath on my face. I realize now that I think of them as freaks, some of whom are harmless and some who aren't. "How are you?" I ask loudly, self-conscious as a teenager meeting his first date's father, knowing every word I say will be repeated by the beaming receptionist, a country woman whose brown hair is pulled tight in a bun behind her head. Homer grins sheepishly, as if he had been told an off-color joke in the presence of his mother.

I turn and look at the woman who orders, "Let go of his hand, silly!"

I think she is talking to me and pull my hand away just as he pulls his back, and he and I both giggle nervously. I'm beginning to feel like I'm the newest resident. Homer now studies me with unconcealed glee. He knows a soul mate when he sees one.

"Who're you out here to see?" the woman asks amiably, her voice crackling with humor as she files away the story. I thought he was his brother he acted so dumb! "You didn't write in who you're visiting."

I take a good look at my interrogator. She has a dimple on her left cheek as deep as a small well and her eyes are a sparkling green behind steel bifocals. She could be anywhere between forty and sixty. "I'm here to see Dr. Chapman."

Her dimple disappears instantly as her cheeks swell with disapproval. "I saw you on TV." Unvoiced is her unimpeachable indictment of me: You're his lawyer.

I confess that she probably did and ask, "Can you tell me where his office is?"

"Homer," she snaps, "take him upstairs to Dr. Chapman on your way back to your unit."

I don't know whether I am to take this as an insult or a high honor, but Homer, who seems to have permanently grasped the power of positive thinking, appears ecstatic. He nods eagerly, and without another word I follow him through an unmarked door. Once through the door we make a series of turns, and I realize immediately I am lost as we come upon two elevators. Happily, we take the stairs (though Homer appears entirely harmless, I'd just as soon not spend a couple of hours between floors with him). On the stairs we pass a little black male surely no older than twenty. He points at me and laughs hysterically. Homer frowns and says something that sounds unmistakably like "Fuck off." It begins to dawn on me that if I stayed out here a week, I'd understand everything he is saying.

Upstairs, we pass through a set of double doors, and to my left is a group of obviously retarded men sitting on sofas watching a soap opera. This strikes me as strange, but why should it? It's not as if you have to be a rocket scientist to watch "All My Children." In the same area further ahead we pass a card table around which three employees (two men and a woman) dressed in ordinary clothes are sitting. I assume they are staff (I realize I expected to see nurses in starched uniforms sweeping by me on their way to patients' rooms). Yet the residents, as strange as they look, are not, for the most part, sick, though I assume some are on medication to control their behavior.

Before I can speak, the woman, who seems to be sorting some papers as the men look on, says, "Homer, where're you taking him?"

Without breaking his shuffling gait, Homer makes a series of noises, the last part of which sounds to me like "Lapland." Chapman. The three give me a hard stare but say nothing. Everybody in America knows a lawyer when they see one.

Andy is reading what appears to be a textbook in a small, dingy office with the door open and looks up as Homer brings me into view. The green concrete walls are mostly bare except for a calendar and an empty metal shelf. It is as if Andy has already been packed up.

I explain, "Homer brought me."

Andy smiles, his eyes crinkling with pleasure at the sight of Homer, who now looks relieved to have discharged his unpopular task. "Thank you, Homer," he says formally. "You did a good job. Go on back to the dayroom."

Homer nods and moves off, his peculiar old-man's gait no longer as distracting to me as when I arrived.

Andy rises and gravely offers his hand. "Have a seat. I've been transferred up here out of harm's way," he says, his voice sounding sarcastic and at the same time embarrassed.

Wearing a short-sleeved sky-blue knit shirt over a pair of comfortable-looking pleated khaki pants, he is dressed far more casually than I expected. But then, I suppose Homer doesn't mind. I sit in a metal folding chair opposite him, already feeling closed in. "What are you supposed to be doing all day?" I ask, trying unsuccessfully to read upside down the title of his book.

"Right now I'm reviewing our training literature," he says mock-importantly, and then mutters, "as if it matters."

I pick up the book from his desk. It is entitled: *Nonaversive Intervention for Behavior Problems: A Manual for Home and Community*. I flip through the pages, realizing I know zero about what is expected of retarded people. "Doesn't it?" I ask.

A bitter look crosses Andy's face. "It's supposed to, but there's so much turnover," he says, looking past me into the hall, "Homer isn't going to do anything the rest of his life except wander these halls."

"What about that suit to shut down places like this?" I ask, feeling the waxy cover of the book beneath my thumb.

Andy gives me an indulgent smile and for the next ten minutes lectures me on the myths of what he calls the dein-stitutionalization movement. "You get all these utopia training models like this," he says, pointing at his book, "but it's not the real world. What good does it do to put a non-verbal, severely retarded man in a group home? There's no place for people like that in American society. Retarded people are, by definition, the losers, the bottom of the barrel, in a country that insists on competition from the moment a child is born. Sure, the mildly retarded can learn enough adaptive behavior to get by, but the Homers of the world don't fit in anywhere. In a consumer society people like him won't ever be accepted because they don't have any value."

I nod, more interested in the emotion in his voice than in what he is saying. I'll be the first to admit I don't want Homer moving in next to me. The price of real estate in my neighborhood is already low enough without having to worry about Homer coming over to peep in Sarah's window. What I want a jury to hear, though, is that Andy cares about these people even if they don't. And it won't hurt if they agree with him. All Andy was trying to do was stop this child from mutilating herself—he wasn't trying to move her into the half-million-dollar homes overlooking the Arkansas River. To get him to talk more, I deliberately bait him. "You don't sound too liberal on this subject. I thought you'd tell me that retarded people were like blacks—just give 'em a chance to show they're regular folks."

Andy gives me a look that reminds me of the first time I talked to him in my office: Is this white asshole educable? "The people who write these books and lead these movements are basically ideologues, no matter how much they've worked with the developmentally disabled. It doesn't matter whether you call them liberals or conservatives. They have this grand vision of how things ought to be. Frankly, I think they're dangerous as hell," he says, softly slapping the table in front of him.

Feigning disapproval, I cross my arms in front of me, anxious to keep him going. A jury has got to be made to see the guy's no Dr. Strangelove rubbing his hands with glee at the thought of Armageddon. Down deep, Andy is paternalistic. He just wants to stay down on the farm and take care of his retarded folks. He is probably deeply conservative, like most Arkansans. If so, I want to exploit that identification at the trial. "You're going to play into the prosecutor's hands," I say, believing just the opposite. "She's going to try to paint you as a real Neanderthal, the kind of professional who's keeping Arkansas in the Dark Ages. Shocking defenseless children, keeping them locked up in institutions."

Andy stands up and looks out his window. I can't see what he is looking at, but probably he is staring off into the woods. He says, after a long pause, "You really think desegregation, when you weigh the pluses and minuses, has benefited most blacks? Look at where a lot of blacks are in the average school. Special ed. The slow classes. Or out of school hanging out, getting stoned on drugs and killing each other. In the United States there can only be so many winners. For whatever reason blacks aren't ever going to win in America. Sure, there are exceptions. The liberals will trot out a black who's made it to prove integration is working. But you don't prove anything by how your best kids do; they would have made it anyway. It's your average kid who proves whether the system is working or not, and for most black kids it's going to be the bottom, and it's not really getting any better."

His voice trails off, as if I should be making a connection. What is it? Is he conceding black inferiority, or what? Is he saying blacks are like retarded people—too stupid to compete? I stare at his back, unable to try to read his face. I have lost the thread somewhere. "It's too late to go back to Africa, Andy," I say, wondering whether he will take this as a slur.

He turns around and gives me a wintry smile. "All I'm talking about is a sense of identity. These reformers have decided retarded people should be a part of the American rat race as if that were a good thing. I'm not so sure the Homers of this world would be better off competing and losing in a society that values only winners."

I look toward the door, wondering if I should get up and close it. We are at the end of the hall, so it hardly seems worth it. The fire has gone out of Andy's voice as if he has gotten stuck. Perhaps he has. Somebody is always ahead of us, but that doesn't mean we have to slit our wrists. Normal everyday life has compensations other than just winning. Maybe, though, if you're forced to compete and you usually come in dead last, it's hard to see the virtue in lining up for the next race. I say carefully, "I want the jury to see you have a point of view, but I'm not sure a racial analogy is going to be appreciated, however sympathetic it is."

Andy props one leg against the wall and leans back against the windowsill with both elbows resting on the edge. He says sarcastically, "You really believe in this legal crap, don't you?"

My right ear itches and I dig at it with my little finger, a pleasure so sublime I scratch until it hurts. Is that how a self-abusive child begins? How to explain I don't "believe" in the law. "A friend of mine," I say, remembering Dan Bailey's beatific expression after he won his first jury trial "once said the law is like toilet paper; sometimes it works and sometimes it doesn't." I study Andy's puzzled expression and decide to spell it out for him. "His point was that there're more efficient ways to clean up a mess, but it's what we're used to in this country, and consequently a lot of people swear by it. I don't swear by our legal system, but I'm getting used to it."

Andy wrinkles his nose slightly at my remark. He is too

proper to appreciate it. The truth is that I am surprised he was willing to get his hands dirty enough even to get close enough to Pam to touch her, much less shock her. I ask, "Can you get away with giving me a tour?"

"I think so," he says. "It'll have to be a quick one, but you need to see this place to get a feel for what's going on."

In the next twenty minutes I see more than I want to. With me trailing Andy, we cover four of the six buildings on the grounds. It is the locked wards that give me the creeps. Somewhat surprisingly, Andy still has a set of keys, and though all eyes are on us from the time we enter a ward until we leave it, Andy acts as if I am about to make an offer to buy the place. As we stride briskly through a ward in which some of the men are tied to their beds, I get a feel for the first time what Pam must have been like. Though none of them are in a position to abuse themselves, it is possible for me to picture some of them ramming their heads against their beds. One hideously deformed man (his eyes look turned inside out, and he has scar tissue for skin) rhythmically rubs his head against his sheets.

On this same ward several men, none with intelligible speech, gather around us. They seem starved for human touch, but, like Homer, they are hideous to me, and there are too many of them. The level of noise is astonishingly high, but I can't understand a word. All I want to do is get out of here. Two male aides, one black and one white, walk over to us and greet Andy warmly. Andy acknowledges that he is showing his lawyer around, and we leave them shooing the men back toward a group of chairs and tables in the corner by a TV. Reading my mind, Andy says, "Homer's ward is higher-functioning. You'd get used to it and see them as distinctive individuals. It's the aides who don't see them as individuals that give us the problems."

One of the men, wearing only a pair of jockey shorts, bends down like an animal searching for food, picks up a cigarette butt, and brings it toward his mouth. The black aide catches him by his wrist and forces the man, who is babbling angrily, to drop it into his hand.

"That's called pica," Andy says as I watch dumbfounded. "Some of them will try to put anything in their mouths that's not nailed down. Including their feces."

Outside, I realize I have been holding my breath, and exhale. As we walk toward a building on the western edge of the campus, Andy points to a similar structure directly across from us. "Pam lived over in Findley. I could take you in there, but some of the women, like the men, like to take off their clothes, and it would cause more of a ruckus. Since it's about the same, we'll go to the boys' building."

As we approach the brick building, I feel myself becoming claustrophobic again. "How do people keep working here?" I ask, shaken by so much abnormality in one room.

"They don't," Andy says. "As I've told you, the turnover among aides is ridiculous. They hardly get paid enough to live on, and yet, they are the people who provide the primary care."

As we enter the boys' ward, I realize that Rogers Hall, the unit for the criminally insane that I used to visit as a public defender, was a piece of cake compared to what I'm seeing. As blunted and spaced-out as the men at Rogers Hall were, at least they looked halfway normal. Too many of these people look as if they were drawn by the guy who comes up with "The Far Side." I tell myself that I shouldn't be so revolted by the way they look, but I can't help the queasy feeling in my stomach. If there is a God, what divine purpose could be served by such genetic mistakes? Free will, the priests at Subiaco, the Catholic boarding school I attended, would say, I suppose. The boys' ward is at the same time less and more depressing. It is smaller, but the sight of children obviously zombied out is hard to take. There must be no more than twenty boys in this room. We walk past showers and I see several boys (one of whom is old enough to have a sparse patch of pubic hair) being hosed down by a woman. A male aide is with her trying to help them wash themselves. It seems like a good way to give them a bath, but Andy whispers, "They sometimes wash the men and women the same way. It can seem pretty degrading, but they don't have the staff to make sure everyone has privacy."

"Together?" I ask, titillated by the thought. One of the boys laughs with glee as the nurse sprays him in the face.

Andy gives me his professional frown. "Of course not," he says, holding out his arms as one of the boys gets away from the aide and comes running to us. The child is naked and wet, but Andy lets him jump into his arms as if this strange-looking child were his own son. "Toddy," Andy says, smiling, "you're all wet!"

For a response, Toddy, who somewhat resembles a gremlin from a Steven Spielberg movie, burrows his head against Andy's chest like a small animal. If we could have Andy's trial out here on the grounds of the Blackwell County HDC, I think Andy would be acquitted in about five minutes. It is easy to paint a sinister picture of an institutional world in a courtroom, but not quite so simple if you're out here.

The female aide puts down her hose and takes Toddy from Andy's arms. "Dr. Chapman," she apologizes, "he just loves you to death."

Andy pats the child's back before returning him to the woman, who obviously is a friend. "There are worse crimes, I suppose," he says, a deadpan expression his face.

Back in his office, we talk in detail about the upcoming trial, which is two months away, in September. I have waited a week to come to see him. I have wanted us both to digest the probable cause hearing and the publicity surrounding it. In the interval, fortunately, we have gone from the worst judge possible in Blackwell County to the best—Harriet Tarnower, a female appointee whose intelligence and fairness is already becoming a model in Blackwell County. If we care anything about competence, we will elect her to a judicial slot.

Andy tells me he has run down the names of three possible

experts who will at least be willing to talk to us. He tears a sheet of paper from a fat notebook and gives it to me. The names mean nothing to me—only the states: Mississippi (we used to say, "Thank God for Mississippi," until it pulled ahead of us in spending for education), Texas, and Pennsylvania. My bias toward Southern-accented expert witnesses is generally appeased. "I must have called ten who as soon as they heard the word, 'litigation,' practically hung up on me," Andy says ruefully.

Surely this shouldn't surprise him. Who wants to say he's an expert with a cattle prod? I take the paper and slip it into my briefcase, knowing this way I'll get back to my office with it, I may not be able to find it because of all the other junk I'm carrying around, but at least I will have it there, and that's getting to be a major accomplishment as I pick up clients. I've acquired five more in the past week, thanks to the publicity. Since we hardly put on a defense, I felt I must have looked pretty much like an idiot at the probable cause hearing, but I guess it hasn't hurt me. I ask, "What'd they say?"

"Nothing much," Andy sighs. "I doubt if we're going to be able to get anyone to testify who currently uses shock. As soon I mention that I am facing a criminal charge, they start sounding real busy."

I play with the zipper on my briefcase and warn him, "Whoever we get won't come cheap."

As usual, the subject of money does not faze him. "I know."

Though it is none of my business, I blurt, "Do you have a rich uncle or what?" Though I have no proof, I have the overwhelming suspicion that Olivia is bankrolling his defense; and, if this is true, it could mean all kinds of trouble.

Andy stiffens, his back arching slightly. "You could say that."

Once I start, I have a hard time stopping. "Olivia?"

His eyes flash angrily. "No."

I believe his body language over his words. I think he is

lying, but I do not say so. The blacks I know don't have the kind of money it takes to defend this case. "If that were so," I warn him, "it could hurt you if it came out."

Without a doubt I have touched a sore spot. His voice is ugly and guttural. "Do you ask your white clients where they get their money?"

I feel my own anger rising. I don't like being taken for a fool. "I didn't have to at the Public Defender's Office," I say, conveniently ignoring the fact that I have been gone quite a while.

"I didn't think I had hired a racist to defend me," Andy says, shoving his chair back and scraping the concrete floor with a sound that sets my teeth on edge.

I nearly swallow my tongue to keep from telling him that I was married to a woman more nearly his color than mine, but after so many years I would sound like those racists who assure everyone that some of their best friends are black. I'm not the man I was when Rosa was alive, and for some reason I can't pinpoint, I'd rather choke on my own spit than try to reassure him how wonderful I am. Maybe I am racist, but I suspect there is racism in everybody if you scratch hard enough. I do know that I don't want to risk losing him as a client. "I'm sorry," I say, "but it's my job to know as much about your case as possible. What would be wrong if she did loan you some money? I think it would be the least she could do," I add disingenuously.

Andy shakes his head as if I still don't get it and lectures, "You make the assumption that all blacks, including me, come from poverty. That's racist."

Big deal, I think, and lean back in my chair, relaxed by his tone which now has more of a scolding quality than the scorching anger of a moment ago. "If that's my worst sin," I defend myself, "I'm way ahead of most people."

Andy gives me a wry smile, breaking the tension. "I doubt if that's your worst sin."

I laugh, glad this is behind us and suddenly think I understand. Andy doesn't consider himself particularly black. He probably thinks he is superior not only to blacks but whites as well. "You're right," I acknowledge. "It was racist. I'm sorry."

My apology seems to mollify him, and we spend some time talking about the people the state will call who didn't testify at the probable cause hearing. Andy seems convinced that neither David Spath, the administrator of the Blackwell County Human Development Center, nor Yettie Lindsey, the social worker who was to chart the number of shocks administered to Pam, will be of much help to us. I leave Andy's office to talk to both persons, hoping that just possibly Spath may have known what Andy was going to try. Granted, as Andy points out, Spath is a state bureaucrat, not a psychologist, but his testimony that Andy wasn't too far out of line could mean the difference between a manslaughter conviction and a Class A misdemeanor charge of negligent homicide, which carries a maximum penalty of a year in jail. Andy's dismissal of Yettie Lindsey seems more reasonable: according to her statement to the prosecutor, as a witness to the accident, she has nothing to add to what is already known. Yet surely, if she is willing, she, now that Olivia has apparently begun to backtrack, could testify how desperate the situation was and how shock, even with a cattle prod, was the only alternative.

I walk downstairs to the first floor to be told that David Spath is not in and won't be back the rest of the day. But Yettie Lindsey is in, and I walk two doors past Spath's office to find a young, pretty black woman sitting in her office behind her desk with the door open. Yettie (her real name? Whites are too afraid of ridicule to be so creative with names), I would guess is in her middle twenties and is short and busty with bangs and a kind of ponytail. She is wearing a maize turtleneck cotton dress that accentuates her figure. Her nose is characteristically wide; she has a lovely mouth and enormous eyes that are more green and yellow than brown. Her skin has a copper tone, and the old phrase embedded in my eastern Arkansas upbringing, "a nigger in the woodpile," pops into my head. Although she is too dark to be what was called a "high yellow," somewhere along the line, as with most African-Americans, she must have had a white ancestor or two. I tell her who I am and more or less invite myself in to visit. After preliminaries about my role, I say, "I thought that perhaps you might be able to help Andy show a jury there is another side to all of this—that, at least, his heart was in the right place when nobody else wanted to get involved."

Her elbows on the desk in front of her, Yettie Linsey leans forward and cups her chin in her hands as if she is considering her response. Thus far, her comments have been, if not unfriendly, monosyllabic. Finally, she says, her diction more elegant and refined than I expected, "I really don't think you want me to testify for you."

Surprised, I ask more sharply than I intend, "Why not?"

"In the first place, I don't agree with what Andy did. Pam was a human being whose life wasn't as horrible to her as it was to her mother and Andy. Being in arm restraints all the time isn't particularly fun, but there're lots of people who can't use their bodies the rest of their life, and nobody says they're better off dead, which is what I've heard Olivia say on more than one occasion."

I am drawn to Yettie's left hand as she tugs down at her skirt. It seems as small and delicate as a butter knife. No ring. What is her motive in spilling out this warning to me? Am I to be some kind of messenger to my client? If she gets on the witness stand with any of this, an Arkansas jury will listen as carefully to her as they would to a scientist predicting the next earthquake. Her voice has an earnest quality that is compelling, and if the men on the jury get tired of that, they can stare at her face and her chest. "Isn't that a fairly typical comment from a parent who's frustrated by the system's inability to help her child?"

Yettie's face now has a smug expression, as if finally she is about to bring me up to speed. "Olivia works the system pretty good. She's got Andy wrapped around her little finger so tight he has trouble taking a deep breath.''

As if she is prompting me, I reply, ''So you think they're having an affair, huh?''

She raises her eyebrows as if there is no other conclusion that could possibly be drawn. ''You know where he lives?''

Before I can even nod, she says, ''You think they're any black women there?''

I resist the urge to doodle for fear she will think I am taking notes and force myself to hold my hands in my lap, as if we were discussing what the residents are having for lunch. Knowing the area, I say, ''I'd be surprised if they even have a black janitor.''

It is her turn to nod. ''You don't have to be a genius to figure out your client has a thing for white women.''

Her face is angry now, and I can see rejection written all over it. A lot of things make me nervous about this case, but until now black racism wasn't one of them. ''That's not a crime—anymore,'' I add, feeling I had better get what I can out of her before she clams up. ''Do you have any hard evidence Andy's involvement with Pam's mother was more than just professional?''

A fake smile plays on Yettie's lips, perhaps at my poor choice of an adjective. ''All you have to do is watch them,'' she says contemptuously.

Since the same thought had crossed my mind, it is difficult for me to protest her vagueness. I risk asking, ''Would it be fair to say that at one point you might have appreciated it if Andy had shown a little interest in you?''

Yettie brings her hands to her face as if the indignity of this question is too much for her to bear. Finally, she answers, her voice trembling a bit, ''How many black professional men do you think I know?''

Her honesty is stunning. She probably doesn't know personally twenty black men close to her age with even a master's degree. ''Not many, I guess,'' I say stupidly, feeling I should say something.

"Look," she says, her voice suddenly weary, "I know I sound like a black bitch from hell. All I'm telling you is that you don't want me as a witness, because I'll tell everything I'm asked."

I sit for a few moments, but there is nothing else to say.

"Fair enough," I mutter and stand. "Thanks for your time."

She doesn't reply.

10

DAN BAILEY STANDS in the middle of my doorway looking as mournful as a man beginning a diet the day before Thanksgiving. He pleads, "I know it sounds hideous, but it's right down your alley."

I rock back in my chair and roll my eyes in mock horror. "An eighty-four-year-old woman caught having sex in a closet in a nursing home, who wants to dissolve her guardianship? Thanks a lot."

Now that he has me talking, Dan tries to hide a manila folder behind him and edges through the door like an uninvited insurance agent. "You were the best attorney at that mental health garbage at the state hospital when we were at the PD's Office. Come on, if I could get another continuance, I would."

I put my feet up on my desk as I watch Dan ease into the chair across from me. He is as inevitable as a mudslide. Obviously, he was hoping his client would die before he had to try the case. "You know how to flatter a guy, Dan."

Dan balances the dog-eared folder, which looks as if he has been snacking on it, between his knees. "She was a friend of my mother's, and before Mama would die, I had to sign a pledge in blood I'd try to help Mrs. Gentry if she ever wanted out."

I smile, remembering the list of chores Rosa gave me before she died. Polish the table, water the tomatoes. It was as if she were going on a weekend trip. I haven't missed a week with the table. "When's the hearing?" I ask. Hell, I owe

Dan. He has given me outright four legitimate cases in the two weeks I've been in solo practice and referred me two others. The trouble is that this is the kind of case where you lose credibility. Not only does it waste the judge's time but it also runs the risk of a Rule 11 motion for an attorney's fee from the other side.

"Next Tuesday," Dan mumbles, daring to edge the folder onto the corner of my desk. "Our plane is supposed to leave at eleven. Brenda and I'll never make it even if she's my only witness. The nursing home would leave half their patients sitting on bedpans to have their witnesses in court to testify in order to keep somebody from busting out."

I look down at my desk calendar. It has a big hole in it next Tuesday, but it would be nice to fill it up with some clients who pay their bills. If it weren't for Andy and my rat-burner case (and she is beginning to call too frequently), I'd be running a one-man Legal Services program. Besides those cases, I've got fifteen clients (mostly women who want divorces) and have managed to collect a grand total of nine hundred dollars from them since I moved into the Layman Building. "Go ahead and hand me the fucker," I say irritably, "and quit trying to slide it up my pants leg."

Dan snickers and hands me the folder, which is sticky as well as ragged. If I licked it, I could probably get a sugar high from all the candy Dan handles between meals. I open it, and a single sheet of paper falls out. On a half-sheet of yellow legal paper Dan has written the words "Wants out." I pick up the folder by my fingertips. "Impressive amount of research," I say and drop it into the wastepaper basket.

Dan, now that I've taken this turkey, props his own feet on my desk. "I got it all in my head," he says, pointing with his finger at his thinning brown hair, now speckled with gray. "Besides, you're getting a nice fee."

I get out a pad in the vain hope he will at least tell me how to get to the nursing home. "Forgive me for being so cynical," I say, looking for my pen, "but somehow I doubt if Mrs. Gentry's got control over her assets."

Dan, grunting from the effort, reaches across to the corner of my desk to where my red Flair pen has rolled and flips it to me. "I was about to add," he grins, "if you get her sprung."

For the next fifteen minutes Dan tells me the story of his mother's friendship with Mrs. Gentry, which has nothing to do with her case. Finally, since it is nearly the time the cafeteria opens, he gets to the point. A year ago, with the aid of the family doctor, Mrs. Gentry's son hustled his widowed mother through a guardianship proceeding (she was slowly recovering from surgery), and had her transferred to a nursing home, where Dan's mother met her. Instead of shriveling up and dying, as she was supposed to, she has made a full recovery, according to Dan.

"Have you ever seen her?" I ask, totally skeptical at this point. With my family history, I can't imagine even living to sixty-five, much less thinking I'd be able to get it up in my eighties.

"She's looks just like Dr. Ruth!" Dan cackles. "And talks about sex ninety to nothing."

I rub my head. I can believe the first part but not the second. Dan will hype any story, anytime. "Is she really eighty-four?" I ask.

His face benign as a cherub's, Dan beams at me. "If she's a day," he says, struggling to his feet. "That I can swear to."

I nod. Meaning the rest is bullshit. I write on my calendar, "Dr. Ruth" and, determined to get something out of this, get up to go downstairs and eat lunch with Dan. I will go out this afternoon to the nursing home to get this travesty under way. As we pass the receptionist's desk, Julia nods, and picks up a pencil and taps her teeth with it. "Tweedledee and Tweedledum off to the chow hall again. Maybe we can get a direct phone line installed down there."

There is no doubt in my mind who is Tweedledum. About

the second week I started getting used to Julia's malevolent comments and have come to accept them for the truths about myself they contain. "Would you see about that, sweetie?" Dan coos at her.

Julia pushes her cheeks out at Dan and pats her poochy stomach. She is dressed today in mauve pants and a lavender silk shirt, reminding me of a big grape. "Whatever you say, Porky," she says, smiling at Dan.

"By the way," she says to me, "while you were in the crapper earlier Mona Moneyhart called again. Should we be installing a direct line for her too?"

I roll my eyes at Dan. I'd like to trade him Mona. Somehow, I've got to learn to charge divorce clients by the hour if I'm going to earn any money. I say to Julia, "I'll call her back after lunch."

Julia pitches the pink message slip in the wastepaper basket by her desk. "It'd save time if we got a little cot for her and put it in the corner of your office."

I nod at Dan, who is grinning now that Julia has shifted targets. "Let's go eat."

In the cafeteria we are joined by Frank D'Angelo and Tunkie Southerland, attorneys from our floor. Frank, who is as wiry as Dan is fat, puts his salad down on the far edge of the table across from Dan. "It's not that I don't trust you, Dan," he says, watching Dan spoon in a mouthful of cherry cobbler, "it's just that I haven't eaten since last night, and it doesn't look like you're slowing down."

Dan moves his hand toward Frank as if to grab his plate of mostly lettuce and cucumbers and then waves it away. "It's not worth fighting you for, D'Angelo." He turns to Frank's companion. "Tunkie," he says loudly, "how was your AIDS test?"

Tunkie Southerland is said to be so shy it's rumored he doesn't know whether or not he has been circumcised. A tall, clumsy man who wears bifocals even though he is at least a decade younger than the rest of us, he pulls his neck inside his collar like a turtle.

"Lay off the Tunk," I tell Dan, who is looking around to see if anyone is laughing, "or he won't write your next brief for you." Tunkie (God only knows how he got his nick-name—he won't say) is the only lawyer I know personally who has had a case at the United States Supreme Court. At least he ghosted the brief. He writes beautifully, but watching him greet a client in the lobby is painful. If the client is a woman, Tunkie's eyes actually begin to water. Why some people feel they have to become lawyers I'll never under-stand.

"How's your big case going?" he asks, changing the sub-ject as he sits down next to me. Despite his timid demeanor, Tunkie dresses well. He is wearing a blue banker's-stripe broadcloth shirt and a burgundy tie. If he is as timid as he seems, I wonder how he can bear to look in the mirror long enough to get his knot so straight.

Dan, who is gulping his lunch down with coffee still too hot for me to do more than sip, answers for me. "Which one? He's got two now."

I let Dan explain and watch Tunkie's face go crimson as Dan announces my newest client is eighty-four and was caught having sex in a closet. "If I can get it up when I'm that age," Dan finishes loudly, "I'll go down to the middle of Main Street and let Tunkie sell tickets to it." We all laugh, and even Tunkie smiles at such a ludicrous thought.

"How's your murder case coming?" Frank asks, after Dan quits hooting at himself.

"Accidental death," I say, wincing at my memories of my conversation with Yettie Lindsey yesterday. Instead of im-mediately confronting Andy with what she told me, I called Rainey at the state hospital and asked her to plug herself into the social-worker gossip line. She knows Yettie only on sight, but the state is too small not to find mutual friends or enemies in common.

"Sure it was," Tunkie says, carefully spreading the cloth napkin that held his silverware onto his lap. "The mother probably wanted her kid put out of her misery and paid this black dude to electrocute her.''

Improbably, Frank tries to rescue me. "It'd be a lot easier just to forget you ever had a child like that.''

Dan wags his finger at all of us. "A man might try to forget," he says, "but a mother can't. Too much guilt. At the age of seventy, my mother still called every week to tell me what to do.''

I say, laughing, "For good reason." We talk generally about why people do things and decide no one has a clue. Maybe it is as simple as the principle of behavior modification: we do what reinforces us. But if that's true, what was the stimulus that led a black social worker to spill her guts to a white lawyer she didn't know from a hole in the ground? Unrequited love? A bad evaluation? If anybody can find out, Rainey can. Odd how she is willing to do anything for me except make love. A lot of the women I've known since Rosa's death have been just the opposite.

Rosewood Convalescent Center is like other nursing homes I've visited—a prison disguised as a rest home for the elderly and infirm. While they think they are being watched, the employees, who are in mufti, wear cheery expressions, at least until they find out who I am. Still, there is no hiding the guard post—the nurse's station that sits strategically at the midway point of the entrance to the building. Two wings form forty-five-degree angles from this central point, and I would bet the lunch Dan graciously paid for that it takes a key to get out the back door.

After being required to show my Blackwell County Bar Association card to the assistant administrator, an anxious young woman who seems to regard my card as a confession that I am a convicted rapist ("This man claims to be her attorney"), and to the administrator, a man, whom I mentally dub Smiling Jack because of the frozen sneer he wears during our conversation, I am silently led by an aide to Room 142, which we reach after a series of turns that leave me completely lost. It must be nap time or perhaps time for their favorite soap, because we come upon only one resident, a trembling old man in bathrobe and slippers pushing a walker who seems as much at sea about where he is going as I am.

The aide, who appears to be a high school kid, knocks as she opens the door, and if my client is again having sex, we will be sure to catch her at it. Instead, we come upon two people, one woman curled up in a fetal position in the far bed nearer the window, and another woman sitting at a desk next to a dresser. It will be just my luck if Mrs. Gentry is the old lady who looks as if she is in a coma, but the aide points out my client in the metal folding chair as if she is identifying her in a police lineup. "That's her."

The aide leaves, and I awkwardly introduce myself. Mrs. Gentry turns in her chair, and I am pleasantly surprised by her healthy appearance. Though her skin is somewhat discolored by liver spots, she has a strong, masculine face that reminds me of an aunt who is now dead. Her hair, more gray than white, is thinning, but it is combed and pulled neatly into a bun at the back of her head. She is wearing turquoise trousers and a beige smock that covers a heavy but not obese body. Holding a pen in her left hand, she waits patiently until I am finished with my lie that Dan has to be out of town, and then asks if her hearing has been canceled for Tuesday. Her voice, I note, has an old woman's cracked quality, but is strong. I tell her that so far as I know it is still set, and that I need to talk to her in private.

With a right hand almost as big as my own, Mrs. Gentry gestures dismissively toward her roommate, and says dryly, "We can't get much more private than this. Eloise can't hear."

I glance at Eloise, who doesn't even appear to be breathing and then back at Mrs. Gentry and smile. Though I get into trouble occasionally, I tend to make snap judgments about my clients, and I decide I like this old, mannish-looking woman. I may not be able to help her, but I've got a little time to give it a shot. I need to stop obsessing about Andy's case for a while and get some perspective. After all, it is still more than a month off. "The judge will want to know why you want out," I say, as I drag over the other chair in the room. "What will you tell him?"

Mrs. Gentry stares at me as if she hasn't made up her mind whether I have any sense or not. I begin to be aware that she hums constantly under her breath when she is not speaking. Finally, she begins, sending forth her words in a torrent. "I never wanted to be in here in the first place. For six months, I was horribly sick and almost died. Gall-bladder problem they probably didn't diagnose right at first and lots of infection. They had to take it out, and most of my pancreas, too. I'm on oral insulin, but that's all except vitamins. I'm still a little weak but I don't need to be in here. My son got tired of waiting for me to die, and by now he's probably wasted half of my money. Tommy thinks he's a businessman—wants to sell Arkansas rice to the Japanese. Who doesn't? Now I can't even get a drink of water without having to ask six people if it's okay. Would you want to live like this?" she asks and immediately begins to hum again.

"No, ma'am," I say, and scan the room. The walls are a dull mustard color, and there is a smell of urine and disinfectant coming from her roommate's bed. What in the world could be more depressing? "Can you take care of yourself?"

She folds her arms across her chest and clears her throat. "I don't want to take care of myself. I was in one of those retirement places—decent food, alcohol, somebody to play bridge with, my own apartment, even some privacy, darn it." Suddenly, tears come to her eyes. "Obviously, I'm not going to live forever, but I don't want to die in here if I can help it. Would you?"

I decide not to ask her about the sex-in-a-box business right now. It is irrelevant and of only prurient interest. Though Dan will be disappointed if I don't come back with details, surely he can survive without knowing the sex life of an eighty-four-year-old woman who looks a bit like the pictures I've seen of Gertrude Stein. I get her to sign a couple of releases so I can look at her records and talk to her doctor. Since she has no control over her money and can't hire her own doctor to examine her, we are at the mercy of the nursing-home physician, who, if he knows anything, surely is aware which side his bread is buttered on, but it can't hurt to talk to him. I visit with her for another thirty minutes, and as I am picking up my briefcase to leave she clears her throat and says, dropping her voice, "There's something else you ought to know."

As I cram my notes into my briefcase, she begins to hum. "Yes, ma'am?"

Mrs. Gentry looks over at her comatose roommate and says, with great dignity, "I'm still sexually active."

I nod, unable to bring myself to tell her that I am aware of this remarkable fact.

She says, "They discourage that sort of thing here. In fact, they treat you like a child and make you feel dirty. You have to sneak around." Her voice has become a whisper. "I have a friend here whom I've known ever since my son admitted me. He and I were caught in kind of a compromising position a couple of weeks ago in the food pantry. I would die if that comes out in court."

Mrs. Gentry's spotted, wrinkled face has turned a bright red. "I think it's totally irrelevant," I assure her, "and I'll object if your son's attorney tries to bring it up."

Mrs. Gentry sighs, apparently relieved, but it occurs to me that the incident would be wonderful evidence that she shouldn't be here. As I try to suggest this, however, the humming grows louder until it seems to fill the room. It sounds like "Sentimental Journey," but I couldn't swear to it.

Hell, I don't blame her. A person ought to be able to screw in peace. Still, it would be nice. As I finally leave, telling her that I will see her again before the hearing, she looks at me as if she has known all along that lawyers are perverts.

Rainey scrapes the bottom of her empty yogurt cup like a chicken scratching for food. A kiddie-size cup hardly seems worth the trouble, but Rainey, as I have learned to my regret, has the self-discipline of an old-fashioned nun. "I have some information for you," she says and then licks the white plastic spoon. "It's all gossip, but since it's about sex, you'll pay attention."

This reference is prompted by my disclosure that I have a date with Kim Keogh tomorrow night. We could never work out lunch, so I swallowed hard and asked her out to dinner. Rainey and I have gotten to the point where we tell each other about our love life, or at least parts of it. It seemed strange at first, but since we have become such good friends it was probably inevitable. "She's probably home looking at herself in the mirror," I say gloomily. Now that I've asked Kim out, I've started to worry that we don't have anything in common. I scoop out an M&M from my cup and pop it onto my chocolate-and-vanilla-flavored tongue. God, if chocolate tasted any better, it'd have to be outlawed. "What's the deal?" I ask, remembering that I have asked her to find out what she could about Yettie Lindsey.

As if she has forgotten, Rainey stares for a moment at the traffic whizzing through the intersection of Davis and Edgemont and then back at me. She is wearing pink twill jeans and a soft, clingy aqua top. She brushes a strand of her frizzy red hair back from her temple in the humid, oppressive night air, raising her left breast in the process. "Yettie supposedly used to have a thing for your client," she says, "but apparently he wouldn't give her the time of day."

I watch as some teenage boys who don't look old enough to shave pull up to the red light in a 280 Z and then scratch off. "Why wouldn't he?" I ask, thinking I know the answer. "She's attractive, young, and available. At least she wasn't wearing a ring."

Rainey snaps her spoon against the table, splintering it into two jagged pieces of plastic. "What you mean is that she's got a figure that would wear out the elastic in your jockey shorts."

Somebody has given Rainey a good description of her. I dig into my yogurt. "If a woman that good-looking were to come on to me . . ." I say, letting my voice trail off.

My friend takes her napkin and wipes her mouth. "It doesn't take much to set you off," she says. "Maybe she just wasn't his type."

An M&M goes down the wrong way, and I launch into a fit of coughing after I say, "I think he's the type who likes white women."

Rainey watches me unsympathetically as I hack until I think I'm going into convulsions. "That sounds so racist. I thought you were married to a black woman yourself. Is that how you choose women—by color?"

Her voice is sharp, even hostile. I wonder what I have said that is so offensive to her. "Not particularly, but some white women, for example, prefer black men," I say, trying to defuse the subject. "It's just a matter of taste."

Rainey sniffs, as if this subject is far more complicated than my simple-minded statement implied. "Anyway, he has never even asked her out once and it pissed her royally, according to my sources."

I try one M&M at a time. "Have you heard any rumors about my client and Olivia Le Master?"

"No," Rainey says irritably. "You know, I might as well get on your payroll."

I wish I could afford her. On the way to her house to drop her off, I get Rainey to promise she won't breathe a word of what I'm about to tell her and then give her the whole story. If I am violating any of Andy's confidences, then so be it. I would trust her with my life. We pull up in front of her house and sit in the dark in the car until I finish. "Do you think there's a chance anything funny could have been going on, or was it just an accident?" I ask.

Rainey sits with her back against the door of the Blazer. Apparently mollified that I have told her about the case, she says, "It's all too problematical. If that aide who was holding her hadn't let go, Pam wouldn't have been electrocuted."

My eyes have begun to adjust to the darkness. I respond with my latest theory, "Unless he was in on it, too."

Rainey snorts, "You're beginning to sound like those people who still write books about the Kennedy assassinations."

I grin in the darkness, yet I am serious. Ever since the Hart Anderson murder, I see conspiracies everywhere. "Well, what do you think happened, based on what I've told you?"

Rainey opens her door, and the dim, dirty car light comes on, causing her face to appear harsh and prematurely old. "It sounds like a tragic accident to me, but I know I think that your client should never have shocked that child!"

Her tone is almost shrill, on the verge of being out of control. Why is she so mad? I wasn't the one who used a cattle prod. Irritated, I shoot back, "Hindsight doesn't take much courage. If she had been your child, wouldn't you want somebody to try to give her as normal a life as possible?"

Rainey fairly yells, "Not that way, for God's sake!" She pushes open the door and takes a deep breath. "I guess I'm just tired, Gideon. I'm sorry."

Tired myself, I take her at her word. "That's okay," I say. She must be getting her period. Poor women. "I'll call you this weekend and let you know how my date goes."

"Fine," she says shortly, and I wait until I see the light in her house go on before I drive off. It is a bad sign that Rainey's reaction is so unsympathetic to Andy. Other than being much more liberal, Rainey shares many of the characteristics of the average Blackwell County juror: a middle-aged white female who has at least one child. If she thinks that Andy is in trouble, I suspect he is. I wish I knew the guy well enough for him to level with me. But maybe he has. Can't a black man try to help a white female without everyone thinking that sex is involved?

I turn into my driveway and walk into my stale, hot house. Woogie stretches but does not get up to greet me as I turn on the light. "The dog days of summer," I say to him. He makes a squeaking sound that I take to be assent. I drink a beer and go to bed.

11

KIM KEOGH'S APARTMENT (only two blocks south of Rainey's house) is much smaller than I had imagined and quite a bit funkier, too. In fact, it appears to be hardly more than a one-room efficiency. Maybe there is a bedroom, though from the couch where I am sitting I cannot identify which door leads to it. On the wall behind me, on each wall actually, are blown-up pictures of old-time movie stars: Marilyn Monroe, Clark Gable, Greta Garbo, Bette Davis, William Holden, Ingrid Bergman, Grace Kelly, but also current ones like Robert Redford, Cher, Tom Cruise, Eddie Murphy, and my favorite, Michelle Pfeiffer.

We managed to do nicely at dinner—a seafood place on the Arkansas River, where she considerately declined my invitation to order lobster and instead had catfish and salad. She talked mostly about herself (which is fine with me, since in the back of my mind I am worried she will try to pump me about Andy's case). Despite Rainey's snide comment about how well she conceals her makeup, she is gorgeous—beautiful blond hair and the longest natural eyelashes I've ever seen on a human. She is sitting encouragingly close to me on the couch, which is so slick it seems inevitable that we slide toward each other.

"I was going to be a model," she says, sipping on a glass of white wine while I drink beer, "but I wanted to do something really meaningful with my life, you know what I mean?"

"Sure." I nod, thinking that her ambition to be a TV

anchor would be judged, when the big meltdown comes, hardly to have qualified, but there is no doubt this woman takes herself quite seriously. And for all I know, she may be the next Barbara Walters.

She is wearing a jade cotton jersey dress that comes modestly below her knees. There is something touching to me about ambitious women who are in fields where they are required to rely on their looks. She has said enough for me to realize she has enormous doubts about herself, and with good reason. She seems to sense that it is only a matter of time before someone notices a few wrinkles that can't be hidden and asks her to start filling in on the 6 A.M. farm show. I find myself giving her a pep talk about how much she has achieved already. "Half the women in Arkansas would switch places with you in a New York minute," I tell her. "You're beautiful, poised, and talented. What else do you want, for God's sake?" I do not add intelligent, because it is apparent she is probably below average in this department, which will probably be her professional death.

For this rhetorical question, she has already thought about an answer. She crosses her legs and balances her wine against a thigh. "I'd like to be quicker, smarter," she admits, "I don't really understand a lot of the stories I cover," she says.

I sip at the Coors she has brought me. There is a sad, sweet quality about her that is touching. I feel heat rising as if someone had lit a boiler under me. Women want so badly to be taken seriously and listened to it is almost embarrassing. I have promised myself that I will not get involved quickly with the next woman, but I hear myself lying, "You're a lot brighter than you give yourself credit for. I've watched you too many times cover difficult stories not to believe that."

She pats her lovely hair self-consciously and gives me a hopeful smile. "Are you serious?"

As I gulp at my beer, trying to cool down, I look at the pictures on the opposite wall. Humphrey Bogart, Sally Fields.

She is living in la-la land. Please don't do this to this woman, I tell myself. She doesn't want to go to bed on the first date, but she will if I handle her right. "You're your own worst critic," I say, putting my beer on the cheap coffee table in front of the couch. All her money must go into clothes, I think. This place is just short of a dump. "They wouldn't have hired you if they weren't certain you could do the job."

She puts the wineglass to her lips and finds it empty. I pour her some more from the beaded, sweaty bottle in front of us. Over the years I've found that it doesn't matter if you look like an orangutan—all you really have to do is listen.

From her bedside table she reaches over and pulls open a drawer. I watch her right breast swing free as she strains to reach a brown envelope. I've had better sex the first time but not with anyone less inhibited. The alcohol must have loosened her up, because, until the last hour she has been almost ploddingly serious. The bottle she brought into the bedroom is almost empty. I am expecting marijuana, but instead she pulls from the packet a handful of pictures. Incredibly, they are of her naked in various poses. She looks at me through the harsh glare of the lamp and says in a slurred voice, "I had these made when I was twenty. What do you think?"

She looks incredible—slim hips and small but attractive breasts which appear larger because of the way she is bending toward the camera. My immediate reaction is embarrassment, not arousal. I am too recently spent for that. Why is she showing me these? I look slowly through them. Was she trying out for *Playboy* or what? I have a slight headache from the six pack of beer I have drunk and rub my head. I say truthfully, "They're stunning."

She nods, her right hand stroking my back, the other holding the pictures up for her to see in the light. "I think they're good, too," she says, her voice sodden with the liquor.

Finally, I understand why she has shown me these pictures. She is almost pathetically insecure. Somehow, she considers the photographs are proof of her value. I say, "No matter what happens, you'll have proof what a knockout body you have."

She tosses the pictures onto the table instead of putting them back into their envelope. She smiles and rests her head on my chest. "How'd you know that?" she says. "My body works a lot better than my mind."

I stroke her hair, noticing that Rainey was right. This close I can see her makeup. "The old mind/body problem," I say. I am a little drunk myself.

She reaches down and peels off my condom and holds it up for us to inspect. Waving it over my head like a pennant, she says, "Wanna hear a joke?"

Fearful that she is going to spill my jism onto my head, I lean back but say quickly, "Yeah."

She pulls the condom down and rests it on her pubis. "You know what the rubber said to the diaphragm?"

I pat her right thigh. "Naw, what did it say?"

She turns her head and smiles crookedly at me. "Was it good for you, too?"

I begin to laugh and find I can't stop, shaking the bed and her body in the process. The truth of the joke has struck some nerve I can't begin to understand about my own life. I guess the joke works because our protection against each other has become the most important element in the equation. At some level we have become merely matchmakers for our own technology. I glance across the room, noticing again that the largest picture she has in her bedroom is a picture of herself. It is enormous, an eleven by fourteen, probably a promo by her employer. Kim Keogh, the latest and prettiest member of the Channel 11 news team. I wonder but do not have the courage to ask if she has had her name changed.

She reaches across me and casually tosses, like a worn-out sock, the swollen condom into the wicker wastepaper basket beside her bed and says sourly, "It wasn't that funny."

For some reason she thinks I am laughing at her. I roll her off my chest and cradle her in my arm. "It was a good joke."

She snuggles against my chest, "I like you," she says, "You understand me, you know?"

So I will not have to answer, I kiss her hair, which is damp from her exertions. In three minutes she is sound asleep, snoring gently against my shoulder. For all her nude pictures, aggressive lovemaking, and vanity, the always kind and pleasant Kim Keogh who appears on TV is the dominant personality. Alcohol and a sympathetic ear have uncovered a wilder side, but before she got halfway through the bottle of Chablis, Kim moved me with her own unpublicized work as a volunteer tutor for the last two years to black girls who live in Needle Park. A nice woman, I think, sleepily, nicer than she'll sound if I ever tell someone about the pictures. . . .

Remembering Kim's joke and my extreme reaction to it, for some reason I think of Amy and wonder if she had an abortion. I should call but realize I'm not anxious to be confronted by either of the choices available to her. What would I do if Kim becomes pregnant and wants to have a baby? I yawn so loudly Kim stirs beside me. Somehow, I don't think either Sarah or Rainey would be pleased. . . .

I awake feeling pain in my rectum and notice a growing need to defecate. I turn my head and check the luminous red dial on her clock. It is just after three. I have been asleep only an hour. Kim has turned over toward the wall, and I slide carefully out of the bed, trying to remember the location of her bathroom. After opening a closet door, I find it and sit on the commode hoping a good shit will take away the pain. Though I strain like a man who has been constipated for weeks, nothing doing. It feels like someone is going into my bowels with a corkscrew, and I break into a sweat as I stand up and look into Kim's bathroom mirror.

"Gideon," Kim calls through the door. "Are you okay?"

I come into the room almost dancing with pain. She turns on the light, and I would feel embarrassed were I not hurting so much. "Something's wrong," I admit and explain my symptoms as if she were a physician making a house call.

Perhaps sobered somewhat by what she is being forced to witness, she pulls the sheet over her breasts. "Has this happened before?"

I would be less alarmed if the corkscrew feeling were in my stomach. Food poisoning would be bad enough, but I might live. There is no mistaking the location however. I begin to put on my clothes as fast as I can. If I am going to die, I don't want to do it like this. I can see Sarah's face as they tell her, "Your dad's ass started hurting, and then drunk and naked as a jaybird he fell over dead on top of a pile of nude pictures of some TV reporter he had known only a few hours." I catch my big toe on a belt loop and fall sideways on the bed. She scoots backward as if I were now trying to rape her. "No," I say, looking sideways at Kim as I slide up my pants. "Please tell me if you do," I beg. "Do you have AIDS or some disease?"

Kim bursts into tears. "No!" she shouts at me. "How do you know you don't?"

I try to think of the women I have slept with in the last year. There have been only three since I met Rainey, and, of course, they swore (as I did) that they were practically virgins. I wore a rubber, but as one worried woman told me, even the best roof will eventually leak. "I just know, damn it!"

The last five minutes, which seems like an eternity, have sobered her as no coffee could. Clinging to the sheet, she whimpers, "I'm sorry you're hurting. I'm just terrified I'll get AIDS from you!"

Thanks for the vote of confidence, I think. I have to get

out of here. I cram my socks into my pockets and slide on my loafers. The pain, bearable, however, is constant now, coming in steady waves. "I'll call you," I say politely.

She nods, apparently too afraid to move. In the Blazer, I pop the clutch as badly as Sarah used to do before she figured out it wasn't a device to strengthen your knee. Where to go? I noticed there was no blood. At least I'm not hemorrhaging to death, but I am even more frightened by the pain than when it first began. Desperate, I turn onto Fairfax, Rainey's street. If I'm going to die, I don't want to be like some animal that crawls off into the woods.

I ring her bell and pound on the door like a wild man. In just a few moments I hear her yell through the door, "Who is it?"

I scream back, "Gideon. I'm sick!"

She throws the door open, and standing there in a thin cotton robe, cries, "What's wrong?"

I tell her and beg, "Will you take me to the St. Thomas emergency room? I'm having horrible cramps."

Looking dazed and scared, she says, "Of course, wait just a second," and disappears into her bedroom while I sit on her couch.

In less than a minute she appears, dressed in shorts, a T-shirt, and tennis shoes. Her hair is still a mess, and without makeup she appears like a ghost, but at the moment she has never looked better. In her car, she asks, "Where were you when it started hurting?"

There is not hint of snideness in her voice. She is wondering why I didn't call first. I want to say that I just happened to be in the neighborhood but don't feel up to it. I swallow hard and admit, "I was watching the local news." Rainey taps the steering wheel sharply with the palm of her right hand. She doesn't require much explaining. "How interesting," she says, her voice taking on a characteristic drollness.

I look out the window into the darkness. There are a dozen snotty things she could say but won't. Still, I feel like some lowlife snake running back to his wife after playing around and getting into trouble. Why do I feel this way? We've agreed to be just friends. For God's sake, we've never seen each other naked, yet guilt begins to bubble up like boiling oil alongside the pain in my rectum. What is a friend for if you can't tell her something without feeling guilty about it? Maybe it is true men and women can't be friends.

She whips into the St. Thomas emergency room parking area, and brakes to a halt at the security guard station. A black guy who looks a hundred sticks his head through the window on Rainey's side and asks, "Is he going to need a wheelchair?"

Through the light shining through the windshield, I can see the barest hint of a smile on Rainey's face. She says, "I think he can walk."

Embarrassed now, I hiss, "Of course I can."

Fortunately, it is a slow night at St. Thomas. Only a couple of people are waiting, and they look so miserable I can't tell whether they are family or patients. I look at Rainey, who yawns and says, "I confess that there is a part of me that hopes you're really sick."

An hour later (the pain began to recede thirty minutes ago, but I am too embarrassed to admit it has gone away entirely) I am told I am simply middle-aged. "Prostatitis," says the intern who had stuck his finger halfway to China. "How old are you?"

"Forty-four," I say, wishing his pants were a little cleaner. Dr. Wacker, according to his nameplate (for all I know he may be an orderly pressed into service because the regular doc is off sniffing glue with one of the nurses), looks about Sarah's age but not as responsible. "Does this mean I'm going to lose my prostate gland?" I ask. Hell, maybe it would be a relief if I couldn't get it up anymore. All it's done since Rosa died is cause me trouble.

"Shouldn't," the baby doc says casually. "You've got a little infection, but an antibiotic should take care of it."

With a twenty-five-dollar prescription for a bottle of pills

(Septra) I walk into the waiting area feeling relieved but a little foolish. Rainey's face looks frozen in worry. She stands, holding her hands together as if she is about to pray. I had told her the pain was better, but I didn't tell her how much before I went in.

"Prostatitis," I mumble to Rainey as I come out into the waiting area. "Just an infection. I've got a prescription for it."

I head for the door. Do I just imagine it or are the nurses smiling? Rainey walks beside me and says loudly, "You got me out of bed at three in the morning for prostatitis? Women have infections all the damn time."

Outside, it is humid and sticky as we walk to her car. I feel like an idiot. I had given the hospital my group insurance card from Mays & Burton, but I have little hope I'm covered. "It hurt like hell," I say, realizing I am whining. "I thought I was dying."

Rainey unlocks her door. In the brightly lit parking lot, she looks as exhausted as I feel. She stares at me over the roof of her car. "You're such a baby!"

We ride in silence to her house. How did I have the nerve to put her through this? I wouldn't wish me on my worst enemy. Still, I can't suppress the feeling entirely that I've dodged a bullet. I turn my head toward the window and smile. I'm okay. After a moment, I say sincerely, "I panicked; I'm really sorry I put you through this."

Rainey's voice is harsh as she pulls up in front of her house. "Damn you, Gideon, you had me worried to death!"

I stare straight ahead. I have already apologized once, and I'm getting a little tired of being cussed out. Sure, I overreacted; most people would if they thought the plug was about to be pulled on them. I'm sorry I ruined her beauty sleep, but supposedly that's what friends are for. "I'll call you tomorrow," I say and open the door to get out.

She shakes her head angrily and turns off the lights and motor. "I can't wait," she says as she gets out of the car and stalks into her house.

I drive home, whistling, thrilled I don't face surgery to-morrow. What is her problem? She is the one who wanted to be friends. I turn onto my street. What am I supposed to do—wait until I'm seventy for her to decide I'm good enough for her? I yawn until I can't see. I wonder if she thinks that I am playing games with her. I have committed a lot of sins in the sexual wars. But that is not one of them. Not con-sciously anyway.

12

ON DIRECT EXAMINATION Mrs. Gentry proves to be a real trouper. If we could stop the trial right now (not likely, since she is the first witness and hasn't even been cross-examined), I am convinced Judge Fogarty, the probate judge hearing her case, would let her leave the nursing home. For an eighty-four-year-old woman still weakened by the trauma of a serious infection and gall-bladder surgery, Mrs. Gentry seems to have made a decent impression on Judge Fogarty. It is control over her property that is going to be the problem. She has become confused about what she owns and how much income is being generated, but, as I will argue at the end of the trial, why shouldn't she? Her son has completely cut her off from her money for the last six months. Fogarty, one of the smarter judges in Blackwell County, also has lived up to his reputation of treating everyone with respect. When she began to grow upset because of the difficulty of her memory, he told Mrs. Gentry to take her time and allowed me to lead her when it became obvious she was having problems.

As I turn to leave the podium to allow Ferd ("Nerd" of course, behind his back) Machen, the opposing attorney, to cross-examine Mrs. Gentry, I hear a sound like the buzzing of a power line. I have seen her twice and have never heard her hum this loud, but she is going at "Shine On, Harvest Moon" as if she were making her debut at Carnegie Hall. I know it will stop as soon as Ferd begins to cross-examine her, but he is going to stay glued to his seat until Fogarty makes him get up. I had reminded her for the second time right before the trial began not to hum, but, to my horror, she is becoming a one-woman band right in front of our eyes. "Your Honor," I plead, "can we have a recess for a moment?"

Her asshole of a son is smirking as if his mother had been caught trying to pull down her pants in the courtroom. Judge Fogarty stands up. "Why don't we take five minutes?" he says, smiling benignly at Mrs. Gentry.

Typically, as soon as someone speaks, she becomes quiet so she can hear what is being said. It is the silence she has to fill. I invite her to step outside with me. As we walk by the counsel table, I begin to hum "Stars and Stripes Forever." Screw them all.

The Nerd grins, then tugs at my sleeve and whispers, "You'll never see a dime of it."

I shrug as if this were a pro bono referral from Legal Aid. Yet, I have discovered in the last week that Mrs. Gentry is loaded, or was, having assets of well over a million dollars, more than enough to live comfortably in any retirement community of her choosing and to pay her newest lawyer a generous fee. Out in the hall by the water fountain, I take Mrs. Gentry's right hand in mine to calm her down. "Do you remember we talked about your humming when nobody is talking, Mrs. Gentry?"

Her face flushed with embarrassment, my client stares miserably at the floor. She seems shrunken, and for the first time she looks her age. Maybe she ought to be in a nursing home. Yet why should a person be locked up because of a little humming? She is wearing a bright emerald-green dress and matching pumps with little high heels. This morning when I saw her at the nursing home, I had a fleeting thought that we had a chance. Mrs. Gentry moans, "Some people bite their fingernails when they get nervous. I hum."

True, but not so loud they can be heard a block away, I think, but then I get an idea. I pull from my right pants pocket an unopened pack of five-flavored Life Savers I bought in the courthouse coffee shop this morning and hand it to her.

"When nobody's talking, take one of these out and suck on it like your life depends on it."

She squints warily at the pack of mints in my hand as if I were trying to get her to take drugs and then bends over the fountain to drink. When she is done, she straightens up and takes the mints, sighing, "I'll try."

Back in the courtroom, the mints don't rescue her completely, but they help. A couple of times during her cross-examination, she sounds like someone humming with a Life Saver in her mouth, but at least the volume is way down. Unfortunately, Mrs. Gentry is becoming more confused than ever about what she owns, and there is nothing she can do about it, since Judge Fogarty won't sustain a single one of my objections. It is apparent that she needs a guardian of her estate but not so obvious at this point that she requires a guardian of her person, as the law distinguishes the two. Rustling through his papers, Ferd pretends to pause, hoping he can get her humming again, but I point to her mouth, and she pops in a Life Saver just as she begins "The Blue Danube."

The Nerd waits as long as he can and then asks, "Isn't it a fact that three weeks ago you were caught in a closet . . ."

I shoot out of my seat, cutting Ferd off, "This is irrelevant, Your Honor!"

Judge Fogarty, who for some reason suffers fools more gladly than most judges, says mildly, "I can't rule on your objection, Mr. Page, until I hear the question."

There is no jury to keep from hearing the question, so there is no excuse to approach the Bench and argue the point quietly. I look at Mrs. Gentry and know she is beginning to die up there. She pops her last Life Saver in her mouth and stares at me with such a forlorn expression I feel a lump forming in my mouth.

Ferd, whose normal clientele is about as scruffy as mine, finishes his question, ". . . in a closet at the nursing home having sex with a Mr. Peterson?"

I am livid. I turn to Mrs. Gentry's son as I speak. He is in his sixties, squashed down in his seat as if he knows his mother will never forgive him; nor should she. "Your Honor, this question is probative of absolutely nothing, is a total invasion of Mrs. Gentry's privacy, and is simply to harass and upset her."

Taking off his reading glasses and rubbing his eyes, Judge Fogarty, laconic as usual, says in a monotone, "What's the relevancy, Mr. Machen?"

The Nerd, for no apparent reason, points theatrically at my poor client. "Your Honor, Mrs. Gentry is old and sick; she could have gotten hurt or even locked in the closet. She may well have been given a social disease. It is just another example that this old lady has no idea what she's doing and needs to be protected."

Judge Fogarty stands up, and crooks a finger at us. "I'd like to see the lawyers back in my chambers right now. Court's in recess." He walks into his chambers without even a backward glance at us.

Ferd and I shrug at each other, wondering what's up. We haven't exactly been Clarence Darrow and William Jennings Bryan, but we've each done worse, I suspect. I tell Mrs. Gentry she can come sit at the counsel table, but she glares balefully at her son and shakes her head. He is finally beginning to seem embarrassed by what he is putting his mother through and glances sheepishly at her.

Clarence Fogarty's chambers are impersonal as a public urinal, without a single plaque or diploma on the walls. His office looks as if he moved in this morning. In fact, he is new, having only recently been elected, but he has had six months to unpack. He is a bachelor (shades of Justice Souter). On his desk, at an angle, I can see a single picture of, presumably, his parents, since he looks just like his mother: a woman whose most distinguishing features are almost thread-thin lips and a chin so triangular that it reminds me of a snake's head. No beauty queen, but at least not bovine-looking, as my father used to say of half the girls he saw on the streets in Bear Creek in eastern Arkansas.

Behind closed doors Judge Fogarty's manner changes. Gone is his laborious, painstaking, and diffident manner. He grabs the volume of the Arkansas code containing the guardianship statutes from a shelf by his desk and flips through the pages in a rapid, irritated manner. His reputation is that he takes so long to make up his mind on difficult cases my client could be dead by the time he gets around to making a decision. I glance at the Nerd, who looks smug and confident, as if he has only begun to humiliate my client. It crosses my mind that I am putting Mrs. Gentry through hell. Perhaps, I should tell the judge we will take a voluntary nonsuit and dismiss the case. From the way it has gone in the last ten minutes, it might end up taking six months off Mrs. Gentry's life no matter who wins, and at her age she doesn't have that much time to give.

Judge Fogarty looks up over reading glasses considerably more expensive-looking than mine, and says to Ferd in a low, intense voice, "Mr. Machen, do you know what the probate code says is the purpose of the guardianship statute?"

Ferd leans back in the imitation-leather chair provided to the judge's visitors, and says in an offhand manner, "To protect the ward."

"Do you know?" Judge Fogarty asks me.

I rack my brain, fearing I'm about to be embarrassed. In taking the case over from Dan, I haven't exactly knocked myself out reading up on guardianship law. I glanced over the statutes, but I didn't memorize them. There's too much law to keep up with all of it, especially if you're not getting paid. Usually, judges, like lawyers, exhibit a paternalistic attitude when dealing with incompetents. Surely I can't go wrong with the Nerd's answer. I guess, "I don't think Ferd is too far off." The judge draws back in his chair in obvious disgust with both of us. "Let me read you both something," he says brusquely. "I'm quoting here. 'The purpose is . . . the development of maximum self-reliance and independence of the person, and shall be ordered only to the extent necessitated.' " He pops the bright red book shut and says to Ferd: "My suggestion to you, Mr. Machen, is that in the next fifteen minutes you get together with your client and consider settling this matter along the following lines: Mrs. Gentry does not appear in need of a guardian of her person; however, she would seem to require the services of a guardian of her estate. Unless Mr. Page is going to present evidence of severe mismanagement or fraud, I see no reason why her son should not be appointed guardian of his mother's estate so long as she is permitted to leave the nursing home and resume her former quality of life. If you want to try this case, it's fine with me. But let me warn you that I'm not inclined to keep the elderly locked up in nursing homes because it's convenient to do so. You embarrassed that poor old woman out there by that ridiculous question about sex. If she wants to have sexual relations with another consenting adult, she should be able to do so in the privacy of her own apartment or house instead of being forced to have them in a closet. I'll resume court in fifteen minutes to either continue the trial or dictate into the record a settlement."

Ferd leans back in his chair as if he can't believe his ears. "Judge, she's batty as she can be!" he protests, pointing at his head and rotating his right hand in the time-honored manner. "She sounds like a chain saw if you give her a chance!"

Fogarty leans forward on his desk and peers over his glasses unpleasantly at Ferd. "Mr. Machen," he says, "the world is full of eccentric people, but we don't institutionalize them in this country simply because they're odd. For your information, my mother is in her eighties and hums as loud as Mrs. Gentry, and she does the crossword puzzle in the paper every morning before breakfast!"

The Nerd, whose face has turned almost as red as the statute book on the judge's desk, says, "Yes, sir," and he and I leave, chastened as schoolchildren who have been sent to the principal's office for disrupting class.

After a talk alone with our clients, within ten minutes we witness a reconciliation between mother and son. As Ferd and I watch, our clients embrace in the hall outside the courtroom, I marvel at the capacity of some humans (at least) to forgive and to trust once again people who have wronged them. I wouldn't want her son near me, but as I watch the tears run down his mother's cheeks, I realize she really loves him, regardless of how he treated her. However, at her age, she doesn't have a lot of choice, leaving me to speculate what, if anything, was going on in that closet. Her boyfriend, a man at least a decade younger, refused to talk to me and wasn't worth a deposition I couldn't afford. Subpoenaed to testify by Ferd, he has been sequestered with the other witnesses, but with this settlement, we will never know, and, for once, I am content to leave my prurient curiosity unsatisfied.

Judge Fogarty, again relaxed and in good spirits after learning Ferd's client has swallowed the settlement the judge rammed down his throat, tells me to prepare a petition for an attorney's fee for my representation to be paid from Mrs. Gentry's estate, but hints, as I feared, that the amount won't be overly generous, since he was less than impressed with the quality of representation by both attorneys in the case. He tells Ferd bluntly that he won't be able to charge the estate at all for his time in court. My cheeks burn, but Mrs. Gentry is happy. She tells me to come visit her any time. When Eagle Savings and Loan forecloses on my mortgage, I will remember her invitation.

Cooking in the July heat, I walk back to my office wondering what lessons I have learned from this case. In the future, reading the law might help. I realize now that despite what I had told myself, I was only going through the motions, never expecting to win, never expecting to be paid a dime, so I didn't prepare adequately, relying mainly on my instincts from the days when I represented mental patients at the state hospital as a public defender. If the state hospital wanted a patient badly enough to go through a commitment proceeding, the judge wasn't going to get in its way. The patients rarely had a chance, so I assumed Mrs. Gentry wouldn't either. My clients won't always be so fortunate as to have a judge rescue them.

Across the street, waiting for the light to change, Martha Birford waves at me and yells, "Gideon, wait a minute!"

Nonplussed by this effusiveness after our last meeting at the Hardhat Cafe, I stand above a steaming gutter, wondering if another snotty remark is on the way.

"I got a job!" she says gleefully, pounding across the pavement toward me.

Good for you, I think, meaning it. Dressed in a red suit I've seen half a dozen times, Martha looks as happy as a woman who's been told she doesn't have ovarian cancer. Instantly, I forgive her for her remark at the Hardhat about me landing on my feet. We may talk about sex as if we can't live without it, but it is our work that defines both men and women these days. "Great!" I say, touching her arm as if for luck. "Who's the lucky firm?"

"Verser and Jeffcoat," she says, naming a partnership that has come together in only the last year. "Actually, I'm only kind of a glorified paralegal, but it's a start."

A paralegal! I maintain my grin, hoping it has not become a grimace, but inwardly I feel embarrassment for her. True, at Mays & Burton we got the shit cases, but at least we got to see the inside of a courtroom. Poor Martha. Those idiots at Verser and Jeffcoat will probably never discover how much money she could be making for them. A few more bromides about our mutual good luck, and I head off in the opposite direction, once again glad I'm not a woman or black. As sloppy as my performance was today, I realize I'm one of the primary beneficiaries of discrimination. I may be a capitalist now, but damn if I like competition.

On my floor in the Layman Building, Julia, seeing my scowling face, greets me cheerfully, "Lose another one, Giddy baby?"

I check my box for messages. "Not quite," I say, noting her outfit. This is sex week, I decide. Everything so far has been skintight or see-through. Today, underneath a sheer white blouse she has on a purple bra, which matches her eyeshadow. The effect is that she appears to have two badly rotted grapefruits under her blouse. I have a message to call David Spath, administrator at the Human Development Center, who keeps playing telephone tag with me. "Actually," I say, my eyes drawn like a bomber pilot's to her chest, "the judge ruled mostly in my client's favor." I am careful not to say that I did anything to win the case. Gossip from the courthouse spreads like poison gas, and if Julia gets wind of the hearing, she will throw back in my face anything I say.

She nods sourly. "Don't you lawyers have a saying that even a blind hog can find a few nuts?"

In more ways than one, I think, looking at Julia, but I do not say anything. I have found it is crucial to let her have the last word. Once some people think they have the better of you, they treat you better, and Julia, who turns out to be the niece of the owner of the building, will be here long after I am gone. I go to my office and surprise myself by getting David Spath on the phone. In a British-sounding voice, he tells me that an appointment has canceled for the afternoon, and he will see me if I have the time. Since I had scheduled Mrs. Gentry's trial for all day, I am free and I agree to meet at two in his office.

It is close to twelve, and I take the elevator down to the cafeteria to put my own spin on Mrs. Gentry's abbreviated trial. I find Tunkie Southerland and Frank D'Angelo seated at a table against a window overlooking the Arkansas River.

Tunkie, who avoids even nonjury trials whenever he can, preferring the written word to the spoken, chews on the lemon in his glass of tea. "She got what she paid for," he comments, defending my laziness. I have not spared myself in my telling of the morning's events, though I have made Ferd Machen sound even more cruel and venal than he probably is.

"Every lawyer screws up," Frank says, folding his napkin on his plate, "it's just a question of who catches you and what they try to do about it."

Truly, misery loves company, but so does incompetency, I realize. Yet, in their own areas, they are not incompetent. Along with Dan, these men are becoming my friends. There is not a soul at Mays & Burton I miss. Why? These guys aren't so rapacious, but maybe they just don't have the drive to make it. I wonder if I do either.

Tunkie belches into the back of his hand. "At any rate, Dan will be delighted, . . ." he begins.

". . . That you took him off the hook." Frank finishes, grinning at me.

On the drive out to the Blackwell County Human Development Center, my mind returns again and again to Mrs. Gentry's hearing. I decide I have a real talent for overlooking the obvious. This case must have stuck out like a sore thumb, because most judges wouldn't have gotten past the fact that Mrs. Gentry is eighty-four years old and had undergone an operation that required her to enter a nursing home. But Judge Fogarty took the "purposes" clause of the guardianship statute seriously, as almost no one ever does. Is the prosecutor's case against Andy this crystal clear and I can't see it? Maybe the real lesson is that the law be damned, what judges (and juries) do is justice. If the judge's mother has a right to hum in her own house, then Mrs. Gentry should have that right or the judge's mother will give him hell when he goes for his Sunday visit. Is Andy's case really about what people can identify with? Isn't it similar to a situation in which a mother authorizes a doctor to use experimental cancer drugs to save her child's life? The problem is that Pam's life wasn't in danger as long as she was in restraints. Yet what Olivia feared was that sooner or later Pam was going to end up like those men I saw—tied to their beds. No mother should ever have to accept that. Maybe that is the argument I should make to the jury: the choice Pam faced was being kept under virtual lock and key until she died. Because shock is currently (an unwitting pun I'll have to avoid) out of fashion, her doctor felt he had no choice but to keep quiet about it until he could present proof it worked. In fact, ladies and gentlemen, you should think of Dr. Chapman as a kind of a brave pioneer . . . maybe that's a little thick.

Unexpectedly, David Spath is a bit of a dandy. With a mustache so trim it looks as if it has been stitched into place and an English accent straight out of World War II movies about the RAF (he surely possesses the stiffest upper lip in the state), Spath seems a foreign visitor instead of a man who has spent a career climbing a bureaucratic ladder. No wonder he hired Andy—he likes the way he dresses. Spath is wearing a striped blue chambray long-sleeved shirt that looks so smooth and neat it seems made of silk. Against the blue of his shirt, he has on a gold tie dotted with small, black, castlelike designs. His pants are Yorkshire cords that I recognize out of a Lands' End catalogue my boss used to keep in her office at the Public Defender's. Though it seems entirely useless information, I immediately assume this man is gay. There is an overrefined quality to his sensibility (I can't put my finger on it—suffice it to say he is like my best friend, Skip, who just last month pitched a promising commercial art business and moved to Miami with his lover) that connotes a sexual orientation different from my own.

Given his lip, I expect a bone-crusher handshake, but his hand is as soft as that of an English gentleman visiting his country estate on the weekend. Instead of tea, he gives me a cup of coffee, and I sit across from him, wondering how this man got to be here. Even his office is decorated with English themes. Instead of pastoral scenes with hunting dogs and men in red coats on horseback, the pictures are of Dickens' England—harsh industrial cityscapes done in gray, brown, and black. Gently, I try to bring up the subject of Andy by asking how long Spath has known him. Spath sips at his cup of coffee, obviously studying me, "I first met Andy," he finally says, "when he was working for the state hospital. He's a good man. A good clinical psychologist. So why would he go off on his own and try electric skin shock without going through the process of getting the Human Rights Committee's permission? I haven't got the slightest idea.''

So much for easing into the subject. I try to keep in mind that Spath's job has been jeopardized by Andy's actions. If Andy is going to be helped by this man on the witness stand, it will have to be in bits and pieces. A good man here, a good clinical psychologist there. I try to back up. ''Why do you think a mother would let someone try shock on her child?''

Spath's mustache, probably intended to give his face a more masculine look, almost succeeds, but not quite. His face is not so much soft as it is delicate. His nose is as thin as a communion wafer, and his tiny ears (partially hidden by a mass of thick brown hair) remind me of a bat's. ''To try to help her, of course,'' he says archly. ''But the problem is we don't know how to help children like Pam, and Andrew knew that.''

I fold my arms against my chest to keep them still, reminding myself not to argue with this man. My hope is that he will bring himself to admit (assuming it is true) that he knew Andy was going to try shock and will have the courage to admit it. I say innocently, ''I thought the literature shows that shock works.''

For a moment I think I see real conflict in Spath's face, which seems to collapse downward, but despite a brief nod, he says curtly, ''The literature doesn't prove anything from a statistical point of view because there hasn't been enough research.''

This statement doesn't qualify as a denial, and I press on. ''If you had a child that was retarded and self-abusive, wouldn't you be tempted to try everything possible to help her?''

''Mr. Page,'' Spath says, a note of exasperation creeping into his tone, ''from a purely personal point of view, I sympathize with Andrew. I like him; I hired him because I thought he was qualified, and because I think this state needs to educate and hire more black professionals. I don't even try to imagine what care for retarded black children was like before integration. But if a treatment plan involves aversive stimuli, we follow a certain protocol, and Andrew ignored it.''

I look over his shoulder at a picture of a grimy child working, presumably in a cotton mill. Something, I don't know what, tells me this man knew in advance what Andy was doing. He doesn't seem like the conventional cover-your-ass manager I used to see when I worked for the state as a social worker investigating dependency/neglect cases. "If he had gone through the human rights committee," I ask, "is there a chance it would have approved shock?''

Spath doesn't hesitate. "I seriously doubt it. Highly aversive techniques are no longer in vogue today.''

I note that he didn't say they don't have their place in treatment of the retarded, but I can't figure out how to use it to my advantage. Spath turns his back on me to pour himself a cup of coffee. He is fussy as an old maid, painstakingly measuring out a teaspoon of sugar as if that were all he had been put on earth to accomplish. I say, "This, I'm sure, won't come as any surprise to you, but Andy told me that he thought he could talk you into purchasing remote-control shock equipment once he demonstrated that Pam was responding to shock.''

Spath silently stirs his coffee. If he at least concedes that he might have considered the idea, I can argue to the jury that what Andy did wasn't so rash after all. It was just a matter of no one's having the courage to try a controversial treatment. Had there not been an accident, Andy would have been regarded as a hero even if nobody had the guts to say so publicly. Spath finally removes the spoon and lays it upside down on a clean napkin. "I'm afraid it doesn't work that way," he says, giving me a strange, false smile as if he knows perfectly well that ends invariably justify means, since history is written by the winners.

"Why not?" I press him, still hoping for a miracle. "Isn't the point to help people?''

"This is not a field in which people are encouraged to free-lance," he says. "What happened to Pam, I think, proves that."

I watch Spath sip at his coffee. I don't hear any conviction in his voice. He sounds like one of those C.I.A. flacks who routinely refuse to acknowledge we are engaged in subversion of other governments. I want to say: I think you're lying. You let Andy try shock on the condition that he not implicate you if something went wrong. Instead, I keep silent, afraid to alienate this man, who, if he were willing, could deflect much of the blame from my client, although at the risk of further damaging his own career. He hired Andy; he'll be damned if he'll try to save him. They must have talked about aversive measures like shock many times. Andy is the only Ph.D. on staff at the moment; the facility is too small (only 150 residents) for them not to have been in frequent contact. There is bound to be a conspiracy of silence among Olivia, Andy, and Spath that I haven't yet breached.

Spath is willing to discuss other things—his background (a master's in the administrative side of social work), Olivia (a desperate parent consumed by unjustified guilt), deinstitutionalization (a misguided movement that will lead to unimaginable horror stories of homeless, abused, and ill retarded people), his institution (woefully underfunded, which is the reason for the lack of meaningful training programs for people like Pam). It is as if I were talking to Andy. The only difference is the accent. As I get up to leave, I ask, "Do you miss England?"

Spath gives me a weary smile. "Never been there." Before I can ask what must be a tiresome question, he says, "My father was from London. He gave me my accent and for some reason I've never lost it."

I leave, realizing for the hundredth time since I started practicing law that my assumptions are my worst enemy. I resist the temptation to go by and see Andy. I am coming back out here in a couple of days, but I want to see if Olivia is willing to talk to me first. Of the people in this suspected alliance, she has nothing to lose by the truth, since she has already lost everything she possibly can. I drive home, thinking I'd be a decent lawyer if I could read my clients' minds. Right now, I'd settle for some facts.

13

AS OLIVIA LE MASTER inspects my office, I note an unexpected air of contrition on her part. She seems to be looking for something nice to say about my office, which will require a major feat of diplomacy. Two weeks ago Rainey brought by a philodendron to hang from my ceiling; however, I have already begun to violate my blood oath to water it. Instead of having a healthy, sleek, green appearance, its leaves are brittle, yellowish, and paper-thin. Typically, I don't notice it until Julia comes in and stares in horror and makes snotty remarks about how some people shouldn't be permitted to own living things.

Olivia refuses my offer of a cup of coffee and swallows hard before saying in a small voice, "I'm sorry about the way I testified at the hearing. When I got on the witness stand, I realized I felt some anger toward Andy I hadn't been aware of."

Guilt. God, I wish I owned the patent on it. I lean back in my chair and snack on a piece of ice, my newest weight-loss device. I've gained five pounds just watching Dan eat. "I confess I was extremely disappointed in your testimony," I respond, relieved I don't have to try to figure out how to initiate this topic. Scolding witnesses is a tricky business. "I really thought you'd be more supportive of him than you were." I stare back into her troubled eyes.

Obviously unaccustomed to apologizing, she shifts uncomfortably and fixes her gaze on a spot on my wall directly above my head. "I felt I had betrayed him after you finished

173

asking me questions,'' she says, her voice rising. ''It was only when the prosecutor started in on me that I wanted to defend him. But even right at this moment, I think he probably should have told me to forget the idea of shock treatments.'' Her voice is anguished. This is a battleground she must revisit often.

Jump on 'em while they're down, I think, and hit her with my gossip. ''While we're clearing the air,'' I say, watching her carefully, ''I think you better be aware there's some evidence you've had an affair with Andy.'' Evidence is too strong a word, but I don't have to prove it. Unexpectedly, her face turns a bright red and her eyes begin to fill with tears. Score one for Yettie Lindsey's female intuition. ''You didn't expect to hide it, did you?'' I ask, needing a confirmation. I don't always know why women cry. I hand her the box of tissues from my desk. My office may not be pretty, but now at least it has the necessities.

She nods, a look of genuine misery on her face, and wipes her eyes with fingers as white as chalk. It seems as if all the blood in her body has rushed to her neck and head. ''I didn't think anyone knew.''

As if in celebration of getting the truth, I tap another chunk of ice from the cup into my mouth. My lips are already so numb I doubt if I sound normal. I must be taking some perverse pleasure from this exercise in ruining the few decent teeth I have left in my head. Embarrassed to spit the ice back into the cup, I swallow it whole and begin to cough. ''It's hard to do things in secret,'' I sympathize between wheezes, almost in tears myself from having forced the ice down my throat. My concern for her, however, is genuine. My own life is Exhibit A. I can go to the seediest bar in town in the dead of night, and the next day I might as well have taken an ad out in the paper, so many people will have seen me. ''How do you think Andy will handle the news becoming public?'' I ask, leaning in against my desk. I am overselling the danger of exposure (as far as I know, no one has so much as seen them holding hands), but I need to get her perspective on what it means.

Olivia brings her hands up to her mouth and begins to nibble on what was, until now, a perfect nail. "He'll worry about what it will do to me."

Nervously, I begin to tap the cup against the edge of the desk. Saint Andy the Unselfish. This won't do. "You realize this is all the more reason he shouldn't have been working with Pam."

A sad smile comes to Olivia's face as she forces her hands to her knees. "What you mean is that the typical juror, whether it's conscious racism or not, will punish Andy for having an affair with a white woman."

That, too, I realize, but she is one step ahead of me. I take the cup, which still has ice in it, and drop it into the plastic wastepaper basket beside my desk, realizing that though this woman may be upset, she can still think. My lawyer's mind was worrying about the hammer this information, if disclosed, would give to Jill Marymount. In her place, I would argue that Andy's professional judgment as a psychologist was hopelessly compromised by his relationship with the child's mother. Yet, as Olivia has suggested, perhaps infinitely more powerful will be the unvoiced argument that society must punish Andy for the transgression of one of the few remaining American sexual taboos. Whatever the cost, a hint of this must not get to the jury, or the real trial might not ever begin. I resist the urge to lecture her. It is my client whom I need to take to the woodshed. I tell her, "If we can prevent this from even being hinted at in court, Andy has a chance. If not, as you surmised, he's beaten before we get started. I would guess that even blacks on the jury, and there will be a couple for sure, would resent it."

Her head cocked at a slight angle to the right, Olivia shifts slightly in her seat. "Are you asking me to lie to the jury?"

"No," I say automatically, noting her tone didn't convey much surprise, "but I don't want you to lie to me either." At this stage I have to assume she is what she seems—a

distraught but honest woman caught in a mess. Do I want
her to lie? Yes, but I am forbidden to permit her to do so. It
isn't fair that racial bigotry could decide this case regardless
of the lip service that race has nothing to do with it. Black
defendants have been subject to prejudice for years because
of their color, but not until I entered private practice have I
gotten this bent out of shape over their treatment. Since the
outcome of this case will have an effect on my practice, I can
feel my indignation rising at the injustice of racial discrimination. At the Public Defender's Office, we used to play Ain't
It Awful? with this issue, but the paychecks kept coming
whether we lost or not. I doubt if paying clients will be that
tolerant. "When did this start?" I ask, wondering how many
other people suspect what Yettie Lindsey intuitively knew. I
fold my hands across my chest to keep them still.

Olivia studies the ceiling for an answer, further exposing
her long, graceful neck. "Since about two months before
Pam died," she says, again composed.

I study this woman, whose normally cool demeanor has
returned. Women, like men, are not averse to using sex to
get what they want. Unlike men, they can, if the occasion
demands, be subtle about it. I ask, hoping my sudden skepticism isn't apparent, "Whose idea was it?"

As if she knows what I'm thinking, she gives me a wan
smile, barely exposing straight, milk-white teeth. "Mine. I
felt enormously grateful to him. How could I not fall in love
with the one man who was trying to help my child? Andy
doesn't think or act like other men. He doesn't stop and
figure out the cost. By the way, he didn't try to seduce me; I
seduced him." She gives me a fierce look, as if she expects
me to react, and continues, "But now that Pam is dead I'm
really confused about how I feel about Andy. Maybe he did
use my child to get to me. I don't think so, but I don't know."

Andy using her? A nice twist, putting the idea in my male
mind. I lean back in my chair, trying to decide if she was
simply ready for me or whether she has been extremely can-
did. Yet my own reading of Andy doesn't change. As ideal-

istic as he is, he could have been thinking he was embarking on the great love affair of the century. Maybe they're both for real. Who knows? My chair begins to squeak, and I stop the rocking I have unconsciously begun. As Olivia herself has pointed out, few people serving on an Arkansas jury will sympathize with either of them. "I don't know about his personal motivation," I admit, "but as a professional psychologist he's going to be held to certain standards."

She nods soberly, and I am forced to conclude that she is telling me the truth. So what if she came on to this guy to get him to try to help her child? People have gone to bed for a lot less noble motives. What we call "love" always has a price. I feel my own blood begin to quicken. What is it that this lanky, angular woman has to offer Andy that couldn't be better satisfied by a younger, more voluptuous female of his own race? Is it the forbidden fruit that tempts us all? I have wondered more than once if that wasn't the initial reason I was attracted to Sarah's mother. Southern boys at one time had a long history of crossing to the other side of town. I ask, "Who have you told about this relationship?"

Now seemingly more relaxed, she slumps back against her chair. "No one, of course. Who has seen us?"

Now that some of the tension in the room seems to have dissipated, I notice my stomach growling. It is almost time for lunch. "Yettie Lindsey has seen all the signs, but I doubt if she can implicate you directly."

Olivia's eyes narrow and she once again becomes alert. Competition is good for the circulation. "She does everything but take off her clothes in front of Andy."

I keep from nodding but just barely. "She feels like you're moving in on what ought to be her territory."

"Did she say that?" she asks, now rigid in her chair.

I would not want to go one on one in a dark alley with her. "Not in so many words," I say mildly, "but I can understand that point of view. Good men, I hear, are few and far between." The smile flickers but doesn't quite come back. From where she is sitting she can see Sarah's picture on my desk. I follow her gaze and explain. "At least that's been my daughter's experience."

Her expression softens as she listens to me brag about Sarah. It is somehow easy to forget she was a normal mother at one point in her life. In the last few moments she had become more like some kind of predator. Even as vulnerable as she sometimes seems, I cannot think of her cuddling a child. Perhaps, had I endured her life, I would be equally intense.

Olivia merely shrugs when I finally ask about Andy's statement that she, too, felt certain that David Spath would go along with ordering remote-control equipment once it had been demonstrated that shock worked on Pam. "Andy was more optimistic than I was, but he and David were good friends. I had to trust Andy. Usually, the administrators of these places will never go out on a limb, but Andy swore David would come around once he could see Pam was no longer hitting herself."

I write down the words "not certain at all" as if they are the key to the case. Fat chance. Tomorrow I won't even remember what they mean. Clearly, Olivia feels too conflicted to make a strong witness on Andy's behalf. "What's your opinion of David Spath?" I ask, thinking of my fruitless interview with him. The only thing I got out of him was that he wasn't from England.

A look of consternation comes over Olivia's face as though she has met her match in Spath. "David's an expert at massaging parents. He knows how guilty a lot of us feel and tells us what we want to hear; in retrospect, I think Andy may have overestimated him. Honestly though, Andy was really putting him on the spot by not getting consent of a human rights committee first."

I scratch my right ear with my pen. All of a sudden it is Andy alone who is responsible. She has forgotten she was part of this plan. "You don't think it's possible Spath might have known in advance Andy was going to try shock?"

As if she is resisting me, Olivia stiffens her back against

the chair. If she knows something I don't, she isn't telling. "Not David Spath," she says, her voice hostile. "I can't see him leaving himself open that way."

To make certain she isn't totally abandoning Andy, I ask, "How much of what happened occurred without Andy talking about it with you first?"

She looks at me warily but admits, "I knew about all of it."

I nod, knowing she is slipping away from Andy as we get closer to trial. The possibility that her affair with him may become public isn't helping. "I admire the hell out of what he risked for you," I say, trying to keep her on his side. "As you say, nobody else would do anything but massage you."

She starts to speak but doesn't, and I ask the question that has been on my mind since Andy gave me his check. "Have you given him any money for his defense?"

She begins shaking her head even before I have finished. "He would never take money from me. He'll probably never tell you, though, that he has a very successful brother in Atlanta who thinks he's a saint for working with the retarded."

"No," I say weakly, feeling like an idiot. Despite what he had said, I was absolutely positive it was from Olivia. If his own lawyer is this blind to him, what can he expect from his jury? I dread this trial.

After a few more questions I walk Olivia to the elevators. There is no need to caution her about the need to cool down the relationship between her and Andy until after the trial, since that is obviously on low pilot now anyway. She gets a commitment from me to let her call him first to tell him she has admitted their affair to me. I see no harm in this and was not looking forward to having to leap in headfirst when I see him tomorrow.

As I walk back through the reception area, Julia, who is dressed almost normally for once (her polka-dotted blouse looks as if it is on backward, but I am no fashion expert), says from behind her computer terminal, "You look way in over your head on this one, buddy boy."

Buddy boy? I laugh out loud, realizing for the first time
that Julia is a romantic stuck in a 1940s time warp, all the
way down to the fashionable shoulder pads that look like
bean bags underneath her blouse. All of this business must
be from old movies on TV, because I have a sneaking suspicion, based on her spelling and punctuation, that she is no
great shakes as a reader. All we need on our floor is a couple
of investigators and she would be in absolute heaven. "You
guessed it, sister," I say, doing a quick Humphrey Bogart,
and roll my shoulders to indicate that I may be in trouble
now but I'll get out of it.

Julia narrows her eyes at me, surely wondering if I am
mocking her. "Guess who called for the hundredth time."

"Mona Moneyhart."

"Give this man a cigar," she says to no one in particular.

There is supposedly a key to understanding everyone's
frame of reference. Too bad I don't have one for my main
client. Back in my office I stare out of my sorry excuse for a
window (I could see the river if I could hang by my feet) and
wonder what really happened in this case. Unfortunately, bad
lawyers are always the last to know.

On my kitchen table near the nearly empty box of Ken-
tucky Fried Chicken and french fries confronts me like an
indictment. Grease stains and bones are all that remain of
my dinner. Since Sarah has been gone this summer, I find I
am eating more junk and fat. If she leaves Blackwell County
to go off to college next year, I will need to get a grip on my
eating habits or I will end up like Dan, whose heart surely
must be beginning to resemble a stopped-up garbage disposal.

Seated beside my chair, his spine and legs straight in a
rare demonstration of good posture, Woogie reproaches me
with his soft brown eyes: if you can eat that junk, at least
give me the bones. "No!" I say, rising from the table with
the box in my hand. If I throw the bones in the trash can in
the house, the smell will drive him crazy, and though the

bones, stripped of meat, seem almost flimsy, the disposal
has been making a funny noise recently, as if it has been
asked on too many occasions, much like my stomach in the
last few weeks, to digest difficult objects. I head for the back
door, with Woogie at my heels hoping I'll spill the box or
relent at the last moment. I go through my backyard to the
metal trash cans by the diamond-shaped fence that separates
my property from my neighbors'. The heat (it still must be
close to ninety) of this long July day has begun to lift, but I
do not linger outside, dropping the Colonel's image uncere-
moniously into a plastic bag filled with the remains of a
week's garbage, and return immediately to the house to read
Sarah's latest letter, which I have saved as my dessert. Again
seated at the kitchen table with Woogie and a Miller Lite for
company, I rip open the envelope, but not before marveling
that the return address is written in a hand (except for the
way she makes the number seven—Americans risk confusing
ones and sevens, but Colombians, like most of the rest of the
world, do not) almost identical to her mother's. Her initial
torrent of correspondence has diminished to a trickle (a sign,
according to Rainey, she is no longer homesick). In fact, this
is only the second letter since I took her back over two weeks
ago. She will be home Saturday—barely twenty-four hours
before she leaves for "Camp Anytown," her religious and
atheist do-gooder camp sponsored by the National Conference of Christians and Jews.

Dear Dad,

*We just had a mock trial, and I served on the jury.
Everyone else wanted to be a lawyer or star witness, so it
was easy to get my first choice. It was a murder case. In
some ways, it was just a chance for the boys to try to show
off. Is that why you become lawyers or is it the money?*

*I think I'm beginning to have more confidence in myself.
I was the only one on the jury who voted at first for an
acquittal. They got mad and said I was just being stubborn.*

I wouldn't give in though (I knew there was a reasonable doubt!). It was cutting into our free time, so everybody else changed their vote. What I wonder is whether I would have the courage to do that in real life? People like you a lot more if you go along with them. Some of the kids are still irritated with me!

I've decided my biggest problem is that I want everyone to like me, no matter what. I've always gotten a lot of attention at school because I look so much like Mom. It's easier just to smile and keep my mouth shut. Was she really intelligent? You never have told me whether she was really good at her job or not. Did she want to be a doctor or did she think they are such jerks it wasn't worth it? I'd like to know more about her—what she was really like as a person—not just a mother.

I think it's important that I go far away to college and get out of the South. It's okay, and people are nice and everything, but it kind of lulls you to sleep—like the most important thing is whether the Razorbacks (Razorblacks one of the kids here calls the basketball team) win or not. I know I sound like a snob (some of these kids are but most are not). I realize how loyal you are to Arkansas and everything, but I think I need to go and see for myself what other places are like. Do you have the money to send me to college next year out of state? If not, I understand. But maybe I could get a scholarship and work part-time. If I had some math and science brains, I'd have more options!

I have no idea what I want to do with my life, but at least most of the kids here don't either. If they all did, I'd really feel stupid. After this mock trail, I don't think I want to be a lawyer. Too many egos and silly rules. It is hard to believe you were ever in the Peace Corps or a social worker. You don't seem the type. I'm not putting you down, but you don't seem to care that much about other people. I mean, I know you care about me (and maybe Rainey), but really, that's about all. You have sort of an "us against the world" attitude. I wish I had known you

*and Mom back when you were in the Peace Corps. I bet it
was neat! Remember I'm going to the NCCJ Camp Sunday.
Thanks for getting my money in!*

 *Love,
Your non-legally interested daughter, Sarah*

 I put the letter down and grab a beer and check the freezer:
a half-empty sack of Harvest Foods crushed wheat (no cho-
lesterol) bread, and enough ice to build an igloo. No wonder
I'm eating fried chicken: I'm starving to death. It seems so
hot in the house I'm tempted to sleep in the refrigerator. I
might as well use it for something. I sit back down at the
table and, still irritated, reread Sarah's letter while I sip at
the Miller Lite. I realize my feelings are a little hurt. You
can't spend your whole life trying to save the world, damn
it. Marriage and a family change things. Sarah can go off
and escape our provincialism, but somebody has to pay for
it. Woogie whimpers as if he is about to stroke out. His
panting tongue, pink as a slab of bacon beginning to fry on
the stove, makes me think of Rosa's Lamaze classes. I walk
into the living room and check the thermostat. Damn, no
wonder he is about to go into labor. It is eighty-five in the
house even though I have it set on seventy-eight. Great. Another bill. Out the back door Woogie and I go to investigate
the fuse box, which is behind a holly bush underneath my
bedroom window. After scratching my hands on a leaf, I
open the metal container to find that the circuit breakers are
still in the ''on'' position. Having exhausted my technolog-
ical knowledge, with Woogie at my heels I go back inside to
cool off with a shower.

 The cold water on my back sends an exquisite shock down
my spine, but tingling with the mixture of pain and pleasure,
I weenie out and switch the nozzle to warm and let it gently
knead my neck muscles. When I open my eyes, it is painfully
obvious that the pinkish tile in the shower could stand cleaning, but if it's not going to bother me, then I won't bother it

tonight. Alcohol, heat, and water have their own healing qualities, and I feel myself begin to relax. After a while, with a little help from (as my kindergarten teacher used to call my hand) Mr. Thumb and his four friends, I soon get myself into a pleasant state thinking about Kim Keogh. Each time I have thought about sex in the past week and a half, my musings have been accompanied by a mental picture of my prostate swelling to the size of a watermelon and then exploding. Following my premature hospital admission, Kim, sounding hung over but anxious, called the next morning, probably to see if I had died. Relieved at the truth (she had merely slept with a middle-aged man who is beginning to deteriorate), she shyly hinted that she would like to see me again. But feeling I had received a warning, I put her off, saying I would call her. I haven't. Why don't I have the guts to say that I am not interested in pursuing a relationship with her? Too hard. For once, I feel deeply ashamed. She bared more than her body. No wonder women think men are jerks. I can hear the phone ringing and grab my towel.

"Gideon, what're you doing?" Rainey asks. She sounds happy. I have been afraid to call her since I got her out of bed to take me to the hospital.

"Right now?" I ask, looking down between my legs. A disappearing act is taking place before my very eyes. "Not much."

"Want to get some yogurt?" she asks, running the words together as if they were the words to a song. No longer do I allow myself to think of Rainey as I have been thinking of Kim Keogh. I always feel too morose later.

I begin to rub myself briskly with the towel as Woogie, who has come into the room to keep me company, licks my wet legs. "I'll pick you up in fifteen minutes."

I slip on a pair of denim cutoffs, a T-shirt, and my running shoes, thinking that forgiveness is a wonderful thing. Like the rain, it falls on the just and the unjust. Thank God for that.

She is waiting for me on her front steps. We are dressed

identically, even to our T-shirts from the Blackwell County Pepsi 10K race two years ago. "Twinkies," I tell her, as she slides in beside me.

She barely glances at me and says, as she buckles on her seat belt, "I don't have a prostate."

One of the things about Rainey I like is that I don't have to wait long for her to slip a knife between my ribs. I smile, inordinately pleased to see this woman. Her curly red hair is cut shorter than I've ever seen it. In profile her face looks boyish. I resist the urge to reach over and playfully squeeze her leg as I do Sarah's. "I kind of panicked the other night," I apologize to her as we head west on Maple to the nearest yogurt emporium. "I think I was born without a pain threshold."

Rainey's laughter is refreshing as a cool breeze. "Gideon, you're just awful! Poor Kim Keogh. I saw her on TV tonight and she looked frazzled. You're really great for a woman's ego, you know that?"

I can hear Kim telling her friends: the last guy I made love to had to go to the hospital an hour later. "I'm too old for somebody like that," I admit, turning my head so I can see her. She is sitting so straight it makes my back ache. If I had her posture, I'd be an inch taller.

As if she is commenting on the weather, Rainey, watching the road for both of us, says offhandedly, "That's how men your age die—a massive heart attack and—poof!—you're gone. Think of the guilt for the poor woman."

As we climb the hill into Blackwell County's most exclusive area, the traffic increases as if the heat had driven even the rich into the streets tonight. The poor woman? I feel a sudden twinge in my prostate, as if it is an early-warning signal for the rest of the body. "Surely, it doesn't happen all that often," I argue weakly, wondering what the statistics are. "It sounds like a line of bull cooked up by wives who won't put out anymore themselves but who want to scare their husbands into lifelong celibacy."

Rainey reaches over and pats my knee. "I'm not your

wife," she says with mock tenderness. Her hand, as light and soft as a first kiss, immediately returns to her lap.

I turn onto Bradshaw and see the lights of the section called Riverview, a yuppie heaven for central Arkansans who demand proof we have the potential to be like everybody else. Antique shops, pricey women's clothing stores, pretentious restaurants with snotty-sounding names (Pompidieu's, the Lion Tamer), business offices (a favorite area of therapists, dentists, and accountants) daintily line the street. A little too cutesy for me, but Rainey, however, has decided tonight that Turbo's has the best yogurt in town, and obligingly, I turn into the drive-through lane, which, through a stroke of blind luck, isn't backed almost into Bradshaw this time of night. "You might as well be my wife," I say as we pull up to the order window. "I read a survey recently that married people hardly ever do it after a few years. Like just a little over once a week."

After we order (she gets her pathetic kiddie cup), Rainey says, "God, Gideon, you sound like Rosa's been dead so long you can't remember what it was like to be married to her."

Rainey hands me a five-dollar bill. It's her turn, and she has become scrupulous about paying her share since we have decided to be friends. As I get her change from the girl at the window (she looks about nine—have the child-labor laws been repealed or does it just seem as if kids are quitting school in the third grade to go to work?), I think about my sex life with Rosa. Have I been romanticizing that, too? It was good, but like everything else, it became a routine. In my present state though, it seems wonderful. Oblivious to the ritzy Buick full of kids that has just pulled in behind me, I roll my white plastic spoon around in my medium-sized cup, mixing the chocolate syrup and the yogurt together and then digging out as big a bite as I can manage to get into my mouth. If this is going to be my only sensual pleasure in life, then I'm going to get it right now.

We drive back to her house and sit on the sweltering concrete steps with the porch light out so as not to attract bugs. Across the road, lit by the streetlight on the corner, two small children run shrieking through one yard into another chasing each other. The leader of the two, a girl about nine with a long ponytail and short, stubby legs laughs excitedly and blasts a tin can five feet into the air without breaking stride. "No fair! No fair!" her pursuer, a little boy of no more than seven, wails, throwing himself despondently on the high grass in front of the house as she continues around the corner. When I was a child in Bear Creek, we played endless games of Kick the Can, and my older sister, before she became obese, was that ponytailed tomboy across the street. Dejectedly, the boy gets up and retrieves the can and places it upright on the sidewalk. Putting his head down on his chest, he trots around the corner, still muttering to himself. I lean back and look up at the humid sky, which is packed with misty stars. Under my now sticky T-shirt I can feel drops of sweat slipping down my sides. "My air-conditioning went out tonight," I say glumly. "If it's not one damn thing, it's twenty or thirty."

Rainey, moving toward me but not touching, titters at my hyperbole. Her laughter is like tinkling glass. "How you do go on, Gideon," she says lightly. "Do you want to sleep on my couch?"

I think for a moment. How nice it would be just to glimpse the woman I have loved for over a year in her nightgown. Underneath she would be solid, her body still firm from five days a week of Jazzercise. Yet I know I would lie awake all night listening futilely for my name. Our friendship is too delicate to carry such a weight. Maybe in five or ten years, I think irritably. "Better not," I mumble, not daring to look at her. "But thanks for the offer." Above us I can hear the whisper of a breeze in the maples that flank her house, but ground level it is hot and still. Incessantly busy locusts provide a kind of white noise around us for the now half-dozen children who occasionally come charging into view from out of the shadows across the street.

I think I hear a sigh, but she is gasping at a shooting star
that flashes by us from left to right. "Look!" she says, touching my arm. For perhaps a second I trace the star which then
winks out of sight.

"Incredible," I mutter, but I am thinking of the relationship between men and women. Why are things so difficult?
I have tried as earnestly as I know how to accept the terms
of friendship she has offered, but times like tonight when I
can smell the heat in every living thing around me, including
Rainey, it is not easy.

We talk for about an hour. She tells me that she has begun
to worry that she may lose her job at the state hospital. The
state is struggling to convert itself to a community-based
system, and the census is way down. Her offer to loan me
money becomes even more astonishing. I'm so cheap I even
hate to lend Sarah money. "I probably could get a job at a
community mental health center somewhere," she says offhandedly.

The idea of Rainey moving anywhere shocks me. Ever
since Rosa died, I have told myself not to expect permanence
in any situation, but as usual, I am always surprised and hurt
by the prospect of change. How dare anyone disrupt my life?
I scrape desperately at my empty cup. "It won't come to
that." Yet it might. Nothing stands still. As usual, she lets
me talk about Sarah. I tell her about the letter I received
tonight. "She doesn't want to be a lawyer, that's for sure,"
I say irritably. Since I have been in private practice by myself,
I have quietly entertained the thought that someday she would
go to law school and then come into practice with me.
Page & Page, Attorneys at Law.

The right side of her face pressed against her arms which
cradle her drawn-up knees, Rainey looks like a sleepy child.
"Who in their right mind would?" she asks, breathing deeply
in the dense air. "Some day historians will look back and
regard lawyers as the dinosaurs of our culture. All you did
was eat and fight. This country better learn quickly we can't

afford you, or we all better start learning Japanese and Korean.''

Absently, I lick my spoon, which has long been clean, and taste nothing but plastic. ''We're like cops: nobody likes us until you need us.''

Rainey raises her head and gazes up at the stars again. ''That's the problem. We only think we need you because nobody trusts each other in this country. It's everybody for themselves. That's what is killing us as a society. There's no sense we're part of each other. It's white against black; rich against poor; everybody against everybody and nobody for each other. We don't even have large families anymore. I think it's a pretty sterile mentality we have in the United States with all this never-ending individualism.''

I am surprised at the passion in her voice. Rainey doesn't make many speeches; yet, I have heard this again recently. Where? Sarah's letter, of course. Us against society. Well, that's how it looks to me. Yawning, I lean back on my elbows until I am almost horizontal on the concrete stoop. ''It's easier said than done,'' I say, knowing I sound glib, but there is no quick cure for the national mind-set that is enshrined in so much patriotic nonsense.

Rainey takes my cup from my hand and places her smaller container inside it. ''You're just scared that Sarah will go off to college and never come back.''

I nod. Scared to death.

14

FOR MY FIRST meeting with Andy in over a week I can tell him that it appears we have an expert witness. A psychologist in New Orleans has referred a colleague, who, in the spirit of the calling card of an old TV gunslinger, has implied that he "Has Electricity, Will Travel." A series of phone calls has also produced a résumé and a potential fee ($150 an hour, plus $300 an hour in court and travel and hotel expenses). Dr. Kent Goza, a clinical psychologist with a private practice, in the suburbs of Jackson, Mississippi, has insisted to me that he successfully uses shock treatments to stop head banging and other self-destructive behaviors in retarded children and is sending me the research (as yet unpublished) to prove it. Once again, thank God for Mississippi.

In the main office on the grounds of the Human Development Center, I am told by the woman at the reception desk that Andy has just been called into a meeting and is not available at the moment. Even though I am still the enemy, this country woman is basically too friendly to be rude and confides, "He said to tell you he tried to call you but you had already left your office." Separated by a dirty pane of glass (is there a fear the residents will steal a notepad or the visitor sign-in sheet?), we smile at each other for the first time. I notice her nameplate on her desk: Mattie Moss. With a name like that, she must be closer to sixty than to forty, though as it seemed to me the first time I came here, her emerald eyes appear ageless behind her indestructible-looking steel-frame glasses. "That's okay," I assure her. I wasn't looking forward to this meeting anyway. "Is Yettie Lindsey in?"

As I say this, Yettie walks by and allows me to follow her to her office. I note that this view of her is as positively reinforcing as the front. She is wearing a pair of jeans whose snug fit would make the principal shareholders of Levi Strauss weep with happiness over the design of their product. Yettie is none too pleased to talk to me but has consented to give me ten minutes. I don't need more than that; I just want to check in with her to make sure Jill or someone from her office hasn't been snooping around. A male resident, an older man of thirty, whose ears and face seem to have been at one time caught in a vise, passes me and sniggers as if he knows what I am thinking. Irritated by Yettie's coldness (though I understand it), I give him a jaunty salute as if to say that all men, regardless of their mental age, think with their dicks, so what's the big deal about a normal brain?

Yettie's office, formerly lime green, is now the color of pumpkin pie. Though I'm hardly an artist, I think I would have taken a raise instead. On the wall behind her desk is an elaborate bright yellow God's Eye, which I apparently didn't notice before because I was too busy concentrating on her rather well-endowed chest. For all I know, the ornament on the wall may have been nailed into place five minutes ago, but her expression, sullen as a sulking child's, as she orders me to sit, indicates she is not in the mood to suffer a fool gladly.

I sit down in the one seat available to me: an unpadded and corroding metal folding chair and instantly wish we were conducting this chat on our feet. It is as if I can feel bits of iron working into my butt. Since she hasn't offered me coffee (I'm not going to have trouble staying awake in this chair), I resist making a snide comment and simply ask, "How are you doing?" I find that I mean it. Her honesty last time has produced in me a sympathy for her (despite her hostility) I wouldn't believe existed. Maybe, though, it is that she looks as delicious as a chocolate ice cream cone would taste right about now. I have gotten in the habit of walking across the street with Dan to Beaumont Drugs for ice cream at about three in the afternoon. Hunger, as Dan points out almost on a daily basis, unlike sexual desire, can be satisfied any time and in public.

"I've been better," she says abruptly, though examining her fingernails as if she had all the time in the world. "What do you want now?"

I look up at the God's Eye instead of her blue cotton knit sweater and try to think of a believable lie, but can't and offer the truth instead. "I was out here to see Andy, but he's in a meeting, and so I just thought I'd stop by to see what you think of a co-worker."

From beside her desk she picks up a ball of yarn and knitting needles and astonishes me by beginning to knit on what I take to be an orange sweater. I hadn't seen a woman her age knit since Rosa and realize the God's Eye is probably her handiwork. "What're you talking about?" she asks suspiciously, making tiny clicking noises with the ivory-colored needles.

Now that I'm out here, I might as well ask something that has been in the back of my mind since the probable cause hearing, but I'm not sure how to put the question. Leon Robinson, in some ways, is directly responsible for Pam's death. He could help Andy enormously if he would cooperate. "What do you think of Leon?" I ask lamely, my mind a desert. This girl, still hardly a woman to me at my age, is an oasis for my eyes, however, and I forsake the God's Eye to stare shamelessly at her sensual full mouth and oddly colored irises of green, yellow, and brown.

"I can't stand him," Yettie says, not missing a beat with the needles that she flashes and whirls like small swords. Two swift thrusts and she would have two more eyes for her collection.

My eyelids throb spastically at the thought of the damage the needles could do to them, while my mind goes back to the hearing. The sight of Leon's crying suddenly has stayed with me. I was touched by his emotion and thought he could be brought around to testify if I knew how to handle him right. He was hostile, but I thought I understood the reason, since he had taken care of Pam for years. Maybe there are some feelings of guilt I can exploit. "He didn't seem so bad," I say, rubbing my left eye to still it. Perhaps she will give me a clue to his personality. "How come?"

"He hates blacks," Yettie says flatly, not even bothering to look at me. Rosa wasn't as dark as Yettie, but there is something that reminds me of her. Maybe her body.

I am fascinated by the needles: I can't follow them at all. God, she is bitter. Does she like anybody? For all I know, the sweater is for herself. "How do you know?" I ask, more urgently than I intend. "Has he ever said or done anything?"

Yettie shrugs, refusing to look at me. I could develop an ego problem around this woman. The needles click for what seems like a full minute. Finally she says, "You can just tell."

I suppress a sigh and decide to leave. More female intuition. It seems to me a lot of blacks think all whites are racists. It gets old after a while. I doubt if I would be too crazy about blacks if the only one around was Yettie Lindsey. Still, I may need her. "My wife used to knit," I say, leaning forward to get a better look at her hands. "She wasn't as fast as you, though."

Yettie puts down the needles and looks at her watch. "Anything else?" she says.

Andy comes for me in half an hour. During that time it seems I have gotten more information out of Homer, my retarded escort the first time I was here, than from Yettie Lindsey. Homer, who saw me sitting in the waiting room on his way outside, greeted me as if I had come to take him home. Unfortunately, I didn't understand a word he said. He didn't seem to mind as long I kept smiling. I wish I could make everybody that glad to see me.

Andy doesn't seem any happier to see me than Yettie was.

"Got called to a meeting," he explains tersely. We walk side by side in the wide corridor to his office, our silence interrupted only by a retarded man who greets Andy with such genuine enthusiasm that Dale Carnegie himself (were he not dead) would approve of his effort. Though I am on Andy's shit list, Jake, who looks normal except for his crossed eyes and jug-handle ears, is not: My client lets Jake pump his hand as though both of them expected oil to spurt from Andy's mouth. I know Andy resents my talking to Olivia about his affair. Clients want you to help them, but they hate like hell for you to do it.

Andy's office, I see, has not been repainted. In fact, the room has an even more temporary look than it did before. On his desk is a cardboard box filled with books as if he were moving in or moving out. Before I can comment, he lights into me.

"You had no right to ask Olivia about our relationship!" he says, closing the door behind him. His voice is under control but just barely. Standing in front of his door, he has balled both his fists, but I doubt he has ever physically fought another man. Even with his face stretched tight with anger, he looks too elegant. His goatee and mustache look freshly trimmed this morning, and there is not even the hint of a wrinkle in his tan poplin slacks. Mine always make me look as though I have an accordion on my lap five minutes after I've put them on. I can imagine Andy fighting a duel with pistols at fifty paces but not in a street bawl.

I turn my back on him and sit down across from his desk, wondering how to handle him. The best defense is a good offense, especially with a cream puff like Andy. As he comes around behind his desk, I say softly, "You sure as hell weren't going to tell me." Though his office is at the end of the hall and the door is closed, there is no sense trying to sell some tickets to this conversation. "I hope you're not going to tell me an affair with Olivia isn't relevant to your case."

Andy is more formally dressed than the last time I visited him here, in a turquoise gingham shirt, blue sports coat, and maroon tie. All heated up, he discards the coat. "It won't be if no one knows about it!" he says, still taking time in his rage to hang up his jacket properly and place it on the coat rack in the corner by the door. Neatness counts with this guy, I think, as he goes back behind his desk.

"I suppose," I say sarcastically, "that you think nobody has a clue to what's going on."

Folding his arms across his chest like a used-car dealer who won't let a sucker get his money back, Andy purses his lips and says disdainfully, "Nobody can prove a thing."

I resist a smile. This attempted guile has its own charm in a man who usually displays the naïveté of a scientist: Who, me blow up the world? This bomb is purely for research purposes. Andy must have lead an unusually sheltered life for a black person. The ones I have encountered have no illusions about whitey's power. "If the prosecutor ever gets hold of it, she'll bring your used rubbers into court if she has to."

Andy narrows his eyes at me in pure hatred. There has never been a messenger of bad news in the history of the world who hasn't been despised, and I'm no exception. I know how crude I must sound, but he has to start living in the real world.

I fairly yell at him: "Don't you realize you have to tell me the things that will affect this case? I can't represent you in the dark. I'm not a magician who can pull a trick out of a hat at the last moment and save you, goddamn it! Frankly, I couldn't care less whether you're shacking up with the Queen of England, but you can be awfully damn sure the prosecutor is going to try to get that information to the jury, especially since the Queen is white."

Andy's expression changes from one of contempt to disgust. "I know all that," he says wearily and leans back hard in his chair.

I continue to press him. "You don't act like it. You're the one who doesn't want race to be an issue at your trial," I say, remembering his words. "I can't do it without your help."

This last point seems to mollify him somewhat, and his face loses some of its intensity. He shifts restlessly, as if he is trying without success to think of a comeback. "You could have asked me first," he says lamely.

This is a minor point to concede, and I try to do so graciously. "I should have," I admit, "but I was afraid you wouldn't tell me the truth and would try to stop me from talking to Olivia about it."

A frown spreads over Andy's face as he looks at me for a long moment and then says, in a voice stiff with formality, "I've given you absolutely no reason to distrust me."

I soften my tone and try to smile at him. "My experience is that we all lie when we're cornered, Andy. It's really nothing personal." Candor is an overrated virtue, since often I resort to it when I need to manipulate somebody, I think, but don't say.

"How patronizing," he retorts, glowering at me as he shoves his chair back and turns away to the second-story window directly behind him. "There was a time right when I first met you," he says, his voice so quiet and flat I have to strain to hear him since his back is almost directly to me, "when I thought after this was over you and I might be friends. You seemed to be taking my situation personally, and I found I appreciated that."

Perhaps, as a defense mechanism, I find myself beginning to shrug, but I am uncomfortable: not only do I like this guy, I finally recognize that I have begun to admire the hell out of him. Unless he has managed to fool me completely, his life has awakened in me a memory of the idealism I must have felt over twenty years ago when I joined the Peace Corps. His color-blind stubbornness and his commitment to the Homers of the world are so naive, he seems from another world. I believe he made a serious mistake in using shock on Pam, but unlike so many of us who live our lives virtually indifferent to the horrific suffering that is an inseparable but ignored part of daily life, he made an error of commission, not omission. He is in trouble precisely because he was willing to care and risk himself for other people. It is rare that a lawyer has the opportunity to represent a person in a criminal case whose life he sees as a positive force. At best, my other clients have been, and are, victims. Andy, I have come to believe (unconsciously until this moment I realize) is much more than that. Doubtless, he will appear unaccountably quixotic to a jury composed of ordinary Arkansans; but Andy, I hope I get them to see, though not blameless, should not be judged so harshly that his life and career are destroyed. Under the circumstances, Pam's death is punishment enough. This man is willing to make himself as vulnerable as a teenager who falls in love for the first time. "You're absolutely right," I admit, squaring my shoulders to the desk and looking him in the eyes. "I put all my clients in the same box, and I'm wrong to do that. In fact, I admire you a great deal."

His brown eyes lose some of their hurt look. "I'm not looking to be admired," he instructs, "but by explicitly categorizing all people as being willing to lie, you've illustrated what whites do to blacks when they make judgments about us as a race."

I nod, my agreement automatic, thinking that Andy is obsessed by the issue of race. Though surely he doesn't intend it, his effort to pretend his blackness isn't the defining quality in his life merely emphasizes that it is. Since he insists that he is honest, I have no qualms about testing it. "Why does Yettie Lindsey hate your guts?"

Andy blinks rapidly. "I won't go out with her."

A button has been punched here. There is something more going on here than a case of hurt feelings. "That's all there is to it?" I ask, remembering Rainey's gossip.

Andy sighs and, as if he felt a sudden chill, hugs himself by squeezing his arms against his sides. He says, "If you're black, Arkansas is a small state. Yettie's family and my family have been friends for years. When I was in high school in Fayetteville, she was still a child, but our families used to kid each other that we'd end up together. Actually, it's not a coincidence that Yettie is here. Before she graduated from Arkansas State in May, because of our families' friendship, but also because Yettie's going to make a good social worker, I persuaded David to give her an interview, and she got the job, largely because of my recommendation. I see now that she thought I had something else in mind.''

I tap my pen against my pad as if to applaud, appreciating the depth of Yettie's disappointment. It is likely that she has been in love with Andy for many years. What she had hoped was coming true. He was sending for her, but when she arrived, finally ready to begin an adult relationship, she found out that she, a black woman, was nothing special to him. Like the fools men are, Andy probably thought she should be happy just getting a job. Black people in love! It occurs to me that since Rosa died (she was the exception), I have never really thought that the complexity of their inner lives mirrored my own. I equate their material poverty with an emotional poverty as well, I realize. No wonder I can't figure this case out. I'm such a racist I can't even imagine them. Poor Andy! She hates him now, and he didn't even realize it. I lean forward to ease a sudden crick in my back and try to empathize. ''If Freud couldn't figure out what women wanted, why should you?''

Andy tries to smile, but his heart isn't in it. He is a behaviorist and won't find much consolation in the befuddlement of Sigmund Freud. I close my eyes and see old Mrs. Whitelaw, my high school English teacher, swaying back and forth before thirty bored and horny small-town and farm kids and quoting in a voice choked with rage: ''Remember, always remember, 'Hell hath no fury like a woman scorned!' '' I warn Andy, ''We've got to treat Yettie with kid gloves. So far, she hasn't volunteered anything to the prosecutor's office. I wouldn't do anything to upset her further if I were you.''

Andy nods, a preoccupied expression on his face, and I

move the subject to our Mississippi expert witness. As we talk, Andy seems to be thinking about the past. Why didn't he fall in love with Yettie? Who knows? I got my wife in a foreign country: I can't really assume he would want to marry his next-door neighbor any more than I did. Does it bother me? Obviously, or I wouldn't be wondering about it. After a few minutes of desultory discussion (Andy doesn't seem much interested right now in our expert, though I have to assume he is relieved somebody is willing to come to Blackwell County to justify shock), I head back to my office, thinking how a New England jury would react to a psychologist from Mississippi who proclaimed the virtues of a cattle prod. I can hear the discussion in the jury room: ''They probably used cattle prods on blacks, so shocking retarded kids is no big deal.'' Outside the Blazer, which is close to overheating, the central Arkansas countryside, shimmering in the summer heat, appears on fire. Prejudice is everywhere.

15

"GIDEON," JILL MARYMOUNT says, her hectoring voice
crackling through a bad connection, "in about five seconds
after I get off the phone, I'm walking down to the clerk's
office to file a charge of capital felony murder against Andrew Chapman. You want to come over to my office and see
what we have?"

The client sitting across from me, a middle-aged man
whose paycheck has just been garnisheed on a judgment taken
by a health spa (he had signed a lifetime contract and discovered he wasn't *that* interested in trying to keep a thirty-
two-inch waist), must be able to read my reaction, because
he looks as if Julia had interrupted me to say the building
was on fire. Furious at what I am hearing (in the last two
weeks I had begun to have some hope I could persuade a
jury to come in with a conviction of negligent homicide and
let Andy off with probation), I reply sarcastically, "I appreciate the advance notice," and wag my finger at my client,
who surely must think I am warning him instead of trying to
reassure him. "I'll be right over." I hang up and exhaust my
knowledge of debtor-creditor law in one sentence by explaining that he can't be put in prison for debt, and that
an emergency has come up requiring me to postpone our
interview.

"I can come back tomorrow," Mr. Welford says gratefully, absurdly relieved. I know nothing about bankruptcy
law and have no idea what to advise him. With as few clients
as I have, I can't afford to refer him out, and I tell him I'll

see him on his lunch hour. This way I'll have time to run down to Frank D'Angelo's office to find out what to ask him. When he had made the appointment, it sounded like a contract dispute, but with a legal judgment against him, it is past that stage. Like a man who has a tumor the size of a tomato in his testicles, but who says he is just having a little problem passing water, Mr. Welford, a salesman in the men's department at Sears, had told me only that he owed a little money on a debt he thought he shouldn't have to pay. I dial the Human Development Center and am told that Andy is not in his office. I leave a message for him to call me in an hour and say that it is urgent.

Finding I am almost sprinting to the courthouse, I force myself to slow down to a brisk walk; otherwise, in this heat, I'll be as sticky and nasty as a sponge soaked in blood. The thermometer outside First Capitol Bank across from the courthouse reads 101. They ought to give the humidity. It's got to be almost 100 percent. I am angry and confused. What evidence could there be that Andy deliberately killed this child? To charge him with first-degree murder, Jill will have to show intent, and to my mind, that leaves only the possibility that somehow Olivia is in on this.

"Hey! Don't be actin' like you don't know me!"

I squint into the glare across the street and see the old woman from the jail. An orange jacket covers part of the filthy black dress that reaches the top of her red high-top tennis shoes. Her hair is as wild as ever. I don't want to encourage her, but neither do I want her to begin screaming at the top of her lungs. "How're you doing?" I call to her, moving toward the courthouse at the same time, as if I'm late for a hearing.

"Where's that half-nigger who you had wid you?" she screams as two men come out of the bank beside her. Despite the heat I break into a run up the south steps into the courthouse. This is an explanation that will only get worse with the telling. We all assume the worst, and sometimes no amount of explaining can help. I realize I hadn't doubted

Andy until I got the call from Jill. The most I thought he was guilty of was bad judgment. Damn it, ever since I saw that kid jump into Andy's arms, I've thought the guy was unique. A black male as smart as he is doesn't have to be stuck in the boonies covered up with people who can't even say their own name, and yet that's what he had committed himself to doing with his life. Damn Olivia. Why couldn't she leave him alone? She has to be behind this. I don't want him to have deliberately ended this child's life, even if somehow he thought it was the right thing to do.

The receptionist, obviously forewarned, waves me on back, and I walk knowingly back into the maze of offices as if I worked there myself. I wonder if my old pal Amy Gilchrist knew this was coming. I would have appreciated a tip.

Jill, wearing a dressy red pantsuit that, perversely, reminds me of the orange jumpsuits county prisoners are given, is standing behind her desk with a telephone clamped to her ear. She waves me on in as if I were a long-lost friend instead of someone she clearly does not like. Holding an earring in one hand, she laughs and whispers, "See you later," and hangs up. A personal call to a lover? Not likely, I'm afraid. Every person has secrets, but I doubt if sex is one of Jill Marymount's. Oddly, she seems relaxed, as if filing a capital murder charge has discharged the tension within the case instead of creating a great deal more.

"Why don't you close the door, Gideon," she instructs me as she attaches her earring, a plain silver hoop the circumference of a half dollar, "and we'll have a little talk after you read what we think your client has been up to."

Confidence. Jill's borders on smugness. I wish I had some about this case. I shut the door while she sits down and opens a file on her desk. "I was beginning to have some sympathy for your client and wonder if I had overcharged him," she says, handing me the document in which the formal allegations of capital murder are contained.

I notice that though the dozens of pictures of the children remain on the walls, she has changed the desk in her office.

Replacing the exquisitely handcrafted wood with its delicate finish, a museum piece I openly coveted, is a metallic surface a jet fighter could land on, reminding me of the Persian rug my old boss at the PD's Office replaced after repeated coffee spills. Women keep trying to humanize the workplace, but work keeps getting in the way, I suppose. Sitting down across from her, I read the "Information," as the formal charging document is called, and learn nothing new. Murder, as opposed to manslaughter, is, of course, a question of intention, a conclusion, and is easily stated.

"So what do you have?" I ask, clutching like a security blanket the briefcase on my lap as I wait for the bad news.

"We've known since the girl died that the cattle prod had very little tape insulating the handle," Jill explains. "It was a lethal weapon in the hands of somebody who knew what he was doing with it."

To give myself time to respond, I pretend to study the paper in front of me, remembering Andy's apparent lie to me that he had carefully wrapped it and couldn't understand what had happened. God knows how many others he has told. If I've ever had a client who didn't lie about something, I'd like to meet him. I say, "Obviously, I'd like to examine it. Do I need to get an order?"

Jill shakes her head as if I'm missing the point. "Still, I gave Chapman the benefit of the doubt until we found out this," she says, shoving at me a fourteen-year-old Blackwell County Circuit Court Consent Judgment that is styled: Pamela Le Master, by her Mother and Next Friend, Olivia Le Master, and Olivia Le Master, Individually, versus Dr. Hamilton Corbin, et al. Ham Corbin is a now retired obstetrician who owns a major chunk of the First Capitol Bank. What I'm looking at, I quickly realize is a copy marked "confidential" of a structured malpractice settlement in which Pam was awarded slightly over three million dollars, to be paid in increments to Olivia on her behalf, over her life. At her death the balance was to be paid to Olivia. "Where'd you get this?" I ask, knowing it doesn't matter. I'm in a daze as I try to catch up. Olivia must have decided that not only would Pam be better off dead but that she, as her mother, would as well. So how come I'm not reading about Olivia?

"Marvin Hippel has a long memory," Jill says, flipping through her own file. Her posture makes my back ache. I couldn't sit up that straight if I had a rod of reinforced steel inserted into my spine.

"The same Marvin Hippel who passes out his cards to doctors after he speaks at their meetings?" I say, remembering a seminar I attended when I first went to work at Mays & Burton. So what? Now that lawyers can advertise, I wouldn't be surprised if I saw some of my colleagues walking up and down the street in front of the Blackwell County Courthouse wearing those front-and-back sandwich placards with their phone numbers in glitter on them.

A glint that might pass for a smile steals into the corners of Jill's eyes. Hippel, who is a partner in one of the largest firms in the state, is notoriously shameless about hustling business he wants. Like our part-time state legislators who labor as employees the rest of the year on behalf of the industries for which they vote tax loopholes, Hippel professes not to have a clue as to the propriety of his conduct. "They say he's great in the courtroom, too," Jill says, her voice sarcastic. "Anyway, Hippel finally started hearing about the case and immediately came forward to let us know he had some information we would be interested in."

Feeling perverse as well as powerless in this situation, I slump disrespectfully further into my seat. "I'm sure the fact that he would like to torpedo what's left of the settlement has nothing to do with the exercise of his civic duty."

Jill, who now has removed a nail file from her drawer (we could be a husband and wife sniping at each other), says sweetly, "I wouldn't be too holier-than-thou. There's a rumor going around that you stole Chapman from Mays & Burton after you got fired, but I'm sure there's not a word of truth to it. By the way, there was quite a bit left—over two million dollars."

What have I ever done to this bitch? She hates my guts, or maybe she is just tough. I bite my tongue, telling myself she wants to goad me into something that will implicate Andy further. I wish I knew something. Now I can't believe a thing out of his mouth. "So what?" I say, feigning a casualness I don't feel. "My client didn't stand to benefit from it."

As if she has been waiting for me to say exactly this, Jill puts down her nail file and reaches into her desk drawer and takes out a document and hands it to me, making me straighten up. "That's not what Yettie Lindsey is going to say on the witness stand."

Yettie has signed a statement for Jill, dated only twenty-four hours ago, in which she says that outside Andy's office approximately a week before Pam died she heard Olivia tell Andy (among other things) that "there'll be more than enough money for you to go back to school for as long as you want." Yettie admitted that she has been trying to eavesdrop, and that someone had come up behind her and she had not heard anything further that she can remember. Yettie's statement goes on to say that she had not previously disclosed this information to the prosecutor's office because she had not understood or remembered the remark until it had been disclosed to her (by Jill, obviously) that Olivia stood to gain financially from Pam's death. Nor had she divulged until now that it was her belief that Andy and Olivia were romantically involved because she had no proof (only her suspicions from the way they looked at each other and talked together) and because she was jealous of Olivia.

"It's still a pretty thin case," I say more bravely than I feel. I am furious for talking myself into believing there was nothing more to this case than a tragic accident. My problem is that I allowed myself to like my client too much. Damn it, I still do.

Jill picks up her nail file again and begins to go to work on the nail on her left pinkie, reminding me again of my old boss at the Public Defender's Office. Her actions are totally unprofessional, but Jill is so calculating that I have to believe her studied casualness is a form of contempt. She looks up at me and says, "Come on, Gideon, your client has told more than one person he thought he had the cattle prod insulated. I assumed he just didn't know what the hell he was doing, and that's why I only charged him with manslaughter. Obviously, I didn't have all this other evidence when I charged him the first time."

I stand up, unable now to keep still. "So why haven't you charged Olivia?" I say angrily. But as soon as the words are out of my mouth, I realize Jill needs Andy's testimony to get her. Without it, she doesn't have enough even to charge her. With it, Olivia will go to jail for life. It flashes on me, too, that I know now why Kerr Bowman, her lackey assistant, is not in this room. Jill had said in front of him, in a moment of self-righteousness, that she would never offer Andy a deal, and now she has to if she wants to get the woman who instigated this. I know what Jill's version of this conversation will be: "I made him beg for it."

She blows on the nail file to rid it of her dead skin. "There's no hurry."

Bullshit. Despite knowing where this is heading, I rise to the bait. "You wouldn't get past a motion for a directed verdict without my client's testimony," I huff, "and you know it." Now that I'm on my feet, I have no place to go except out the door. Still, I have to see where she's heading.

Jill begins on her ring finger. Her nails are clear and appear from where I'm standing to be perfectly buffed. "Now that I know what happened," she says, "I have no doubt there's a lot more evidence out there. Your client won't be going anywhere, will he? I think I would like to increase the bond a bit though."

Thoroughly disgusted, I jam my hands in my pockets. "You expect me to ask for a deal."

She can't suppress a smile. "Not right now," she purrs, holding her fingers up to the light for us to admire. Her fingers are long and surprisingly sensuous. "But maybe you'll want to after you've had a little talk with him. By the way, we've asked for a bond hearing first thing tomorrow. I don't think I'll be quite so generous this time,'' she finishes, her face now a frozen sneer.

What crap, I think, as I pick up the Information, the Consent Judgment, and Yettie's statement from her desk. "We'll be there,'' I promise. As I walk toward the door, I notice again the photographs of children on both sides. I halfway expect to see Pam's round face mounted on the wall like a trophy.

An hour later I pull into the Clearwater Apartments to meet Andy in his home. Soon the media will be swarming over us like teenaged girls over Florida during spring break, as the news of his murder charge boils out of the courthouse. Though over the telephone at the Human Development Center he had sounded shaken (but not nearly as stunned as I would have preferred), I know that from now on I won't trust anything he tells me. Parking the Blazer near the manager's office, I note that Andy has gotten about as far from downtown as possible. But why not? Crime is all over Blackwell County, but it is worse downtown. I pass the pool area on my way to his building and see four young women in bikinis—all of them white, of course. Probably teachers on summer vacation who are sharing two apartments. Clearwater isn't cheap. Stretched out on bright yellow loungers, two of the four have their shoulder straps down, and I can't resist staring at them. One of them glances up at me. Her bored expression tells me I can look, but I better not even nod. If there are other blacks out here, I bet most of them cut the grass. Again I wonder where Andy is getting his money. The admiring-brother story is beginning to sound a little quaint.

Andy, his face grave, opens the door and invites me in. "Want something to drink?'' he says politely, leading me past an area that encloses his kitchen. "It'll cool off in here in a minute.''

Apparently, he has been home long enough to change clothes, but even in faded jeans and a blue work shirt rolled up at the cuffs, he looks better than most guys I know dressed in tuxes. I take off my suit coat and fold it over my arm. It must be close to ninety degrees in here. I'd love a beer, but take ice water instead. "Nice pool," I say, as he drops three cubes of ice in my glass. Though I am ready to jump on him, I want to ask the questions. I am curious where he will go first.

He fills the glass from the tap and hands it to me. "School-teachers," he confirms casually, as if I'm a bachelor interested in becoming his neighbor in a singles complex instead of his lawyer trying to defend him on a murder charge. "There're out there all the time. I don't know why they're not dead from skin cancer. The two blondes are damn nice-looking though."

Given his involvement with Olivia, I wonder how much he has seen. I gulp the water, all the while glancing around the kitchen. Most single guys live like pigs. Not Andy. Not even a dirty dish in the sink, which, unlike my own, is as white as his teeth. Surely he doesn't have a maid, but why shouldn't he? Maybe one of those white school-teachers comes over and gets on her hands and knees and scrubs the floor until she can see her face in it. As I follow him into his living room, it occurs to me that I haven't been in a black person's house since before Rosa died. Despite her conservatism, Rosa moved easily between both worlds; I was the token white at the few parties I went to with her in our neighborhood in the late sixties and early seventies after I had come back from the Peace Corps and still believed it was just a matter of time before blacks would be just like us. Just a matter of enough Head Start classes and compensatory education and after a while we wouldn't be able to tell if they were white or black if they called us on the phone—like Andy the first time he called me. I never felt comfortable despite my liberal pretensions at the time. I always felt most at ease with the women.

Why? Was it sex? Or was it that I was secretly petrified that beneath the bullshit that passes for party talk one of the men was waiting to get enough bourbon in him to unload on the nearest male honkie. At my insistence, we always went home early before the booze kicked in and turned them sour.

"Have a seat," Andy says, his voice still calm. If I were in his place, I'd be climbing the walls.

"I like this room," I say. I mean it though. Dark colors, but the space still seems light, airy. Part of it is the plants. If I look at something green, it dies. Chapman has several—a veritable tree in the corner, a bush hanging from the ceiling, a couple in pots around the room, and they are thriving yet not overgrown. On the walls are Van Gogh themes— sunflowers, peasants in fields, etc., perhaps the real things stolen from museums, for all I know. My knowledge of art blossomed and withered one spring in Fine Arts 101, but there is one picture directly behind Andy's chair that gets my attention. It is the only hint that he is black—a painting of an old African woman, judging from the load on her head and her dress. There is suffering in her weathered visage, but it is the kind that is mastered somehow by the victim and becomes merely a part of the geography and history of the face. No self-pity in those bones.

I can't contain myself. "You realize if you're convicted of this new charge," I say urgently as I sit down on the couch, a tan-and-green jungle-colored monster that blends nicely with the straw-colored wallpaper in the room, "you could either die or spend the rest of your life in prison trying to keep from getting raped."

He perches on the edge of a wicker chair across from me. "I swear to you," he says, his voice intense for the first time since I've been in the apartment, "I didn't kill Pam deliberately."

I sip at the remaining ounce of water in the glass, watching his face for a clue. He is as impassive as ever. How can he not be devastated by a charge of capital murder? Maybe he is, and is hiding it behind that black mask. Or maybe he realizes he's been found out. I've been lied to by clients who waved their arms and screamed at the top of their lungs that they were innocent; yet, I've had clients whisper their lies to me as quietly as penitents given their confession. "I suppose you didn't have the slightest idea," I say sarcastically, "that Olivia was scheduled to receive about two million dollars by Pam's premature death."

Andy narrows his eyes at me as if I were suddenly having a stroke. Finally he says, "I have no idea what you're talking about."

I unzip my brief case and take out the documents Jill gave me as I tell him about the malpractice settlement, wondering as I do if it is possible that Olivia has set him up. He wouldn't be the first man ever fooled by a woman. I can vouch for that. But how can he not know? They were lovers. They could have spent hours setting this up. "Come on, Andy," I say, feeling anger flow into me as I pick up Yettie's statement, "you were going back to school after you got married. Who was going to pay for that?"

For the first time I get a strong reaction. His head jerks down sharply as he leans forward to see what I have in my hands. "How do they know," he asks softly, "that we were talking about marriage? No one knew that."

The telephone rings, startling me almost out of my chair. The media surely have the story by now. It will be only a matter of time before they are here camped out by the pool. "Don't answer that," I instruct him. "It's a reporter."

In two strides Andy is in the kitchen. "It might be Olivia," he says, picking up the phone from the counter that separates his kitchen from the living room. "She's been trying to reach me since eleven this morning."

"Say, 'No comment' and hang up if it's the press!" I yell at him and rise to my feet. If it is Olivia, I want to hear what he says. Jill, I realize belatedly, must have had someone talk to Olivia this morning to try to catch her in some lies; and she has been attempting to warn Andy. Had Jill gotten an additional statement from her, she would have told me. Obviously, Olivia was shrewd enough to shut her mouth. I hear Andy mumble that he has been advised by counsel to make no statement and watch him put down the phone. He is beginning to appear shaken, and, sitting down again, I read him Yettie's statement.

"We had begun talking about marriage, but I'd been thinking about medical school," he mutters as I finish reading. He is trying to appear relaxed, but his arms are folded tensely across his chest. "Olivia said she was considering selling her business, and there'd be enough money after we were married from that to do a lot of things."

The phone rings again, but I shake my head. "Were you really seriously thinking about getting married to this woman?"

He turns his back on me and picks it up. "I've got to see if it's Olivia."

I watch as the anxiety on his face changes to irritation. He says brusquely, "I have no comment," and hangs up. What is going through his mind? If he is not in on this, it won't take him long to figure out a woman has made a royal fool out of him. But what if they're both innocent? After all, Olivia hasn't even been charged. I'd just as soon blow my money at the dog races in West Memphis as bet on that possibility at the moment.

As if he can make the phone cease to ring by ignoring it, Andy walks back to his chair and sits down. "As you know," he says, answering my question, his voice ironic, "it's not illegal."

No, but murder is, I want to shoot back at him. I struggle to contain my anger at my growing sense that this case is out of control. "For God's sake, Andy," I say urgently, "if you and Olivia decided to end Pam's life, now is the time to tell me. I can make a deal for you with the prosecutor that will keep you from spending the rest of your life in prison. Jill Marymount needs your testimony to charge Olivia.''

Like a child taking a dose of milk of magnesia, Andy squinches his eyes shut in distaste and swallows, his Adam's apple bobbing like a cork. Lawyers are often no more than messengers; yet there is an art to delivering bad news. Too bad I haven't mastered it. Is he wincing at the truth and preparing to accept it, or is he offended by the thought that I can believe him to be guilty of plotting to kill a helpless child? Squinting at me, he says in a choked voice, ''Neither she nor I wanted Pam to die!''

I begin to roll up Yettie Lindsey's statement into a scroll until I realize what I'm doing. ''How can you be so sure about her?'' I ask him as the phone begins to ring again. ''It wasn't too long ago when Olivia admitted to both of us in my conference room that Pam's death was a relief.''

Andy looks over at the phone and lets it ring. ''That's a natural reaction anybody would have,'' he says, but I think I detect a note of uncertainty in his voice. For all I know, however, he may be trying to con me. ''She loved Pam.''

The damn phone. ''People are murdered every day,'' I say loudly as if I can drown it out, ''by family members who love them.''

Andy is oblivious to the ringing now. He shakes his head. ''Not to get their child's money.''

Still thirsty, I stand up and walk back into the kitchen for another glass of water, thinking this motive is not all that rare. ''Maybe it wasn't for the money,'' I call from the sink, not believing myself for a minute. ''Maybe Olivia simply couldn't stand Pam's suffering any longer.''

I look up. Andy has followed me into the kitchen. He says, ''And talked me into electrocuting her. That's what you want me to admit, isn't it?''

''Is that what happened?'' I ask.

''No, it's not,'' Andy says resolutely. ''It was an accident.

If you can't believe that, I don't want you representing me any further.''

I turn off the nozzle. The ice cubes have shrunk to the size of aspirin. What the hell? It's not cold, but it's still wet. I drink anyway, pleased to receive this ultimatum. I'm not so jaded by the system that it doesn't matter whether my client professes to care whether I believe in his innocence. Do I believe in his innocence? I don't know. But now is not the time for a lecture on the lawyer's role, for I can't afford to lose him as a client. I set the glass down on the counter, which doesn't have a crumb on it. Andy may be a murderer, but he's clean. "If you tell me you're not involved," I lie, "I believe you, but you can't expect me to be so certain that Olivia hasn't set you up. I know you can't accept that as a real possibility right now, but it's something I have to keep in mind.''

I watch in amazement as Andy comes over to the counter and takes my glass and puts it in the dishwater. If my watch had emotions, it wouldn't be any more compulsive. "How could she have set this up?'' he asks, either implicitly entertaining the thought or carrying out the role of trying to con me.

I have been wondering this since Jill Marymount told me she was charging Andy. Looking for a cooler spot, I go sit down over a vent at a small table across from the dishwater. "Did she have access to the device''—I will not say "cattle prod''—"that electrocuted Pam?''

From a cupboard under his sink Andy takes a sponge and wipes the counter. "I don't see how she could have without my knowing about it,'' he says, needlessly rinsing out the sponge. "I kept it in my office.''

"Easy,'' I say, feeling with my hands the surface of his table. He keeps it as well polished as my own breakfast table. "She obviously was out there quite a bit at this time. Getting a key duplicated takes about two minutes. It would have been simple for her to slip in and remove most of the insulation from the handle before you shocked Pam.''

For good measure, Andy swipes at a spot on the handle of the cabinet above the counter. The guy is a one-man cleaning service. If he runs out of money (which doesn't seem likely), we can barter our services until he goes to jail. He shakes his head. "What keeps your theory from making sense is that electrocution doesn't automatically result just because the handle isn't well insulated. In order for that to occur, Pam has to make contact with the device at two points of her body."

Andy's face is in profile to me as he continues to work on the cabinet. I can't really see if he understands the implication of what he has said: Olivia needed his help to kill her child. I spell it out for him. "And guess who was holding the device when Pam came into contact with it? The prosecutor is going to argue that you and Olivia were in this together."

Finally, Andy puts down the sponge and faces me. "But if Leon had held on to Pam the way he was supposed to, she never would have been able to grab the handle."

"And Leon testified that he had no idea how hard Pam was going to resist when she was shocked. Jill Marymount will argue you knew how much it was going to hurt Pam, and knew she would fight like an animal to grab the shock stick to keep it away from her. He had no idea how strongly she would react, and you did."

Andy's expression grows sullen. "I told Leon it would really hurt her and make her try to pull away. He just let her go."

I look down at the table and see the outline of my own glum reflection. I seriously doubt that. Pam was a big kid, and though she couldn't have been too terribly strong, all that mass when the electricity began to flow through her would be hard to hold down unless you knew what to expect. Leon isn't likely to want to take the rap for a child dying. We can't expect him to admit it was his fault. "I doubt if he's going to say that, Andy, given his testimony at the probable cause hearing."

Andy sighs. He knows we have an uphill battle. He bends down and places the sponge underneath the sink. Neatness counts, but I'm afraid it won't keep him out of prison. I turn the talk to our more immediate problem: the bond hearing tomorrow. As I discuss the likelihood of the judge's requiring a significantly higher bond, there is a knock at the door. Maybe it is one of the blondes in her bikini wanting to borrow a cup of sugar, but somehow I doubt it. "You don't make any comment, okay?"

He nods, and I open the door to face a television camera. Ah, the media. My client is innocent! What else do defense attorneys know how to say?

16

"YOU LOOKED SHELLSHOCKED this afternoon." Rainey giggles sympathetically into my ear on the telephone. "You see these attorneys who smile into the camera as if their clients were announcing to run for President instead of having been charged with murder, but your teeth were clenched so tight I could barely understand you."

Standing in the doorway of my kitchen as the ten o'clock news on Channel 4 ends, I hear the bathroom door shut, signaling the beginning of my daughter's shower. "Sarah told me I looked like a ventriloquist whose dummy just died," I admit. After half a six-pack I can laugh at my performance—a little. "Do you think Andy's guilty?" I ask plaintively.

There is a short but pregnant pause. On the TV is a commercial for a douche. Damn. The way things are going on TV it won't be long before they show a woman using it. "Are you asking me?" Rainey asks, her voice almost high enough to shatter glass. "I have no idea. People will do anything for money."

"That's for sure." I nod, staring at the model's face. She is so gorgeous I almost forget what the ad is all about. I wonder what she got paid. "Are you watching Channel 4?"

"Isn't she a knockout?" Rainey says. I imagine her feet tucked under her on her couch, the way I have seen her dozens of times.

"Would you still think so," I ask, "if she said, 'I usually stink like hell, but this stuff works even on my worst days!'?

216

I mean, sometimes there are situations when it's hard to open your mouth. I guess it's no secret that I wasn't prepared for Andy to be charged with murder. It's hard to be objective.''

Rainey laughs, used to my nonsense. ''You're his lawyer. You're not supposed to be.''

I carry the phone, whose cord could practically extend around the outside of the house, into the living room and bend down to turn off the TV. It's been a long day. ''Of course I am,'' I protest, ''but my clients are always duping me.''

Whimsical as ever, Rainey sings to a tune from my youth, '' 'Dupe! . . . Dupe! . . . Dupe of Earl'. . . . So you really think he's been lying to you? He's such a nice guy.''

''The 'Duke of Earl,' '' I say, surprised she's old enough to remember. What in the hell was that song all about? I like the Dupe of Earl better, too. ''Obviously, they think the mother is in on it, but they don't have . . .'' The phone beeps, indicating a call is waiting. I hate being interrupted, but Sarah pleaded and agreed to pay the extra amount from her job. Naturally, I haven't collected since the first month. ''Just a second, okay?'' I tell Rainey and push the button. ''Hello?''

''Gideon,'' a female voice gushes, ''you were just wonderful on TV tonight!''

I rack my brain and then realize, God forbid, it is my rat-burner divorce client, Mona Moneyhart. It seems as if she has tried to call me almost every day since she was in the office the first time, but this is the first call at home. ''Mona,'' I say, my teeth on edge, ''do you realize how late it is?''

''You weren't asleep, were you?'' she coos. ''I just had to tell you how proud I was when I saw you tonight. My son asked if you had false teeth and were ashamed of them, but I told him you talk like that when you're trying to be firm with me.'' She giggles at the very idea.

I open my mouth as wide as I can and still speak: ''I . . . am . . . on . . . another . . . line . . . I . . . have . . . to . . . hang . . . up . . . now. . . .''

"That's okay," she says cheerfully. "I'll talk to you tomorrow."

I click Rainey back in. Why can't I just tell her that if she calls me again I'll put out a contract on her? Julia, no easy customer herself, now screens my calls, but Mona has become a woman of a thousand voices and usually manages to get through. "That was a client," I tell Rainey.

"At ten-thirty at night?" she says. "Sure."

I sigh. I wouldn't believe it either.

In bed that night I toss and turn and it dawns on me how little I have really thought about what happened in Andy's case. At the Public Defender's, we assumed that over 95 percent of our clients were guilty, and invariably they were. The job consisted of seeing how much off the maximum sentence we could get for them, usually in a plea bargain. From the beginning, I have assumed Andy was guilty of professional negligence—but deliberate murder? Not in my wildest dreams. My brain shut down after that. If I'm going to survive in private practice, I won't be able to afford the luxury of my assumptions. What have I done wrong here? I saw a nice guy in trouble, one who, I thought, reminds me a little of myself, in that he had fallen in love with a woman outside his race. Is that even true, or is that part of the plot, as well? Part of my problem, I realize belatedly, is perhaps my own latent racism in this case. Andy is a nice black man. Well dressed, well spoken, he has been especially easy to like. How could a guy (especially a black one this sharp, my racist mind runs) be part of something so evil? I never let myself entertain the thought for five minutes. Yet the possibility has been there all along, and I have ignored it. Actually, it is not that I mind defending someone who is guilty (I accepted the game at the PD's of figuring out what was the lie and what was the truth of my client's story); what do I mind? (a), being taken for a fool, or (b), acting like a fool? Probably (a), but to be charitable to myself, I'll choose (b). Well, no more Mr. Nice Guy. I yawn, finally sleepy, knowing I've been sleepwalking through this case. And yet Andy, as I've thought all along, may be not guilty of anything more than bad judgment. Tomorrow, I think, my head finally still on the pillow, I'll get to work.

"Dad," calls Sarah, who has been back from Camp Anytown for two weeks, "there's someone to see you."

I put down my coffee and the section of the *Arkansas Democrat-Gazette* with a front-page article about Andy and hurry into the living room. Surely not even a reporter would come to the house this time of day. Woogie's furious barking at seven-thirty in the morning is particularly obnoxious. "Hush," I holler at him as I come around the corner and see Mona Moneyhart standing inside the screen.

"I just brought you and your daughter some fresh blueberry muffins for your breakfast," she says, handing Sarah a plastic bowl with a paper towel over it. "Your dad's my lawyer in my divorce," she says smiling sweetly at Sarah, "and after I saw him on TV last night I was so proud of him I just had to get up early and whip these up."

My eyes begin to tear as I smell the warm, slightly acidic odor of ripe blueberries hidden in the plastic. I think I'm going to throw up. Mona is dressed in almost nothing. In red running shorts cut high on the sides and a gray threadbare T-shirt labeled, as I feared, "Let Being Be!" she is braless and apparently pantyless as well. My stomach flips as I think of her oven. I feel sweat popping out on my forehead. I expect to see a rat's tail dangling over the side of the bright blue bowl. When I do nothing except swallow, Sarah, who looks a little stunned herself, says brightly, "How nice of you to do this! They smell delicious."

My mouth thick with the saliva that accompanies nausea, I finally manage weakly, "Sarah, this is Mrs. Moneyhart."

My client beams as if she has been introduced to a member of the royal family. She offers Sarah her free hand. "Do you want to be a famous lawyer like your dad?"

Sarah, realizing fast that Mona may not be a candidate for the world's most well-adjusted person, extricates her hand after it has been given a vigorous pump, and says dryly, "One's enough in the family. Dad, we've got to hurry."

Turning to leave at last, Mona gives me a wink. "Jealous of her daddy's time. I don't blame her one bit."

Sarah looks at me as if I have invited a whore over for breakfast, but Mona, either happily oblivious or unconcerned, is bouncing out the door, her small breasts rolling around underneath the skimpy material covering her chest. "Gideon, I'll call you later."

After she is gone, Sarah begins to take a muffin. "God, she was weird! You're beginning to drool!"

Swallowing hard, I snatch the muffins from her, shaking my head. "You can't eat these!"

Sarah herself is dressed for her second day of her senior year in a well-worn pair of Levi's and a University of New Mexico T-shirt. (She contends, with logic on her side but little else, that students should be allowed to wear shorts if they are made to start school in August.) She stares at the offending muffins in my hand. "Why? They look okay."

Holding the bowl at arm's length as if it were a container of nuclear waste, I carry it into the kitchen and force six muffins down the garbage disposal. I sit at the kitchen table and tell Sarah about the rat roast in my client's oven. Sarah, who has inherited a low vomit threshold from me, places her hand over her mouth. Her eyes begin to tear, and she pushes away the bowl of Froot Loops she has poured for herself. "Poor Daddy," she says between her fingers. "Are all your clients this bad?"

I look out the window, halfway expecting to see Mona turning cartwheels in the yard. "People wouldn't need lawyers if they didn't have problems."

Sarah carries her bowl to the sink and rinses it out. "Please swear to me she's not a new girlfriend!" she says.

"Thanks a lot," I say archly, bending down to scratch Woogie, who also seems in need of reassurance. "I don't date my clients." That's crap, of course. I probably would if I liked one enough.

"What's wrong with us?" Sarah asks dramatically over the dishwasher. "Our love lives are the pits!"

I try not to smile. Sarah has gone perhaps only two weeks straight without a date since the dam broke over a year ago when she had her first boyfriend. At least she's not dating anybody steady. That's when I get nervous. I watch Woogie lick where his testicles used to be. Maybe that's my solution. "Nobody wants you when you're old and gray."

Sarah nods in agreement as she puts the bowl in the rack to dry. "These little sophomore girls think they're so cute. They act like they've never seen boys before."

I think of all the lawyers in Blackwell County. We seem to breed faster than rabbits. "Competition is an overrated virtue in this country," I say, glad that Sarah's mind is back on her own business, and not mine. She was genuinely distressed when I showed her the paper earlier. I suppose I have talked more to Sarah about Andy than I have intended. I look down at the *Democrat-Gazette*. The headline looks like reading material for the blind: PSYCHOLOGIST AT STATE CENTER CHARGED WITH CAPITAL MURDER. Only the media love trouble more than the legal profession. Suddenly depressed, I stare unseeing out the window into my backyard. Maybe Andy thought of it as a mercy killing.

"I hope Dr. Chapman's not guilty of murder," Sarah says, coming over to hug me. "I know you like him."

Absently, I pat my daughter's back. How can I like somebody who has murdered a child?

Later, in my office after Andy's bond hearing, I have occasion to ponder his defense. Dan, sprawled over two chairs across from me, growls, "You should have brought the muffins to work. I wouldn't have sued you if I had gotten sick."

Andy's bond has risen from five thousand dollars to one hundred thousand dollars, but he arranged for a ten-thousand-dollar certified check as if he were a billionaire donating to his favorite tax write-off. I think back to the first bond hearing only a few weeks ago. "It's odd, isn't it?" I muse, now able to nurse a cup of coffee without my stomach heaving,

"Bruton, who almost held me in contempt, accepted a bond worth peanuts, and Judge Tarnower, who has the best reputation in the county, almost went through the roof when I tried to argue that Andy's bond should stay at five thousand."

"Jesus, Gideon," Dan wheezes, "your guy's probably a child murderer. She could have gone a lot higher. I think she's got the hots for you. You should have seen the way she stared at you when you sat down."

It's hard not to laugh at Dan. He thinks that if a woman even blinks twice at a man she wants to go to bed with him. "She was pissed," I say, but the truth is I'm still delighted with our luck of the draw. I wouldn't have kept on going so long about the bond if I didn't think there was some chance I could push some guilt buttons. Before she took the bench, Harriet Tarnower had the reputation, rare among our judges, as a liberal in Arkansas politics. At least she'll give Andy a fair trial if she doesn't bend over too far the other way, thinking she has to prove something.

The phone rings, and fearing it is my rat burner, I hand the phone to Dan. "If it's Mona Moneyhart," I say, my hand over the mouthpiece, "tell her I'm at St. Thomas having my stomach pumped."

He snickers, but says in a surprisingly professional tone, "This is Dan Bailey." A moment later, Dan's eyes widen in anticipation. He hands me the phone, saying, "Olivia Le Master."

I wait for Dan to get up and leave, but he is all ears. What the hell. He knows everything anyway. I push down the button on the speaker phone to allow him to hear. "Olivia, this is Gideon."

"I just want you to know," she says in a firm voice, "that despite everything, Pam's death really was an accident. You have to believe that."

I put my finger to my lips as Dan rolls his eyes. "There's a lot you didn't tell me."

"We didn't think you needed to know," Olivia says, her

voice sounding hollow and unconvincing through the speaker.

"Obviously," Dan mouths, shaking his head. Suddenly, I realize that if Olivia were suddenly to implicate Andy, Dan would be a witness and could testify. How stupid can I be? Of course he would never do that. Still, I am made nervous by his presence and say, "Olivia, why don't you come to my office this afternoon? We need to talk face to face."

Dan, leaning forward on his haunches, is on the edge of his two seats. "Do you want to represent me?" she asks. "Obviously, I'm a suspect."

If I did, I might get the truth out of her. Dan nods vigorously, but I reply, "I'm sorry, Olivia. There's a potential conflict of interest between you and Andy. I suggest you get your own attorney." Dan jabs his finger repeatedly against his stiff shirt, which contains so much starch I can hear it. I shake my head. He knows too much about Andy already.

"Oh," she says after a long silence. "Well, let me call you back about this afternoon."

"Fine," I say and hang up.

Dan is about to have a fit. Rocking backward, his shirttail coming out of his pants, he reminds me of our days together in the Public Defender's Office when he was a skinny slob instead of a fat one. "First you don't bring the muffins; now, you knock me out of a great referral. What kind of friend are you?"

I begin to make notes of my conversation with Olivia on a yellow legal pad. "If she's set Andy up," I say, "we wouldn't be friends long."

Dan, reverting to an old habit, wipes his face with the bottom of his shirt, a button-down pink pinpoint Oxford. "So your guy's guilty as hell, huh?"

I laugh, continuing to write. Dan is shrewder than he looks. "He swears he's not," I say. Since early this morning an idea has been cooking in my brain. "You know any lawyers in Benton who would check out Leon Robinson for me? I remember he testified at the probable cause hearing that's where he's from.''

"The aide who let the girl go?" Dan asks, a puzzled look peeping through the fat around his eyes. "You think Olivia paid him to let go of her daughter?"

I shrug, throwing down my pen. It isn't much of a conversation. "I've got to start somewhere, don't I? The trial's less than four weeks away.'' I did not ask for more time at the bond hearing, thinking the longer Jill Marymount has to poke around in this case the worse it will be.

Lost in thought, Dan, exposing his throat, looks at my ceiling. If he ever needs an emergency tracheotomy, somebody better have a whale knife. Finally, he says, "Let me work on this for a little bit. I went to school with a couple of guys who ended up in Saline County. Maybe Leon was promised some money instead of your client.''

The phone rings again. This time I don't hand it to Dan, who seems permanently encamped in my office. It is Andy.

"I've just been fired," he says, his voice discouraged. He had been told to report to David Spath's office as soon as the hearing was over.

"I guess we shouldn't be surprised," I say, drawing an imaginary knife across my neck for Dan's benefit. Actually, I suspect if he wasn't black, Andy would have been fired after he was charged with manslaughter. David Spath could only do so much for him. "Are you going to be able to make it to the trial?''

His voice a whisper, Andy says, "I've got all my vacation pay coming.''

"Good," I say, shaking my head in wonder at my client's seemingly inexhaustible supply of money. I couldn't ask for any more if I were representing a cocaine dealer. Yet Jill has surely already checked to see if Olivia has transferred money to Andy. "I'll call the psychology board and tell them you're voluntarily giving up your license until this is resolved. I don't want them investigating this too, right now.''

"Whatever you think's best," Andy says, knowing the noose is being tightened.

"I think we need to do that. There's no sense picking another fight right now." We had had an informal deal with the board that it would not act against Andy until after the original criminal charge was disposed of, since David Spath had assured them that Andy would be permitted no professional contact with the residents at the Blackwell County HDC until after the trial. Now, with a charge of murder, we can't very well expect the board to act as if nothing has changed. We arrange a time for him to come in tomorrow after I tell him about Olivia's call. "She sounded supportive," I say, trying to cheer him up. Olivia had not come to Andy's bond hearing, although I couldn't honestly blame her. Talk about a media circus! With a case promising the revelation of secrets involving interracial sex, big bucks, and murder, what else can I expect? Kim Keogh had been there, her beautiful eyes silently accusing me of the worst sin a man can commit: I have never called her back. She had tried to be tough in her questions, but she is fundamentally too nice to be a good reporter, even for local TV, which doesn't expect much except a nice hairdo. My conversation with Andy fizzles out. Being fired takes the wind out of whatever sails you have left.

As soon as I put the phone down, it rings again. Finally, Dan pushes up from his chairs to leave.

"Gideon," Mona Moneyhart says, her voice brimming with disapproval, "I had to pretend I was a reporter for *People* magazine in order to get through today."

I motion for Dan to sit down again and push the speaker button so he can hear. If I have to listen to her, he should too. "Mona, I really don't think it's a good idea for you to come over to the house." Grinning happily, Dan collapses back into my chairs, a cheek on each one.

"Didn't you and your daughter like the muffins? I made them from scratch."

Dan whispers, running his fingers across my desk. "I bet

she did.'' Even now, my eyes begin to tear as I imagine the ingredients.

''They were delicious,'' I say weakly.

''Gideon, your little daughter is just precious! But you're gonna have to watch her like a hawk. Girls her age are hideously promiscuous. It's just so obvious she needs a mother. Why haven't you remarried? That's the least you can do for her. Don't you think she deserves a mother?''

His hand over his mouth, Dan begins to laugh uncontrollably, making a sound like a lawnmower motor trying unsuccessfully to start. ''Uh, uh, uh . . . uh.''

''What do you want?'' I ask. I watch Dan's red face as he begins to choke. I hope he dies.

''There's no way I can live on two hundred dollars a week child support. I just can't do it.''

Dan pulls out a handkerchief and mops his face. He has begun to make little hooting sounds.

''We've had this same conversation three times. He's paying more temporary support than the child-support chart requires him to. His lawyer thinks he's a fool.''

''He is a fool!'' she begins to cry. ''What are those horrible sounds you're making?''

I point to the door and Dan staggers out, his whole body shaking. ''Talk about fools,'' he mouths as he goes out.

17

THE SOUND OF clicking billiard balls is the first thing I hear when I enter the Bull Run, which is only ten miles from the Blackwell County Human Development Center. The Bull Run is apparently one enormous room, with enough floor space to work on a 747. To my left, all in use, are six tables surrounded by almost as many women as men, which tells me I haven't been in one of these places in years. Most everyone, fat or thin, is dressed in denim, shod in cowboy boots, and hatted in Stetsons or baseball caps. Directly in front of me is a large dance floor (the two-step and Cotton-eyed Joe obviously require more space than the postage-stamp-sized dance floors of the clubs I've frequented over the years) and a vacant deejay booth with so much hardware that it looks like Mission Control in Houston. In front of the pool tables are over a score of mostly empty Formica-topped tables, each with a full complement of canvas-backed chairs. It is still a half hour before nine, so the dancing, which is advertised in foot-high red script over the Bull Run front door as "The Best Country in Central Arkansas" has not yet commenced. To my right a brunette with a head of hair almost down to her tiny waist is bending over a shuffleboard table as she lines up a shot. The thumb and forefinger of her right hand encircle a blue-and-silver puck. She runs the disk back and forth over the smooth blond wood, which has been made slippery by sawdust, and then it flies from her hand, hitting nothing in the process and dropping off the end of the surface into the trough that rings the wood. "She-it!" she exclaims to her opponent, an older guy who could have posed (with a little work on his gut) as the Marlboro Man in the old TV commercial.

As I head for the bar, the jukebox by the shuffleboard table begins an old favorite from my brief country music period: "D-I-V-O-R-C-E" by Tammy Wynette. Even her fast songs (and this isn't one of them) seem to me slow and sad. A small plane could take off and land from the bar, and so, to avoid standing out in this still sparse crowd of about six drinkers, I plant myself on a red-cushioned stool toward the end nearer the entrance. Since it is a Saturday night, I would have figured on a bigger crowd, but there is still a little light outside, and I assume the real partying doesn't begin until dark. Waiting for the barmaid (she has some ground to cover in this place), I am impressed by the selection of alcohol. Besides what I'd expect in the way of whiskey and bourbon, within my sight there is gin, rum, vodka, wine, and even two liqueurs—coffee and chocolate almond. Damn. Am I still in the South? But on the wall above the beer nozzles I spy a Confederate flag, and I know I'm in the right place.

The Bull Run, among other stories I've heard about it in the last twenty-four hours, has been rumored to be the de facto headquarters of a white-supremacist group known as the Trackers. It also is supposed to be Leon Robinson's favorite watering hole. Remembering Yettie Lindsey's remark to me about blacks, I decide Arkansas is a small place for whites as well. With only five days until the jury is impaneled my hopes of somehow implicating Leon Robinson in Pam Le Master's death have come to nothing. There is no evidence that Leon has lied about his involvement, nothing to dispute his story that Pam simply jerked out of his grasp when she was shocked. Finally, Eben Crawford, who was a classmate of Dan's in law school, phoned me yesterday and said that he has found out in bits and pieces that Leon is divorced, has no police record, is an avid turkey hunter, and likes to chase women at the Bull Run. We may not know much, but, by God, we know our neighbors' business in the

South. This would have been a snap if I had hired an investigator, but I didn't even bring the subject up with Andy. If he knew what I was up to, he would fire me.

I order a Pabst Blue Ribbon from the barmaid, who gives me a friendly smile. Hell, if she isn't one of the more attractive-looking women I've seen in a while! As far as rough places go, according to Eben, the Blue Run's reputation is only middling, but there is already enough smoke in here to choke a horse, and the faces of women who tend bar don't usually look this classy after a certain age. She has silky, soft blond hair and the kind of high cheekbones I've seen in magazines advertising expensive perfume.

"You're new, aren't you?" the barmaid asks, sizing me up. She is about thirty, I would guess, and is wearing a T-shirt that says "Lobotomy Beer," which is tucked neatly into skin-tight jeans.

I'm a breath away from asking the brainless question of what's a nice girl like you doing in a place like this, but manage instead, "You have on my daughter's T-shirt."

In the background, Tammy wails, " 'Me and little J-O-E will be goin' away. . . . ' " I wouldn't mind a little trip with this woman. Her hands on her hips, she looks down at the front of her shirt, which swells out nicely. "I'll be danged if I don't," she drawls, grinning at me and showing a dimple in her left cheek. "Tell her I'm sorry."

I let some of the Pabst slip down. Cold with a nice sour bite. Until this moment, I have forgotten I used to like it. Right now I wish I wasn't supposed to be figuring out how to make Leon look like the worst racist this side of Mississippi. I try not to stare at the woman, but I suspect she is used to it. With no admissible evidence to back it up, my plan has been reduced to suggesting to the jury that Leon hates blacks so much that he deliberately let go of Pam so she would attack Andy. My thinking is that if I can get a couple of blacks on the jury, at least one of them might hold out if I can obtain some evidence on this point. Is this cynical on my part? Without a doubt. I decide I'd better act before she gets too busy. "She'll be relieved," I say finally, "it's in good hands."

The woman rolls her eyes as if this bullshit is about par for the course, but she doesn't move away. "I bet she will," she says dryly. This woman has surely heard a lot of crap, but, like the smoke, it comes with the territory.

I put my mug down on a Coors pad. "Actually, I'm looking for Charlene Newman. She ever come in here?" This morning at the Saline County Chancery clerk's office, my plan appeared to come to a screeching halt. Leon's ex-wife, who I hoped would be willing to talk about Leon's racial attitudes, has resumed using her maiden name and apparently left no forwarding address after the divorce was final.

Placing both hands on the bar (no ring I notice), Blondie raises her eyebrows in mock disapproval and confides, "You can do better than Charlene."

Fighting the urge to smile at my good luck, I feign embarrassment. "My cousin went to high school with her," I mutter and duck my head. "He said now that I'm divorced I ought to look her up."

Blondie shrugs and turns to the other barmaid a few feet away, who is drying glasses and putting them on a shelf behind her. "Hey, Betty, where'd Charlene go after she and Leon split?" Blondie calls to her.

The much older woman, whose hair is a peroxide platinum, picks up a burning cigarette from the corner of the bar and puffs on it as she contemplates. Her strong face, wrinkled by smoking and age, has an indestructible quality to it, as if nothing in the last forty years has come as a surprise. "I heard Hot Springs," she says, exhaling, her voice a throaty contralto. "Who wants to know?"

I remain motionless, since I don't want to attract attention to myself, but I'd like to leap across the bar and kiss her. Blondie nods at me with her chin.

I gulp my beer, ready to leave. I'd just as soon Leon not hear too much about this conversation if I can help it. Betty, who is wearing a pair of starched jeans and a man's long-sleeved blue work shirt, cocks her hip at me. "Shit, he can do better than Charlene."

I lean across the bar. This woman reminds me of women I occasionally picked up in bars after Rosa died. Big in the chest, brassy, horny. "You don't sound like," I say, unable to resist opening my mouth, "Charlene's best friend."

Folding her arms across her breasts, Betty, friendly until now, gives me a hard stare, as if whatever signals she was putting out have suddenly been switched off. "Charlene's okay," she says, her voice now scratchy and defensive. "You old guys are something, you know it?"

Old? Thanks a lot. I turn to Blondie, but her eyes have turned cold, too. What is going on here? One minute we were getting along great, and the next I have become their worst nightmare. I turn and stare directly into the eyes of Leon Robinson.

"What are you doin' here?" he says. It is not really so much a question as a demand. Leon is an inch or two shorter than I am, perhaps ten pounds lighter, but fifteen years younger. He is wearing a red Razorback cap jammed down over his eyes that proclaims "Woo Pig, Sooie!"

For some reason I look down at his cowboy boots, I suppose, hoping the toes aren't reinforced by steel. I may not be on my feet much longer. Cover your balls, I think. Even if by some miracle I can take out Leon, I suspect he has a few friends here, and I don't see any of mine. Discretion, every lawyer learns in his career, is sometimes the better part of valor. The odds of the women covering for me (assuming he hasn't already overheard them) are abysmal, but if I want to be a good liar, I have to take a few risks in life. "I was just visiting a friend in Benton and stopped by on my way home. Can I buy you a beer? I'd like to talk to you about the case you testified in almost two months ago," I say, hoping I'm coming across like a friendly aluminum-siding salesman who is having more luck today than he can stand. I can feel a river of sweat pouring down my sides under my arms. The Bull Run must have air-conditioning problems, too.

Leon runs his right thumb past his nose, a gesture whose significance I can't interpret. He puts his hands on his hips and makes a snorting sound as if he has caught the odor of fresh road kill. "Randi, this is the son of a bitch who's defending that nigger that killed Pam." Although there was not much noise at the bar before, I can now hear all the way across the dance floor the sound of a cue ball kissing a break. No more Tammy either. She and Little J-O-E have slipped out the back door.

I should throw a punch now (I'd like to salvage some honor if I can), but my fear that every male in here will kick me in the face is still too strong. I glance around me. The bar, which seemed fairly empty when I sat down, has attracted a nice crowd, or maybe it is that everyone just seems a little closer to me. Ever since I've been an adult I have owned only one weapon, and it's suddenly stuck against the roof of my mouth. Which is Randi? The real blonde, I bet.

Blondie reaches across the bar and touches Leon's bare arm. "Take him outside, Leon," she whispers. "They'll try to shut us down if there's another fight in here."

In no hurry now to leave, I pick up my mug and tilt it back as far as I can to get the last of the beer. "What's your problem with blacks, Leon?"

Leon gives me a snotty grin and turns and crooks his finger at a man at the door. Either he wasn't there when I came in or I was temporarily blind. By his size, I judge he can have only two possible occupations—a nose guard for the Cowboys or a bouncer.

Accepting the fact that my question will likely go unanswered for the moment, I try to remember precisely where I parked the Blazer and stride to the door with Leon and several others close behind me. Something just tells me that Leon may not be my only opponent. Don't run, you chickenshit, I think, and manage to saunter past the doorman, who, as I pass by, helpfully takes my arm and shoves me through the door into the sweltering September night. If I can make it to the car quickly enough, maybe they will let

me leave. In the few minutes I was in the bar, it has grown
dark. The lights in the asphalt parking lot behind the Bull
Run will win no security awards this year, but I have plenty
of company as I head for the Blazer. I estimate seven men
have come outside. As I stick my right hand into my pocket
for my keys, Leon clouts me with a right to my jaw, sending
me careening on top of the Blazer. Unable to free my hand,
I roll off onto the pavement on the other side. For a moment
I think of running. What prevents me is the fear that they
have guns in their vehicles and I will be run down and shot.
The others are fanning out around me, so there is no escape.
If I had only Leon to fight, it might not be too bad. Furious
at letting myself get poleaxed without being in a position to
defend myself, I come around the car and pop him directly
in the nose as he lunges for me. I couldn't hit him that square
in the face if I fought him another ten years.

For perhaps three seconds Leon stops and feels his nose
as if this wasn't supposed to happen. I hope I have broken
it.

Behind me, a hoarse voice commands, "Get the son of a
bitch, Leon!"

I should plow into him, but I am hoping he won't have the
sense to realize how lucky my punch was. If he quits now,
we'll be even, like two small countries who have fired one
missile each, and are thinking of declaring victory and announcing the end of the war. My hands are raised in the
classic fighter pose, my right guarding my aching jaw, my
left forward. Every boy pretends at one time to be a prizefighter, but in my case it is strictly for show. At various times
Sarah and I have pretended to box. Even with my own daughter I have difficulty warding off blows before we collapse
against each other laughing at the silliness of what we are
doing. It is too dark to see Leon's eyes, but I think he is
afraid.

Another voice is more insistent. "Get the fucker!" It is
shrill, and I wonder if it is that of a woman, but I don't dare
take my eyes from Leon to search for the speaker. Leon's

hands are up in front of his face, but he looks as awkward and silly as I do. A coward, now, I'm convinced, he will be sure to attack if he thinks I'm not looking. The old saying pops into my head: "One's afraid to fight, and the other is glad of it."

Probably fearful of what will happen if he doesn't, Leon comes for me, swinging furiously. As with Sarah, I block most of his wild blows, but a couple slip in, including a crisp chop on my right ear. In this kamikaze assault, I panic, forgetting to swing at him. Instinctively, I try to wrestle him to the asphalt, hoping my weight and advantage will help me. Caught off guard (he is no more a fighter than I am), Leon trips and I fall on top of him driving my elbow into his stomach as we go down. His head hits the parking lot with a sickening pop, and for a flash of an instant, I think I have knocked him out, but the asshole immediately tries to bite me while I pin his arms in the classic grade-school style. My last coherent thought before the others get to me is that I won.

Only when I am kicked in the balls and kidneys do I scream for help, thinking in a moment of extreme panic that I am being killed. The noise is frightening. One man is crying, "Kill the dumb shit!" and there is yelling and snarling sounds that verge on the inhuman. After three blows to my mouth with somebody's fist, a front tooth flies out across my face, and I wonder if I will lose consciousness but don't. A beating takes energy, and apparently it is too hot for my attackers to really enjoy it, for after a couple of minutes (though it seems much longer), they suddenly stop.

Someone says, "Let's get the shit out of here!"

Leon bends down and whispers, "Don't you ever come back here, you motherfuckin' bastard! You hear me?"

I raise a hand to signal that I do, and lie panting in the dim light, feeling my entire body begin to radiate pain. I wait until I hear cars pulling out of the lot, and stagger to my feet, dazed, but deeply grateful I am alive.

I lean back against the Blazer and fish out my keys. I can

hear the band, which has begun to play. I don't recognize the tune, but I don't think I'll go back inside to find out. The front of my light blue short-sleeved shirt is dark with blood, and I realize I must look like hell. Sarah has a friend spending the night, so I can't go home looking like this. Poor Rainey, I think, as I drive away from the Bull Run. I need a nurse, not a social worker, but what are friends for?

"Good God, what happened?" Rainey cries as she opens her screen door. The expression on her face is alarming. Is one of my eyes hanging out? My entire face feels swollen. In the thirty-minute ride to her house I have convinced myself that I have no broken bones, though my ribs on my right side feel as if someone had been trying to separate them with a pitchfork. At least I haven't wakened her. It is still before ten, and she is dressed in her usual summer weekend attire: shorts and a T-shirt.

Gingerly, I let myself in, and close the door behind me. "You're a sight for sore eyes," I say, pleased I can still speak. The power of speech is about all I have left. "Believe it or not, I was winning a fight against Leon Robinson, when his friends decided I was too tough."

Rainey, seeing I am not in too much pain to brag, yells, "Have you gone crazy? You're a grown man, for God's sake! Follow me into the bathroom!"

What does being a grown man have to do with anything? I think as I make my way through her living room. Grown men do a lot worse to each other than this. Yet for the first time in an hour I begin to relax, knowing Rainey will take care of me. Walking behind her, I notice how nice she looks in blue short shorts. Super legs to go with such a trim ass. Wonderful! The last thought I will have before I bleed to death will be about sex.

She snaps on the light in her bedroom. "Take off your shirt!" she commands, opening her medicine cabinet. "It's about to make me sick to my stomach."

I look in the mirror and wince. The assholes. My face

looks like mincemeat. At one point it was rubbed into the blacktop of the parking lot, not a beauty tip I would recommend. Little black pieces of tar and dirt make my grimy cheeks look like a coal miner's. Rainey says, "I'll get some ice for your eye—stay right here!"

Not quite feeling up to a trip, I sit down on the seat of her commode and get out of my shirt and T-shirt. Both are soaked with blood. Even my right hand aches from the one punch I threw. A lover, not a fighter, I think, looking around Rainey's bathroom. Unlike mine, it is sparkling clean. I inspect the sink—not even a single hair. Even the soap dish in the shower gleams. Each week Sarah and I take turns cleaning the bathroom, but this weekend it will be all I can do to keep my head from rolling off into the commode because even my neck aches. The body has only so much room for seven people to beat.

Rainey, it develops, isn't the gentle nurse of my dreams. "Ouch!" I mutter more than once when she washes my face. The washrag is nice and warm, but it feels as if she has decided my chin is a silver tray that needs polishing.

"Hold still!" she orders, her left hand on the back of my head, presumably so she can dig in better. "I have to do this or it'll get infected. Is this tar or what?"

"They kind of rubbed my face around on the parking lot," I admit, trying to hold my head still. I'm beginning to think she is enjoying this. "I feel like you're mashing a hunk of Monterey Jack through a cheese grater. You're not exactly Florence Nightingale at this, you know."

She pushes the rag harder against my burning face. "Why don't you get up and go on to the emergency room? They probably have a room now just for you. Oh, for God's sake, Gideon, they've knocked out a tooth!"

I nod miserably, running my tongue to the vacant spot and tasting congealed blood. "What am I going to tell Sarah? She's got a friend spending the night with her. I'll scare them to death."

Rainey bobs her head in agreement as she throws the

washrag into the sink and picks up the bag of ice from the porcelain ledge and hands it to me. "Now, hold this against your eye while I dab on some hydrogen peroxide," she says opening a cabinet drawer under the sink. "Tell her the truth: that you're an idiot posing as a normal human being. She'll forgive you. We always do."

As she rubs my face with a square cotton pad soaked with the medication, I feel my flesh is being barbecued. If smoke begins to rise from my face, I won't be surprised. I close my eyes. Poor Rainey. She deserves better. So far this friendship business has been a one-way street. Besides looking like a lawyer from hell, I stink from sweat, tar, smoke, and alcohol, but she hasn't even wrinkled her nose. "I'm sorry I keep showing up," I say, as she moves the cotton around my face, "when I'm in trouble."

Sure I am. Rainey doesn't even bother to protest this lie. Finished, she screws the cap down onto the jar containing the medicine. "Why on earth were you fighting Leon Robinson?" she asks, her green eyes flashing at me. "Isn't he the aide who was holding Pam?"

I nod and stand up to look into the mirror. It's not a pretty sight. My right eye, now purplish in color, is almost shut; parts of my face now resemble raw hamburger; my neck is abraded; and, of course, a tooth is gone. What do I tell her? She hates lawyer games. Though I have told Rainey much about this case, I have avoided mentioning my idea to argue to the jury that Leon let go of Pam because he hates blacks and he wanted her to attack Andy. Why? Because I know, like Andy, she will object. "It's a long story," I say wearily. For the first time since I've known her, I notice strands of gray among the red hair that has always attracted me. She is still pretty at the age of forty-one, but her face, especially under the eyes, has lines that were not there when I met her. I am aging this woman. What can she possibly see in me, even as a friend? I sigh, looking at my own torso in the mirror. Rainey, I realize, has never even seen me shirtless, and suddenly I am embarrassed by the roll of fat around my middle and the white patch of hair sprouting from my chest, an appetizing picture when my mutilated face is thrown into the bargain. "I'll tell you if you'll let me use your bathroom to take a shower."

Without a word she opens a cabinet and hands me a clean blue towel. "Don't wash your face again," she commands as she closes the door behind her, "or I'll have to put the hydrogen peroxide back on you." Is there a hint of malice in her voice, or am I just imagining it?

When I emerge ten minutes later, I am feeling one hundred percent better. While I was in the shower behind the curtain, she opened the door and left a man's V-necked T-shirt on the counter for me. Where did she get this? It's none of my business, but because it looks old, I can resist asking—not that I would get an answer. When I heard the door opening, for an instant I had thought she might get in the shower with me. Wishful thinking, as usual. Instead of about sex, she's probably thinking that it would be nice if somehow I could get a job in another state. She is waiting for me in her living room, curled up with her feet drawn up under her in her favorite chair across from the couch where in our courting days we necked like teenagers. An opened Miller Lite is sitting on the table by the couch. Underneath it is a napkin. I sit down, thinking what she would do for me if I were good to her.

"I thought you could use a beer," Rainey says, staring at the T-shirt. It is a little large, but I'm not in a position to complain.

"Thanks," I say, sincerely. My face feels as if it is glowing. "I'm not quite ready to go home and face my daughter yet."

Rainey barely lifts a shoulder in reply. I know she thinks I worry too much about Sarah. She will be fine, Rainey has said, if I don't smother her. Obviously, I'm the one who needs looking after. It isn't Sarah who is dragging in with a black eye and a tooth knocked out. Yet I worry that she will worry. If the old man isn't out chasing women, he's off get-

ting his face bashed in. "You're just about smooth nuts,"
Rainey says, sipping at a glass of water she has picked up
from the polished floor beside her chair. Her latest project,
taking up the carpet in the living room and finishing the
wood, has just been finished this week. She seems inexhaustible.

"Smooth nuts?" I ask. I never heard that one, but somehow it fits. What was I doing in that bar by myself? For the
next few minutes or so, I try to explain what I've been up to,
but the mask of disapproval on Rainey's face is in place before I get thirty seconds into my story, as I knew it would be.

"Even if you could show that Leon Robinson was the
biggest racist in the entire state," Rainey objects, cradling
her empty glass in both hands between her knees, "what
should it have to do with Andy's case?"

Relevance. I sip at the beer and put it down. According to
the Arkansas Uniform Rules of Evidence, relevant evidence
is that evidence which tends to make a proposition at issue
more or less true.

"If I can make a jury believe that Leon deliberately let go
of Pam," I explain, "don't you think that should have some
bearing on Andy's guilt or innocence?"

Rainey rolls the plastic container in her hands as if she
were a potter. "I guess I don't understand criminal law."

The alcohol and the shower have lowered my heart rate
substantially. I'm beginning to feel normal again. "I'm not
sure I do either, but let me take a crack at it," I say, leaning
back against the couch. "The jury has to find at a minimum
that Andy acted recklessly. I will argue that no one can reasonably believe that Andy should have anticipated that one
of his assistants would deliberately release control of Pam.
The crucial act that resulted in Pam's death was Leon's letting
go of her, not Andy's decision to use shock."

Rainey purses her lips and shakes her head. "But what
evidence do you have that Leon deliberately let go of her?
You told me last week you didn't have a shred of evidence
that he and Olivia Le Master cooked this up together. You

said that Olivia has clammed up and might even invoke the Fifth Amendment and refuse to testify, which means she's guilty as hell.''

I correct her. ''I said she might. Her attorney said she hasn't decided yet.'' I finish off the beer. ''But to answer your question, I don't have any evidence except Leon and his friends don't like me coming into their bar,'' I go on, not willing to tell Rainey that my evidence is living in Hot Springs. She will be furious that I am going to try to drag someone else into this. I stand up. ''I need to go on home. I told Sarah I'd be home by eleven.''

At the door Rainey surprises me by reaching up and brushing my lips with her own. ''Promise me you won't do something this stupid again,'' she says, her voice a quiet whisper against my ear.

''I promise,'' I say, thinking that it has been over a year since we have kissed. Worry—the surest way to a woman's heart. I thank her again and leave. If I didn't know better, I would think Rainey still loves me.

At home Sarah and her friend Chris are watching a movie. Fortunately, it is dark in the house, which is lit only by the glow of the TV set. I carry my bloody clothes in a paper sack Rainey has provided me. Engrossed in some horror flick, Sarah barely speaks, and I escape to my bedroom after murmuring goodnight. Tomorrow will be soon enough for her to see my wounds. I take a couple of aspirin and sit down on my bed. Woogie, perhaps drawn by the medication, tries to lick at my face until I push him away. He is even a more inept fighter than his master and has perpetually sore ears to prove it. Before I turn off the light, I tell him, ''They would have knocked every one of your teeth out.''

He turns his head away and settles down at the end of the bed as if to say he would never have gotten himself in such a mess.

The next morning every bone in my body feels as if someone has taken a hammer to it. Thank God I don't have to get out of bed today, because I can't move. Of course I do have to get out of bed or risk wetting it. As much as I ache, it is tempting just to say to hell with it and see if I can reach the window. I could always blame it on Woogie. As if sensing disaster, he hops down off the bed and scratches at the door. At least he is civilized. Shamed by my own dog, I slip on some pants and creak into the bathroom. If anything, my face looks worse. Today there are streaks of yellow and green under my eye. I look forlornly at the spot where my tooth was. Even as bad as the others look, chipped and dingy, at least they are present and accounted for, and not in the parking lot of the Bull Run buried up to their roots in the tar. Depressed, I limp into the front yard with Woogie, hoping nobody is out. Accustomed to more of a walk, Woogie contents himself with lifting his leg over my neighbor's petunias. What the hell. If his wife needs flowers, Jewell Patterson, a tall black man in his fifties, can bring home all he wants from patients' rooms at the VA hospital, where he works as a registered nurse.

His brick home, the color of ginger, has three bedrooms to my two, and Jewell has a snow-white Lincoln Continental in the garage that he'll wash this afternoon. Carol, his wife, is a schoolteacher. If we're all outside in the yard and hear the sound of a gun being fired from the direction of Needle Park, Jewell will mutter, "Damn, those niggers!" and order Carol to go into the house. The second week in September, the morning, in contrast to last night's humidity, is sharp and clear, a beautiful day for a walk, since Needle Park is usually quiet on a Sunday morning. Even drug dealers have to sleep some time. My bones ache too much to go further, however, and I turn around, disappointing my dog. This is what old age must be like. "Pick up the paper and hand it to me," I tell Woogie as I dodder up my driveway. He looks at me as if I were crazy, and I stoop in slow motion. Thank God, he can't talk. He'd give me hell, too.

Normally, I would make some coffee and sit at the kitchen

table and read the paper until Sarah gets up. Not today. I collapse back into bed and doze off after reading the funny papers, the last thought on my mind Margo's underwear in Apartment 3-G.

"Dad, are you okay?"

I awake with a start. I had been dreaming about the fight and apparently was talking in my sleep. I look at my watch. It is almost ten. I haven't gone back to sleep in the morning since I was in high school. But I haven't been beaten up since high school either. "I guess," I mutter. "Come on in."

"What happened?" Sarah exclaims immediately as she comes through the door. Her eyes redden as soon as she sees me. She is wearing her blue summer dress I haven't seen since the spring, a strand of fake pearls her aunt Marty got for her at Christmas, stockings, and her white flats. Mass—what else? What has prompted this? So far as I know, she hasn't been inside a church in a couple of years. Then I remember her letter and our conversation on the way home from Conway during Governor's School.

I put a finger to my mouth and motion for her to close the door. I assume Chris is still in the house. I feel as sheepish as if I had been caught with a woman in my bed. "Just a little problem last night," I say, pulling the sheet up to my chest. "Sit down on the bed, and I'll give you a real quick summary. Looks like you're on your way to Mass. You look great."

Obediently, Sarah sits on the bed, a horrified look on her face. "Did somebody beat you up?"

God, she looks beautiful. My heart is about to burst as I realize how much she looks like her mother on our first formal date. We went to an outdoor seafood restaurant, not more than thirty yards from the beach in Cartagena. It was January, windy but still warm, and the waves crashed so loudly against the shore we almost had to put our heads next to each other to be heard. "I was out at this redneck bar looking for some information about that case I have in four days involving the black psychologist, and a guy who obviously hates my client jumped me in the parking lot.''

''Oh!'' Sarah says, jostling the bed and sending a wave of nausea through me. I shouldn't have had that last beer at Rainey's last night. ''Your eye looks terrible. I'm so sorry.''

I try to smile, but it probably looks like I'm wincing. ''I'm fine.'' Except for the last two words, I've at least told some of the truth. There is no sense in trying to tell her the whole story right now. ''How come you're going to Mass?''

Leaning forward on the bed, Sarah wails, ''He knocked out your tooth!''

I lean up and pat her hand. ''It was the chipped one— probably about to fall out anyway. I'll get a fake temporary one tomorrow. It'll look ten times better. Don't worry.''

''Did you call the police?'' she asks, tears beginning to trickle down her face, ruining her makeup. I wish she wouldn't wear it.

I reach over and grab a tissue from the nightstand beside the bed. ''Quit this,'' I say handing her the flimsy paper. ''Chris is going to think I've been abusing you.'' Call the police? I think not. I wouldn't be surprised if a couple weren't there giggling as that monster at the door hustled me outside. At least he didn't come out with me. ''Nay, calling the cops would have been sissy in that place,'' I say.

''Oh,'' she says, laughing in spite of herself, ''where was it?''

''Go on to church,'' I urge her. ''I'll tell you more about it later. It's no big deal.''

She looks down at the cheap Timex watch I gave her for her birthday last week. Seventeen. She's been kissed, but I hope that's all. A black boy from her Christians and Jews camp has called her a couple of times, but she says they're just friends. Given who her mother was, how can I complain? ''Are you going to be okay?'' she asks, pushing up from my bed. ''I can stay home. After not going for two years, it's not like I'm trying for a perfect attendance record.''

''I've been a great father, haven't I?'' I say, forcing a

smile. I run my tongue through the latest hole in the rapidly deteriorating dike that is my body. At least they didn't knock out four or five.

"You've been a great father," Sarah says, her voice trembling and hoarse with as much emotion as a radio evangelist's.

Lighten up, kid, I think. It's not as if I am trying to make a living as a prizefighter. "Say a little prayer," I instruct her, "that my dentist won't enjoy fixing this too much. That's what I'm worried about."

I get the grin I want, and five minutes later I hear the front door slam. Woogie, pushing open the bedroom door, clicks into the room and sits on the floor looking hopefully at me. His toenails are starting to look like bear claws. He could use a trip to the vet, but so could I. He wants to jump up on the bed, but he doesn't deserve it. Lying flat on my stomach with my left hand under my pillow, which is down by my waist (my sleep position since Rosa died), I have to strain to see him. "You wouldn't have bitten a flea last night." Disappointed I won't let him up on the bed, he settles down on the floor. I yawn, hoping Sarah won't retail this all over St. Michael's. The way gossip spreads, when I wake up Father Curtis with the earnest pop eyes and bad breath will be standing over me, administering the last rites. I can't stop yawning. Good, sleep. Blessed sleep.

18

I AM AWAKENED out of a fuzzy dream by the sound of the telephone ringing in the kitchen. I was dreaming I was in a boxing ring, and my opponent (some guy I don't recognize) kept hitting me after the bell. Stiff as Sheetrock, I limp into the kitchen, remembering that Sarah said she and Chris were going to McDonald's after Mass. Did I tell her I was driving to Hot Springs this afternoon? I can't remember. "Hello," I say, clearing my throat, my raspy voice more a moan than a greeting.

"Gideon," a female voice says, "it's Kim Keogh. Did I wake you?"

Guilt feelings for not having called her rouse me from my lethargy. If she's calling to give me some hell, it's just another chicken coming home to roost. I look down at Woogie, whose own expression seems downright scornful. You deserve this call, jerk. "Well," I say, my tongue seeking out the hole where my tooth was, "I had to get up to go to Hot Springs this afternoon." Go ahead and ream me out. I'm leaving anyway.

Her voice is soft, almost a whisper. "Have you got a minute?"

Mournfully, I run my fingers over my wrecked face, yet grateful I still have one. How did my nose survive? Last night when it was being ground into the tar of the parking lot, I was certain it would be in the shape of a pretzel this morning. She still wants to go out with me! Maybe she thinks I'll die this time. "Sure," I say. "I've been meaning to call you."

There is a pause as if she is filing this lie away for future reference. "I have a proposition for you," she says finally. "Want to hear it?"

This is amazing, I think. I've treated her like shit, and she's going to invite me over for lunch. Maybe I can eat with a bag over my head. I'm not up to competing with the movie stars on the walls of her apartment today. "I'm all ears," I say, a little cocky, thinking this isn't too far from the truth. The left one, at least, feels the size of a small boxcar. Even as bad as I feel, I'm all for being propositioned.

"I've got some information that can affect your case, but if I give it to you and you can use it," she says, her voice firm and steady, "I'll want you to agree that when the trial is over you and Andrew Chapman will give me an exclusive interview on camera."

I try to think what she could possibly have. I can't imagine. "You're asking me," I complain mildly, "to buy a pig in a poke." I'm not anxious to make this kind of bargain. Since I've been in private practice, I've tried to be friendly to all the reporters who cover the courts. Free advertising is the best kind. "Besides, I can't bind my client without talking to him anyway."

Kim, not a subtle negotiator, asks, "What about you?"

After last night I'm not as eager to jump in headfirst. "Let me talk to Andy first," I insist. "He's the kind of guy who would regard this as a form of reverse blackmail if he's not handled right."

Kim sounds as young as Sarah. "Are you serious?"

I shift from my right to my left leg. Even my hips are sore. "You claim to have useful information but won't part with it without a price," I point out delicately. "But I suspect most of us would regard this as a part of the American free-enterprise system."

Her voice frosty, Kim retorts, "It's my professional duty to try to get a story nobody else gets."

I try flexing my knees to ease the pressure on my spine, wondering if I might need to go to a chiropractor. The media, God bless it, have perfected the maxim that the ends justify the means. Surely, if most reporters made a decent living, the general public would hate them as much as it hates lawyers. "How come you can't break this on your own?" I ask, changing the subject. If I hurt her feelings too much, I'll scare her off.

"I can't confirm it," she admits. "If this is just a rumor, I'll get sued for libel."

Ah, it might be about Olivia, I realize. I'm getting an appetite. Still searching for a painless position, I lean back against the kitchen wall. "It's your station they'd be interested in suing."

Kim, perhaps sensing my interest now, asks, "You want to come over about seven if you're back from Hot Springs?"

I look at my watch. It is only noon. I'll have plenty of time. "Sure," I say, "but you'll have to disregard my appearance. I've been going through a second childhood recently and have acquired a few nicks since you saw me last."

Guessing, Kim says pleasantly, "Somebody beat the shit out of you, huh?" Her voice contains no hint of surprise, as if she expects lawyers to brawl.

Embarrassed, I admit, "Something like that." I guess she doesn't have to be a genius to figure out the damage middle-aged men can do to themselves.

After I hang up I immediately dial Andy's number but get no answer. I wonder if he is at church. Do psychologists believe in God, or has Freud shamed them out of it? I'll try to reach him later, I decide, and stumble toward the bathroom to see if I can shave without screaming.

As I reach the outskirts of the tourist town of Hot Springs, a torturous two-day stage coach drive in the 1840s but only an hour's drive to the northwest from the house this afternoon, I think that it would be an interesting, even exciting, place to live—over a century ago. In the 1880s rival gambling interests shot it out on Central Avenue; Al Capone sedately walked the streets in the 1920s. Along Central, the main drag, illegal gambling flourished alongside still viable attractions such as Bath House Row, the Arlington Hotel, and first-class horse racing at Oaklawn Park. And all along the way, showbiz people as bizarre as Phineas Barnum's midget, General Tom Thumb, trooped into town over the years for the purpose of entertaining luminaries as diverse as Yankee Civil War General William Tecumseh Sherman and Helen Keller. How could Baptists have so much fun? It apparently got to be too much for the state, for in the 1960s, under the administration of the so-called black-sheep Rockefeller brother, Winthrop (though he had more integrity and compassion than many of us wanted), Arkansas's first Republican governor since Reconstruction, the state police conducted a series of late-night raids, confiscating slot machines by the carload, and suddenly, after a century of notoriety and excitement, Hot Springs, left with only its natural beauty and legalized horse track, became respectable and now confines itself to the normal appetites of more typical small-town corruption and tamer tourist entertainments such as I.Q. Zoo, the Alligator Farm, and the Mid-America Museum.

In ten minutes I am standing in front of the door to Charlene Newman's apartment and am presumably separated from her by only the length of a security chain. I got her number from the telephone company, and less than two hours ago called her and told her the truth—that I am a lawyer in a criminal case in which her ex-husband is a witness and needed to drive over and talk to her in absolute confidence. She said okay, but now that I am here, if this is Charlene Newman behind the door (my introduction of myself has elicited no response), she is having second thoughts. Perhaps it is the neighborhood that invites such caution. It is in a seedy, cheap part of the downtown area. The hallway in her apartment building is dimly lit, dirty, and is as confining as the inside of the corroding, stained gutter that runs along the outside roof. After almost a minute of dead silence, the door comes to as the chain is unhooked, and then a slender but well-built young woman dressed in faded jeans, a blue halter top, and sandals, slides through it, revealing not so much as a couch in the background. "Let's go for a walk," she says, her voice pleasantly hillbilly.

With her straight dark hair the color of black shoe polish, thin lips, and an aquiline nose, Charlene Newman surely has Native American blood coursing through her veins. She leads me out of her apartment with her arms folded across her chest Indian-style, as if she were auditioning for a part in a movie that spoofs bad westerns. She is not a princess, but not a squaw either. If she would smile (assuming her teeth are good), with her high cheekbones she could be pretty. "What's Leon got hisself into now?" she asks. She leads me in the direction of the mountain behind the Arlington Hotel. My own jeans feel like a rubber suit in the humidity and heat. Fall is only a week away, but it might as well be midsummer. Though a walk might relieve some of my stiffness, I hope we aren't going far.

Walking uphill on a wooded path past benches populated primarily by elderly retirees, many of whom are Yankees permanently escaping snow and ice, I summarize Leon's involvement in Andy's case, uncertain, despite the divorce, how far I can go in trying to paint Leon as a villain. "He and his friends at the Bull Run beat me up last night pretty good," I say, removing my sunglasses and baring the gap in my teeth. It ought to be good for something. "All I did was sit down at the bar for a few minutes."

A few yards off the path, Charlene points to a vacant bench, and I nod gratefully. Her voice, surely a product of the Ozarks, cracks slightly as she sighs, "When he's had a couple, Leon's pretty good at that."

Though we have been walking only a few minutes, I am ready to sit. The back panels of the wooden bench, painted Astroturf green, creak as I collapse against them. Fortunately, it is in the shade. "Did he ever hit you?"

From where we are sitting, apart from a few old people with their brown canes and white heads, the predominant color is, though this is September, a lush green. The park, a sanctuary of hardy survivors, is neatly hidden from the town. Charlene must come here to escape the bleakness of her apartment. Her unpainted lips press against teeth I still haven't seen. Questions like this when asked by strangers are never innocent. Finally, she says, ''Only when he was drinking. If I could of kept Leon from his friends, we would have done all right.''

The old phrase ''If wishes were horses, beggars would ride,'' flits through my head. I have never understood it, but somehow it seems to apply to Charlene Newman. If Hot Springs is Camelot, she seems destined to spend her life fishing for carp with the ''gentlefolk'' in the moat. Out of the corner of my eye, I notice to my left an old man who reminds me of how my father would have looked had he lived to be an old man. A Harry Truman look-alike, his eyes (unlike my father's, whose soupy lenses were troubled by the paranoia that often accompanies schizophrenia) gleam with small-town self-satisfaction behind gold-rimmed eyeglasses. Sure, I dropped two atomic bombs, but it was either us or them. Yet, I remind myself, I don't need or expect a complete surrender from Charlene. ''At the probable cause hearing a few weeks ago, Leon started crying when he talked about Pam,'' I say, hoping for the right note of empathy. ''I think he felt guilty for turning her loose.''

Charlene squints at me as if I had asked her to do long division in her head. ''Why would he have jus' let go of her?''

Harry, who apparently has no need at this stage of his life to be concerned with appearances, lays a forefinger against his right nostril and shoots the contents of his left onto the bench beside him, his message being, I suppose, If you don't like it, don't watch. Too late, I turn my head back to Charlene, but somehow not until I am reminded of the tobacco-stained brick streets freshly spotted each Saturday in my eastern Arkansas hometown of Bear Creek by farmers of both races. Poor woman. I can see the emotion in her eyes. Like the fools most women are about men, she still cares about him. "I think your ex-husband hates blacks so much," I say as gently as possible, "he'd do a lot of things if he thought he could get away with it, even if for a moment it meant hurting somebody he really cared about."

Charlene's long legs push out against the grass underneath the bench, making me fear I have offended her. "Leon wouldn't kill nobody," she says, her voice stubborn, suggesting I have indicted her as well—and I have. Who wants to have married a murderer?

"I don't think Leon ever intended for a second for her to die," I say quickly, holding her gaze to establish my own sincerity. "I just think he let the girl go, hoping she would attack my client."

Charlene ponders this possibility. "How did you know," she says, lowering her voice though we are at least a good fifteen feet from Harry, who is using a clean handkerchief to wipe the corners of his mouth, but not his nose, "Leon's got a thing about niggers?"

Niggers. She says the word as easily as her own name. Though not a candidate for membership in the Rainbow Coalition either, out of loyalty to my client (or is it to Rosa or even frayed values from a more idealistic time in my life?), I flinch at the word but try not to show it. "Somebody told me," I lie, "that he's a member of the Trackers."

For the first time since we've been seated on the bench, she won't meet my gaze. Watching Harry stand up, she asks, slipping out of her natural twang, her voice too guarded for it to be an idle question, "Who told you that?"

Pretending indifference, I stand up and jam my hands in my pockets. "It doesn't matter." For the first time it clearly occurs to me that Leon, like Yettie, knew Andy and Olivia were having an affair. As a member of the Trackers, he was enraged by it and had every reason to punish Andy.

Charlene, her voice listless, hunches her shoulders. "What do you want with me?"

I stand over her like a father reprimanding a child. "Only to tell the truth at my client's trial if you're subpoenaed to testify about Leon being a member. If he admits it, you won't even have to take the stand.''

Charlene bites her lip but doesn't cry. "I thought I was away from him for good.''

Marriage, I'm finding out from my divorce clients, is forever. I look back over at Harry, who is now watching us suspiciously. I could use a good caning for upsetting this girl, his expression says. "This won't get him in trouble,'' I say, too glibly. Lawyers tell people this all the time, when, in fact, we may be setting off an avalanche that will maim them for life.

"It's not him,'' she says, still no inflection in her voice, "I'm worried about.''

But it is, I think, as I watch Harry dodder toward us. Through his thin white shirt I can see the outline of the straps of his old-fashioned ribbed undershirt, which again reminds me of my father, who fascinated me as a small boy by the painstaking way he tucked his shirt into his pants each morning before going off to his drugstore. All Charlene had to do was hang up, keep the chain in place, or even lie to me in a convincing manner. Humans are even worse than canines when it comes to hanging on to bad relationships. "How long were y'all married?'' I ask, curious about the amount of violence in their relationship. Maybe in private Leon was as cute as a French poodle, and she laughed her head off, but somehow I doubt it. Raised to be polite to my elders, I nod at Harry, who stares at us with the frankness that is only permitted to certain groups of our society. Disgusted, he shakes his head. Thirty years ago, he might be standing over this young woman, but he wouldn't be making her cry.

Charlene, perhaps unnerved by such interest (or maybe just bored) stares at the ground. "I was fourteen when he and I made it legal. I'm twenty-one now.''

Charlene, the tease. I do not ask, but I wonder how old she was when she first had sex. "Any kids?'' I ask. What other reason would a girl have for giving up her youth?

Now that Harry is past us, it is our turn to stare at him.

From the rear he is trim as Nancy Reagan and is nattily attired in white bucks and blue seersucker pants. Maybe there is a Bess at the Arlington restlessly checking her watch. Time for a massage and then, who knows? After Charlene he seems a little pumped. Her forearms resting against the bench, Charlene shakes her head. "My mama and daddy had so many yard apes runnin' around, I swore I wouldn't never have a one, and I haven't," she says proudly.

"Good for you," I say, wondering how she has managed it. Leon doesn't seem the type to accept rejection well. Though I doubt if Charlene was social chairman for the Saline County Planned Parenthood Board, I have detected a spunkier side to her than I thought existed. She may tell the truth about her husband in court yet. "He may come looking for you," I say. "The women at the bar may have told him I was looking for you."

Charlene shrugs and says, more bravely than she surely feels, "I'll worry about that when I have to."

At exactly seven o'clock Kim Keogh, dressed in baggy jeans, a shapeless gray man's shirt with the tail hanging out, tennis shoes, and white athletic socks, opens her door to me. "God!" she exclaims. "Somebody didn't just get mad—they got even, maybe a little ahead."

Perversely, I am a little disappointed. Though I wasn't expecting her to run down to a beauty salon this afternoon, I guess I wanted her to make more of an effort. After all, we did go to bed together, didn't we? Instead, she has barely run a comb through her normally stunning hair and could stand some lipstick. Damn, I'm awful, I think. Presumably I'm here on business, and I want her to look as if this is our wedding day. I move on into her living room and still an urge to gather up the Sunday papers, which are scattered on the couch, and to pick up a dirty coffee cup and spoon and take them to the kitchen. The movie stars are still up on the walls. Clark, what do you think? I nearly ask aloud. Would your feelings be a little hurt by such casualness? He probably didn't give a damn about that either.

Kim, shoving the *Democrat-Gazette* aside to make a space for me, doesn't seem to be aware of the impression she is making. "Have a seat," she says absently. She sits down across from me on the one chair in her living room. I'm glad I'm not hungry or thirsty, since it doesn't appear I'm about to be offered anything. "Did you talk to your client?"

"Can't get hold of him," I confess, having tried three times before I gave up. "I'm in though," I tell her. "And I'll do my best to convince him this is in his best interest." I am afraid I will miss out on something important if I play this too cool. Kim is holding the only card available. If my only chance is Charlene Newman, I'm in deep trouble.

She is leaning forward on her knees as if she were a hungry animal trying to decide if the meat she sees is real or part of a trap. "Why should I trust you when you wouldn't even call me back?"

Good question. Why should she? My face warm, I begin to fold up her papers to try to stall for time. "I'm much more trustworthy when the subject isn't women," I mumble. "Actually I've been involved with this other . . ."

She cuts me off. "You don't have to explain that." Leaning back against the back of her chair, she folds her arms under her breasts. "I've been given a tip that Olivia Le Master had a child taken from her several years ago because of child abuse, but since the records in juvenile court are confidential, I can't get them."

Another child? I touch my lower lip, measuring its puffiness. Olivia, to the best of my recollection, has never even mentioned another marriage. A lot could have happened since she had Pam. People don't stop living their lives because of a single catastrophe. "How do you think it's relevant?" I ask.

Kim, now slightly defensive that I'm not reacting more positively, says, "The word on the street is that the prosecutor would love to charge Olivia Le Master with murder but she needs more evidence. If she intentionally abused one child, wouldn't that be relevant in showing her state of mind toward the one that died?''

I have my doubts about its admissibility. If it were admissible, it could be dynamite. Unfortunately, it might hurt Andy as much as Olivia if a jury believed he was a part of a plan to kill Pam. The one thing I know it will do is make Andy rethink the possibility of a plea bargain. Somewhere a noose is slowly being tightened around somebody's neck: if it's Andy's, he'd better take the opportunity to slip his head out of it while there is still time. Simply screaming "racism" in this case won't be enough. "I don't know whether a judge will admit it or not," I say candidly. "You can be sure Jill would try her damnedest." As I watch Kim nod, a satisfied look on her face, I realize what she is doing does amount to blackmail. Probably Jill Marymount would find this information more useful in court than I would. As far as I'm aware, she might already know. Kim is way ahead of me, but I'm beginning to think it doesn't take much. "What year was this supposed to have happened?"

My inattentive hostess shrugs. "I'm not sure, and don't ask how I found this out. I can't reveal anything."

After a few more minutes during which I learn exactly nothing, I head back home, having promised my story in exchange for a rumor. What I have learned, however, is exactly how little I know about Olivia Le Master. I have assumed she was what she seemed: a woman caught in a seemingly endless nightmare that her desperate effort to end turned into a tragedy. Instead, for all I know she could be a sadistic bitch who has never blinked once in her life.

In the car on the way home I decide to verify this information before I tell Andy. I have a theory that he doesn't know everything about Olivia either. Knowing Andy, he will discount it as gossip unless I confront him with some evidence. As an old social worker for the Department of Human Services in Blackwell County, I have a friend who, if she will, can speed up my research.

* * *

Sarah says, bringing me the phone from the living room, "It's Mr. Bailey. I think something's wrong. He sounds weird."

Dan must be drunk, I think, putting down my pen to take the phone. I am working in the kitchen on direct examination questions for my Mississippi expert. With the trial only three days away, I have begun to panic. Though Olivia seems intent on testifying and not invoking the Fifth Amendment, that has been my only good news. Andy has become uncharacteristically morose and distant, which has had the effect of further convincing me that he knows more than he is telling me. While he continues to maintain his innocence, it is as if he realizes he has been fooled by Olivia but can't quite bring himself to admit it. I put the odds at his implicating her at the last minute at fifty-fifty. It is still not too late to cut a deal with our prosecutor.

"Gideon," Dan says in an agonized voice after I speak his name into the receiver, "I've been arrested, and I'm down here at the police station."

I nearly drop the phone. Dan, I realize, is my best friend. Despite his juvenile nature (or maybe because of it), he and I have become as close as brothers this summer. What on earth could he have done? He doesn't sound drunk. An argument with Brenda that led to a shooting? Dan is a gun nut and has a workshop in which he makes his own ammunition. "What's happened?" I ask, trying to keep my voice normal.

"They say I shoplifted a Twinkie!" he says, his voice screeching against my ear. "Can you come down here?"

For God's sake, I think, looking at Sarah and rolling my eyes back in my head to indicate this phone call is surely more nutty than tragic. What next? I look at my watch. It's almost nine. "I'll be down in fifteen minutes."

"What's wrong?" Sarah asks, as I hand her the phone. If she hadn't already washed her hair and wasn't in her robe,

I'd take her with me. Every kid ought to see a jail at least once.

"Middle age," I groan. "Dan's gone middle-age crazy." I tell her what he told me. "Don't you gossip about this," I warn her. "I'm sure it's all a misunderstanding."

Unfortunately, it is not. "I'm guilty as hell," Dan confides as I drive him back to his car, which is still parked in front of the Quik-Pic, an all-night convenience store five minutes from his house. "All of a sudden I just scarfed it up before I had paid for it," he says miserably. "A little piece of the wrapper was even hanging from my mouth when this security guard pops up out of nowhere and starts screaming as if I was gonna try to crawl up through the ceiling. I must be nuts."

Turning to the Quik-Pic parking lot, I agree but do not say so. Dan would have been released on his own recognizance if he hadn't given the cop, who had just pulled in to get a cup of coffee, so much lip. With Brenda out of town and five dollars in his pockets, I have had to put up a minimal bond for him. "Obviously, you had no intent to steal it. They should have waited until you were out of the store. You can sue 'em for a million bucks for false imprisonment."

Dan leans his head against the window on his side of the Blazer. "You can't go in and suck down a package of Twinkies and expect to get away with it."

I turn off the engine which has begun to shudder in neutral and listen to ominous sounds coming from the hood. From the noise it sounds as if someone is trying unsuccessfully to shut down a nuclear power plant. "Why in the hell did you do it? Maybe we can get a doctor to testify that you suffer from some eating disorder."

His head still against the glass, Dan cuts his eyes to me. "I do," he says grimly. "I eat too much damn food."

I look through the window at Quik-Pic and see a good-looking blonde in shorts at the magazine rack. She must be looking for something to read before bed. For a society as obsessed with sex as the United States, we don't spend much time actually doing it. "That's not a crime," I say, losing the thread of our conversation.

"Stealing is," Dan says wearily, as he opens the door. "Look, why don't you just go in there and ask her to come home with you. You can tell Sarah this woman was going to have to sleep down at the jail and you took pity on her."

I laugh and turn to look at Dan who, incredibly, seems about to cry. "We've got to do something," I say, now ashamed that I let myself be so easily distracted. "This could be really humiliating if they make it stick."

Dan's eyes are red. "Thanks for that insight," he says dryly.

"Well, damn it," I argue, "you just can't plead guilty."

Dan sighs, making a mournful sound through his nose. "Why the hell not? Because it's not the American way? Do we have to litigate everything in this country? I ate the damn things! I've done it before, if you can believe I'm that stupid. Why? I haven't got the slightest idea."

Jesus Christ, I think, now uncomfortable with what I am hearing. He really *is* middle-age crazy. Is this Dan's idea of living dangerously, or what? Some guys get a sports car; others inhale Twinkies. What do *I* do? Sleep with women almost twenty years younger, I guess. For the first time in weeks I think I feel a twinge of pain in my rear. I got caught, too, I realize glumly. I pat Dan's shoulder. "Everybody does stupid things," I say. "This doesn't have to make you want to jump off the Arkansas River bridge."

Dan stands outside the door and bends down to peer inside at me. "I'm so fat I couldn't climb over the side if I wanted to," he says smiling, albeit wanly, for the first time tonight. "I'd have to roll down the bank."

I grin, feeling better. If he can joke about it, he is all right or will be. "Well, you've got a free lawyer, ol' buddy," I say, sticking my hand through the window. "You think about it tonight and I'll do whatever you want."

His big paw, which is as moist as an ink blotter, clamps

down on mine. I look down to avoid the tears in his eyes. Hell, I might be crying, too. The *Arkansas Democrat-Gazette* will carry this story. Reading my mind, Dan mumbles, "I can't wait to read the paper tomorrow."

I return the pressure but still can't look him in the eye. "It'll seem more like a joke than anything else," I say, unable to deny the story will make the rounds.

As usual, Sarah, like a long-suffering wife, is waiting up for me. "What happened?" she asks from the couch, still in her robe, just as I left her an hour and a half ago. In her lap is a European history book. Woogie, who is sitting primly by his mistress's side, looks at me suspiciously as if he has no intention of buying a cock-and-bull story about a late-night client.

I sit down by her on the couch and begin to pet Woogie, who quickly rolls over on his back to have his stomach scratched. When all is said and done, it doesn't take much to make my family happy. If I were to go strictly by our code of ethics, I would never have told Sarah a word about Dan. A lawyer is bound to keep his client's confidences, but she would only think he had done something worse than he has. Still, I am at a loss to explain his behavior.

"He's a lawyer!" Sarah exclaims as I try to minimize his actions.

Woogie's eyes looked glazed with pleasure. This is as close as he will ever come to an orgasm. "But not exactly a serial murderer."

Sarah, who ought to be more charitable after reading her history book, with its unending story of mass slaughter, will have none of it. As if banging a gavel at me, Sarah's hand moves Woogie's muzzle in an up and down motion. "Behavior like this is exactly why people don't trust lawyers."

Actually, it's for stuff a lot worse, but she is missing the point. "My own theory is that lawyers' worst sins are of omission," I say, noticing for the first time how gray Woogie is getting. He probably thinks the same thing about me. "There are lots of people we refuse to help or just go through the motions because they don't have the money to pay us. If there's a hell, those are the kind we'll burn for.''

Woogie hops off the couch. All this attention is beginning to get to him. My daughter nods, but I suspect she is still too young to feel comfortable with the various shades of gray that stipple the middle-aged human organism. There is only one cure for that, and with luck, it's a good thirty years off.

As I'm brushing my teeth before getting into bed, it occurs to me that the partners in Mays & Burton would consider me a far worse thief than Dan. I'm glad I have never told Sarah when I acquired Andy as a client. As someone who hasn't stolen even so much as a boyfriend, my daughter probably wouldn't be very sympathetic.

19

THE NEXT MORNING in municipal court, Daniel Blackstone (I never knew before what the initial stood for) Bailey pleads guilty to the crime of theft of property which has a value of less than one hundred dollars.

"You're sure you want to do this?" Darwin Bell, our black judge, says more to me than to Dan, who is resplendent in an expensive charcoal gray pin-striped suit from Dillard's. The suit makes Dan look like some visiting dignitary rather than a petty thief confessing his sins. Tunkie Southerland and Frank D'Angelo, who with me form Dan's male support group, are in the front row. I turn and glance at their solemn faces. It is as if we are expecting Dan to be sentenced to die in the electric chair.

I nod in the direction of my friend Amy Gilchrist, the prosecutor in this case. Amy, whom I realize now I haven't seen in weeks, has obviously been sent down to the minor leagues as punishment for having an abortion. Amy, who perhaps is sad for a number of reasons, looks somber without her usual jewelry. She says in a puzzled tone, "I haven't talked to the defendant's attorney about this, Your Honor."

Patting down an out-of-fashion Afro (only acquired since the election), Darwin Bell, who seems destined for a much higher judicial calling (except for his hair, he is developing a reputation for conservatism) squints at Amy as if to ask: Why is he pleading guilty if there is no deal? Amy's small palms turn out to her sides in a gesture of frustrated ignorance. Normally, there is a litany of formal questions the judge will ask to assure himself (and to protect himself on the record in case there is an appeal) that he has a guilty client in front of him who is voluntarily pleading guilty and who knows the court is not obligated to accept the prosecutor's sentencing recommendation, but here Dan is simply throwing himself on the mercy of the court with no questions asked.

"Judge, my client would like to make a statement about what occurred," I say, confined by Dan to an embarrassingly small role in this drama.

Plainly puzzled by what he is witnessing, Darwin looks past us to the rest of his morning's docket seated impatiently behind us. Lawyers are served first. For a group that contains a high percentage of drunks, druggies, street persons, and irritable cops, the men and women sitting behind the railing are remarkably restrained today, though not entirely silent. In federal courtrooms (I've been in a total of two—one when I carried Oscar May's files in a diversity of jurisdiction car accident case and last week on my first appointment in a minor, federal firearms violation case involving an alien from Panama), a majestic dignity pervades. There is no such mystique in municipal court. Darwin, whose already big shoulders look immense beneath his black robe, says casually, "Please do."

Dan begins in a dignified, quiet voice that is several octaves below his normal gossipy, breezy tone. "Your Honor, what happened is that I opened a package of Twinkies in the Quik-Pic on Texas Street and ate them. I had no intention of paying for them because I would have been too embarrassed to admit what I had done. I'm sorry and I apologize to the court and to the manager and to every member of the bar."

Darwin Bell rubs the bridge of his nose as if a headache has settled in between his deep-set eyes. A fat white lawyer stealing Twinkies. What next? Amy Gilchrist, who had seemed on the verge of tears, says cheerfully to the judge, "Your Honor, for the last five years I've known Mr. Bailey to be an honorable and valued member of the bar, and I recommend that the court accept his guilty plea and order him to pay costs and to stay out of the Quik-Pic, and if there're no other incidents of this nature within a year, to expunge his record."

Looking squarely at the reporter from the *Democrat-Gazette*, the judge pauses for what seems like an eternity, then barks gruffly, "I'll accept the prosecutor's recommendation."

Dan, blinking back tears, nods gratefully at Darwin Bell and whispers in a choked voice, "Thank you, Your Honor."

Tomorrow there may be headlines charging lenient treatment for lawyers, but today justice reigns in Blackwell County. I wink at Amy, who manages a thin smile from hollow cheeks. She must be going through a living hell at the Prosecutor's Office. Until this morning, I had never seen her perky face when it wasn't bursting with energy and high spirits. This might have cost her job today. As Darwin hastily calls the next case, I make a note to call her. I know Dan will.

Before noon I swing by my old place of employment. It is virtually impossible to call the Blackwell County Division of Social Services office because of their automated telephone-answering service. They might as well have dug a shark-filled moat around the building, so effective is the system at denying access. After ten minutes of "dial this" and "dial that" with no results, I decide to hell with it. In sixty seconds I am back in the office of my old supervisor from my days as a case worker for the agency.

"Been seeing you on TV, Gideon." Shelley Jenkins grins from behind her desk. "But you're looking a little rougher even in person."

"Got any openings, Shel?" I ask, mugging for her so she won't think I'm serious. At the rate I'm going, I ought to consider it. "With this phone system though, I guess you're trying to lay some people off."

She cackles mournfully, "Isn't it a disgrace?" Shelley, an obese woman in her early sixties with sad eyes, took a special

liking to me for some reason. Actually, it was Rosa she probably enjoyed. When we had her to dinner, at least once every
year, like a mother and daughter-in-law they conducted a
comprehensive discussion of my shortcomings that covered
my performance at home and at the office.

"I need some help," I tell her after a few minutes of office
gossip. The state is being sued because of the lack of resources and management problems in the Division of Child
and Family Services. The papers have had a field day docu-
menting the failures of the child welfare system. Rumors
about mass firings crop up every month, according to Shelley. I worked in this building for more years than I cared to
remember, primarily as an investigator of dependency-
neglect cases. Over the years I investigated scores of allegations of sexual and physical abuse in Blackwell County,
but more often situations involving neglect. I have no memory of Olivia Le Master being in the system, but Shelley,
who kept up with all the cases in the office, might, and I tell
her what I'm looking for, "Olivia Le Master wouldn't have
been our typical poverty-stricken welfare mother. She's a tall
white woman who owns River City Realty. You've seen her
ads on TV."

"Threw the damn thing out ten years ago," she mutters,
opening her desk drawer. As I have seen her do so many
times in the past, Shelley takes out a calligraphy pen and
begins to doodle on green graph paper while she thinks.
"Around what year are we talking about?"

I shift in the uncomfortable wooden chair. If they keep
this furniture much longer, they can sell it as antiques. This
is one agency that doesn't get in trouble for spending state
money to redecorate bureaucrats' offices. "Maybe close to
fifteen years ago," I say, wondering if Olivia had another
name back then. For all I know, she could have been married
four times since her divorce.

Abruptly, Shelley stands, telling me, "I think I know who
you're talking about. I'll be back in a minute."

While she is gone, I look around her office, stilling an

urge to go see who has my desk. Shelley has told me only three people remain in the entire office from the time I was there, which was only three years ago. The turnover is enormous. Insufficient staff, low pay, and unqualified people who shuffle paper until the next tragedy hits the news have long made the place a revolving door. Why did I stay so long? Much of the time I felt like a voyeur of horror. I know I would have gone crazy if I had accepted a supervisor's job. In a system this bad, you have to prove that a case worker lay in bed drunk for six months before you are allowed to fire him. Ordinary incompetence and negligence are part of the job description. On Shelley's wall is a sign she has lettered herself. "IF YOU GET YOUR PANTIES IN A WAD BEFORE 10 A.M., YOUR MEDICINE ISN'T STRONG ENOUGH."

Shelley returns, panting a bit as she comes through the door and shuts it behind her. Her blue polyester pants, freak-show size, strain against her hips as she turns the handle on the flimsy door. "If you reveal where you got this information, I'll be in bad trouble."

I watch her ease her huge body into the chair, thinking she could set the governor on fire and no one would touch her. "You know I'd never do that." What motivates *her* to stay? She's been here twenty-five years. Low pay and bad working conditions only explain part of it. Actually, I know the answer. Without making a federal case of it, she is totally convinced there is nothing else on earth she could do with her life that is more important.

"Don't you remember this?" She grins happily, delighted by her superb memory. "Good, good talker. We were about to file once before and she talked us out of it. This case was not your run-of-the-mill, attractive middle-class single white woman struggling to sell real estate and raise two small children; and we kept getting calls she was neglecting the one-year-old. The older child, a girl, was retarded. We never exactly understood the problem, but when there was an incident with boiling water that burned the boy, she agreed to a placement with her mother in Ohio and we closed the file. We never went to court. We'd file on a case like that now instead of having an informal agreement.''

I feel a chill run down the back of my neck. Olivia has never mentioned a word about any of this. Boiling water? Give me a cattle prod any day. I think of her commercials. She is a damn good talker all right, but, I suspect, a better actress. ''Can you live with a subpoena?'' I ask. ''All of a sudden my memory's crystal clear.'' It isn't, of course, but I have no qualms about lying to protect her.

My old friend's smile becomes a smirk. ''You better say that,'' she says, squinting at the file in front of her. ''And I didn't tell you a damn thing.''

After getting a few more details (Olivia would admit only that her infant might have pulled a pan off the stove but had no answer when Shelley pointed out he wasn't tall enough to reach it), I thank her and leave through the rat's maze of cubicles, watching the workers at their desks, some gobbling sandwiches and talking at the same time. Almost always it is the poor who get caught up in abuse and neglect proceedings. Was Olivia that down and out? This child would have had to have been born only a year or so after Pam but before the settlement with the obstetrician came through. Her husband left her, so maybe at one time she wasn't all that much different from the terrified parents who are sitting across from the desks of my former colleagues. I look into the eyes of a young black man sitting in my old cubicle. Does Andy know about this part of Olivia's life? I seriously doubt it. Just because she abused one child and let it be sent away doesn't mean she wanted Pam to die. Yet, if I were a prosecutor, I'd be rubbing my hands with glee and wondering what else I could find out about the past of the star of the River City Realty Commercials.

''My brother's a little naive,'' Morris Chapman says soon after Andy introduces us. He flew in this morning from At-

lanta and has accompanied Andy to my office for our final
interview before the trial begins tomorrow.''

"You've noticed,'' I say, unable to resist sarcasm now that
I have an ally. Morris Chapman does not have his brother's
flair for clothes. For this visit at least he is dressed in a drab
blue business suit that in no way announces its wearer's presence. Taller than Andy, he is also skinnier, but the family
resemblance is there around the eyes and mouth. Yet, where
Andy's intelligent face mirrors his emotions even beneath his
trim beard and glasses, his brother has a wary, pinched look
as if he has an internal computer clicking off prices that he
knows aren't ever coming down. So this is where the money
has come from, I think, already wishing this guy had been
around for the last couple of months. His long fingers,
clenched until this moment like talons around the arms of
the chair, finally uncurl but do not relax. He lives in the real
world; his brother does not. Uncertain how he will take the
information about Olivia, and still wondering how to use it
at the trial, I have not yet told Andy about what I learned at
the Blackwell County Social Services office.

Andy, who seems to have returned to his more open and
accessible personality now that his brother is here, flashes
his first smile in days. "Just a few days in prison will make
me like y'all,'' he says easily, crossing an ankle over a thigh.
The half grin, half smirk on his face suggests to me that some
of the weight he has felt in the last two months has been
shifted to his brother.

"Not that normal,'' Morris replies, shrugging, each digit
of his hands now a blunt poker testing the strength of the
wooden arms of the chair. "Any dude dumb enough to get
involved with a white bitch in your circumstances needs a lot
of work.''

His crudeness crashes over his brother's face like a tidal
wave. I lean back in my chair, content for now to watch the
family dynamic work itself out. Andy cocks his head at his
brother as if he is amazed that Morris can use such terms,
and especially in front of me. Yet his tone, when he finally

speaks, is mild. "White bitch?" he says, laying equal emphasis on both words. "Mo, you haven't even laid eyes on her."

"Damn straight," Morris says dispassionately as he looks squarely but blandly at me as if I were a poorly painted bowl of fruit in a frame on the wall. "She's played you for the starry-eyed, guess-who's-coming-to-dinner nigger aristocrat you've always wanted to be. If you had to have some respectable pussy, what's wrong with Yettie? She's always gone into heat every time your name comes up. You've dragged Yettie down to work with those shit-for-brains fuck-ups and now you won't even look at her 'cause you're too busy sniffing white pussy. Damn, Andy, the only way they'll let more than one nigger at a time in that bunny hutch where you live is in a maid's uniform."

As awful as Morris sounds, I have to resist the urge to hug him. I have thought everything he is saying. But white people can't talk to blacks that way. Afraid I will end what is becoming an embarrassing but revealing harangue, I stare into the space between the two brothers, wondering how much more of this Andy will take. Yet surely Morris is no surprise to him. Everything comes with a price, and perhaps Morris is merely presenting his bill. After a few polite minutes of chitchat to show him I was real, I had intended to ask Morris to wait outside, but now I wanted him to stay. Despite his crudeness, he is delivering some badly needed reality therapy to his brother, who, amazingly, doesn't seem angered by it.

As if he were a child learning to pray, Andy brings his hands together and touches them to his lips. "My brother's living proof," he tells me, "of my theory that the most rabid racists and chauvinists are black men."

Feeling somehow that Morris, Leon Robinson, and I are not all that different, I shake my head. "I doubt that."

Brother Morris, clean-shaven and almost burr-headed, so closely clipped is his bristled head, clearly couldn't care less about our sociological speculations and now gives me a hard stare. "I should of figured Andy'd get a white law-yer, but I hear you don't mind leaning on people. Can't he agree to spill some shit on this Olivia Le Master and still cut a deal?"

Perhaps I should feel insulted, but I can live with the word "lean." Morris understands the game, but surely he doesn't know how prescient his remark is, and I doubt he knows how deeply involved Andy and Olivia are. Quickly, before Andy can interrupt, I reply, "Sure he could, but he says she hasn't done anything wrong except trust his judgment."

"Bullshit!" Morris explodes, slapping the arms of the chair. "According to you," he says, turning to his brother, "she was gonna pocket a couple million off her own kid's death."

Implicit in Morris's question to me is the suggestion that Andy conspired with Olivia. More probably, Morris, cynical beyond words, thinks as I do that Andy may have been duped. Andy returns his brother's stare. He is younger, but he isn't about to be bullied by him. "Olivia's only mistake in this nightmare," he says stubbornly, "was to let me shock her daughter."

I watch Andy's lips curl into a rare but now familiar pout, signaling he won't even begin to be budged. If this were still a charge of manslaughter, I'd have another guilty plea on my hands. It is as if it has taken his brother's presence for him to admit he has some responsibility for Pam's death, something that can't be easy to accept when all his energy has been directed toward fighting for his freedom. How ironic that his streetwise, misanthropic brother has had the effect of stimulating his conscience. "And your mistake," Morris replies to Andy but flicking a glance at me, "was to pull your pants down when she started wagging her white ass at you."

Maybe Morris knows more than I think. Andy, who rarely uses profanity in my presence and never refers to women in sexist terms, merely winces as he says to me, "Morris is a real liberal, isn't he?"

Never having had a brother, and not being particularly close to my only sister (we blow hot and cold), I don't get it. What binds these two except blood? "I think that species," I reply, "has gone out of business."

"I hope to hell you're right," Morris says benignly. "They were about to kill us black folks."

Despite my vow to keep out of this, I laugh out loud. Morris probably thinks Franklin Roosevelt was part of a Communist plot to overthrow this country, while his brother may well pray to him every night. Still, they must touch something in each other. Maybe it's just as simple as sleeping in a room together for a number of years and calling the same man and woman your parents. "The composition of the jury could be crucial for us," I say, having called attention to myself and feeling forced to speak. I would like to be able to discuss my plan to force Leon Robinson to admit his membership in the Trackers, but I am afraid of the reaction I'll get from Andy. Despite a concerted effort in the last few days on my part to get some information on Leon, I still have no evidence that he deliberately let go of Pam. Yet, surely it was as obvious to Leon as it was to Yettie that Andy and Olivia were romantically involved; and, given his feeling about blacks, Leon wouldn't miss an opportunity to act upon his pent-up hatred. Too bad I can't prove it.

"Damn straight," Morris says emphatically, giving the chair a rest and slapping his knee with the palm of his hand. With his height and aggressiveness, Morris could have been a point guard in basketball had he gone to college. Owner of several businesses and some real estate in downtown Atlanta, according to his brother, Morris had better things to do than dribble a basketball and waste his time fantasizing about the pros. "It only takes one to hang up a jury," Morris says, looking at me for confirmation. When I nod, he says, "On the other hand, no nigger I know, man or bitch, is gonna like it when it comes out Andy was messin' with white pussy."

I've almost gotten used to Morris, but when he says the

"N" word, I flinch. For the last two days I've worried that there will be no blacks on the jury. Since Blackwell County is about twenty percent black (though its percentage of registered voters from whom the jury panel is selected could be lower), there should be at least a couple. But this is the kind of no-win case that makes prospective jurors, especially blacks, suddenly remember they are about to miss their mother's funeral in Cleveland.

As if we have touched on something sacred, Andy pointedly changes the subject. "Tell Morris about our expert," he says to me.

Morris, like a dog with his favorite bone, shakes his head. "You're not gonna pull this shit about race not being an issue," he says to his brother.

Again, I feel relief that Morris is here. "It's the most important thing in this case," I tell Morris, convinced that only he can bring Andy around on this subject. "As a psychologist Andy has got to appreciate more than either of us that the jury is going to be influenced by their own racial biases. We just can't sit there while the prosecutor takes advantage of that and we don't," I plead, hoping Morris will work on him.

For the first time today, Andy's magnificent eyes begin to smolder behind the gold frames of his glasses. "You know exactly how I feel about this," he warns me, his voice a low rumble, "and you gave me your word. You are not going to pander to the racist instincts in the courtroom, and that is final."

"Using peremptory strikes to keep whites who won't admit their racism off the jury," I say, somewhat disingenuously, "is hardly pandering." Andy and I have previously discussed that in a capital case the defense gets to eliminate up to twelve potential jurors without having to disclose a reason, and the prosecution gets to eliminate ten. This tradition, not required by the United States Constitution and purely a creature of state law around the country, has as its purpose the selection of an impartial jury.

Like a law professor lecturing the statistically inevitable bad apple in his ethics class, Andy adjusts his glasses as if he would prefer not to see me and thunders, "You just want to use the system to get a black racist on the jury."

Instinctively, I shake my head. Hell, I want both. I want to win his damn case for him. His long arm striking like a snake, Morris bridges the space between their chairs and clutches his brother's arm. "Jesus Christ!" he yells. "Every person on this earth is racist. I don't give a damn who you are. You think you aren't one the way you run after whites? You hate us niggers so bad it makes you sick to look at us!"

Andy recoils as if Morris were trying to spit on him. "I don't live where I do," Andy says icily, "because I hate African-Americans."

Morris laughs, sending an ugly barking sound through my small office as he holds the arm of Andy's chair so he can't pull back further. "You're scared shitless by us. You always have been. Even when you were a kid, you wouldn't go play basketball if it was just a bunch of niggers."

"I wasn't any good and didn't enjoy playing," Andy observes coolly. "And I live where I do because of the crime downtown."

Disgusted, Morris gives Andy's chair a shove. "Bullshit!" he snorts. "Every other black person you see looks like a mugger to you."

"That's ridiculous," Andy scoffs, meeting his brother's now malevolent gaze. Watching this, I wonder how close to the truth Morris is. Their shared history has to count for something. Though I doubt if I would call for Morris to come hold my hand while I struggled through a life-threatening illness, I'm glad to have him now because I don't have the guts to challenge Andy this way. And I can't imagine he is making any of this up for my benefit. By the expression on his face he is as frustrated by his brother as I am.

"If you get convicted," Morris says, his voice dropping,

''we'll get a chance to see how scared you are, 'cause the penitentiary is full of us!''

Maintaining his composure, Andy looks at Morris and me as if we are necessary but inescapably inferior beings. Maybe we are, but when this case is over, it seems highly likely that Morris and I will be going home, while he goes to jail.

20

IT IS LATE afternoon when Olivia arrives with the attorney for her company for a meeting that has been postponed twice. Karen Ott is no more a criminal defense attorney than I am a real estate lawyer. If Olivia is eventually charged, undoubtedly Karen will bow out before the ink is dry on the warrant for Olivia's arrest; but for now, she is here and plainly uncomfortable with her role. Andy has seized on Olivia's failure to go out and hire the best criminal lawyer money can buy as proof of her innocence. I'm not so sure she hasn't already done so and is only appearing to be represented by Karen. Olivia may be as pure as new-fallen snow, but I no longer trust a word out of her mouth.

"It's just going to be you, your client, me, and Olivia," Karen says nervously after I tell her that Andy wants Morris to sit in with us. She is wearing a silk designer blouse that has never seen the inside of a courtroom, and has admitted in a previous conversation that it is difficult for her to refuse Olivia, especially since she does all her title business. I have kept to myself Olivia's attempt to employ me.

"If you're going to insist on it," I say, pretending reluctance I do not feel, "I'll tell him." Morris, though he has promised to be merely an observer, is too much of a loose cannon for this meeting, which may soon take on the overtones of something other than a final get-our-stories-straight session. At some point I will take this opportunity to remind Olivia of her past.

I have reserved the conference room for this meeting. Four

people make my office seem a little close, especially under the circumstances. Andy and I take the east side of the table. His former lover and her lawyer sit directly opposite from us. I do not offer coffee and Cokes. If they want something, they can ask for it. Andy is wearing a light gray suit with one of those wild, flowered ties in fashion that I can't bring myself to buy. Even Morris, no clotheshorse either, is wearing one. Andy looks everywhere in the room except at the face of the woman he told me he loved. Maybe he, too, is finally having second thoughts about Olivia's innocence.

Though I have requested this meeting, Karen begins it by asking me if I think Olivia should consider taking the Fifth Amendment and not testifying, which is another way of asking me if I have any knowledge that her client bears some criminal responsibility for what happened. Though she doesn't practice criminal law, nobody has ever said Karen was dumb. She is not bad-looking for a real estate lawyer. In addition to being as tall as her client, she looks around the mouth and eyes like that goofy movie star Geena Davis. She has the advantage of being able to claim relative ignorance. Even if my client can't bear to take a good look at his former lover, I can and do. She looks damn nice. Her hair, longer than the last time I saw her, is tightly permed. Her long legs, shaped by black tights under a short teal-green skirt, make her look sexier than I remembered. I guess if I were a woman and knew I was going to be on the front page of every newspaper in the state the day after tomorrow, I'd go shopping and to the beauty parlor, too. Now that I've been handed this opportunity, I say, "I'm beginning to wonder, Karen. This morning I was told that your client"—I watch Olivia's face— "years ago gave up another child she had abused."

"That's not true!" Olivia says, jerking her head sharply in my direction. But there is no mistaking she has been caught off guard. I turn and look at Andy who has become rigid in his chair. Behind his lenses, his eyes, more cinnamon than brown today, are wide and staring like a startled child's, reflecting a mixture of anxiety, surprise, and fear. For once

I have shocked him. "Who told you that?" Olivia demands, her voice shrill with anger.

"I'm not at liberty to say," I say, only half lying. "I don't think Andy or I knew you had another child, Olivia."

"I knew about her son," Andy says weakly. It is clear from his tone, though, that he hasn't been told everything.

"It wasn't child abuse; it was an accident," Olivia says, her voice urgent and loud. "He pulled a pan of water off the stove. I was going through a bad time then and was drinking a lot. In fact, by then I had become a full-fledged alcoholic." This admission does not come easy, and Olivia looks at me with undisguised resentment.

I do not quite shrug in disbelief, but I do not want Andy to think Olivia should be allowed to worm out of this one so easily. "Is that all?" I ask, indicating by my tone that I know more.

"Val had had a couple of accidents before this, and in my condition I couldn't handle going through some kind of child-abuse proceeding, so I let my mother in Ohio take him, and that's where he is today."

What a great mother you've been, I think. "How come you've never tried to get him back?" I ask, drawing the battle lines between us. "Children and Family Services would have worked with you. Both state and federal law requires them to work to rehabilitate the family."

"Val is happy where he is," she says, her voice without a trace of warmth. I have found her guilty of abuse even if there is no court order. "I see him whenever I can."

I am the enemy now, and that is okay with me. I don't like her much either. I say to Karen, "I don't know if Jill Marymount knows this yet or not."

Karen's slightly round face appears deflated by this turn of events. This is more than she bargained for. "Is this admissible?" she asks me.

"It might well be," I say, sensing Andy's discomfort. He has begun to squirm in his seat like a small child who needs to use the toilet. Perhaps this revelation will be like replacing a distorted pane of glass in his bathroom mirror, and when Andy takes a hard look at himself tomorrow morning he might see a different man.

"I want to testify," Olivia says, her jaw set, but her words sound brittle as if she has begun to doubt that she is still in control of her own fate.

Karen says in a low voice intended to soothe her client. "We can talk about it later." Olivia barely nods, and Karen, her gray-green eyes narrowing with obvious distaste at the question she is about to ask, says to me, "What are you going to say in your opening statement? Will you admit their affair?"

I look over at Andy who is studying a blank spiral notebook he has brought in with him. "I don't see how it can be avoided," I say, beginning to warm to the role of the messenger of bad news. If Olivia doesn't testify, by the time we get to closing argument I can consider pointing a finger at her, possibly without running too great a risk that the jury will find the remaining fingers are pointed at my client. I justify this decision by saying, "If Andy is going to stay out of prison or worse, the jury will have to trust him. If he tries to hide anything, it will be extremely difficult for them to accept him, given that most or all of them will be white and will suspect a relationship anyway. His credibility is everything in this case." Without having said so, I have implied her client has none.

Olivia's long, sensuous face dips slightly, as if she knew this part of the story wouldn't be left on the cutting-room floor. Remembering her coldness at the probable cause hearing I ask her, "If you do testify tomorrow, how reluctant a witness are you going to be?"

Instead of looking at me, Olivia stares at Andy as she answers, "I had no intention of hurting Andy's case last time."

"But you did," I reply, not bothering to conceal my anger. This is ground that Olivia and I have covered before, but it can't hurt to remind her. "When I questioned you, your manner suggested you wanted to put as much distance as you possibly could between your own participation and what occurred.''

"That's understandable,'' Andy says, gently rebuking me. "Olivia was not only angry at me but also upset at herself.'' Since he has been in the same room with her, his large and soulful eyes, the color of pennies found on a river bank, have become melancholy.

"It may be understandable,'' I say, irritated by his defense of her, "but she's got to be a hell of a lot more forthcoming next time or she shouldn't testify at all.''

There is an air of unreality in the room. We might as well be rehearsing *Our Town* for the high school senior class play. More sullen than she has a right to be, Olivia asks, "How specific do I have to get?''

With her Queen of England attitude, this woman is fast getting on my nerves. I explode at her: "Tomorrow's going to be the second most horrible day in your lives! Jill Marymount will eat you alive, and the judge is going to let her, no matter how many objections I make, so you better be prepared to be pretty goddamned specific if you want to come out of this with any credibility. You're going to need an explanation for everything that both of you did starting from the day you met and ending with this meeting today, and if you're not prepared to do that, you better keep off the witness stand.''

For the first time since I met her, Olivia looks scared, as if she is about to cry. I can't say that I blame her. I can't always explain my own life even to myself, much less to the people I love. How much more difficult would it be for her to have to justify her life to twelve people, some of whom will regard her as an evil witch as soon as Jill finishes her opening statement. Pour boiling water on one child and then give him up? Put her other child in an institution? Have her shocked? Love a man (a black one, for God's sake!) who is willing to send enough electricity into the child's body to kill her? Even if you forget the damn money, how innocent can she be if she is willing to admit to all of that? If I didn't dislike Olivia so much, I'd feel sorry for her.

My speech gets some results, after a bit of hemming and hawing, and for the next two hours I get to play the role of Jill Marymount and ask every question I can think of that will incriminate either of them. When I am finished, I don't have a clue as to what a jury will do with Olivia's testimony, but at least she has a complete story. "Are you in love," I finish up, as mockingly as I can, "with the defendant at this very moment?"

Love! The burdens we place on that word. Olivia, exhausted as we all are, shakes her head. "I don't know how I feel anymore."

At one time I would have believed her, but no longer. I now think she has manipulated Andy every step of the way. Her past has grown too long. Honesty, a scantily clad virtue usually born of necessity, is Andy's only hope. The trouble is that people lie so much it is hard to recognize the truth when it appears. Without enthusiasm, I follow Olivia's rehearsal with an abbreviated reprise of my opening statement: "Whether you approve of it or not, ladies and gentlemen, this is what happened and why it happened. . . ." On the assumption she will testify as she has rehearsed, I summarize many of the events from Olivia's perspective, but barely mention the issue of race. If I can put enough of a tragic spin on Olivia's story, perhaps the white women on the jury (and they should be in the majority) will empathize with her enough to realize that if their circumstances had been different, they could have been faced with the same choices. Though I do not say it (so as not to set off Andy), I firmly believe white women are less racist than white men.

By six o'clock, when we have finished, the emotional climate in the room precludes idle chitchat. Olivia looks as if she has learned she has two months to live, and Andy doesn't seem much better. Saying goodbye in the conference room, I let Andy escort Karen and Olivia to the elevators and go look for Morris. He is in my office, on the phone, with his feet propped up on my desk. Barely glancing up at me, he continues his conversation, apparently to someone in one of his businesses in Atlanta. I wonder if I'm paying for his calls. His speech is laced with the most profane epithets and scatological references imaginable. Yet at this moment I'd rather talk to him than to his brother.

When Andy returns a moment later, he tells me he wants to talk to me, and we return to the conference room and sit down on opposite sides of the table. "Why didn't you tell me," he demands, his voice angry, "what you were going to say to Olivia?"

I am sick of his defending her, but I keep my voice level. "I didn't want you to tip her off. As far as I'm concerned she's still got a lot of explaining to do." At this moment Morris walks in and sits down beside me. It is as if he and I are the relatives in this case.

"She doesn't owe you the time of day," Andy says, his voice more hostile than I've ever heard it. "Her life's been a living hell, and all you can do is try to set her up." Quickly, for Morris's benefit, he recounts Olivia's latest problems.

Morris, who has nervously begun to drum the table with the knuckles of his right hand, stops. "You're still fucking the bitch," he says sharply, "aren't you, brother?"

As if charged with electricity, Andy's eyelids flutter twice, as obvious as a stammer. "Hell, no."

The hell he isn't! I can't believe I have been so stupid. By the way Olivia had been acting, I was certain they weren't seeing each other. "Of course, he is!" I say to Morris, jabbing his arm with my finger. "She's still playing him like a goddamn violin." Why didn't I see this? Andy's so pussy-whipped he can't remember his own name. Needlessly, I add, "She couldn't manipulate him any better if he were a hand puppet."

Morris shakes his head mournfully at his brother. "You stupid, stupid little nigger."

Andy pushes back from the table and in an agonized tone, pleads, "Can't either of you understand that I love this woman? Olivia's gone through more in the last sixteen years than most people endure their entire lives. Neither of you knows her at all!''

I look at this man, who is as intelligent as anybody I know, and wonder how he can possibly be this dumb. Black people have been getting screwed by whites in Arkansas for more than 150 years, but Andy is competing to be this year's poster child. ''She's about to love you to death,'' I say, more to Morris than to him.

Morris chuckles ruefully, looking at his brother. ''The boy's been fucked blind. The bitch could shoot six people dead, and you'd say her finger just got stuck while she was testing her gun.''

Andy stares balefully at his brother as if they were picking up an old argument. ''I don't really expect you to understand, Mo,'' he says, his voice dropping to a whisper. ''You've always hated yourself as much as you hate whites.''

In a bored tone, Morris replies, ''Now, don't start trying to fuck with me, boy. I came to terms with myself a long time ago. I'm not gonna be the one with my pecker hanging out in the middle of the courtroom tomorrow.''

Anxious to avoid open warfare, I put my hand on Morris's arm to restrain him. ''Andy, if there's more to this than an accident,'' I say quietly, ''there's still time to make a deal with Jill Marymount.''

With a look of utter disdain, Andy stalks out of the room. Morris watches him go and surprises me by commenting after Andy is out of earshot, ''He probably does love her. He's never happier than when he's taking care of a cripple.''

I stand up and stretch. My back feels as if it has calcified since this morning. After this trial I've got to start getting some exercise again. ''I wish now I'd insisted that you sat in on this,'' I say. ''I can't figure her out, but I doubt if Olivia Le Master fits into the category of a cripple.''

Twisting his hands outward Morris pops a thick, hairy knuckle and stares at his fingers. ''Oh, I can see how the bitch could get all twisted.''

I walk over to the window and stare at the street. Morris has put me in my place—he doesn't seem the compassionate type, but even he is willing to concede Olivia has had a hard time of it. "Maybe so," I admit, "but lots of people with retarded children don't go to the extremes she has, and I'm not even talking about whether she's guilty of murder."

Morris scratches his sparse, graying hair. "I don't know," he mutters softly, "you white folks don't handle bad shit too good sometimes. When that silver spoon gets taken away from you, it's mighty easy to get withdrawal symptoms."

"Could be," I shrug, unwilling to argue. As long as he is writing the checks, Morris is free to put a racial spin on whatever he wants. For all I know, he may be right. If you don't expect much, you sure as hell can't claim to be disappointed. And yet there is his brother, who refuses to interpret anything through the lens of racism. Why should I be surprised? We all do what works. "You think Andy would let himself be talked into taking Pam's life?" I ask, lowering my voice.

Morris stands and comes over to the window by me. "He wouldn't do it for the money," he whispers, "but damned if he couldn't think of a whole shit load of other reasons."

I look down on the rapidly emptying street and think of the nightly preoccupations that await these people who are still scurrying out of the Layman Building. TV. Children. Some will work. Maybe a few will even read a book. How many are going home to have sex outside of marriage with someone of a different race?

"What do you think your chances are?" Sarah asks. She had come into the kitchen for a glass of milk. As the product of a mixed marriage, Sarah would be the ideal person to try this case for Andy. She wouldn't have to say a word to get across Andy's point that race should not be an issue in this trial.

I look up from the table, which is covered with my papers. Though I have nailed down their stories (Andy admits to five "meetings" with Olivia since he was initially charged; through Karen, Olivia agrees with this number), our case stinks. As soon as Andy opens his mouth, he will be on the defensive. Once the jury hears about the money Olivia was to receive upon Pam's death, that is all it will be thinking about. Yettie will testify that she heard Olivia say Pam would be better off dead than alive, etc., etc. Jill will build facts and motives on top of each other until they reach the top of the courthouse. And then the jury will hear they have slept together as recently as last week. "About the same," I say, smiling at my daughter, who is wearing ragged cut-offs and a T-shirt the size of a circus tent, "as the chances of the universe randomly coming into being."

Woogie, his long nails tap-dancing on the linoleum, has ambled in from the couch perhaps to hear this discussion, but more likely in hopes that Sarah is opening the door to get him a snack. Sarah, who has attended Mass every Sunday since returning from Camp Anytown, cracks, "Well, they must be pretty good since it happened."

I watch Sarah, who now has a white mustache, unwrap from its plastic a slice of cheese, break it in two, and throw the smaller part to Woogie, who catches and swallows it in a single motion. "Do you do this often?" I ask, exhausted, and wanting but unable even for an instant to forget the trial. Ah, the science of reinforcement. Somehow, it's difficult to imagine Albert Einstein with a cattle prod in his hand.

"If all you were allowed to eat was dog food," Sarah says reasonably, "you'd hope somebody would throw you a little cheese, too."

"He doesn't even taste it," I protest, putting down my pen and watching it roll off the table. "It's like throwing him a quarter every time you do it."

"More like a dime," Sarah says, throwing him the rest of the slice to spite me.

This commentary on my cheapness rolls straight off my back. I bend down to pick up my pen. "If you want to chip in for your food, it's fine with me."

Sarah gives me a stricken look. "Are things that bad?"

"They're great," I lie. To hell with Andy, I think. I ought to be worrying about myself. If he goes down the tubes, my venture into private practice may not be far behind him. Getting your client the death penalty doesn't make for such a great referral. "I've got more clients at this stage than I ever dreamed." Too bad they don't pay. I refuse to worry Sarah. My mother worried about money so much after my father died I thought at any moment I would be sent into the streets to beg for bread. It was never that bad, and if she had been a little less dramatic, I might not be such a tightwad now. I want Sarah to enjoy her senior year and not spend her time wondering whether I can pay the mortgage. The phone rings. As my daughter flies to the phone, I say, "See, there's a client now."

In one fluid motion Sarah shuts the refrigerator door and snatches the phone from the wall as if she is expecting the President to call and give us his opinion on our finances instead of one of a half-dozen nightly calls she receives from her friends. "Hi!"

Sarah's features knit into an uncharacteristic frown. "Just a moment, please," she says, bringing the phone, its cord a long corkscrew tail, to the table for me. "I've heard this voice, but I can't place it."

Mona Moneyhart, I think dejectedly as I take the phone and identify myself.

"Gideon," Mona says, her voice, its normal breathy purr now that she has me on the phone, "your little daughter doesn't let you get far away from her, does she?"

"Mona," I say angrily, "I'm getting ready for a murder trial that starts tomorrow, and I haven't got time to listen to you. What do you want?"

"Why, Gideon," Mona says, "you've never been ugly to me before. Is your little daughter having a fit about something?"

I get Sarah to smile as I roll my eyes back in my head. "It's nine-thirty, Mona. What's the problem?"

"I just wanted to tell you," she says sounding like Shirley Temple as a child, "that Steve and I have reconciled. We're together now. Would you like to talk to him?"

"No, no, that's all right," I say hastily, imagining Steve desperately setting rattraps out all over the kitchen, tightening screws on the stove, doing whatever he can to guard against the inevitable morning he will be again served rat muffins for breakfast. "Congratulations! I'll call his lawyer as soon as I can."

"You can keep all the money I've paid you," Mona says. "It's not worth suing you over."

"Thanks," I say, winking at Sarah. I figure with all her calls I've made about twenty dollars an hour off her case at this point. "I honestly feel I've earned it."

"And you know I haven't got that kind of time," she declares. "You know my motto."

"I sure do know your motto," I say, repeating the words simultaneously with Sarah, who has guessed our caller. "Let Being Be!"

After Sarah hangs up the phone for me, she leans back against the kitchen wall and asks seriously, "Do you think she could be committed to the state hospital?"

"Not even close," I say, thinking of all the clients I used to represent out there. "She's probably as sane as the rest of us. Just a little more obsessed."

Sarah laughs. It doesn't take much to be weird in her eyes. Still, Mona Moneyhart seems the genuine article.

Fifteen minutes later, Sarah is bringing me the phone again. "Rainey," she says approvingly. "She's probably calling to wish you luck."

I smile, thinking of the differences between women. Mona Moneyhart is the original client from hell; Rainey makes me glad just thinking about her.

"Gideon," Rainey says, her voice solemn and small, "I promised myself I wouldn't bother you with this tonight, but

I'm so scared. I had a mammogram this afternoon, and my doctor has arranged for me to see a surgeon next week.''

I can't take this. I'm just not going to be able to go through it again. I wait for Sarah to disappear around the corner of the kitchen. In the moment this takes, all the fear and panic come back. It is as if Sarah has taken all the oxygen from the air with her. ''Who's your doctor?'' I ask, knowing I should be saying something else.

''Connie Havens,'' Rainey says, mentioning the name of a busy gynecologist who is the only female in a group of five men.

I have never heard her voice sound so dead. Usually, it is like a musical instrument. Even when she is exhausted from a week's work, she still usually manages to sound like a piano being played with one hand. ''How long have you known you had a lump in your breast?'' I ask, trying not to accuse her. Rosa, who, as a nurse, had absolutely no excuse, was lax about examining her breasts monthly, even though she knew the statistics. Women, I read the month before Rosa died, wait an average of five to six months before going to the doctor *after* they discover they may have a problem. During this time the tumor can grow from the size of a pea to the diameter of a golf ball or much larger.

''I didn't know,'' Rainey says. ''It was just a part of a regular checkup.''

My mouth is so dry I can barely swallow. Breast cancer is the leading cause of death for women Rainey's age. ''Did she say how big the lump was?'' The beauty of a mammogram is that it can pick up tumors small enough to be cured.

''You won't believe this,'' Rainey says, her voice a whisper, ''but she told me and I've forgotten. Something like four centimeters or six.''

If I remember what I've read, that number can make a huge difference in her chances, assuming the tumor is malignant. I look across the lighted kitchen to the darkness in the den. I feel myself becoming angry. Rainey knows enough to get all the information she needs. ''Maybe it's just a cyst.''

"I've been going to Connie for years," Rainey says dully. "I know when she's worried."

I feel like I'm suffocating and reach over with one hand to push up the window across from the table. It has finally turned cool this week. A gust of air rushes over the window sill through the screen as if it were being sucked in by a pump. Rosa's doctor had been certain she had a malignancy. "What day is it?" I ask, knowing my own voice sounds like a computer recording. I have to give more than this, but I don't think I'm going to be able to.

"Wednesday morning at ten," Rainey says, her voice a little brighter. "Have you heard of a surgeon named Alf Brownlee? Connie swears by him."

There is no way the trial will last until then. Wednesday morning is free, but there is no way in hell I'm going to be there. "Yeah," I say. "He's supposed to be superb." Of course, he couldn't save Rosa, but he gave it the old college try. "Why didn't you write down some of the things she told you?" I sound like the world's greatest asshole, but I can't stop.

"I don't know," Rainey says, beginning to cry for only the second time since I have know her (the first was when she broke up with me at a point in the relationship when I was about to propose to her). "I guess I was in shock."

She is waiting for me to say I will be there with her, but that's not going to happen. I just can't do it. "I've got to be in court Wednesday," I lie. She has a lot of social-worker friends at the state hospital. They'll know what to say to her. "Maybe Edna can go with you."

There is silence at the other end. Finally, I think I can hear her sigh. "Maybe she can."

"I'm sorry for you, Rainey," I say. I'm sorry, all right. But I just can't do it.

A couple of minutes later I hang up, but working on the case is now out of the question. I stare at the mass of paper in front of me, but all I can think of is the nightmare of Rosa's last year. Was it as bad as I remember? I get up to pour myself a glass of water. Yes and no, I think. Afterward, I began to think of it as paying for all the good times we had had together. A bill coming due much sooner than we expected. I would have preferred to pay as we went instead of having a big balloon payment that we couldn't quite make at the end. At the very end, Rosa saw her death as a release—a part of God's Grace. Maybe she was right, and I am wrong, but I do not want to repeat the class. I knock on Sarah's door.

"Come in," she says primly, as if she is living in her own apartment. I go in and feel the sense of dismay that always accompanies me when I see her room: clothes, books, tapes, magazines, Coke cans, candy wrappers, and other debris litter the floor. How can she stand it? Seated cross-legged on her unmade bed with her European history book between her knees, she is not happy to see the old man.

I blurt, "Rainey may have breast cancer!"

"What?" she gasps, the thick book snapping shut as her legs jerk together.

I nod, "Her gynecologist has referred her to a surgeon." Unable to stand the pain on my child's face, I let my eyes go out of focus and look at the dozens of pictures of her friends she has mounted on a board behind her.

"Oh no!" Sarah cries, her tears released as suddenly as tap water.

I wade through the junk on the floor and sit on her bed and put my arm around her. "She's going to the same surgeon as your mother did."

Against my shoulder, Sarah shakes her head. "It's not fair!"

I close my eyes, wishing that fairness had something to do with life. But maybe I shouldn't. "No, it's not," I agree, tasting salt in my own mouth.

"Is Rainey by herself tonight?" Sarah asks, clearing her throat.

Her face against my shoulder feels as warm as a heating pad. "I guess so."

"You can't let her stay by herself tonight. Go on over

there. I'll be fine," she says, drawing back from me so she can look me in the eye.

Sarah's mascara is smeared, and I wipe her left cheek with my knuckle. How can I tell her that I don't even have the guts to go to the doctor's office with Rainey? "I'm not going to leave you alone tonight," I say.

Sarah wipes her eyes on her bedspread, making me wonder when she last washed her sheets. "I'll be fine."

Brave words, but I know if I leave her alone, she won't sleep five minutes. She's not as old or strong as she thinks she is. Besides, she loves Rainey . . . probably as much as I do.

We compromise. I tell her that I will go over to Rainey's and try to persuade her to come spend the night with us. "I can sleep on the couch," I say, never having done so. After a fight with Rosa one night, I spent five minutes on it sighing as loud as I could before she came and got me.

"It wouldn't horrify me," Sarah says dryly, "if she slept with you."

I stand up. I guess it wouldn't. Sarah probably thinks Rainey and I have slept together before when she has spent the night with a friend. It doesn't seem the right time to admit otherwise.

In ten minutes I am standing at Rainey's door. When I see her face, I'm glad I have a daughter who is a better person than her father. Whether Rainey spends the night or not, I will be there for her Wednesday.

21

THE COUNTY'S LARGEST courtroom has been set aside for the trial, and it is packed until Judge Tarnower announces that in her court prospective jury members in capital murder cases are interviewed in chambers by the judge and lawyers to determine bias. As Judge Tarnower, her hands as expressive and lively as a symphony conductor's, apologizes for the limited parking around the courthouse, I notice that she has had her hair done for the trial. Her usual mass of blond curls, a slightly lighter color today, sits higher than ever on her intelligent head. All is vanity, and why not? We all want to look good for the TV cameras that are parked outside the door. When the elevator doors popped open this morning, the first face I saw was that of Kim Keogh, who, unless I wholly imagined it, winked as if to say that if my fly is unzipped, the cameras will not lie.

I think of Kim, and the picture of Rainey, lying in my bed asleep this morning when I went in to get my clothes, forms an overlay in my mind through which I am still filtering all other thoughts. Yet why should I have been surprised that she would accept my offer to spend the night? The fear etched in her voice when she first called and then gratitude imprinted on her face when she came to the door needed no explanation. Like a eunuch who is uncertain what his job entails, I offered to sleep fully clothed in my bed with her, but perhaps out of deference to Sarah, she asked me to sleep on the couch. No matter. Her face asleep on my pillow when

I came in to get my clothes made up for all the sex I've never had and may never have with her.

I glance back at Morris, who is seated in the first row behind the defense table. I wish I were defending him instead of his brother. Dressed in the same suit he wore yesterday, which is now rumpled, Morris would at least be some help. Beside me, Andy, natty as ever in a gray suit and dark tie, seems determined to do some jail time. But after wrestling with it since five o'clock this morning, I have decided his attitude that he is responsible for Pam's death may play well with the jury, given what I intend to do. He will be furious with me, but I'm not campaigning for his vote.

I catch the eye of my Mississippi expert witness and nod, my heart beginning to sink. If there was ever a witness whose testimony looked bought, Kent Goza has to be right around the top of the list. If the jury can get past his looks, maybe he will do us some good, because the guy is intelligent. Over the telephone Goza sounds authoritative, but in person his words slide out the side of his mouth as if he is trying to give you a deal on some choice Florida swampland. On Dr. Goza a perfectly respectable brown polyester suit looks like the by-product of a chemical used to make plastic explosives. We should have demanded that the guy send a video of himself, but after five long-distance conversations with him, it never occurred to me that he would come off looking like a door-to-door salesman of child pornography. When a doubt did cross my mind, I dismissed it. How weird could an educated white professional from neighboring Mississippi be? Well, now I know the answer. Still, this greasy-haired, wormy anorexic from the Magnolia State is convincing about the efficacy of shock in stopping self-abusive behavior in retarded children. Maybe, as Dan suggested yesterday after he had seen him in the men's room, I should ask the jury to put bags over their heads when he testifies.

It is Olivia who is attracting all the attention. As she waits at the back of the courtroom with her real estate lawyer, heads seem to swivel 180 degrees as the crowd strains to get

a look at her. Now cut off from my view at the defense counsel
table, I have had a good look at her. It is not as if Olivia is
trying to hide from the attention. Wearing a red dress whose
color might be more appropriate for Valentine's Day, she seems
amazingly at ease. For all I understand her, she is smiling
because she thinks this case may be great for business. By
focusing on what is in the human heart and mind, the criminal
law seeks to measure what it can never truly know: the intent
of the accused at a particular moment in time. We pay a king's
ransom daily to highly trained specialists to understand precisely our motivations in this country. The problem is that "intent," "heart," and "mind" are philosophical constructs that
for thousands of years have plagued far wiser humans than are
gathered in this courtroom today. Science may evolve to the
point where future historians will giggle hysterically while they
examine judicial artifacts of this period. Given the limitations
of our criminal justice system, if Olivia were my client, I would
advise her to keep her mouth shut the rest of her life, no matter
how innocent she claimed to be. Innocent, of course, she is
not. Less than twenty-four hours ago she was lying to my face
that she and Andy had not seen each other in weeks. My message to her last night via Karen that if she truly cares about
Andy (I do not trust her to tell the truth) she will invoke the
Fifth Amendment and not testify seems doomed to be ignored.
However, as a subpoenaed witness, Olivia will not formally
be making that decision until she is called to the witness box.
There is no way she and Andy can keep their stories straight,
and it will be Andy the jury will punish.

    Judge Tarnower's chambers (actually Judge Rafferty's) are,
by way of contrast to the courtroom, rather cramped. Potential jurors, like job applicants, come in one by one and sit at
the head of a small conference table. Jill and Kerr Bowman
face Andy and me. Judge Tarnower, motherly (she has five-
year-old twin boys) and businesslike at the same time, pre-
sides from the other side of a desk perpendicular to the table,
clucking directions at her clerk, a bailiff, and the court re-

porter who round out our group. Andy and I have reached a compromise of sorts. He agrees with me, as he must to be logically consistent, that any potential juror exhibiting bias, racial or otherwise, should be struck by the judge for "cause," as the law calls it, or by us using one of our peremptory challenges if we suspect bias but cannot persuade the judge of it. But he is adamant that I also question potential black jurors along with the judge and the prosecutor to determine a bias against whites or in favor of blacks simply based on race. This kind of scrupulousness, in my opinion, is unheard of, and unnecessary in an adversary system. That is the business of the prosecution and the court, not mine. "My client, Your Honor," I explain drolly to the judge before the first jury panel member is brought before us, "takes, as no client of mine ever has before, the ideal of an impartial jury, as you shall see, very seriously."

Matters that are essentially trial tactics and strategy are decisions to be made by the attorney, not the client, and while ultimately a client has the theoretical right to fire his lawyer, no judge will permit a defendant to hold the court's docket hostage to a decision by the accused to fire his attorney in the middle of a trial. Still, I see no harm in humoring Andy's obsessions at this point. Perhaps he will score some points with Judge Tarnower, a liberal, who may be persuaded to see Andy for the unique piece of work he is. At any rate, Andy will be furious with me before this trial is over, if all goes according to plan.

When I ask a young black accountant about Andy's age whom I would love to have on the jury if he would be any more likely to be sympathetic to Andy because of his race, I get an expected negative reply. Who wants to admit to any bias at all? We're all one big, happy family. Sure. Though Mr. Bert Williams doesn't know it, I want him very much. Actually, it was a safe question, since Jill has worked this area to death, hoping to find a justifiable excuse to strike him. The U.S. Supreme Court has generally hacked away at the rights of criminal defendants for the last twenty-odd years, but it will no longer let a prosecutor get away with striking a black juror just on the mere assumption that the juror will be biased. If Jill tries to use one of her peremptory challenges to strike this guy, who, like Andy, lives in an integrated part of Blackwell County, she knows I will challenge her and put her to the test of offering a racially neutral explanation of her decision. Of course, if he were to admit to racial bias, he would not be allowed to serve, but this guy, whose breezy manner suggests he might swing a little if he got some pot or alcohol in him, says he likes everybody and everything. I doubt it, but since when has saying you're an optimist been against the law?

It is the matter of interracial love and sex that naturally consumes the most time. "Are you opposed to whites and African-Americans being involved romantically?" I ask a forty-six-year-old white mother of three who is temporarily at home raising her children.

Mrs. Hyslip, a red-haired woman who could be Rainey's sister except for her large, rubbery lips, gives Andy an embarrassed glance and says, "Well, I'm from a small town, and that sort of thing was frowned on when I was growing up."

Since Arkansas is practically devoid of urban areas, she hasn't said much, but she is no different from any other potential juror who has been asked that question. What I would love to know but don't dare ask is whether she could ever imagine under the right circumstances being involved with a black male. Since the judge won't strike anyone for cause who answers affirmatively (we couldn't have a trial within the state), I have to ask if she could be fair and impartial in her deliberations knowing that the defendant and the mother of the dead girl had talked about marriage at one point in their relationship. To their enormous credit, five whites and one black answer that question honestly, and Judge Tarnower strikes them for cause, saving me my peremptory challenges. Mrs. Hyslip hesitates so long before answering and is so tentative before she says, "I'm pretty sure I could," that I resolve to use one of our strikes.

Despite a long list of other questions designed to reveal their racial prejudices (Judge Tarnower lets me ask all the clubs and organizations anyone has ever joined, including any groups that espouse the superiority of one race over another), we move much faster than any of us thought we could; and by eleven o'clock we have a jury composed of six white women, four white males, and two African-Americans, a man and a woman. Besides Bert Williams, Jill has failed to strike a middle-aged nurse at St. Thomas who squinted at me when the judge asked her if she knew me, but said she didn't. I am betting she might have known Rosa and liked her and made the connection I was married to her. Still, a black woman on the jury makes me nervous. Will she, like Yettie Lindsey, punish Andy for wanting to marry a white woman? Picking a jury is little more than a crap game. I have used our peremptory challenges to keep off anybody I suspected of being a redneck. My rule of thumb, unscientific and prejudiced, is that if I had absolutely nothing else to go on and other things were equal, I struck whites who lived in the southwest part of the county. That area is considered the most racist, but I am glad I don't have to offer a public explanation. The Supreme Court has not as yet gone so far as to require lawyers for black defendants to offer a "racially neutral" explanation of why we choose to strike certain whites from the jury list.

Jill's opening statement to the jury prepares them for the sermon she will give in her closing argument: the only thing less sacred than the bond between a child and her parents is the relationship between a child and her doctor. I am tempted to pretend I am gagging, but the jurors are instantly captivated by Jill's manner, which is somehow preachy but effective because of her utter sincerity. As if she is in mourning, she is wearing a black dress, no jewelry, except for plain earrings barely visible underneath the shining, lustrous dark hair that is her only concession to femininity. Unlike some

other female attorneys, who withdraw part of their retirement
pensions to buy clothes and accessories for a big trial, Jill
refuses to call attention to her striking features. Even her
shoes, low-heeled black pumps, say to the jury that she is
telling them a shocking story that deserves everyone's respect
and full attention. She comes from behind the podium and
stands in front of the rail that runs in front of the jury box.
Stooping slightly she reviews the evidence she will present,
staying away from a possible motive until just before she sits
down. "Mr. Page will tell you that Pam's death was a terrible
accident, but as you listen to the testimony, I want you to be
thinking about what was occurring between Andrew Chapman and Olivia Le Master and what they had to gain by Pam's
death."

I watch the jury's faces as they hear her describe the malpractice settlement and Yettie Lindsey's expected testimony. It is as if the issue of race were the last thing on Jill's
mind. Andy leans over and whispers to me, "She's really
good, isn't she?"

Concentrating as hard as I can, I do not answer, but I want
to tell him that a prosecutor doesn't have to be great to keep
a jury interested in this case. Yet this jury is hoping for the
details, and they will be disappointed. There will be no description of any salacious practices that will have the spec-
tators gasping with delight. Not for the first time I consider
telling the jury that I, a small-town boy from eastern Arkansas, was happily married until her death to a woman whose
skin was almost as dark as that of two of its members—that
under the right conditions any of us might and do choose
against all we've been taught and believed. Yet, as I study
the jury, I lose courage. The risk is too great that some of
the whites on the jury (maybe the blacks as well) might decide to punish me for presuming to preach a text few want
to hear. It is enough that Andy is on trial; I don't dare add
to his burden. Instead I tell the jury a version some of them
might be able to accept.

"Ladies and gentlemen," I say standing at the podium

after Jill has taken her seat, "what happened in this case is unfortunately what happens in real life: two people who have no need, desire, or intention of doing so fall in love and, instead of living happily ever after, see their lives become an unintended tragedy. Though I could give you a hundred examples from everything from Shakespeare's *Romeo and Juliet* to the tritest made-for-TV movie, we all know it happens in the most inappropriate of situations: it happens at work; it happens in wartime; it happens between neighbors; it happens in institutions for the retarded. The prosecuting attorney has painted a picture for you of a man who is so evil that he would take the life of a child to satisfy his own lust for a sexual relationship and money beyond his wildest dreams. The truth is a lot less sensational but a lot more lifelike. The accident that I'm about to describe, which resulted in the death of the child of Olivia Le Master, has been emotionally devastating to her and to my client as well." I come around the podium and grasp the jury rail. "Because of our culture and our history in the South, some of you may be thinking, 'So what?' since they should never have been involved with each other in the first place. But if you are and can't get beyond this feeling simply to accept it as a reality, you won't understand what happened in this case, and why my client and Olivia Le Master now feel as they do—"

Behind me, Jill interrupts. "I'm loath to break in, Your Honor," she says, as I turn to her, "but Mr. Page is making a final argument instead of an opening statement."

From the barrier separating me from the jury, I tell Judge Tarnower, "I should be able to tell the jury why some of the witnesses will be testifying a certain way, Your Honor. This alleged crime is all about intent. If I'm wrong, I'll be contradicted by them."

Judge Tarnower shrugs, as if this is no big deal. "I don't see that Mr. Page is out of line, Mrs. Marymount. Your objection is denied."

I turn to the jury and waste no time in getting specific. "An interracial relationship in the South makes us all uneasy, ladies and gentlemen, whether we say we are liberals or conservatives. Even the most accepting of us knows the difficulties of such a union and the reactions that occur in some quarters. It comes as no surprise when I tell you that sustained love between two people with everything going for them has a fifty-fifty chance, and sustained love between people of different races, especially in the South, to most of us is a matter of hope over reality. When you add to it the accidental death of a child, you get at least two, and actually more, very conflicted people, as you shall see when they testify. . . .''

As I sit down, Andy leans over and whispers, his voice scratchy with disapproval, "I never told you I felt conflicted.''

For the jury I place my hand on his sleeve as if I am thanking him for complimenting me on a fine opening statement. This guy is one in a million.

After lunch the courtroom fills up again. Most of the crowd had expected voir dire to take at least the entire morning. Jill calls as her first witness Dr. Warren Holditch, who had been her expert witness at the probably cause hearing. Knowing the municipal court would send Andy to trial and since I was not really prepared to do so, I didn't cross-examine him. Now I have my chance. Holditch, a behavioral psychologist who seems even more emaciated than he was a couple of months ago (I am tempted to ask him if he is treating himself for anorexia), essentially repeats his opinion that shock is dangerous and Andy should never have used a cattle prod and should have gotten the consent of a human rights committee.

Since I have heard this before, it is difficult to gauge the effect on the jury, but since he is only the first witness and they are not tired yet (though I see one lunch-induced yawn), they pay close attention to his explanation of the different behavior-modification procedures he says Andy should have tried before he attempted shock. In a new wrinkle, Jill introduces as exhibits two commercial shock sticks as well as a remote-control device complete with a helmet. She is protecting her manslaughter charge in case the jury won't go for murder. As these are passed around the jury, the male jurors barely resist poking each other with them while the women pass them quickly on as if they were hot to the touch.

On cross, I get Holditch to admit that one of the most widely published researchers in the field has reported using a cattle prod to suppress self-abusive behavior. Though I know Jill will come back on redirect and reinforce his testimony that safety considerations have made this research obsolete, except for the point that shock can work, I want the jury to know it is something that a man, with many more credentials than Warren Holditch, has employed successfully.

Before I sit down, I ask Holditch, "Isn't it a fact that if Leon Robinson had not loosened his grip on Pam she would be alive today?"

Jill objects loudly that Dr. Holditch isn't qualified to answer this speculative question, and I don't fight it, having made my point.

Jill ends my own speculation by calling Olivia next. Despite everything Olivia has said, there is the possibility she will invoke her Fifth Amendment right not to testify, now that the moment of truth is at hand. Led in from the witness room by a black female bailiff, Olivia, smiling as she walks through the door at the back of the courtroom, seems as confident as a reigning heavyweight fighting out of his division. But as she passes by our table, I see that it is all an act. Her smile looks soldered into place. She is scared to death, and I don't blame her. With a single slip she can cook her own goose, and everybody in the courtroom knows it. I glance at Andy to see how he is reacting to her presence, and like a small child who is afraid his playmate is about to tattle on him, he seems to be holding his breath.

As Jill leads her through some preliminary questions, it is hard not to think about Olivia's manner at the probably cause hearing. Then she was the grieving mother, a difficult witness for both Jill and me. Today, she is a murder suspect, and Jill will show her no mercy. I presume anything Olivia says that is favorable to Andy will be made by Jill to seem like a cover-up when she makes her closing argument—either the story of a woman concealing her own role in the murder of her child or the words of a woman who was duped by a man who wanted her money badly enough to kill her child for it. If Jill knows about the child who lives in Ohio, I have no indication of it.

Olivia begins to cry at Jill's first hostile question. "When I questioned you at Dr. Chapman's hearing a couple of months ago," Jill asks, holding a volume that contains her testimony, "you didn't mention you were having an affair with him at the time he applied electric shock to your child, did you?"

Everyone, me included, seems to creep to the edge of our seats. Her voice trembling, Olivia says, "No, but I wasn't asked."

Jill, reminding me more and more of one of those old peasant women in *Zorba the Greek* in her black dress (all she needs is a black shawl for her head) booms from behind the podium, "And you didn't mention that you were to receive at the time of your child's death approximately two million dollars as a result of a malpractice settlement against your child's doctor, did you?"

Olivia wipes her eyes with a tissue she has balled up in her right fist. "No, I did not."

Jill backs slightly away from the podium and says softly, "And you didn't mention at the hearing that you had told your lover, Dr. Chapman, that there would be more than enough money for him to go back to school, did you?"

"We were talking about getting married and I was considering selling my business," Olivia says, her voice becoming more defensive with each question.

Jill pauses for a moment to allow these answers to sink in on the jury. She makes a great show of thumbing through the transcript and then asks, "Mrs. Le Master, isn't it true that you suggested to your lover that he use shock to try to stop your daughter's self-abusive behavior?''

Seeing Jill turn to a specific page in the transcript, Olivia answers, ''No other doctor had helped her.''

Coming around from behind the lectern as if to challenge Olivia to a fight, Jill says vehemently, ''Your child died as a result of your lover's help, didn't she, Mrs. Le Master?''

Before Olivia can answer, I am on my feet objecting. ''She's not qualified to answer that.''

''Sustained,'' Judge Tarnower says.

I sit down, knowing I could object to the form of all of these questions, since they amount to cross-examination, but I know Judge Tarnower will allow Jill to treat Olivia as a hostile witness and ask leading questions, and I don't want the jury to be any more aware of the distinction than they already are. I will have an opportunity to allow Olivia to explain her actions as much as she is able, but the damage has already been done. Anything that Olivia says will be filtered by the jury through her admissions. Now that she has whetted the jury's appetite, Jill takes Olivia through her story from the beginning. It all sounds sordid now, each action suspect. Olivia comes across as though she had planned her daughter's death for months. Against the backdrop of her initial admissions, her story that she fell in love with Andy rings hollow. Instead of a poignant and ultimately tragic in-terracial love story, the jury hears monosyllabic responses directed by Jill. I had hoped to convince the jury that Olivia seems ambivalent now because of Pam's death. Instead, she is unconvincing because of what she has admitted she stood to gain.

''How do you plan to spend the money,'' Jill asks sarcastically, now that she has taken Olivia through her story, ''that you expect to receive from your daughter's death?''

I am on my feet objecting, ''She hasn't received any money, Your Honor.''

''Sustained,'' Judge Tarnower says, her first words in twenty minutes.

"No more questions," Jill says, sitting down with a grim smile on her face. It was the question she wanted to leave the jury with, not Olivia's answer.

As I think about where to begin, it occurs to me that Jill has made the same erroneous assumption I had—that Olivia and Andy are no longer sexually involved—and has failed to follow up. But perhaps she hasn't asked this question for a reason: she would be delighted to leave the jury with the impression that the affair is over. Olivia, I decide as I sit down, can't be allowed to have it both ways. Either she must be shown to have manipulated Andy into helping her through an act of seduction or she still loves him, and as repugnant as that may be to a Southern jury, it will be consistent with Andy's feelings when he testifies.

"Your witness, Mr. Page," Judge Tarnower clucks impatiently from the bench. I get up again and begin the arduous chore of trying to rehabilitate Olivia's answers, but, as I have feared, there is little I can ask Olivia that hasn't already been compromised by her admissions. No matter what spin I give my questions, Andy still seems to be either a conspirator with her or a grossly incompetent professional. Maybe she doesn't know how she feels about him, but I will point out to the jury that maybe after all this time she should. If Andy won't turn on her, I sure as hell can when it comes to my closing argument.

"Mrs. Le Master, did I hear you say that you are uncertain," I ask, feigning a genuine air of puzzlement, "about your present feelings for Dr. Chapman?"

If she has a clue where I am going, Olivia doesn't act like it. Calmly, she recrosses her legs as if I had asked her what she had for breakfast. "Although I know Pam's death was an accident," Olivia says calmly, "I can't help but feel very confused about the way it happened. As I have said, I no longer think Dr. Chapman should have used shock."

I lean my arms against the lectern as if I am suddenly wearied by her testimony. Dr. Chapman? She is talking about Andy as if she only met him a couple of times. "Isn't it a fact you told me that it was you who seduced Dr. Chapman and not the other way around?''

Taken off guard, Olivia draws back in the chair as if I have tried to strike her. "I don't recall saying that," she says, frowning. Her face colors slightly, and if I can see it, so can the jury. I am glad I can't see Andy without turning my head, because I know if I do, I will see him going through the roof.

"Isn't it a fact, Mrs. Le Master," I say slowly, now clearer in my own mind about the effect Olivia wants to create, "that you've had sex with my client as recently as last week?"

There are titillated gasps behind me. Olivia, visibly angry, can't resist a look at Andy before saying, "That's not true!"

To heighten the effect, I, too, turn and look at Andy, who seems as stricken as a father who has caught his teenaged daughter in her first act of deception. I turn back to Olivia and keep up the pressure. "Is it your testimony that you haven't had sexual intercourse with my client on five different occasions since he was originally charged in this case?"

Olivia knows she can't retreat, and tears again well in her eyes as she cries in a choked, almost guttural, voice, "Of course not! I've talked to him on the telephone several times, but that's all!"

I pause, wishing her steadily reddening face would burst into flames. "Now isn't it a fact that approximately fifteen years ago the Department of Human Services substantiated child abuse involving your son, whom you no longer have custody of?"

Prepared for this question, Olivia, as if on cue, bursts into tears again and recites the story she gave me yesterday. The jury seems more shocked than moved, a reaction I'll take anytime. I sit down, and while Jill confers furiously with Kerr Bowman, Andy whispers furiously, "Why did you ask her all of that?"

When Jill tells Judge Tarnower finally that she has no more questions, every eye in the courtroom watches Olivia leave the stand. I hedge my answer. "You don't think the jury should hear the truth?"

"You humiliated her!" he rages.

I try to keep from reacting in front of the jury. Only a man in love could worry about such a thing. "Why should she be humiliated," I ask, disingenuously, "if she's telling the truth?"

Unwilling to respond, now that Yettie Lindsey is about to begin her testimony, Andy pulls back and sits rigidly in his chair. He knows what is coming. Even if he could talk me out of asking him what he has admitted as recently as last night, Jill Marymount will have to bring it up, and Andy is one criminal defendant I will not give the benefit of the doubt if he tries to lie on the witness stand. I will not let him lie to protect Olivia. If I were on the jury, I'd be mulling over at least two possibilities. If Andy testifies under oath the affair is still going on, I'd be asking myself whether she is still screwing him because she still loves him, or she is manipulating him so he won't turn on her. At least now, if I judge this correctly, the case will turn on Andy's credibility and not Olivia's.

Bristling with the dignity that only rejection can give a person, Yettie makes the kind of witness lawyers drool over in their sleep. She is wearing a beige knit suit that seems enameled upon her chocolate frame, and her strange, speckled yellow eyes seem to burn with the pleasure of the knowledge that at long last some chickens are coming home to roost. The men on the jury have to be wondering what in hell would possess a black man to kiss off this voluptuous and obviously passionate young woman for a milky bread stick like Olivia—unless, it was, of course, a fortune and a chance to get into a white woman's pants. Tearfully, she acknowledges she was in love with Andy, and you can see the female jurors loving her for admitting it and loving her for eavesdropping outside his office. That son of a bitch, we'll punish him if for nothing else than breaking this girl's heart. Sure, she spied on him, but we wouldn't have cared if she'd set up a hidden camera and microphone under their beds.

Yet despite the visual impact Yettie has on the jury—

indeed on all of us except perhaps Andy—her testimony really adds nothing, since Olivia has admitted at least part of it just minutes before. And she doesn't say the one additional thing that could hurt Olivia (and by extension Andy), and that is her comment to me in her office that Olivia said on more than one occasion that she thought Pam would be better off dead. If she went to Jill with what she had overheard, why didn't she volunteer this as well? Why didn't Jill ask her what else she had heard Olivia say? Perhaps Yettie believes that those comments could have been made by anyone with a self-abusive child, and that it wouldn't, after all is said and done, be fair to mention. I don't know the answer, but now is not the time to find out. Unwilling to give Jill a second bite at this juicy plum, I say, "I have no questions of this witness, Your Honor."

Jill has sandwiched Leon Robinson between Yettie and her other witnesses. As he struts to the witness stand, I feel my heart kick into overdrive. My tongue goes to my false tooth, on which I will be paying for the next six months. My body was sore for three days. If Leon has told Jill that his friends and I got acquainted that night in the parking lot, I haven't heard it.

Judging by the way Leon is sashaying to the front of the courtroom, someone must have told him he is the star witness in this case. In his red cowboy shirt with its requisite whorls, buttoned-down pockets, and fancy stitching and new, starched Lee jeans that slide down over brown cowboy boots that gleam with a military spit shine, Leon, his pompadour waved even higher on his head than at the probably cause hearing, looks cocky instead of nervous. Surely, like Olivia, he must be pretending confidence he can't be feeling. Unless Leon has had a vastly different life from most Arkansans, he hasn't appeared before this many people since the night he graduated from high school.

Jill has him well rehearsed, however, and he testifies in an arresting country voice that for the first time has a little twang in it, like George Jones singing, "I stopped lovin' her to-day."

After reviewing his length of employment (three years, not a record, but unusual given the turnover at the Blackwell County HDC) and training, Jill asks him to describe what happened when Pam was electrocuted.

I follow his testimony in the transcript from the probable cause hearing. He repeats it almost verbatim. "If Dr. Chapman had of jus' told me how bad it was really gonna hurt, I'd of known to holt her a lot tighter," he says earnestly. "I didn't want to hurt her by squeezin' too hard. I liked Pam a lot."

He gets through his testimony this time without tears, though, as last time, his voice becomes hoarse with emotion. Jill has left me as little as possible. As I stand up to cross-examine him, Leon shoots me a look of pure hatred, which I interpret as fear. We are on my turf now. "How much do you weigh, Leon?" I ask as if we are old friends comparing diets.

"About one-seventy," he says, his voice sullen.

"How old are you?"

Not understanding where I'm going, he volunteers, "I'll be twenty-five in October."

"Would you say you're in pretty good shape?"

Too macho to admit he doesn't lift more than a pool stick and a can of beer when he finishes his shift, he says in his George Jones voice, "I'm all right."

"Despite being a hundred-and-seventy-pound, twenty-four year old in good condition, you couldn't hold on to Pam's hands when she pulled away?"

Leon's lower lip puffs out as if a bee had stung it. "I said every way I know how," he huffs, "I would have kept aholt of her if I had been told she was gonna kick like a mule."

Leon's whining cuts through the room like a power saw being revved up. I ask, "How long have you known Dr. Chapman?"

He is wary now, but he has no choice about answering my questions. ''It hadn't been a year, I guess.''

''Would you say you and he were friends?'' I ask, turning as I finish to look back over my shoulder. In the courtroom I have noticed a couple of men whose knuckles look familiar.

Unable to restrain a dry chuckle, Leon looks into the audience. ''I wouldn't say that.''

''But you don't have anything against him?''

No genius, Leon has started going on smell. He sniffs, ''He don' give me no trouble, an' I don't give him any.''

I am in no hurry. ''So you know of no reason why you wouldn't try to do exactly what he said when it came to holding on to Pam.''

I can't resist looking at Jill. She is on the edge of her seat and she knows something is coming. ''Have you ever heard of a group that has the reputation of hating African-Americans and goes by the name of the Trackers?''

Jill shoots out of her chair like a Roman candle. ''I object, Your Honor. This isn't relevant.''

Judge Tarnower looks at Jill and then at me. I'd rather not have to telegraph it all to Leon, though right now the question is like a neon sign blinking on and off. ''Of course it is, Your Honor,'' I say. ''Every one of the jury answered this question.'' This isn't precisely true, but it's close.

The judge, bless her liberal heart, helps me out. ''I'll allow it. Answer the question, Mr. Robinson.''

Thinking he's about to be trapped, Leon says nonchalantly, ''Sure, I heard of it.''

I have been waiting to ask this question for weeks, and I don't waste any time. ''Are you now or have you ever been a member of the Trackers, Leon?''

On her feet again, Jill says, ''I object again, Your Honor!'' her voice anxious for the first time all day. ''I have no idea how Mr. Robinson is going to answer, but all Mr. Page is trying to accomplish is to prejudice this jury.''

''On the contrary, Your Honor,'' I say, ''if Mr. Robinson let go of Pam when she was shocked because he hates black people and he thought in a moment of anger she would attack Dr. Chapman, the jury, in deciding what my client's own state of mind was, should be allowed to take this into account.''

Shaking her head angrily, Jill says, ''That's guilt by association, Your Honor. Just because Mr. Robinson may have been in some kind of club doesn't prove he did anything.''

''The Trackers is not just some kind of club, Your Honor. It's . . .''

Cutting me off, Judge Tarnower says, ''Sit down, Mr. Page. You're not testifying. Answer the question, Mr. Robinson.''

I plop down, trying not to look too relieved, thinking this entire case (unless Andy is lying) is about guilt by association.

Leon, righteously indignant, yelps, ''I've never joined them or nothin' like them.''

After a few more questions, I sit down, thinking that with a little luck, we'll know about that tomorrow.

As I return to my seat, Andy, without even a glance at me, rises suddenly and says in a loud voice to the judge, ''Your Honor, I want to fire Mr. Page and represent myself!''

Staring at Andy as if he has suddenly gone crazy, Judge Tarnower stands up, too, and says, ''I want the lawyers and Dr. Chapman back in my chambers immediately. The court will be in recess for fifteen minutes.'' With that, she flees the bench through a side door.

I turn to Andy and snarl in a low whisper, ''Are you out of your fucking mind?''

In front of the jury, Andy grabs my arm and says, ''You broke your word! I warned you not to do this!''

''Come on!'' I say, furious. ''She's not going to let you.'' Shaking with rage, I look into the stunned faces of Jill and her young assistant as they hurry past our table.

In chambers, the judge has taken off her robe as if she is through for the day. Underneath it, she is wearing a red dress almost identical to Olivia Le Master's. ''What is your client's problem, Mr. Page?'' she yelps at me. Whatever sympathy she may have had for our case seems a distant memory. Judges do not like surprises, nor do they like defendants to represent themselves.

For an instant I consider trying to explain what I believe is in Andy's mind. The truth—that Andy thinks I have wrongly injected the issue of race into this case, when, in fact, that is what it is primarily about as far as I'm concerned—is too bizarre, too threatening. Instead, I say, ''We are having a disagreement over trial tactics, Your Honor.''

''Your . . .'' Andy begins.

The judge loses her temper. ''I don't want to hear from you, Dr. Chapman,'' she yells, pointing a finger at him. ''If you didn't want a lawyer, you should have thought about that a long time before today. I'm not allowing you to represent yourself; I'm not allowing Mr. Page to quit as your attorney, and I don't want you to speak here or in my courtroom again until you're spoken to! Is that clear?''

Andy shakes his head. ''Then I refuse to participate in this trial any further.''

Judge Tarnower looks at me and then back at Andy as if she wants to make pressed meat of both of us. Lawyers are supposed to be able to control their clients, and defendants dressed as nicely as Andy are supposed to behave themselves and go to prison, if not with smiles on their faces, at least with stoic calm. It is not as if I am back at the Public Defender's, representing some dope-crazed space cadet. ''That's fine with me,'' she says grimly. ''You can spend it in a holding cell.''

Great! I can hear the talk on the street: Page can't even keep his clients out of jail during their trials. I look at Jill and send her a silent prayer: we're both lawyers, even if we hate each other's guts right now. There is a smirk on her face as if she is daring me to keep Andy company. Desperately, I look over at the huge bailiff, who seems more than willing and able to take each of us under one arm, and notice the clock. It is after four. ''Judge, it's getting late. Why don't we quit for the day, so I can have a chance to talk to Dr. Chapman? This is a capital case, after all.''

I have said the magic words without ever having mentioned the dreaded word: appeal. It could go on forever if she screws up. No judge likes to be reversed, especially this woman. A thin, bloodless smile comes to the judge's lips. ''That's the first good idea,'' she says firmly, ''you've had all day, Mr. Page.''

Oh yeah, Dan, this woman has the hots for me all right. I nod, grateful beyond words I don't have to go back out there to the defense table alone.

22

IN MY OFFICE, Morris listens to my account of our conversation with the judge and then looks at his brother as if Andy had told Judge Tarnower he had seen her mother in a Juarez whorehouse. "You're one crazy nigger," Morris tells his brother. "We're trying to save your ass, and you want to fuck it up with this stupid shit! You think you're gonna have a rat's-ass chance in hell sitting in a cell while your lawyer does a solo act. That's bullshit, man!"

In a rare concession to the pressure he must be feeling, Andy loosens his tie. "I don't expect you to understand this either, Morris."

Morris, seated across from his brother, has his feet up on my desk. He puts them down on the floor and gets up to pace. "I understand this," he says, his dark face anguished. "You're the most selfish motherfucker who's ever had the nerve to draw a breath! Have you thought one God-damned minute about what it's gonna do to me, knowing you're in prison for the rest of your life or a piece of fried meat in the ground? Forget our mother and daddy's memory; forget their families. They're mostly dead. What good are you gonna do anybody in prison? We don't need another nigger convict. You're throwing away the one chance you have! Even if by some miracle you walk, the white assholes who run these things are gonna bust their asses to keep you from being a psychologist again, and then what will all those shit for brains you're so crazy about do? You think white folks care about a nigger retard? Bullshit! I've been out there and seen the way

311

those little black monkeys climb all over you. Who's gonna give a shit about them while you're in prison getting fucked up the ass by some crazy dude who'll pile-drive you into the concrete after he's stretched your asshole to the size of a manhole cover? This ain't the time," he pleads, his voice winding down to a whisper, "to tell white folks what a shitty place for us this country is."

Morris, to my amazement, is almost in tears. His eyes are red, and his voice is so hoarse I can barely hear him. He probably doesn't understand Andy much better than I do, but there is no doubt about the love he feels for him. Andy shifts uncomfortably in his chair but says nothing. I don't get it. Andy isn't stopping at cutting off his nose to spite his face; he's taking his eyes and ears, too. People who actually do things this drastic on principle are, in my experience, few and far between. The last one in the legal profession was Thomas More. "We've got a chance, Andy," I say, filling the silence. "But you've got to stay and fight. If you don't stick around to explain your side of the story, the prosecutor will fill in the blanks for the jury on closing argument."

Like some kind of black Buddha, Andy stills himself and draws his hands together beneath his trim goatee. I look at Morris, who, judging by the agonized look on his face, has withdrawn into his own private hell. "I know you feel I'm betraying you, Andy," I say, from behind my desk, "but at some point you simply have to start trusting me."

From behind his hands, Andy says bitterly, "Olivia trusted me, and look what she's getting."

I slam my fist on my desk in frustration at this man. "She betrayed you!" I yell at him. "She had the opportunity to convince the jury she is still passionately committed to you even though her child is dead, and she lied!"

Wearily, Andy shakes his head. "She's ashamed," he says, his voice under control. "She can't imagine people would understand how she could be involved with anyone right now, much less a black man, after what has happened."

He has just admitted that the woman he supposedly loves is as racist as the rest of us. I look at Morris for support, but he merely shrugs, as if his brother were another species. I still believe that Olivia is calibrating her performance as best she can, but I don't dare risk fighting this battle again. Andy, I decide, is a lost cause. Yet, even as I think this, I remember the shame I felt in having an affair with a married friend of Rosa's just two weeks after Rosa's death. What was that all about? Probably grief, loneliness, lust. All I know is that I would never have admitted it in court to a group of strangers sitting in judgment over me. Maybe it's possible that Olivia, despite everything I know about her, is as innocent as Andy thinks. But I represent Andy, not Olivia, and my job is not to judge the moral purity of a witness's soul but to be an advocate for my client. While Andy may feel he has the luxury of philosophizing about the motives of Olivia, I do not. "You're going to have to decide," I say harshly, getting up from behind my desk, "whether you want to fight for your freedom or be a martyr. You can't do both."

Andy is silent for once as if he is about to give up on the idea of trying to make me understand he sees no conflict between the two. I leave the two brothers in my office and go to Dan's office to use his telephone to call Charlene Newman to tell her she will have to testify that Leon told her he was in the Trackers. After a tearful phone call from her, I agreed not to subpoena her, so that Leon would not find out she might be a witness. "Leon will find out within two hours if I'm subpoenaed," she had told me. That gives me a lot of confidence in our law enforcement officers, but since they seldom make it into the Blackwell County Country Club, they have to be members of something. Leon has not been in contact with her, proving, I suppose, that the female bartenders at the Bull Run are, if not quite feminists, more loyal to their own sex than to their own race, since they apparently have not told Leon I was looking for his ex-wife.

Seated behind his desk like Humpty Dumpty in a special oversized chair, Dan, happy as ever to eavesdrop, observes cheerfully, "You're doing a hell of a job! Keep this up, and you'll give a new meaning to criminal defense work."

I dial Charlene's number. "Shit happens when your client gives his home address as Uranus," I say glumly. Great. No answer. "Do me a favor and try this number every fifteen minutes until you leave for the day. If a woman answers, come get me." I hand Dan a slip of paper with Charlene's number on it.

Dan squints at the number. He needs reading glasses but won't get them, claiming he is too vain about his looks. "You can't turn a sow's cunt into a silk purse," he says, his face now sympathetic.

"I think that's a sow's ear," I say, happy to smile for the first time today. "The weird part is that my client may really be a silk purse."

"Sure," Dan says breezily, "and the Cubs'll win the World Series."

I am home by seven (with nothing resolved), my briefcase crammed with work, and exhaustion begins to creep up like a shot of Novocain. Walking in the front door to find Woogie and Sarah curled up on the couch, I feel as though I have been gone a lifetime. "What happened?" Sarah asks, anxiously twisting a lock of her springy black hair, which she had decided to let grow. Woogie, probably disturbed from a nap, merely looks grumpy. "Are you really getting fired? Kim Keogh made it sound on TV like it was a disaster today. You seemed a little desperate in the interview."

Well, what the hell? The truth hurts. "I don't know whether I am or not," I say, peeling off my suit coat and tie. I'd love a beer, but with so much work to do I don't dare drink one, tired as I am. "Has anyone called?" I ask, going into the kitchen for a glass of water. Tomorrow I'm probably going to look like the biggest idiot ever. I pour myself a glass of water from the tap, realizing how petty my thoughts are. My client and my girlfriend could end up dying, and I am worried about how I am going to come across on TV when I'm asked why Andy chose to spend the rest of his trial in a jail cell instead of with his lawyer. Self-hatred begins to work into those spaces of my brain not overcome by my growing lethargy.

"Rainey dropped by a casserole about thirty minutes ago," Sarah says, following me into the kitchen. "She said she wasn't coming over tonight, but that she'd be all right. I'm sure she wants you to call her."

I do. Her voice sounds calmer. "Thanks for last night," she says, declining my offer to come over and eat her own cooking and to spend the night again. "I need to spend some time by myself tonight."

I doubt that, but I can understand why she isn't hungry. "I'll call you later," I say, watching Sarah turn on the oven to heat up her gift to us. "You can always change your mind."

"Thanks," she says, her voice warm with gratitude. "I may do that."

Knowing she can come over if she needs to is half the battle. "How're you doing?" I ask, wishing desperately that last night was only a bad dream.

"Better than you," Rainey answers, for a moment her old saucy self. "It was all Kim Keogh could do on the six o'clock news to keep from laughing out loud when she reported that Andy wanted to represent himself. What's going on?"

I permit myself a broad smile, delighted she can tease me. Though it is a breach of my relationship with Andy, I tell her why he feels I've betrayed him. "He's got a death wish you wouldn't believe," I conclude, wondering for the first time if he does. Martyrs don't lose much time getting on my nerves.

"He's always been like that," Rainey says. "He spoke out against affirmative action when he was a psych examiner at the state hospital."

I suppress a sigh. What an attractive political candidate he would make to whites. And unlike other first-time candidates, he would have a record to run on—thirty years in the Arkansas prison system. "What did you do today?" I ask, remembering how quickly she fell asleep last night.

"Went to work," she says. "Your talking was better than a sleeping pill."

I laugh. Even if we had wanted to have sex, we wouldn't have dared. Rosa used to say the walls in our house are so thin that if she so much as coughed in our bedroom it would be damp in Sarah's room for a week. It felt good just to lie next to her for a few minutes. I thank her for the casserole and hang up, feeling good for the first time since I went to work this morning, and then I try Charlene Newman's number again, giving up on the tenth ring. I should never have agreed not to subpoena her, but I was afraid she would lie if I forced her to testify. All she would have to answer is that she had never told me that Leon was a member of the Trackers. I do not remember if she was ever willing to come out and say directly that he was. While I wait for the casserole to heat, I worry that I have misunderstood the conversation with her that day in Hot Springs. What difference does it make? She isn't coming anyway. Damn. I'd fuck up a wet dream.

"What's wrong?" Sarah asks, standing in the doorway of the kitchen. "You're sitting there like a zombie."

I look up and force a smile, hearing the anxiety in her voice. God, she is pretty. "What would you think if I quit my job and became a janitor?"

Sarah laughs indulgently. "No way! You can barely change a light bulb."

"Thanks," I say, pretending not to be hurt. I can usually

manage a light bulb all right, but the truth is that I'm not fit
to do another damn thing in my life except run my mouth. I
get up and try Charlene's number again. Where the hell is
she? I sit down, trying not to sigh. Rainey's casserole is
delicious, but I can't eat it. As I push chicken, cheese, and
broccoli around on my plate and try to keep a conversation
going with Sarah, some weird things start to occur. The phone
rings twice while we are eating, but all there is when I answer
is a click.

"What is it?" Sarah asks, watching my face carefully the
second time I put the phone down. "What's going on?"

"Nothing," I say. I debate telling her. Probably nothing.

After dinner, Sarah, her black eyes no longer trusting me,
comes again into the kitchen where I am working on the table
and says, "Something's going on outside. I can hear a lot
more cars and trucks going past our house than usual."

I listen, and hear the sound of a pickup turning the corner.
The sons of bitches. They are watching the house. I feel the
hair on my neck standing up like cat's fur.

"I don't think it's anything," I lie, not wanting to alarm
her. They are watching to see if Charlene shows up here.
"Sit down and I'll tell you what I think is going on."

For the next fifteen minutes, as I listen for more activity,
I tell Sarah everything that is going on in the trial. "Just to
be on the safe side," I say, "why don't you and Woogie
sleep back in my bed tonight and I'll sleep on the couch in
the den where I can keep an eye on things?"

Sarah's eyes are round with fear and disapproval. "Call
the police!"

Ah, the police. I can't tell my daughter I may not be able
to trust them either. Candor has its limits. Exhausted, I rub
my eyes, though it is only nine o'clock. "Babe, nobody is
doing anything illegal."

Sarah begins to twist her hair again. "They'll hurt
her," she says, her voice almost a sob, "just like they
hurt you."

Not if they can't find her. I watch as Woogie sidles into

the kitchen and rubs against Sarah's legs. Some watchdog he is. The phone rings, scaring me. I get up and answer it.

"Is this Mr. Page?" Charlene Newman asks.

"Where are you?" I ask, barely able to keep my voice under control. Sarah is watching me as if I were taking a call from the President. If anything happens to Charlene, she will never forgive me. "I've been trying to get you all day."

"I'm at a service station on Lehigh and Third."

She is downtown, not far from the bus station. I can hear cars passing in the background. "I think they're looking for you."

"A friend warned me," she says, her voice low and frightened.

Though I do not want to say it, with Sarah two feet away from me, I have no choice. "For your own safety, I think you shouldn't testify. It's not necessarily going to do my client any good. Have you got enough money to get back to Hot Springs?"

There is silence for a moment, and I think she is going to hang up. Finally she says, her hillbilly voice cracking in my ear, "I owe Leon, you hear me? I owe that son of a bitch. You get me a place to stay tonight and a bus ticket to California after the trial, and I'll testify if you want. I don't really care what happens to your client. I just owe Leon for all he done to me."

I look at Sarah. Her face is a stone mask of disapproval. If I thought I had a chance in the case, I'd tell her to walk back to the bus station. Instead, I give her Rainey's address and tell her to call a cab. "Call me when you get there."

After I hang up, Sarah screams, "You can't involve Rainey in this! She's got enough to worry about!"

I dial Rainey's number. "This'll take her mind off herself," I say, hoping she won't go through the roof. When she answers, I say, unable to keep a smile off my face, "I've got a little favor to ask you. . . ."

When I get off the phone with Rainey (as I suspected, she had no problems—I didn't quite tell her everything), Sarah is slamming doors all over the house. "You're horrible!" she screams at me when I track her down in her room. "All you do is manipulate people just so you can win a case! You don't care what happens to the others just as long as you get your client off!"

I stand under her doorway watching her glower at me from her bed where she is seated, her knees drawn up under her chin like two iron bars. Beside her, Woogie cowers as if this lecture were intended for him. "That's what I'm paid to do," I say, already beginning to worry that Charlene is being followed. Rainey is supposed to call me the moment she gets there.

Like a child throwing a tantrum, Sarah kicks out angrily at me as I start to sit down beside her. "You're not paid to use people, and that's what you're doing and don't pretend you aren't! You're using this woman; you're using Rainey! You'd use me if you thought it would help!"

I lean against her chest of drawers. Ugly beyond belief (it looks like a project from high school shop with its knobs and handles of different sizes and uneven brown stain), it was mine when I was growing up in eastern Arkansas, and I can't seem to throw it out. "No, I wouldn't," I say automatically, but I wonder. This case has begun to seem like a war in which no prisoners will be taken. "I'm sorry, Sarah. The dirty work usually gets done at the office."

She throws a pillow at me and begins to cry. "No, you're not! You like this! You should have seen your face when you called Rainey! You get off on it!"

I lay her pillow beside her and retreat from her room to wait alone in the kitchen for Rainey's call. I sit down and begin to go over my questions for my Mississippi expert. There is no sense in lying to her. A part of me loves this crap. In thirty minutes the phone rings. "She made it," Rainey says, a little breathless. "Gideon, she's just a child!"

"I know," I say, a little breathless, too. I want absolution, but now is not the time to ask for it. Maybe I'm right though.

Rainey hasn't mentioned her lump tonight. "Can you see that she gets down to the courthouse tomorrow morning?" I ask.

Rainey sighs. "I guess," she says.

After a few minutes I get off the phone but decide not to chew this bone with my daughter any longer tonight. Sarah will forgive me. She always does.

The morning, at least, starts out all right. Though he is clearly not happy about it, Andy has decided to attend the rest of his trial. Before I went to bed, I had tried to call him, but either he wasn't answering or Morris had taken him out for his last night on the town. Dressed defiantly in his Moby Dick suit, he glares at me as we enter the courtroom as if he is about to testify against me at an ethics hearing to revoke my license.

Morris, who looks as if he spent the night drinking to blot out the nightmare he is having to pay for, whispers across me to his brother, "You keep looking this mean, and there won't be enough left of you for a barbecue sandwich."

Having already notified the judge that my client has decided to play the game by its normal rules, I am content to let Morris scold his brother, since I'm afraid Andy will change his mind if I start in on him. Andy responds with a curt nod, and I will be satisfied if we can get through the rest of the trial without his coming out of his chair at me. I would pay part of my fee to know what finally changed his mind.

The rest of Jill's witnesses roll by quickly. Dr. Beavers, the emergency-room GP on duty who pronounced Pam dead, substantially repeats his testimony from the probably cause hearing. Stubbornly, on cross-examination, he won't admit that he can't say to a reasonable degree of medical certainty that Pam's death was caused by the cattle prod. "Everything I know about this situation convinces me she died as a result of the electric shock," he says smugly as though he were a world-famous pathologist instead of a small-town primary care physician.

"For all you know, she could have had a heart attack unrelated to the electric shock since there was no autopsy, isn't that correct?" I ask, knowing the question is pointless. It's not as if the jury doesn't have any common sense.

"It doesn't seem like much of a possibility to me," Dr. Beavers says, his tone implying that I have asked him a question similar to one about the chances of my being nominated to the U.S. Supreme Court. "But I suppose it could have happened."

Jill's last witness is David Spath. If I had any lingering hopes that Andy's former administrator would suddenly come forward and shoulder some of the responsibility for what happened to Pam, they are smashed thirty seconds into his testimony. Spath, whose English accent delights the jury, must be fighting to save his job, because he acts as if Andy were a rogue elephant who had totally disregarded written policies and procedures that might well have been part of the Ten Commandments. His bird wing of a mustache almost flapping with indignation, Spath turns on Andy with the fury of a petty tyrant. If he knew Andy was going to try shock, he will take the secret to his grave.

On cross-examination, I can't even get Spath to admit that Andy cared about the persons he was supposed to be helping. "The way a true professional shows his concern," Spath says in reply to a question, "is by the way he works with his staff on the most difficult cases. I can't stress enough that highly aversive procedures are never used without exhaustive debate first. In every institution I've worked in that has been the rule, and Dr. Chapman was well aware of that."

They teach you in the trial advocacy course in law school to end any cross-examination with at least some concession, but Spath is so adversarial and difficult to shut up after a while I sit down abruptly, hoping the jury will realize Spath wouldn't publicly say anything good about Andy even if he had been his own father. "Can you answer 'yes' or 'no' if you hired Dr. Chapman?"

"Yes."

"That's all, Your Honor," I say, turning my back on him.

With Spath through, Jill rests her case. After the briefest of recesses in chamber Judge Tarnower, pleasant again now that Andy is acting the part of a typical defendant, perfunctorily denies my motion for a directed verdict, and immediately we begin Andy's defense.

As I have feared, my Mississippi expert is a disaster, since he comes across in person like a former Nazi labor camp guard. Shock is simply not a technique easily justified by even the most distinguished-sounding of experts, and Goza, talking out the side of the mouth, begins to sound more like Jill's witness than my own. After his direct testimony in which he said in his crablike fashion that Andy's use of shock was appropriate, Jill gets Goza to admit on cross-examination that he has not even read of a cattle prod being used on a person in at least fifteen years. He admits his own research has just been published in a journal that is so obscure it hasn't even been abstracted. Human Rights Committees, he concedes, his lips barely moving, are routinely consulted before decisions about procedures like shock are used.

When Goza doggedly defends Andy's decision, Jill, dressed in a dark blue suit today instead of a black dress, asks, "Dr. Goza, would you agree that you're an expert on the amount of pain required to stop a child from hurting herself?"

Forced to answer whether he is the Dr. Joseph Mengele of the Nazi death camps, Goza stared at Jill with the squint of a man who has just been released from a long stretch in prison. "I'm a psychologist," he says, blinking rapidly, surely knowing he has been mortally wounded by this question.

"Paid a handsome amount, I presume," Jill asks, enjoying this piece of cake, "to try to defend Dr. Chapman?"

Coached yesterday, Goza remembers the right answer.

"Compensated for my time," Goza responds haughtily, but it is no use. He is dying up there, and by the time Jill is finished, he is a corpse. Preferring to get his body out of the jury's sight, I don't redirect.

It's now or never, and I call Andy, who mounts the witness stand like a man climbing on a scaffold to put his head in a noose. I glance back at Morris, who is shaking his head. He and I know that the only thing I am trying to accomplish is to save Andy from being convicted of outright murder. It is a foregone conclusion in my mind that Andy will do some time, even if Leon Robinson were to come back in and testify he is the Grand Dragon of the Ku Klux Klan. Andy, sullen and balky, at first comes across woodenly as he gives his credentials as a psychologist; however, as he begins to try to explain himself, he becomes the warm, compassionate man who took me on a tour of the Blackwell County Human Development Center. His defensiveness evaporates and he admits that he might have done things differently if he could begin over again.

"But I was in love," he says, looking directly at the white faces on the jury, "and the child of the woman I loved was in a horrible situation. Olivia was desperate, as are all parents who see their children tearing themselves to bits, and I got caught up in her desperation. . . ." As he speaks, I realize that Andy, in the process of accepting his own guilt, has been finally freed to do what he has always secretly wanted: he is preaching a sermon about an ideal world in which people risk themselves, no matter what the costs. Yet, instead of coming across as an ideologue, he seems a romantic figure from another century. He is no longer intellectualizing about prejudice; his text is the power of love, and in his hands, it is not, despite the results, destructive but liberating. "Every previous psychologist had approached Pam as a problem to be minimized. You could see that in their approach: they drugged her; they kept her in restraints. After I began to love her mother, I could no longer do that. . . ."

I would love to be inside the brains of the jurors right about now. From the podium I sneak a look, but their faces are strangely blank, as if they have no idea what to make of this man who yesterday was ready to fire his lawyer and represent himself. In a sense he has done exactly that: his lawyer has no control over him today, and this one fact keeps his testimony from seeming like pure melodrama. As he testifies, I find myself gently injecting myself from time to time to play to him: "Do you now think," I ask, more as if we were discussing this five years from now over a drink in a bar than like a lawyer fighting to keep his client alive, "Olivia was manipulating you from the very beginning into using a dangerous procedure in the hope that it would end her child's suffering one way or another?"

Jill pops up out of her seat before Andy can answer. "Objection, Your Honor, it's not relevant what he thinks Mrs. Le Master thought."

"It goes to his intent," I argue, "and that's what a murder charge is all about, Judge."

"Overruled," Judge Tarnower says irritably as if Jill had interrupted her favorite soap opera. *She* is interested, and I wish desperately that this case were not being tried in front of a jury.

"Of course not," Andy says. "Every person in Olivia's situation wishes at some point her child's suffering would end through death, because that seems the only alternative. Olivia expressed that wish as any human would. Initially, *I* worried that she thought I was using my willingness to shock Pam to get close to her."

Out of the corner of my eye, I see Harriet Tarnower duck her head slightly as if she is nodding in agreement. Is Andy trying to outsmart all of us? As he tells the jury his version of the story, I stay out of his way as much as I can. As I wind down, I debate whether to risk confronting him with Olivia's denial or to let it go. I decide I have no choice, knowing a denial from Andy will put me in a position no lawyer ever wants to be in—knowing without a doubt his client is lying under oath. Though it is seldom done, a lawyer is supposed to request a moment to confer with his client and then ultimately inform the court if his client persists in his prevarication. If it comes to this, the only way I'll ever get another client is in hell.

I take a deep breath and ask as if I don't have a care in the world, "You heard Olivia testify yesterday that she had not had sexual relations with you since you were originally charged—is that correct?"

For the first time Andy seems flustered, and I prepare for the worst. I have halfway convinced myself his answer won't be crucial enough for me to confront him if he lies, when he says, his voice sorrowful, "We continued to be physically intimate until last week."

I see no need for the details. "Even now, you still love her," I ask, dropping my voice as much as I dare, "don't you, Andy?"

With great dignity, my client says, "Yes, sir, I do."

When I sit down, the jury, especially the two blacks, are clearly wondering whether they are looking at the first entirely honest man they have ever seen or a consummate con artist.

Jill makes the mistake of trying to tear into him, but it is like ripping through a soufflé: there's no resistance, no angry denials, only the faintly bemused air of an African-American male who seems at peace with himself. Gradually, Jill realizes her mistake, and her questions, instead of sounding shrill, become heavy with sarcasm. "You're telling this jury you were just so head over heels in love," she asks mockingly, "that you forgot everything you learned about being a psychologist?"

Andy nods, as if she were a student who is close to the right answer but hasn't quite got it. "It wasn't that I forgot," he says, taking the question literally, "it's that my feelings for Olivia influenced what I did as a psychologist. For those few weeks I saw Pam just as Olivia saw her: without hope, in almost unending pain, in need of someone who was willing to try to save her from the agony she inflicted on herself every time she was allowed to be free.''

He handles everything Jill throws at him. Marriage? Sure, they talked about it; at one point he and Olivia talked about the possibility of his going back to school to become a physician so he could take care of these children's medical problems as well. She revisits each part of the case, and, unlike Olivia, he manages to reinterpret a number of Jill's questions in light of his feelings without seeming argumentative. He tries to place each of his actions in the context of his relation with Olivia.

Finally, Jill shows him the cattle prod and asks him to examine the handle, apparently so the jury will take to the jury room the image of him holding it. It is only at this moment that Andy seems to lose it. He holds it as if he has been asked to inspect a snake with fangs at either end, grabbing it loosely in the middle and holding it at arm's length. His face becomes as stiff as his beard. Clearly, this is an uncomfortable moment for him, one I hope the jury can understand.

''Dr. Chapman,'' Jill asks, giving the jury plenty of time to freeze this moment on their brains, ''would you unwrap the tape from the handle?''

I think to object, but it will only look as if Andy has something to hide. He looks at me, but I nod, and taking the dirty tape which has begun to curl at the end, peels it away from the handle. There is shockingly little tape on the end. No words about how he felt about Olivia will ever explain why he insulated it so poorly. Since I don't know the answer either (and I have already asked him in private the same question), I decline to redirect.

As my final witness, I call Charlene Newman, whom Rainey delivered with a smile to the steps of the courthouse precisely at eight o'clock this morning. She has been waiting alone to testify, in a separate witness room guarded by a black deputy I've known for years. If he is a member of the Trackers, the organization has changed drastically. Charlene's straight Indian hair is permed for this occasion, making me wonder if she wanted to show Leon she is taking care of herself or whether it is simply a periodic change. Instead of jeans and a halter top, her costume the day I interviewed her, Charlene is wearing dressy black pants, a white blouse, a vest, and a bolo string tie, the exact outfit worn by the female employees at a Mexican restaurant in town. What the hell. Maybe she can head for the border when she's through.

She is as nervous as I feared she would be, her voice almost inaudible, and I have to remind her to speak up during my preliminary questions. Her fear brings out Harriet Tarnower's maternal instincts and the judge practically reaches over and pats her hand.

"Do you know Leon Robinson?" I get around to asking when I finally get her voice level up loud enough to reach the jury.

Charlene looks down at the little strings resting on her starched blouse. "He's my ex-husband," she says, raising her eyes to meet mine.

"How long were you married?" I ask, wanting to build up to this but afraid she will begin to change her mind as she looks around the courtroom. Though Leon is not in the courtroom, his friends are.

"A total of seven years," Charlene says, her voice husky with anxiety. I'm afraid she may be having second thoughts. What does she really have to gain by testifying? I have no idea what she meant last night about "owing him." At this moment I would be willing to bet she's ready to cancel obligations all the way around on the theory that she has scared the piss out of Leon. If this happens, I'll have more egg than usual on my face, but I won't have to worry about how long she survived after the trial. There is no federal slush fund for witnesses testifying for defendants. She adds, when I am slow in following up, "I was married when I was just fourteen."

I glance at Andy, knowing he will hate me the rest of my life for what I'm about to do. He is looking down at the table as if he knows he has made a pact with the devil. Maybe he has. I ask, "Ms. Newman, during the course of your marriage did your husband ever tell you he was a member of a group called the Trackers?"

Jill goes through the motion of objecting, but we both know the judge will allow the question. Since she allowed me to ask Leon and he denied it. I can impeach his answer. "Go ahead, Ms. Newman," she instructs when we have settled down.

Charlene pauses, looks squarely at the jury and says, "Yeah, about six months ago he told me he was a member. Leon hates blacks."

I let go of the podium I have been squeezing. The only way her answer would have been better is if she had used the word "niggers." I ask a couple of more questions to lock in her answer and then say to Jill, "Your witness."

Obviously stewing, Jill sits in her chair, still frowning at the judge. She has to make a choice. She can ignore Charlene, which will reinforce her closing argument that Leon's membership in the Trackers is irrelevant, or she can go after her and try to make her out to be a vengeful, lying ex-wife. She leans over to whisper into her assistant's ear. A big smile comes over Kerr's pretty-boy face, and he stands up proudly as if he had been anointed a Knight of the Round Table. As Kerr starts in on Charlene, I realize Jill can't resist trying to have it both ways. By sending in the second string, she is hoping to signal to the jury that Charlene's testimony, if it stands up, isn't a big deal. On the other hand if Kerr can score some points, she'll be happy to use them.

Kerr looks good; there is no question about it. His blond hair is as glossy and wavy as that of any woman in the courtroom. His expensive suit, a three-piece job that is a little warm for September, does not have a wrinkle in it. And, in fact, he gets Charlene to admit that she has developed some real bad feelings about Leon. As a cross-examiner, he's proficient, cutting Charlene's answers off where he wants, controlling her with no difficulty. Yet, as Kerr pushes Charlene around, I notice Jill is squirming because she knows she has made a mistake. Unless Charlene recants her testimony completely, and she will not, Jill knows I will be asking the jury why the prosecution made a big deal out of cross-examination if it didn't think Leon's statement to Charlene that he was a member of the Trackers was relevant. Kerr comes back to sit down by his boss's side as bouncy as a puppy bringing his mistress a dead sparrow between his jaws. On the witness stand Charlene is wiping her eyes. That's okay. She may hate Leon's guts, but she has stuck to her original statement. Jill glared at Kerr as if he hasn't done exactly what she told him to do. "No questions," I say. Sometimes, less is more.

23

"LADIES AND GENTLEMEN," I begin my closing argument, "I have never had a client like Andrew Chapman. Nor do I ever expect to have one like him again. Frankly, I'm not sure I ever want to have one like him again." There is some laughter in the courtroom, and about half of the jurors smile. As expected, Jill had painted a sinister picture of Andy and Olivia, telling the jury before launching into her conspiracy theory, that it would have to find Andy has the mind of a retarded child to allow him to escape guilt in this case. Slowly, I take in each member of the jury. "In all candor, and most, if not all of you, know this to be true of the criminal justice system in America, much of what happens in America's courtrooms seems like an elaborate game between the prosecution and the defense lawyer. It's as if the object of the game is for the prosecutor to jump over a high bar, but the rules let the defense lawyer try to trip up the prosecutor during the attempt. The rules, as you know, are there in our judicial system to protect the individual defendant as well as to safeguard certain values we have said are important in this country. Now, that's all well and good, and defense lawyers like myself at this stage in a criminal trial routinely launch into a speech about how the prosecutor hasn't made it over the bar, and therefore you, the jury, are required to acquit the defendant."

I come around from the podium, and feeling the eyes of the women on the jury, resist an urge to check my fly. "You may have observed," I say dryly, "that Dr. Chapman has not always been happy with me during this trial. At one point, as you saw much to my embarrassment, he asked the judge to allow him to represent himself. While I, as a defense lawyer, have been thinking I would play this game out according to the ordinary strategy that usually prevails in criminal cases, my client has insisted on playing the game differently. He thinks lawyers' games get in the way of the truth, and whether we have liked it or not, he has insisted on telling us the truth, and quite honestly, many of us don't like it, because it involves a white woman and a black man. He has insisted on telling you that he continues to love Olivia Le Master, and that the physical expression of this love has persisted through last week. Now, this makes us all uncomfortable, because there is a little moralistic voice in the back of our brains saying to us: for God's sake, shouldn't a child's tragic death in which they were involved put a screeching halt to all of that? Human nature doesn't work that way. Though it can be made to seem sordid examined clinically, we know we comfort each other in our grief through the act of sex just as we make love out of joy.''

I pause, hoping at least a couple of the jurors will have experienced this need. Though nobody is nodding, a few seem sympathetic. It is not something to dwell on, but I needed to make sure I touched this base. I come up to the railing, putting as much distance as I can between me and Andy. ''There is no doubt in my mind that Andy Chapman sincerely believes Olivia Le Master is a wonderful human being who has been the victim of one tragedy after another. Love has a way of turning worry lines into signs of character: a birthmark becomes a beauty spot in our eyes; and so on. When I first stood in front of you yesterday, I still accepted my client's picture of Olivia Le Master. But having heard her in this courtroom yesterday and comparing her testimony with my client's, *I* can't do that any longer. A person blinded by love can find all kinds of excuses for his beloved's behavior. As the person's lawyer, I am not required to do that. Doubtless, if my client had been permitted to

represent himself, he would be telling you a different story—
one I don't believe would be accurate, but knowing this man,
it would be honest and straight from the heart. The truth is,
I now think that Olivia Le Master set my client up and has
been sleeping with him ever since to keep him from discov-
ering the truth.'' I turn to Andy and see him glowering at
me, and I quickly turn back to the jury. ''No man likes to be
thought of as a fool, but I'm afraid that is what my client is
in this case. I think Olivia from the beginning played him
like a violin and suggested a procedure she already knew
was dangerous. She was around the Human Development
Center enough to have entered Andy's office and removed
much of the insulation tape. She could have worked out some
kind of plan with Leon Robinson, and I'll talk more about
him in a moment. But the prosecutor has just told you how
much Olivia had to gain. . . .'' I want to leave them with
the option of accepting my original opening statement, and
it will do no good to get so far out on a limb I can't climb
back down. Moments later, as I begin on Leon, I sense some
reluctance on the jury's part to switch gears. This is for the
blacks on the jury, I want to interrupt myself and tell them,
but of course, I can't. ''Leon Robinson, by virtue of his
membership in the Trackers, despises Andy Chapman. He
didn't have the guts to admit it, and I had to bring in his ex-
wife to prove to you he has been a member. I think it is
significant during this trial that it has become apparent that
Olivia Le Master and Leon Robinson have told you lies, and
Andy Chapman has not told you a single one. How can you
be sure that Leon didn't let go of Pam deliberately either in
a moment of blind racial hatred or perhaps for a promise of
cash from Olivia Le Master? Because when all is said and
done, Pam would be alive today if he had merely done what
he was told to do by my client, and nobody has denied that.''

Finally, before I sit down I leave the jury with the possibility that it was, as I told them at the beginning, an accident.
''The fact is that after this case is over and you return to your
everyday lives, you cannot be certain beyond a reasonable

doubt that despite all inferences to the contrary, Olivia Le Master is as manipulative as she seems. Granted, it seems clear she has lied to you, but I can't stand up here and swear to you that she is a cold-blooded murderer or that she isn't telling you the truth about everything else." I turn to Andy who is staring down at the table, refusing to even acknowledge my presence. For a moment I wish I had let him make his own closing argument. Truly, he might have convinced them. "The one thing I am one hundred percent confident of is that my client has not lied to you. At a cost few, if any of us, would prefer to pay, I am certain he has told you what he believes to be the truth, and this is no small thing to take back with you to the jury room. He is simply not like anybody else I know. It is not that he is an innocent who got in over his head. What happened to Andy Chapman could have happened to any of us, but particularly to a man who insists that society must become color-blind. It is my hope you will not punish him because he has the courage to live his life in a way that many of us, if we dare to admit, envy. . . ."

Jill finishes strong. Preaching in her usual manner, she storms up and down in front of the jury. "This case is not a love story; it is about responsibility for the death of a child. Mr. Page wants to confuse you. And if he can't do that he wants you to forgive and forget what his client stood to gain; he wants you to forgive and forget his client's total lapse of his professional responsibilities as a psychologist; he wants you to forgive and forget he used a cattle prod when the first rule of any professional is to do no harm. What is easy to forget is that it doesn't matter how Dr. Chapman says he rationalized his behavior. He can say he did it in the name of love; his lawyer can argue racism to blame someone else; it doesn't matter a hill of beans. It's your job to fix responsibility, and you're under no obligation to accept one word either of them says. . . ."

It is not an easy wait for the verdict. Tunkie, Frank, and Dan drift in and out of the courtroom all afternoon to see if there is any word from the jury. Dan, whose conviction, so the rumor goes, is going to draw him only a reprimand from the state ethics people, hangs around much of the time. As soon as the trial is over and the jury has trooped out to begin its deliberations, Andy drops all pretense of civility and leans over to inform me that my services will no longer be needed for an appeal once the verdict comes back. Since then, he and Morris have been sitting together in a corner of the courthouse chatting off and on with a group of blacks, none of whom I recognize. It is a little late for group support, I think sourly. The case was too messy for the local NAACP to unite around. Morris, true to form, comes over to shake hands and to give me the rest of what I'm owed. I'm grateful I'm getting it before the verdict. I'm intensely curious about how he brought Andy around. "How'd you get him to show up this morning?" I ask as we talk in the empty jury box.

"Guilt," Morris says, poker-faced and unsmiling. It is obvious he fears the worst. "If he spends his life in prison," Morris says, looking past me at the American flag by the door to the judge's chambers, "how can he save the world?"

I think of Morris's impassioned plea to Andy and realize it worked. Maybe I should have asked if Morris could make the closing.

Later, Dan, who has brought a bag of popcorn into the courtroom with him, nods at Andy and his group. "That's gratitude for you," he says loyally as I tell him Andy's words to me after the trial.

"Not your average dope dealer from Needle Park," I say, looking over at the group of rednecks sitting near the middle of the courtroom. If there aren't some Trackers waiting with us, I'd be real surprised.

Dan understands just enough about the case to sound like an idiot. "Looks like he wants to play both ends against the middle," he says, nodding at Andy and his all black group.

His lawyer maybe. "Not Andy," I say, wondering if the jury will have to come back Monday. It has been just over two hours. Jill and I have agreed that we jointly will move to sequester the jury this weekend if they can't reach a verdict tonight. They could get a few anonymous calls from somebody in this group. "I could be wrong," I whisper, "but Andy may be one of those one in a million people who mean what they say."

"Sure," Dan says, leering at Kim Keogh, who is waiting by the double doors to the courtroom. "Women fall for that kind of guy every time."

I have to laugh, knowing Dan's views on the human condition. The truth is, between Andy and Morris, I'd take Morris every time. Morris lives out of his experience; his brother lives out of his head. As a behaviorist, Andy ought to know better. I smile at Kim, but I don't go over to her yet. I am going to catch enough grief from the other journalists present when this is over. I will keep my end of the bargain, but I never screwed up the nerve to ask Andy to honor my commitment to Kim. A black female deputy comes through a side door, stopping my heart. Is the jury back? As she comes over, Dan says, "I figure thirty years. You saved him from the chair at least."

I try to swallow but can't manage any spit. Was it that bad? I guess so. I can't imagine how Andy will stand even a year in jail.

Her uniform still starched and crisp at five o'clock in the afternoon, the deputy reads my anxiety and shakes her head. Coming over to the table, she says, "The judge says to tell you the jury reports it thinks it can reach a verdict tonight. They don't want to fool with it this weekend."

Fool with it? My mind seized on these words. What does that mean? I stand up. "Did the jury foreman say that?" I ask.

She makes a face. "No, I did."

Dan chuckles at me, "Down, boy. You did all you could."

As she leaves, the deputy frowns as if to say, bullshit. She's right. You never do enough, and the mistakes you make may be the difference in the verdict. For all I know, the jury re-

sents the hell out of what I tried to do to Leon. Sure, he was
a member of the Trackers, but so what? As Jill said, he loved
that little girl. He wouldn't have let go of her intentionally.
"Mr. Page has tried to smear a man to save his client. A
cheap lawyer's trick playing on the racial fears of the community. Well, Blackwell County is bigger than that. Stunts
like that don't work here. . . ." As Jill was saying this to the
jury, I look over at Andy. His chair was as far away as he
could get it and still be at the same table. It was cheap. Now
I wish I hadn't done it. Still, knowing myself as I do, I'd
probably do it again.

At seven Rainey appears in the middle of the main door
to the hallway and motions me over. In the hall, bearing gifts
from McDonald's, is Sarah. The two together somehow make
me more nervous than I already am. Maybe it is that Kim
Keogh is lurking about. They could all have a nice chat about
me: My dad was ready to bail out as soon as he heard you
might have cancer. Your dad's got a prostate as hard as a
walnut; by the way, did he tell you he screwed me on the
first and only date? Did you know that besides being a jerk
your dad's a first-class demagogue with the race issue?

I wolf down the hamburger and fries so I will not have to
say anything. "I told Sarah," Rainey says dryly, "you'd be
too nervous to eat."

Perhaps smelling food, Dan comes outside. "Ah, the long-
suffering women in your life," he says to me, winking at
Sarah.

"Have some of Dad's french fries, Mr. Bailey," Sarah
says, recognizing him by my description.

Dan bows, simultaneously digging his fingers into the
sack, which has enough salt in it to preserve a herd of cattle,
and says, "A woman after my own heart."

I make the introductions, wondering what they must all be
thinking. They've heard enough about each other. After I'm
finished, I say, "All we need to round out this group is my
rat burner." This gets a laugh from everybody. Confidentiality is not my long suit either. Rainey gives me a wan smile

as if to say that I'm hopeless. For some reason it occurs to me that if she has a mastectomy, I will never have seen both her breasts, but that won't be anything new. For the few minutes we were in bed together, we were as innocent as newborn kittens.

"Where's Dr. Chapman?" Sarah asks. She is wearing a rare outfit, a dress. Rainey's advice, I suppose. I note approvingly that it conceals her lush figure. Usually her clothes are too tight.

"He's waiting in the courtroom," I say, knowing she's curious. "It's not a real good time to meet him." I am worried, actually, about what he might say.

Dan, who is rubbing the salt from his fingers onto his pants, cracks, "It may be her last chance."

While Dan takes Sarah into the courtroom to point out (quietly, I hope) which one is Morris—she has seen Andy's picture in the paper or on TV a half-dozen times, Rainey takes me aside and tells me she thinks she got Charlene on a bus headed west without anyone following her. "She said to tell you that no matter what happens, she isn't sorry."

I nod, thinking I wouldn't have been so brave. What was *her* reinforcement? It surely can't be a two-day bus trip to California. Maybe just the knowledge she stood up to Leon. In her own way, Charlene is probably as stubborn as Andy.

It is at this moment we are told the jury is coming back in. I have a premonition this is going to be worse than I expected. I hope to hell Morris won't try to cancel his check. We hurry back into the courtroom and I motion to Andy to come forward. Jill come hurrying in, followed by Kerr, and I see the look of expectation on her face. She knows it is not a question of "if" but how long. After the jury went back, she admitted she doesn't expect the death penalty—just life without parole. Despite his principles, Andy would kill himself. Who could blame him?

It is a piece of conventional wisdom that if members of the jury look at your client and smile on their way back in to the jury box then you've won. It was my experience at the

Public Defender's that juries almost never smile, no matter what they've done, until the verdict is announced. No one is smiling now. The two African-Americans, at opposite ends of the first row, seem particularly dour to me, and I prepare for the worst. Beside me, Andy stiff as a mannequin, speaks voluntarily to me for almost the first time all day. "They don't look happy, do they?"

I feel nauseous, as a wave of indigestion rumbles through my lower intestines. It is all I can do to nod in agreement.

Judge Tarnower, who now at the end of a long day and a long week looks exhausted, pats down curls that already seem limp (so much for that perm). "Has the jury reached a verdict?"

The foreman, a slenderly built accountant in his mid-forties with a rim of fat around his middle, says, "We have, Your Honor."

I look back over my shoulder at Sarah and Rainey. Twisting her hair in anxiety, Sarah doesn't see me, but Rainey nods, a look of sympathy crossing her face. Wednesday she faces her own verdict. I hope I am more help to her than I have been to Andy.

As Judge Tarnower silently reads the verdict form handed to her by the bailiff, I steel myself not to react if they have come back with the death penalty. I have been here before, but that time the man standing beside me, Harry Potter, who killed two convenience-store clerks deserved to die and, in fact, his appeals exhausted, was executed last week.

"To the charge of capital felony murder," Judge Tarnower reads, her voice solemn, but not without a note of satisfaction, "not guilty." I watch the air go out of Andy's chest. We have exhaled simultaneously.

"To the lesser included charge of second degree murder, not guilty," the judge says quickly.

Involuntarily, Andy clears his throat, but I am not terribly surprised, since they didn't come back with capital felony murder. It is the manslaughter charge I am now worried about.

"To the lesser included charge of manslaughter," the judge

reads, looking up at the jury, "not guilty." With this, the small contingent of African-Americans begin clapping, only to be silenced by Judge Tarnower's quick gavel.

My heart has begun to race. Is it possible the jury will acquit Andy entirely? Again impassive, Andy stares straight ahead, as if he has not heard a word the judge has said.

"To the charge of negligent homicide," the judge says, and looks directly at Andy, "guilty."

I look at Andy, who blinks rapidly, but the maximum is only a year in the county jail. He could be out in four months.

Judge Tarnower continues. "The jury recommends that Dr. Chapman be placed on probation for one year and be required to perform sixty hours of community service." Judge Tarnower looks at the twelve men and women seated to her left and says, "I will accept the jury's recommendation. This court is adjourned."

So quickly I will later wonder if I imagined it, Andy brushes his left eye beneath his glasses. Then, turning to me, he says, sounding for all the world like a priggish old-maid schoolteacher, before Kim Keogh can reach me, "I still don't think the end justifies the means."

Somehow I keep my mouth shut. At least the sanctimonious asshole has the decency to shake hands. Besides, who knows why the jury didn't convict him of murder or at least manslaughter? They may not even know themselves. As Kim Keogh opens her lovely mouth to ask her first question, I think again that I'd take Morris any day.

24

THE SURGERY WAITING room at St. Thomas is so littered with
the debris of the slow passage of time (paper cups, magazines, newspapers, gum and candy wrappers) that I am reminded slightly of the Blackwell County Social Services
office where I once plied my trade as a child-abuse investigator. The difference, of course, is the clientele. St. Thomas
is for mostly the middle class and rich who have private insurance. Down the street is University Hospital, which handles mostly Medicaid patients and people without insurance.
Judging by his bemused manner, Dr. Brownlee, Rainey's
surgeon, seems to regard me as something of a chump: I
keep getting involved with women who have breast cancer.
Correction. May have breast cancer. Only a biopsy can tell
for sure, he said repeatedly, but by his haste in scheduling
Rainey's surgery Brownlee left no doubt what he thought.
Strangely inarticulate for a man who surely earns several
hundred thousand dollars a year, Brownlee apparently lets
his knife do his talking.

Things have moved with such haste that I am the only
family or friend Rainey has in the waiting room. Before being wheeled into the operating room, Rainey told me to bend
down and then whispered into my ear that she loved me.
Since I had told her the same thing the night before, it was
not as if the subject hadn't been mentioned. Still, better late
than never.

Stopping my heart, the female volunteer sitting behind the

scarred, wooden desk at the front of the room calls out, "Mr. Page?"

I find I can barely force myself out of the chair, so heavy is the fear weighing down on me. "You have a phone call over there," she says, pointing to a pay phone booth in the corner.

"Thanks," I say, feeling a momentary reprieve. I have promised to call Rainey's daughter immediately, but I won't be surprised if she couldn't wait.

"Hello," I say, my voice feeling slightly rusty from disuse.

"Any word?" Dan asks, his high voice cracking against my ear.

"Not yet," I report, looking out at the exhausted and anxious faces around me. Good ol' Dan, I think. He would have come with me but he has to be in court this morning. "I'll let you know as soon as I hear."

We talk for a few moments, and I then go sit down, thinking a friend like Dan can be a pain in the butt (he asked me over the weekend to represent him before the bar ethics committee if it decides to bother with him because of his Twinkie conviction), but I wouldn't trade him for the world. We don't talk much about serious issues except our cases, but he knows what is important to me. The ethics committee won't do much, maybe send out a letter of admonition, its lowest level of action. Compared with what some lawyers have stolen, a Twinkie isn't much to get excited about.

I drink my third cup of coffee and stare unseeing at the pages of the *Arkansas Democrat-Gazette*, trying to think about anything except what's occurring in one of the rooms next to me. The papers have been full of stories about Andy's trial. One of the jurors has talked since the verdict, and his comments have proved rather enlightening. Emerson Clawson, one of the white males who kept yawning during my closing argument, has told a reporter for the *Democrat-Gazette* that it never seemed like a murder case to him. Shocking that pitiful child was just a stupid thing to do, a case of poor judgment. Still, as awful as that kid's life was, you could see why somebody would try it. Why such a light sentence? Why not put him in jail to warn people like Andy not to experiment with children's lives, as Jill had demanded of the jury? According to Clawson, the jury figured that somebody has to work with those poor devils and it might as well be somebody who gives a damn and doesn't mind getting his hands dirty. Sure, Chapman had screwed up, but you have to remember he had the kid's mother panting all over him. As far as he was concerned, the dumbest part of the trial had been the defendant's lawyer trying to make an issue of the aide being in the Trackers. He didn't blame Chapman for wanting to fire his lawyer. Lawyers are always trying to use the issue of race in Blackwell County for one reason or another. The prosecutor, he told the reporter, apparently rather indignantly, was right about one thing: cheap tricks like that don't work there. Sure they don't.

The night after the trial I called Amy Gilchrist who told me that from the beginning Jill had been convinced that Leon was in on it—that she was certain he had been paid off by Andy and Olivia but never found the slightest evidence to prove it. When Leon hadn't shown up for work this past Monday, Jill, according to Amy, had nodded and collected a five-dollar bet from Kerr. When she checked with his landlord, she was told that Leon hadn't bothered to ask for his deposit back and had left no forwarding address. Without any evidence to charge him, Jill had been stuck with Leon's story, and then I had really messed things up when I found out about Leon being in the Trackers. She had ended up having to defend a man she thought was guilty as sin! *Conspiracies!* How prosecutors love them! Jill would really be agitated if I told her that last night I got a call from California from Charlene telling me she had called Leon and he had gotten on the plane Sunday afternoon. "I wouldn't of tried to hurt him so bad if I didn't still love him." I could tell Jill this, but she wouldn't believe Charlene. Since I heard Leon laughing in the background, I do. Jill's problem is she's too logical. As the song goes, "The things we do for love!"

After spilling the beans on her boss, Amy had said she was leaving the Prosecutor's office next month. Now that she'd had the abortion, she had no future there. The Layman Building has space, I told her. Yet I am dismayed at the thought of one more lawyer competing for business against me. Amy confided that sometimes she dreams she is having the baby. Regret is the price of freedom, my mother used to say, but I didn't drop this pearl of wisdom on Amy, who promised to come by and see me. Before I hung up, I asked her about the possibility of Olivia being prosecuted. Given the view of the jury that the child's death was accidental, Amy confided, Jill has given up. In turn, she asked me if I thought Olivia and Andy would get back together. I doubt it, I told her, not after her testimony. Andy may be capable of love—but forgiveness? I'm not so sure.

Benign. The sweetest word in the English language. Outside the hospital, I roll up the window of the Blazer on my side to keep out the cool rain. My passenger however sticks her bare arm out the window and waves it around like a naughty child. Her face is wet and shining. "You don't have to go back to work after you take me home," she says shyly.

I smile. My face is wet, too. "I guess I don't," I say. There is something to be said for private practice after all.